KENTUCKY SUNRISE

Also by Fern Michaels . . .

KENTUCKY RICH
KENTUCKY HEAT
CHARMING LILY
PLAIN JANE
WHAT YOU WISH FOR
THE GUEST LIST
LISTEN TO YOUR HEART
CELEBRATION
YESTERDAY
FINDERS KEEPERS
ANNIE'S RAINBOW
SARA'S SONG
VEGAS SUNRISE
VEGAS HEAT
VEGAS RICH
WHITEFIRE
WISH LIST
DEAR EMILY
TEXAS SUNRISE
TEXAS FURY
TEXAS HEAT
TEXAS RICH

FERN MICHAELS

KENTUCKY SUNRISE

KENSINGTON BOOKS
http://www.kensingtonbooks.com

KENSINGTON BOOKS are published by

Kensington Publishing Corp.
850 Third Avenue
New York, NY 10022

All Kensington titles, imprints and distributed lines are available at special quantity discounts for bulk purchases for sales promotion, premiums, fund-raising, educational or institutional use.

Special book excerpts or customized printings can also be created to fit specific needs. For details, write or phone the office of the Kensington Special Sales Manager: Kensington Publishing Corp., 850 Third Avenue, New York, NY 10022. Attn. Special Sales Department. Phone: 1-800-221-2647.

Kensington and the K logo Reg. U.S. Pat. & TM Off.

ISBN 0-7582-0457-4

First Trade Printing: October 2002
10 9 8 7 6 5 4 3 2 1

Printed in the United States of America

Prologue

Babylon Hotel and Casino
Las Vegas, Nevada

Sage Thornton looked across the table at his twin brother Birch. His expression clearly said 'board meetings are deadly dull.' Birch rolled his eyes as if to say, 'I agree, this is boring as hell.'

Fanny Thornton Reed peered at her sons over the rims of her reading glasses. "I wonder, Sage, if you can tell me why the Emperor's Room has been operating in the red for the past two months. The Emperor's Room has always been the hottest ticket in town for fine dining. As far back as I can remember, we've always been backlogged for reservations. The way it stands now, you can walk in off the street and get a table without a reservation."

Sage leaned forward, the better to see his mother. "The chef bailed out on us. She didn't give us any notice, so we shut down for ten days until we could find a replacement. One day she was here, and the next day she was gone. Obviously the new man we hired isn't doing the job he was hired to do. I've been looking for a new chef since the day she left. Five-star chefs are not that easy to come by, Mom."

"Let's try to do better. I hate seeing all these red circles," Fanny said. "I think we're adjourned unless any of you have some business you want to discuss."

Sage glared at the board members sitting at the long conference table. His gaze said there had better not be any new business to discuss.

"Then we are adjourned." Fanny shuffled her papers and booklets into an accordion-pleated envelope. The sound of the rubber band snapping into place was exceptionally loud to those in the room.

The twins waited until the room emptied before they approached their mother. They both hugged her. "Nice to see you, Mom. You should come to town more often," Birch said.

Fanny twinkled at her sons. "What good would that do me, Birch? You're in Atlantic City all the time running Babylon II. As for you, Sage, I only live fifty miles away. You could come to visit. By the way, you are going to Kentucky for the family reunion in May, aren't you? I think it's wonderful that Nealy is willing to host a get-together. Marcus and I wouldn't miss it for the world. Your sisters Sunny and Billie will be there as well as all the Colemans. It should be quite wonderful."

"We'll be there," Birch and Sage said in unison. "Are you staying on, Mom," Birch asked, "or heading back to the ranch?"

"Marcus is waiting for me. I have to get back. How's my mountain, Sage?" Her voice was so wistful, Sage felt his eyes start to burn. He stared at her for a long moment, his heart fluttering in his chest at how old and frail his mother suddenly looked. He blinked. Her hair was snow-white and the fine wrinkles were deeper. Her smile was the same gentle, warm smile of his youth. He made a mental note to go out to the ranch at least once a week, even if it was at midnight.

"It's as beautiful as ever and just as wonderful. The kids love it. I wish you and Marcus would come up and spend some time with us. Iris would love it if you'd come for an extended stay."

"If I were to do that, I might not want to leave. We'll be there for Christmas. I'll say good-bye now." Fanny gathered up her purse and coat.

"How about a trip to Atlantic City, Mom?" Birch asked as he hugged her good-bye.

"One of these days. I like to be close to home. You know I'm only comfortable around my own things in my own place. Marcus is having knee-replacement surgery after the first of the year. Recovery time will be at least a few months. I will think about it, though. Be sure to call me. That goes for you, too, Sage."

"Okay, Mom. Do you want us to walk you to the car?"

Fanny laughed. "I think I can get there on my own. You can walk me to the elevator, though."

Even there on the fourth floor of the casino, the noise from the first floor could still be heard as the slot machines whirred and clanked to the sound of silver.

"Uh-oh, here comes trouble," Sage muttered, as soon as the elevator door closed. He made his way across the deeply carpeted hallway to greet two burly Las Vegas police detectives. "What brings you here at this hour of the morning, Joe? Noah, good to see you again," he said, pumping the second detective's hand. "You both know Birch."

"We're here to ask you about one of your employees. She's got at least twenty aliases that we know of. Willow, Willa, or a variation of that first name. As to her last name, here, take your pick," the detective named Noah said, handing over a sheet of paper. "We have no clue as to what her real name is. She's a cook. We were told she worked here at Babylon."

Sage looked at his brother, a frown building between his eyebrows. "If you're referring to Willa Lupine, yes, she worked for us in the Emperor Room. She's a five-star chef, but she quit a few months ago. She pretty much left us high and dry. Why are you looking for her?"

"Murder."

This time Sage's eyebrows shot up to his hairline. "Murder! Willa? Who is she supposed to have killed?"

"Her husband, Carlo Belez. Also known as Junior Belez. It was in all the papers. Didn't you see it?"

Sage threw his hands in the air. "Hell, it was on the front page of the paper every day for weeks. It didn't say anything about a wife or mention our chef by name. I would have remembered something like that. If this happened two months ago, are you telling me you just figured out Junior was married to one of our employees? I didn't even know Willa was married."

The detective looked sheepish. "So you did know Junior."

Sage jammed his hands into his pockets. "I never said I didn't know him. Every casino owner on the strip knows . . . knew Junior Belez. He was a high roller. Never ran a marker that I know of. He won and lost money in all the casinos. Are you implying our former chef killed Junior?"

"It looks that way. We want to question her. The only problem is we don't know where she is. We have an all-points out, but nothing has come in. We just found out about her a few days ago."

Sage raked his hands through his hair. "Wait a minute. The guy was killed two months ago, and you're just now finding out he was married? What the hell kind of police work is that?"

The detective clenched and unclenched his teeth. "Junior lived on his ranch way out there, maybe twelve miles or so past the Chicken Ranch. He liked privacy. He didn't have a house-keeper but he did have a groundskeeper who sticks his snoot in the bottle from time to time and then has to dry out. He was dry-ing out when this all went down. He came back expecting to pick up where he left off only his boss is dead. He's the one who told us your cook was married to Belez. If it wasn't for him, we still wouldn't know about her."

"She wasn't a cook. Anyone can cook. Willa was a chef," Sage said. "I don't know anything that can help you. She worked for us. She drew customers like a magnet. She was one hell of a chef. She quit and took off. That's the sum total of what I know. Feel free to go to the kitchen and talk to the people who worked with her."

"We'll do that. If you hear anything, call us."

"I will," Sage muttered. He looked at his brother. "Don't look at me like that, Birch. I don't know anything about the woman. The kitchen was strictly off-limits to everyone when she worked here. She was hell on wheels about people going in and out of her kitchen."

Birch shrugged. "You taking me to the airport or should I catch a cab?"

"Do you mind taking a cab? I want to talk to the kitchen staff myself. I have this . . . weird feeling I know something, but I don't know what it is. It's like . . . something I heard. Then again, maybe it was something I saw and didn't realize it at the time. Christ, I hate when that happens. It makes me damn near nuts trying to figure it out."

"No problem. Let me know if I can help."

"Hey, wait just a damn minute, Birch. You're looking kind of smug. You didn't snatch her away, did you? Damn, it would be just like you to pull a stunt like that."

"Sorry. Never saw the lady, and I don't know anything about her. I'm just glad she wasn't my . . . *cook*. See you."

"One of our employees is wanted for murder. I can't believe it, Birch."

Birch bent down to pick up his briefcase. "He said she was wanted for questioning. There's a difference between questioning and murder. She might be a suspect. That still doesn't prove she committed the murder. It's the elimination process to track down the killer or killers. Don't go off half-cocked here, Sage. I'll call you when I get home. We can do that word-association thing we used to do when we were kids. Maybe something will come to you. You could also call that sister of ours. Sunny is great with stuff like that."

Sage watched the elevator door close behind his brother. He felt his stomach muscles bunch up into a knot.

Murder!

PART I

1

Fanny Thornton Reed watched the young dawn creep over her beloved Sunrise Mountain. A sadness, unlike anything she'd ever experienced, washed over her. One small part of her wished she hadn't turned the mountain over to her son Sage. Yet it would have been selfish of her to keep it with just herself and Marcus to enjoy. The mountain was intended for a family, for children to run and play, to hope and dream.

She'd raised her four children there, and it was always the place where she'd come to lick her wounds, to cry in private and bury those close to her.

She looked across the road to the little valley where Chue's family lived. Chue was the young Chinese immigrant Sallie Coleman had befriended and brought to the mountain eons ago. She'd given him a large plot of land and built him a house so he could get married and raise a family. His loyalty and love had served Sallie and Fanny's own family over the years. Chue and his wife were gone now, buried in the family cemetery, but their children remained to care for the mountain and for the new generation of Thorntons.

Twelve children on the mountain. She smiled. Sage's three children and her daughter Sunny's two children plus Chue's seven grandchildren romped the mountain from morning till night.

Fanny reflected on her life on the mountain, where she'd been happy as well as miserable at times. Those other times, the times when she'd been less than happy—they weren't worth thinking about. She was in the winter of her life now, her hair as white as the snow on the tips of the trees in the winter. She was also older, and Marcus was even older. She closed her eyes, wondering what it would be like when it was her time to join those who had gone before her. Tears blurred her eyes. Then she smiled again as she thought about her first husband, Ash, and how much she'd loved him. It was true, what they said, about only having one true love. Yes, she loved her husband Marcus, but it was a different kind of love. Ash was the bells and whistles and the kids' father. Marcus was the steady rock she clung to.

"Fanny, Fanny, you're doing it again. You're stewing and fretting instead of taking action."

"Ash! Oh, Ash, it's good to talk to you again. It's been years and years. I don't even want to think about how many. Yes, I was just standing here thinking about how old I am. If I close my eyes, I can see us here on the mountain with the kids running around. I've been all over the world, Ash, and this is still the prettiest spot on earth."

"Why so sad, Fanny?"

"It's Jake, Ash. If you're so *all-knowing*, you must realize the young man is suffering. He can't seem to find his direction. I know how much you loved him, and he returned that love. I don't think he ever forgave you for dying and leaving him behind. All he ever talked about was being a navy pilot like you. Those gold wings you gave him are his most treasured possession. I think he still sleeps with them pinned to his pajamas. You know he will never be a pilot. It's that damn disease, where he didn't grow the way he should have. We took him everywhere, to every clinic, to every specialist, and there was nothing they could do for him. Right now, he's looking at his eighteenth birthday and doesn't know what to do. He absolutely refuses to go to college. Sunny said he has to accept his condition and work it out, the way she did when she found out she had multiple sclerosis. I think she's right, but it hurts me to watch him."

"I know, Fanny, but there are other ways to fly. I don't mean literally. I'm talking about the same dedication, the same exhilaration. Think about it."

"Ash, I hate it when you talk in riddles. If you have an idea, tell me. I'll do anything for the boy. Anything. Help me out here, okay?"

"That's your problem, Fanny. You always wanted me to do your thinking for you. Use your head. Go inside and turn the VCR on."

"Why would I want to do that? It's only six o'clock in the morning. What kind of tape should I watch?" Fanny asked curiously.

"The one that's in the machine. Come on, old girl, you've been thinking about it but were afraid to say the words out loud. You were always so damn cautious."

"And you were always going off on one tangent or another. I was the one who had to remain grounded for all our sakes."

"Don't be afraid to take chances, Fanny. Get Jake off the mountain before it's too late. If you don't, he's going to turn into another Simon. You don't want that, do you?"

"Ashhhh."

Fanny whirled around when she felt a hand on her shoulder. "Oh, Jake, what are you doing up so early? Couldn't you sleep?" She reached up to tousle his blond curls, the same kind of hair as his grandfather had had.

"I like to watch the sun come up. It's a new day, and I always hope that maybe some miracle will happen."

"Jake, I've lived a long time, and over the years I found that each of us has to make our own miracles along the way. I want you to come with me into the family room and watch a tape. Let's get some fresh coffee first, though."

"What's on the tape, Grandma?"

Yes, what was on the tape? Ash had sounded as if he knew what he was talking about. "You'll see," she said.

Jake sat down next to her on the sofa, his legs barely reaching the floor, weighing only 105 pounds. Even though he was approaching his eighteenth birthday, he looked like a child of twelve. She was thankful the disease hadn't eaten into his mind. He was brilliant, in the top one percentile of his class, and had a photographic memory just like his grandfather Ash, who had always been his idol.

"You have to turn it on, Grandma," Jake said.

"Yes, yes, I do have to turn it on. Marcus always handles the remote. Get ready now." *This better be good, Ash.*

Fanny sat back, wondering what it was she was going to see. "Oh, look, Jake, it's Nealy Clay! I think this is her first Kentucky Derby race. She won two Triple Crowns, and she's your aunt. She was in her fifties when she ran her last race. We didn't know about Nealy for a long time." She looked sideways at Jake. "She's just your size, and she's a jockey. She was very young, not as young as you are, but still young, when she ran her first race. She doesn't look big enough to handle a Thoroughbred, does she?"

"Size has nothing to do with a person's ability to control a horse," Jake said as if he knew what he was talking about. The camera switched to the jockey room and panned the jockeys as they finished dressing. "Look how muscular those guys are," he said, an enthusiasm in his voice that hadn't been there before.

"That was the preliminaries. Now, they're going to show the race. Before it starts, I want you to know one thing. Ash, your grandfather, always said there are other ways to fly than in an airplane. Keep that in mind as you watch the race."

Fanny and Jake watched as the crowd rose to the playing of "My Old Kentucky Home," then fell silent as the gates clanged open.

"And they're off in the Kentucky Derby!" the announcer blared.

"Flyby got away cleanly and moved to the left right at the start. Serendipity takes the early lead and Crusader is on the inside as he challenges early. Celebration is third on the inside with Nightstar fourth. Finders Keepers is fifth, Dark Sire is in the sixth position. Here comes Phil's Choice in seventh. On the outside is Texas Rich at eighth. Leisure Boy is between horses as they round the clubhouse turn and MacInerny takes Crusader to the front three-quarters of a length. Serendipity on the outside is second. Saturday's Warrior in blue and yellow moves to the outside. Finders Keepers is fifth on the outside with Phil's Choice tucked in at the rail and sixth at this point. Dark Sire is seventh, Celebration is eighth, Nightstar is ninth. After that, Saturday's Warrior racing in the tenth position."

Fanny beamed when her grandson leaned forward, his eyes narrowing. "Look, Grandma, she's trying to move to the inside. Look how low she's riding. She looks like she's on the horse's head. She's about eight lengths behind. Wow! Look at that horse! I can't believe we're related to her." Fanny thought her heart would burst at the boy's excitement.

The announcer's voice rose an octave. "Here comes Crusader,

his colors showing the way and in the lead by a head. On the outside, Serendipity is coming off the middle and here comes Phil's Choice, and he's sailing. Celebration swings to the middle of the racetrack. Flyby is fifth and running at the rail. Celebration takes command by a neck. Down the stretch they come. Finders Keepers is on the inside. Here comes Dancer's Flyby, and that horse is *flying!*"

"She's gonna do it, Grandma. Look at her go! The announcer is right, that horse is *flying*. Look at his legs. They're like *wings!*"

Jake was on his feet, his closed fists shooting in the air when the announcer blasted, "What a punch that horse has! And the winner of the Kentucky Derby is Dancer's Flyby! We're talking absolute power here, ladies and gentlemen. Absolute! Cornelia Diamond, owner, trainer, and jockey, takes home the roses to Blue Diamond Farms!"

Fanny leaned back into the softness of the sofa. "Thanks, Ash," she whispered.

"Anytime, Fanny my love. Anytime at all."

"Did you say something, Grandma?" Jake asked, excitement ringing in his voice.

"I said, great race. Flyby looked like he was really flying, didn't he?"

"Grandma, that horse *was* flying. He won by four lengths. Four lengths! He had wings on his feet. I wonder what it felt like—riding that fast."

Fanny smiled. "I bet it was a lot like flying a fighter plane," she said nonchalantly. She shook her head when Sage appeared in the doorway, a sign that he should leave. He obliged.

"But she's a girl!" Jake said, shaking his head in disbelief. He ran to the VCR and rewound the tape to the middle of the race and studied it.

"Now that's a brilliant deduction if I ever heard one," Fanny said.

"Is that what you meant about another way to fly?" Jake asked, his eyes glued to the wide screen in front of him.

"I just repeated the words. Your grandfather is the one who came up with the saying. You know what I think, honey? I think it's not the actual act of flying that you crave, it's the *feeling*, the high that comes with doing something you love. For me it was building this mountain. For your aunt Nealy, it's breeding, training, and racing her horses. I think you could be a jockey, Jake. It's not easy, the training is hard and rigorous. I can almost say with certainty that Nealy would take you on at the farm. If Nealy isn't at the farm, Emmie, then. Who knows, they might have a wonder horse you could ride. Once you learn, that is."

"Grandma, I've never been on a horse in my life. Where did you come up with this idea?"

"You know, Jake, I had a dream, and your grandfather told me about it. I don't dream of him as often as I used to, but last night I did," Fanny fibbed. "Over the years he's come to me in many dreams, usually in a time of crisis. He always seemed to have the right answer."

"And Pop-Pop," Jake said, referring to the name he'd given his grandfather in his early childhood years, "said I should be a jockey?"

"It was a dream, honey. I'm not saying you should or should not be a jockey. It is something to think about. I always pay attention to my dreams because Ash was never wrong. I never figured out how that could be," Fanny said thoughtfully. "I'm going to make breakfast this morning so your aunt Iris can sleep in. What would you like?"

"Anything you make will be fine. I think I'll watch that race again if you don't mind."

"Why don't you watch the others, too? Nealy ran seven Triple Crown races. We're all going to Kentucky the first of May so you can see those magnificent horses in the flesh. And we're all going to take in the Kentucky Derby. I remember Sage saying he taped all six races. I've seen them, and they're very exciting. I imagine they're on the shelf over there with the other tapes. I'll call you when breakfast is ready."

"Okay, Grandma."

In the kitchen, Sage poured coffee, his eyes full of questions.

"I think I might have found the answer to Jake's dilemma. I had this dream last night about your father, and he's the one who came up with the idea. In the dream," she said hastily. "Jake would make a perfect jockey. What do you think?"

"Think! I think that's a great idea. The question is, what does

Jake think? I don't think he's ever been on a horse. We could never get him on a pony, much less a horse."

"He can learn. I think Nealy will take him on. If she's off traveling, Emmie will do the honors. Do you really think it's a good idea, Sage?"

"Mom, it's the best. I think it's Jake's answer. Do you think he'll go for it?"

"He looked interested. I played the first race for him. He's going to watch the other six races now. Let's not overplay it. Let him come to his own decision. In fact, I don't think we should say another word. When we get to Kentucky, he can see for himself. What do you think?"

"As usual, Mom, you're right again. I can't tell you how worried I've been about that kid. Sunny is beside herself. I'll call and tell her when I get to the casino. Iris said blueberry waffles would be nice." He winked at his mother.

"She's right, blueberry waffles would be nice. I'll see you this evening, Sage."

Sage hugged his mother and was out the door a second later.

Nealy Clay Littletree reached for the phone and picked it up on the first ring. "Fanny! How nice to hear from you. Yes, it's been way too long. Hatch and I just got back from some of our travels. Actually, I was just sitting here thinking about the family and missing everyone. How are you, Fanny?"

"Getting older by the day, Nealy. I have a very large favor to ask of you. If you can't see your way clear to helping me, that's okay, too. I've never been one too proud to ask for help."

"Ask away, Fanny. If it's in my power to help you, I will. Your sons came to my rescue, and I didn't even have to ask. Family is such a wonderful thing. Now, tell me what I can do for you."

Nealy looked up and smiled at her husband. Hatch winked at her as he tossed the "Lifetime" section of the morning paper. She caught it deftly as she mouthed the words, 'It's Fanny Thornton.'

"Do you remember me telling you about my grandson Jake?" Fanny asked.

"Yes, I remember. Is he in some kind of trouble?"

"No. However, he refuses to go to college. He won't leave the mountain. I'm sure a lot of it has to do with his size and weight. Even though he's going to turn eighteen in a few weeks, he looks like he's only twelve years old. I understand his mind-set where that is concerned. I was wondering if you or Emmie would take him under your wing and train him to be a jockey. It's a large commitment on your part, but I don't know what else to do. I had this dream . . . No, no, I can't lie to you, Nealy. It wasn't a dream. Sometimes I talk to Ash. He answers me. No, I'm not crazy. I'm just careful who I tell things like this to. Ruby talks to him, too."

"Yes, I do know, and I really do understand. There for a while I was talking to Hunt. What did he tell you?"

"He's the one who suggested all of this. Can you see yourself helping us, Nealy?"

"Of course. I'll do anything I can. I'm sure Hatch won't mind. You are coming to the reunion, aren't you?"

"Wouldn't miss it for the world. I thought it would be a good time for Jake to get his feet wet so to speak. He's a wonderful boy, Nealy, and he got a bad deal like his mother did. Something like this just might be what he needs, to prove to himself he can and will amount to something. I don't know how to thank you."

"Would you do it for me, Fanny?"

"In a heartbeat."

"Then you have your answer. I'll talk to Hatch and get a plan under way. It was nice talking to you, Fanny. Say hello to everyone for me."

Nealy clicked off the portable phone and looked up at Hatch. "How do you feel about us staying on at Blue Diamond Farms after the reunion? I don't know how long, Hatch. It could be two years, a little less, a little more. We could come back here to Santa Fe on long weekends. Fanny Thornton needs my help."

"Then let's do it," Hatch said.

Nealy looked up and stared off into space. God had certainly smiled on her when He brought Hatch Littletree into her life. "Don't you want to know why we're going back?"

Hatch looked over the top of his spectacles. "You said Fanny needs your help."

"Well, yes, she does but it's actually her grandson who needs the help. She wants me to train him to be a jockey. He has a severe medical problem. He never grew normally. He's healthy as all get-out and graduated at the top of his class, but he refuses to go to college. I'm sure image and peer pressure played a big part in his decision. I think he might be able to do it. Train to be a jockey, I mean.

"It's really very sad because the boy wanted to be a naval aviator like his grandfather, but with his condition it isn't possible. He's just the right age, and he's the perfect weight, too. I'd like to work with him. That give-back thing we always talk about when God is good to you. Are you sure you're okay with going back for that long a time?"

"I'm okay with it, Nealy. Metaxas Parish ran his business out of your farm for three whole years while you and Shufly trained. I can do the same thing. Semiretirement allows for a lot of things. Don't look so worried, honey. I think it's a great idea. Maybe he'll let me act like a dad. I'm all for it."

Nealy grinned. "Good, because I told her I would do it."

Hatch laughed, the chair shaking under his weight. "I know. I was listening."

Emmie Coleman leaned back against the board fencing, hooking the heel of her boot onto one of the rails. Hands jammed into the pockets of her jeans, she surveyed Blue Diamond Farms. It had to be the prettiest place on earth. Her home, her sanctuary. She was never, ever going to leave again. She dug the heel of her left boot into the rich soil and wished she could take root. She sighed with happiness.

Thick gray clouds scudded overhead, a sign that it would rain in the next hour or so. If it did, the camera crew would have to wind up for the day. Mitch Cunningham had been true to his word, the crew hadn't interfered, hadn't gotten in the way, but they were always there, always within eyesight. She was so used to Mitch and the crew that when they weren't around she missed them.

The seven-month time frame to complete the movie had gone the way of all deadlines, thanks to the fire and her mother's trip to Thailand for reconstructive surgery to repair her burned face. Now, though, the film was almost near the wrap stage. The thought left her with a feeling of sadness. She'd become very fond of Mitch Cunningham. Perhaps too fond. In the morning she couldn't wait to run to the barn, hoping to see him before she started her day. It was foolish because he never showed up before nine in the morning, and by that time she usually had five hours of work under her belt.

More than ever, she realized that she was just like her mother. She wasn't worldly, didn't know how to play the games men and women played with each other. Her social skills were as pitiful as those of her mother. She could hardly wait to see the film on the wide screen, to see how the young actress played her part. The woman and Mitch had both picked her brain clean. How her life would translate on the screen was still a mystery. She'd heard Mitch call it a modern-day *Gone With the Wind*. God knows he had done as much research on Thoroughbreds and racing as Margaret Mitchell had done on the South and the Civil War. The cast was practically as large, with actors and actresses portraying almost every member of her mother's family, including the Texas Colemans and the Thorntons of Las Vegas. He had even hired actors and actresses to portray some of the office staff and farmhands. Only the horses had played themselves.

He was heading her way now, his long-legged stride unmistakable. The nerves in her stomach did a crazy little dance as she struggled to appear nonchalant. She could see him studying her for a moment. What was he seeing? Obviously something that didn't appeal to him. It bothered her. She tipped her Stetson lower to shield her eyes. He in turn flipped his baseball cap around so that the brim was in the back. All the better to see her with.

"Nice day," he said.

"Summer days are always nice," Emmie said coolly.

"This certainly is a beautiful place. I hope someday I can have something half as grand. I'd like a little ranch out West somewhere. That's so far into the future it doesn't bear thinking about. It's easy to understand why you love it so much."

Emmie nodded but said nothing.

"I need to thank you again for being so gracious and for allowing us to film here. I hope you'll come to the premiere as my guest. Your mother, too. Actually, the whole family. I know it's going to be a huge success. I'm hoping it's Academy Award material. My gut tells me those racing scenes will really put it over the top."

Emmie nodded again. "What's your next project?"

Mitch shrugged. "Don't know. I still have a lot to do on this one. We're going to film your family reunion. That's not to say it will go into the movie, but I would like the footage just in case. The final editing is going to be a nightmare. A definite challenge, but still a nightmare. I'm going to miss this place."

What about me? Are you going to miss me? "You'll forget us soon enough," Emmie said.

"You're like your mother, you know that, Emmie? What is it about me that you don't like? You're always polite, but you're always so damn busy. Do you ever stop to take a deep breath, to smell the roses, to dream? I finally figured out your mother halfway through the film. Do you feel you *have* to be like her? I guess my next question is if the answer is yes, then why? And I still don't understand why you wouldn't allow mention of your daughter or let her be in the film. If this is going to be the epic I think it will be, she might be a little offended when she gets older and sees that she wasn't even mentioned. I don't think it's fair to her. Your mother made it abundantly clear that the deal was off if we so much as mentioned Gabby. Now that we're almost finished, do you want to tell me why?"

"I suppose I am like Mom in some ways. In other ways, I'm not like her at all. It's not easy running a farm this size. From the time I learned to walk, I knew the horses always had to come first. Hard work never hurt anyone. Is that what you have trouble with? My daughter is not part of this conversation, so let's just leave it at that."

Mitch took off his baseball cap and fiddled with it before he plopped it back on his head. "Okay, we'll leave it at that. I don't know if this is the time to tell you or not, but I wanted to ask you out to dinner or just to a movie so many times I lost count. You fix those blue eyes on me and I stop thinking about asking you because those blue eyes tell me 'don't cross that line.' So, I didn't. Before I pack up to leave, I'd like to know if I had asked, would you have accepted?"

Emmie's brain whirled and twirled. "Yes. I wondered why

you never asked. I almost asked you once, but instead I took Gabby to town and went to lunch and a matinee."

Mitch jammed his hands into the back pockets of his jeans. "I thought you didn't like me, that you were just being polite because of your mother. I guess I thought you were just tolerating us, me in particular. So, do you want to go to dinner tonight?"

Emmie smiled. "I'd love to go to dinner with you, Mitch."

He seemed stunned at her response. "You know what, that's great. That's really great. That's just great. I said that, didn't I? Is seven too early or too late?"

"Seven is just fine. I'll see you at seven. I have to get back to the barn."

The camera he was never without came off his shoulder and into his hands. "Say cheese," he said, snapping her picture. He already had hundreds of pictures of Emmie, but he could always use one more. She mugged for him before sprinting off to the barn.

He adjusted the focus and zoomed in on her face. She was a pretty girl, but she didn't have the sparkle her mother had. Nealy Clay Littletree was unlike any woman he'd ever known, and after all this time of popping in and out of her life, he figured he knew her just about as well as anyone could. From the beginning he had pegged her as being a hard nut to crack. It wasn't that she was uncooperative; she was by nature a very private person.

He had taken every care to find an actress who could portray Nealy properly. Actually, he had two actresses. First, a teenager to portray Nealy as the seventeen-year-old unwed mother who ran away from her Virginia home and her abusive father and literally stumbled onto Blue Diamond Farms and into a fortune. Second, a thirty-plus actress to portray Nealy into her fifties with the help of a makeup artist. Both of them had had to be exceptional horsewomen, which had made finding them more difficult, but ultimately worth the effort.

For the racing scenes, he had used actual footage of Nealy winning the Kentucky Derby, the Preakness, and the Belmont Stakes—footage he hoped would make him a legend in his own time. A filmmaker extraordinaire!

* * *

Emmie spent forty minutes checking on things before she was satisfied she could go up to the house and take a bubble bath. She was aching from head to toe. It seemed of late that either one or the other of her joints acted up, causing her to limp, gasp with sudden pain, or just plain old slow down. Her fingers were puffy, too. One of these days she was going to make an appointment to have a physical, something she'd been putting off way too long. She could take a day or so off now that she had a well-oiled machine going full tilt, sterling workers, and a farm manager named Cordell Lancer, who ran the farm with an iron fist. Because of Cordell, and the new workers she'd hired, she was able to spend more time with Gabby, be involved in community affairs, and have some semblance of a life outside of the horses. She didn't do half the things her mother had done, and yet the farm ran smoothly.

She hungered for a man to care about and to love. A man who would be good to Gabby. A man who would want to make his home here on the farm. She didn't think Mitch Cunningham would ever give up the bright lights of Hollywood or the fast-paced life he led, but maybe Mitch would be a stand-in until the real love of her life made an appearance.

She thought about her husband, the man she'd divorced before Emmie was born. Once she'd thought she loved him, and she supposed she had, in a limited kind of way. Buddy was deaf and used sign language the way she had until her speech came back to her. Resentful of his wife's ability to speak, Buddy moved out of her life and went back to Ohio, where he'd been born. She'd never told him about Emmie. Her reasoning was, if Buddy didn't love or want her any longer, he certainly wouldn't want a baby.

Sometimes she had nightmares about Buddy coming back into her life and demanding she turn Gabby over to him. Lately, for some reason, she was having the dreams more and more frequently, a sure sign that she was worried about the reality of it happening at some not-too-distant time. She shivered at the thought.

Emmie gave her head a mental shake to drive away the thought of Buddy Owens. A trip over to the stallion barn to see the two newest colts was in order. She sucked in her breath when she imagined her mother's reaction when she arrived the following week.

She had purchased two colts born from Shufly, each with a different dam, from Metaxas Parish at the Keeneland sale. She had high hopes they would be Derby material.

She entered the dim barn and made her way to Gadfly's stall. The moment he saw her he laid back his ears. Taking a deep breath she moved two stalls down to Hifly's stall. His ears perked at the sight of her. Hifly was small and funny-looking, the horse no one else wanted. When she'd brought him home from the Keeneland sale, Cordell had looked at her, then at Hifly and shook his head. "He's a runt. There must have been a bad gene pool in that dam. Don't tell me you're even considering putting him in training."

Emmie bit down on her tongue. There was something about Hifly that made her want to defend him. He was a spirited yearling, loving and eager to please. Gadfly, on the other hand, was ornery and always out of sorts. The day she'd brought him home, she told Cordell that she and she alone would be responsible for the colts' care. Why she'd done that, she didn't know. What she was trying to prove, she didn't know. All she knew was that she wanted to do it, had to do it.

Soon she was going to have to make a decision since both colts were a year old and training would have to begin. Even if she made the decision to race them, she had no jockey. She knew she was capable of training both horses but she wasn't, nor could she ever be, a jockey. At least that's what her mother told her early on.

Hifly stuck his neck out of his stall to nuzzle her neck, then tried to stick his nose inside the pocket of her shirt for his mint. Mints were her mother's trick for instant bonding. Such a little thing, yet so effective. She handed it over and tried to give him an apple, which he spit out. She doubled over laughing as she reached for more mints in her pocket. He snorted his approval.

"Guess what! I have a date," she whispered. As if this horse really cared. Still, he was someone to talk to, someone to share with. The best part was he didn't answer back.

Tonight was going to be her first date in years. Since Buddy, actually. She felt a little nervous at the prospect, but since she liked Mitch Cunningham maybe the evening would go well.

On the walk up to the house, Emmie childishly crossed her fingers. Inside the kitchen, she almost called out Smitty's name, the way she had every day since the office manager's retirement. Smitty had retired along with Dover Wilkie when her mother married Hatch Littletree and moved to Santa Fe. Emmie had a new office manager now named Agnes Beakman. She ran a tight ship and didn't believe in familiarity, to Emmie's dismay. She also refused to baby-sit Gabby when she got home from school, which necessitated hiring a live-in nanny for the little girl.

Things at Blue Diamond Farms had changed a lot since her mother moved away.

There was a new housekeeper these days, too, named Gertie Zoloff, but she went home at night, leaving Emmie and Gabby alone with Terry Timmins, the nanny. It was a situation that worked for Emmie but wouldn't have worked for her mother.

Emmie found herself grimacing as she made her way up to the second floor. Her mother wasn't going to like all the changes she'd made. She wondered how verbal she would be about her dislikes.

The bathwater steamed upward. Emmie poured her favorite avocado bath salts under the gushing water and inhaled deeply. She tested the water with her big toe and quickly withdrew it. She turned off the hot water and let cold water rush from the tap before she slid down into the silky wetness.

Mitch Cunningham's choice of restaurant was twenty-five miles away. The Picador was small and intimate, with the twelve tables spaced far enough apart so conversation stayed private. Emmie loved it immediately.

"One of my crew found it while he was out riding around. Most of the guys eat here every weekend. The food is quite good, and the service is one-on-one," Mitch said, holding out her chair for her.

"You look so different, Emmie. I don't think I've ever seen you in anything but jeans and shirts. You should dress up more often."

Emmie blinked. She supposed it was a compliment. She smiled. "You look rather nice yourself," she said, indicating his creased khakis and button-down white shirt. His unruly hair was slicked back, but somehow his curls had worked loose and fallen across his forehead.

"When will you finish and wrap up?" Emmie asked, looking around at the greenery that graced the corners of the restaurant. She wanted to remember everything about this first date with Mitch Cunningham, right down to the draperies on the windows and the paintings on the walls.

Behind her she could hear the clink of silver and crystal. The aroma of fresh coffee wafted her way. She sighed.

"Two more days. I already have miles of tape on the pastures, the paddocks, and the bluegrass, but I want more. It's that, from every angle, perspective. I'm going to hang around in town till all your family gets here. We'll do some shooting that day, then I head back to California. The crew will be staying on to film the Kentucky Derby. Since you're all going to attend, I'd like to get that on film, too."

"You really like what you do, don't you?" Emmie asked.

"I do. My uncle gave me his old Brownie Hawkeye along with a load of film when I was eight or so. I had over a hundred pictures of my thumb before I got the hang of it. I really enjoyed it. While my friends were playing football and tennis, I was taking their pictures and selling them to the newspapers. It all just evolved. I would imagine I love my profession the way you love working with the horses. I never realized how *big* those horses were until I got up close to them. I could never in a million years do what you do."

Emmie laughed, a light musical sound. "I still take pictures of my thumb when I try to take pictures of Gabby or Cookie, her little dog." She held out her puffy-looking hand for him to see. When he frowned, she jerked her hand back and put it in her lap. "I couldn't do what you do, either."

"Do you know what really stunned me, Emmie?" Mitch said, leaning across the table.

"What?" Emmie smiled at the serious look on his face as she wondered what was coming next.

"Your families are all so rich. I thought you'd all be snobs and act like those throw-your-weight-around rich people. The kind I have to deal with all the time in Hollywood. You're just normal, everyday, nice people. None of you flaunt your money, you don't wear designer duds, and you don't drive fancy cars. All of you are generous to a fault. You've all had serious setbacks, and tragic things have happened to your family just the way they happen to other people. I find it remarkable. Why are you looking at me like that, Emmie? Everything I said, I meant as a compliment."

"Yes, I know. I guess it's that 'rich' part that bothers me. I don't think about it. I work for my money and I bank it. I live on my salary, and I support Emmie with my own money. I don't think about . . . all the rest."

"That's what makes you all so unique. The rest of your family is the same way. All of you give away more than you keep."

"Can we talk about something else? How is it you aren't married? Forty-two-year-old men are usually married," Emmie said, her face rosy with the question.

"I was married once for about ten minutes. I came close a few other times, but I guess I just didn't meet the right girl. What about you, or is that part of the don't ask section that takes in Gabby?"

"I'm divorced. I was married a little longer than ten minutes. We were childhood friends so it was inevitable we marry. We did, for all the wrong reasons. My ex lives in Ohio. I haven't seen or heard from him in years. I'd like to get married again someday. I found marriage to be very comforting. I'll bet it's downright cozy if you're married to the right person."

"I think you could be right," Mitch said, throwing his head back and laughing. Emmie smiled. She was flirting and loving every minute of it. She could hardly wait to share this experience with her mother.

2

Hatch Littletree watched his wife when she stepped out of the car at Blue Diamond Farms, a look of pure rapture on her face. She was home, and that said it all. He felt out of control for the first time in their year-long marriage.

Nealy had agreed to move to Santa Fe so he could be near his legal firm, which also meant she could be near her son Nick. His stomach started to grind in turmoil as he watched her run down to the barn, where Emmie was waiting for her. He watched mother and daughter hug, and even from this distance could see the tears on both their faces.

Had he made a mistake by taking Nealy to Santa Fe? After this reunion visit, he would know for certain. He listened to their excited chatter. He couldn't remember the last time Nealy had been so animated, so excited. This was her home, and she missed it. Maybe it was time to make some adjustments in their lives.

Hatch walked down to the barn when Nealy motioned to him. "Hurry, Hatch, Emmie wants us to see the two yearlings. Oh, I can't wait to see those two beauties."

"They're in the north paddock, Mom," Emmie said, as she hugged Hatch. She winced when he squeezed her. "It's good to see both of you. Come on," she said, walking away, trying not to limp. Today both her knees and ankles were hurting. She'd put on Ace bandages but they weren't helping. She didn't want to think about how many aspirin she'd taken already, and the day was just beginning.

Gadfly and Hifly were grazing on the spring grass when the trio approached. Gadfly raised his head and looked at Emmie.

"Oh, Emmie, he's a beauty," Nealy said, admiring the horse's conformation. She leaned over the board fencing to see him better.

Hatch could see the sparkle and the love in his wife's eyes and knew the answer to the question he'd asked himself just moments ago. Yes, it had been a mistake moving Nealy to Santa Fe. He'd been selfish trying to keep her to himself. Nealy belonged at Blue Diamond Farms with her horses.

"Where's Hifly?"

Emmie pointed to the paddock farther down. She watched as her mother frowned. "That's the horse you think has potential! He looks like a runt! No! How much did you say you paid for him? For God's sake, Emmie, his legs are too short. He could never run the distance. On top of that, he looks like a plow horse. You actually paid money for this plug!"

Emmie deflated like a pricked balloon. "I disagree. I know he's small and that his legs are short, but he has heart, Mom. I paid five thousand for him at Keeneland like I told you in my letter. He might not look like Gadfly, but his sire is still Shufly. I'm sorry you don't like him, but it doesn't really matter. He's mine, and I'm training him."

Nealy looked up to see Hatch flash her a warning look. She backed down immediately. "I'm sorry, Emmie. I guess I didn't think Shufly could produce anything but large, beautiful offspring. He is small. He's strange-looking, too. What exactly are you training him to do?"

"Maybe some stakes races. Maybe the Derby. If I could find just the right jockey, I think he could run the Derby. I mean that. Take a good look at him, Mom. He's an absolute love. He's gentle, he listens, and he's a quick learner. Gadfly is none of those things, plus he's mean as hell. Mean, Mom. Tell me who Hifly reminds you of?"

"John Henry," Nealy said without thinking. "Everyone remembers John Henry and his rags-to-riches story. He's a legend."

"Nobody wanted this guy. It was actually embarrassing. Metaxas wanted to *give* him to me, but I said no. So I bid five thousand bucks for him, and he's all mine. I think he knew no one wanted him and was grateful to me for taking him. He's good as gold. You know, Mom, you aren't always right. Give me some credit, okay?"

It was Nealy's turn to deflate. "You're right, Emmie. I'm sorry. Do what you think is right. I think I might know a jockey for you. He isn't a jockey yet, but I wouldn't be a bit surprised if the young man I have in mind is the answer to your prayers. He'll be here shortly. I'm going to be staying on for a while to train him."

"You're staying!" Emmie exclaimed. Her face wore a mixture of expressions Hatch couldn't define.

The grinding in Hatch's stomach picked up its tempo.

"Is that going to be a problem, Emmie?" Nealy asked quietly as she correctly interpreted the look on her daughter's face.

"No. As long as you don't interfere with the way I do things. I have a system, Mom, and it isn't like yours. Things aren't the same around here since you left. Smitty is gone, but her replacement is just as good. We have a new housekeeper, and Gabby has a nanny who lives in. I don't go to bed at eight o'clock and get up at four like you did. I have reliable, dependable help I can count on. I have a life outside the farm."

"I see," Nealy said, actually seeing more than she had bargained for. "No, Emmie, I won't interfere." Nealy turned to Hatch, her eyes bright with tears. "I guess it's true, you can't go home again no matter how much you love that home," she whispered so that only her husband could hear the words. Hatch draped his arm around her shoulders in a comforting gesture as they made their way up to the house.

In the kitchen, Nealy looked around. It was different, as was the person standing at the stove. She felt uncertain, unwanted, and out of place when she walked over to the counter where the coffeepot stood. It was empty. She was about to reach up into the cabinet for the coffee can when the housekeeper fixed her with a steely glare. "What is it you want, ma'am, and might I ask who you are, walking into my kitchen?"

Nealy bristled. "I was going to make some coffee. I'm Emmie's mother and I *own* this place. This is my husband Hatch, Mrs. Zoloff, and I'm Nealy. We're going to be staying on for a while."

"I'll make you some coffee, ma'am. I don't like people being in my kitchen when I'm working. You can sit in the dining room, and I'll fetch the coffee when it's ready."

Nealy nodded as she backed out of the kitchen. "I think we'll wait on the front porch instead."

On the porch, settled in Maud's old rocker, Nealy drew her knees up to her chest. "This isn't going to work, is it, Hatch?" She stared off into the distance, her shoulders shaking.

"I don't know, Nealy. Things seem to be a bit different. We talked about this when you turned the farm over to Emmie. Are you thinking you made a mistake in coming back here, honey?"

Nealy looked at the wilted geraniums in their white baskets. Most of the leaves were yellow, and even from where she was sitting, she could tell the soil was dry. Smitty always watered the plants when she forgot. She looked around. The porch was dirty, in need of a good scrubbing. Even the chair she was sitting on was dirty. She fought the urge to cry. "That's exactly what I'm thinking. Obviously, Emmie isn't overworked although she looks tired to me. She doesn't run around the way I remember. The truth is, she *trudges*. It's almost like she's in pain or something. Why didn't she water these plants? I guess 'this life' she has doesn't include such mundane things as watering plants. The porch needs painting. So do all the windows. It's only been a year, Hatch. I feel . . . betrayed. Is that the right word?"

"Nealy, maybe the porch, the flowers, the cleaning, and the painting aren't as important to Emmie as they were to you. Maybe she doesn't like to sit in the kitchen like you used to do. Don't expect too much is what I'm saying. You know, Nealy, we could find a place in town to rent if you don't want to stay here at the farm."

"Or maybe Emmie could go back to her own house and we'll stay here," Nealy snapped irritably. "When I walked away from this farm, everything was in order. There have been rules in place from the days when Maud and Jess ran Blue Diamond Farms. Rules and a system that worked perfectly. The house never needed paint, and the flowers were always watered. Gabby is in school and has a nanny, so she can't be taking up too much of Emmie's time."

"Whoa, honey. Slow down here. You can say whatever you

want to me, but you better be careful what you say to Emmie. I sensed a bit of pride in her. She's running things very well. Perhaps differently than you did, but still running things. I didn't see one thing amiss down by the barns, and those horses all looked great to me. Face it, honey, you don't like change."

Nealy rubbed at her temples. She knew her husband was right. For some reason he was always right. When that happened, it meant she was wrong.

"She's training the wrong horse. That little pygmy she bought is not racing material," Nealy said quietly.

"You don't know that, Nealy. You're questioning her judgment here. Is that wise? You came on pretty damn strong down there in the paddock. She wilted right in front of our eyes. That wasn't fair, Nealy."

"Yes, I do know that, Hatch. I also know Emmie. She's going to do double time to prove me wrong. She'll devote every waking hour to working with that horse. She'll coddle him, sleep in the barn with him, and be there for him twenty-four hours a day. If he has any chance at all, she'll run him in the Derby when he's ready."

The screen door squeaked and then opened. The housekeeper set a tray with two cups of coffee on the table. Nealy thanked her and reached for one of the cups. The coffee was good. She set the cup back down and dropped to her knees. She started to peel off the yellowing leaves on the geraniums.

"And you know this how?" Hatch asked.

"Because it's what I would do if I were Emmie." Nealy laughed. "She's right about him looking like John Henry, too. Now, that was a horse, Hatch. There are so many interesting stories about John Henry. No one wanted him either and he was a gelding. You've heard of Bill Shoemaker, the legendary jockey, right?" Hatch nodded. "Bill rode him in the Arlington Million. He was named horse of the year and moved up to the top of the all-time leading money earners' list with over six and a half million dollars in winnings. He retired the year after tearing the suspensory ligament in his left foreleg. He's staying at Kentucky Horse Park in Lexington until the end of his days."

Nealy stared across at the paddocks. "The grand old man, as he was called, retired with thirty-nine victories and twenty-four places and shows in eighty-three starts and was the all-time leading money earner. He was elected into the Racing Hall of Fame in 1990. I don't know if Emmie's horse is that good or not. If he's half the horse John Henry was, she can't go wrong. She must think he's pretty good."

"So there you go," Hatch said, eyeing her over the rim of his coffee cup. "Anything is possible."

Nealy grimaced. "Emmie doesn't have the guts to work at something twenty-four hours a day. She gives up too easily. She knows how to work but she doesn't know what *hard* work really is," Nealy said, sitting back on her haunches. "I'm going to soak these good, and give them a super dose of plant food. I was hoping everything would look nice when the family got here. I'm disappointed Emmie doesn't have more pride in the farm. I guess I'll have to clean the porch and the furniture myself."

Hatch raised his eyes to see Emmie through the screen door. He was about to say something when Emmie put her finger to her lips for him to remain silent. He looked away, wondering how long she'd been standing there and what she'd heard.

"I'll help you, honey. Let's call it a togetherness project, or, hell, we can just go out and buy some new plants. These do look pretty bedraggled."

"Yes, let's do that, Hatch. Do you have the car keys? On second thought, we should probably take one of the pickup trucks if we're going to buy a lot of plants."

"Sounds like a plan to me," Hatch said, struggling to his feet. "I'll get the truck. You keep the keys on the visor, right?"

"That's what I used to do. I don't know what Emmie does," Nealy said as she finished the last of her coffee.

Nealy carried the serving tray into the house, holding the screen door ajar with her hip. She loved the sound of the squeaky door when it closed behind her. She was startled to see Emmie in the kitchen. She frowned. The frown deepened when she saw Mitch Cunningham walk into the kitchen as if he'd been doing it forever.

"Hatch and I are going to the nursery for some new plants. The ones on the porch are half-dead, and I don't think watering can save them. By the way, did you call the painter to do the windows and porch? The paint is peeling. Nice to see you again,

Mitch." She waited for her daughter's response. When none was forthcoming, Nealy stomped her way out the door, her blood at the boiling point.

While she waited for Hatch, she walked along the side of the house to check on the flower gardens and the morning glories climbing the trellises. All looked bedraggled and sadly in need of water. Weeds were choking out even the hardiest of the flowers.

"Hop in, honey!" Hatch called from the truck. "What's wrong?"

"Maybe it's me, Hatch. Do I expect too much? When things needed to be done, if I couldn't do them myself, I hired someone to do it. All the gardens are going to seed, and it's just the end of April. Those flower borders and the trellises were my pride and joy. They were the color and sunshine in my life from the day I moved here. In one year, my daughter managed to ruin it all. She said she could handle this. She said she was capable. I believed her. Don't worry, I didn't say anything. I bit my tongue. Then that Hollywood guy showed up, just walked into the kitchen like he'd been doing it forever, and he probably has. Emmie had this sappy look on her face. I see what's going on, and I don't like it. Say something, Hatch."

"Not on your life."

"So you're saying I'm going off half-cocked here," Nealy said, using one of Hatch's favorite expressions for when she did something without thinking it through.

"How hard is it to plant flowers? You and I can do it and have the place all spruced up by the time your family arrives on the weekend. I can scrape the paint on the front porch and paint it myself. You know how you love our together projects," Hatch said, hoping to drive the angry look off his wife's face.

"That's not the point, Hatch. I'm talking about responsibility. I hate to think what I'm going to find when I check out the barns."

"Fair is fair, Nealy. You had Smitty to run interference for you. She did a lot around here, and so did your housekeeper. Emmie doesn't have a Smitty. Maybe she's doing the best she can."

Nealy's face set into stubborn lines. "I did it, and I'm a hell of a lot older than she is. Don't throw Gabby at me either. She's in school and has a nanny. And another thing, Emmie took over my bedroom knowing I would be coming back and forth. I saw her robe on my bed and it was unmade when I went up to the second floor to use the bathroom. Why isn't her own room good enough for her? I'm angry, Hatch. I think I have a right to be angry, too."

"Nealy, you need to calm down and decide how important this is to you."

"You know what, Hatch? It is important to me. Did you see all that junk piled up out back? We have trash containers. How hard is it to toss something out instead of dumping it on a pile? There's a soaking-wet crib mattress just lying there with all kinds of rusty junk. That doesn't look good. It all looks shabby and unkempt, and I will not tolerate it. If I have to boot her ass out again, I will. I mean it."

Hatch cringed at his wife's tone. He swerved off the road and pulled into the nursery parking lot and parked alongside a bright red pickup that was being loaded with peat moss.

Hatch turned off the engine and pocketed the key. "Is this your way of telling me you want to stay here?"

"No, Hatch. Not at all. If Emmie can't do the job, then I have to find someone to take over the farm. If you remember, I had misgivings from the beginning. On the surface, it sounded wonderful and right. Daughter taking over when mother retires, that kind of thing. I don't know, maybe she doesn't see things and needs glasses. I don't want to talk about this anymore. Let's pick out the plants so I can calm down. My first day home, and it's all been ruined."

Hatch picked up on the word: *home.*

"How about some coffee, Mitch?"

"Coffee sounds good. I was just getting ready to head back to town. Would you like to take in a movie tonight?"

"Sure. Let's go out on the porch and drink our coffee. Great day, isn't it?" Any excuse in the world to sit down. She was one giant ache. She'd just swallowed three aspirin, and they didn't do a thing for her. She felt like crying. She hoped she could keep up her end of the conversation without gritting her teeth.

"Perfect for filming. I hope it's this nice when your family gets here, and I sure as hell hope the sun is shining for the Derby. Wow, what happened here?" Mitch asked, pointing to the litter of yellow leaves and broken stems that were all over the porch. "I don't think I'll sit down. Doesn't your housekeeper believe in cleaning the porch?" Mitch asked as he looked down at his khaki pants.

The porch was her mother's favorite place on the farm. Emmie looked at it now through Mitch's eyes and then her own. She groaned. "I hardly ever come out here anymore. I just assumed that Gertie took care of it. I see now that it doesn't pay to assume." She looked over the railing at the flower beds and winced. No wonder her mother looked like she'd swallowed a sour lemon. The flower borders, the little gardens, and the trellises with the climbing morning glories were her pride and joy. "Damn, I can't do anything right," she muttered.

"Listen, Mitch, I'm sorry, but I think I'll pass on the movie. I need to weed these gardens before my mother gets back. She's about to pitch a fit. I could see it in her face. She likes things done a certain way, and I think I just screwed up."

"Don't you have a gardener or some kid to mow and weed?"

"We did, but he stopped showing up a while ago, and I never replaced him. Time got away from me, I guess. I'm not going to see this in your movie, am I?"

"No. How about dinner tomorrow night?"

"Okay. Seven?"

"Seven it is. I'll pick you up."

"No, it's out of your way to drive all the way back here. I'll meet you in town. Where do you want to go?"

"How about the rib place. You said you loved spare ribs."

"You remembered?" Emmie asked in awe as she yanked at a stubborn weed.

"Yes. Okay, I'll meet you at seven tomorrow evening. I won't be here tomorrow or the rest of the week. I'll be back on the weekend, and then it's off to California. I'm going to miss you, Emmie. I'll call you, okay?"

"Sure. I'm usually here in the evening. I want to know how the film editing is going. It's all so interesting." She turned away so she could bite down on her lip. Her right knee was sending shooting pains up and down her leg.

"Best job in the world. I suppose everyone says that about their job. I'll see you tomorrow night."

"Okay," Emmie said as she scooped out weeds by the handful. She sat back on her heels and looked up at the porch, then down the length of the flower borders. It would take her days to get the gardens back to their original beauty. How could she have been so stupid, so thoughtless? How? She bit down on her lower lip knowing she was going to cry and hating herself for being so wishy-washy. She struggled to blink back her tears. Work through the pain, her mother was fond of saying. Only weak people get sick was another favorite saying. She wanted to scream but knew she couldn't.

She looked up to see the housekeeper standing on the front porch. "There's a phone call for you, Miss Emmie. She wouldn't say who she was, just that it was important she speak with you."

Emmie bounded up the steps just as the farm's pickup appeared on the road leading to the back of the house.

Gertie placed the phone between Emmie's ear and shoulder so she could wash her hands at the sink. "This is Emmie."

"Emmie, this is Willow. Listen, Emmie, I need to talk to you. It's really important. You're the only one I can trust. Is this a good time?"

Emmie was stunned at the words. "Actually, no, it isn't. My mother just arrived today and . . . she's going to be coming in any minute now. I can call you back later or you can call me later, after eight or so. Nine would be better. Can you do that?"

"Yes. Yes, I can do that. Emmie, promise me you won't tell anyone I called. I'll explain everything when I talk to you. Will you promise?"

"Yes. Call me after nine."

Emmie stared at the pinging phone in her hand. Willow Bishop Clay. The same Willow who married her half brother Nick and dumped him a few days later. The same Willow who went three rounds with her mother. Why was she calling her after seven long years? She shivered as she allowed her imagination to run wild.

Her thoughts chaotic, Emmie watched as her mother and Hatch started taking plants and paint out of the back of the truck. Even from this distance she could see the grim set of her mother's jaw and her stiff shoulders. She squared her own shoulders and marched down the steps, each step painful and jarring as she made her way over to the truck. She likened it in her mind to bearding the lion.

"I guess you're pretty mad, huh, Mom? Look, I'm sorry."

Nealy reached for another flat. "Sorry isn't going to cut it. This place looks like some backwoods shanty gone to seed. Yes, I'm mad, so it might be a good idea for you to get your tail out of here until I calm down. When you're in charge that means you're in charge. You told me you were up to the job. What the hell happened to our yard boy, Toby?"

"Toby graduated from high school this year. I guess he had a lot of stuff going on at school and just didn't want to do this anymore. He said he was going to find a replacement at least for the summer, but no one showed up. I let it slide. I'll call him again."

"The last thing I said to you before I left was to call Mr. Frances to paint the trim around the windows and the porch. Do you remember?"

"Yes," Emmie mumbled. "Mr. Frances slid down the ladder on a job and broke his hip. He said he'd get out here when he could. I didn't want to call anyone else since you said he'd worked for you for years and years. I didn't want to take the job away from him. I guess that was wrong, too." She started to walk away, knowing she was going to cry any second. Not so much with frustration with her mother but with the pain that was engulfing her body. She needed more aspirin. How many aspirin could one person take? Would her stomach start to bleed? Maybe she needed to eat something so the aspirin wouldn't irritate her stomach. What was happening to her?

Her mother was relentless, though. "Just a minute, young lady. Who told you to take over my bedroom? That room is mine, not yours. You have your own room."

Emmie spun around on her heel and eyeballed her mother. "You know what, Mom, you can take this job, this farm, and you can shove it up your ass. I can't do anything right. No matter what I do, I can't please you. Nick was the only one who could please you. Well, guess what, Nick doesn't want this place or this job. That's the only reason you gave it to me to run. I must have been really stupid to think I wanted it. You won't have to throw me out this time, I'll walk out on my own. I hate it, and I hate you when you do this to me. I'm not you. I'm me. Keep your damn bedroom, keep the whole damn place. Stupid flowers, stupid paint, stupid junk. I knew this was going to happen the minute you said you were coming back here. And, another thing, Mother, I didn't take over your room. I've been having trouble with my back, and your mattress is harder than mine. All my things are still in my room. I never used your bathroom either, if that's the next question. Yes, I should have bought a new mattress, but I didn't, so add that to your list, too. I'll be out of here as soon as Gabby gets home."

"That won't be necessary, Emmie. Hatch and I will be staying in town. I apologize. Do what you want. Call me when the family arrives." Nealy's throat closed so tight she couldn't have uttered another word if her life depended on it. She set the flat of flowers down, dusted her hands, and walked toward the rental Hatch had picked up at the airport.

Her hands jammed into her pockets, Emmie watched the Lincoln Town Car until it was out of sight. She had just experienced one of the mystical wonders of the world. Her mother had backed down. She didn't feel elated at all. In her mother's eyes she was a failure. Like hell! She struggled to take a deep breath as waves of pain engulfed her.

Emmie stomped her way up the steps and into the kitchen, where she bellowed at the top of her lungs. "Everyone in the kitchen! *Now!*"

The three office girls, whose names she could never remember, Agnes Beakman, the office manager, and Gertie, the housekeeper, came from all directions. Agnes folded her hands in front of her, her expression saying, 'this better be good,' while the three young office girls twitched nervously. Gertie just looked puzzled.

"Ladies, things are going to change around here starting right this minute. For a long time my family had loyal, friendly help here in the house. You ladies are not loyal; nor are you friendly. I've decided I don't much care for your attitudes. If you like working here, and if you like the generous salaries I pay you and want to keep working for me, things have to change. We're talking about initiative here. Gertie, the front porch is a disgrace. It's dirty, the flowers are half-dead and haven't been watered in weeks. Our family is arriving this weekend, and I want this place spruced up. Big-time."

Emmie fixed her gaze on the three young women. "From now on, you aren't going to have time to read those trashy magazines I see littered all over the office. You are going to weed the gardens and plant flowers. Starting *now!* You will continue to do that throughout the summer. It would also be nice to see some of those pretty flowers on the kitchen table once in a while.

"Aggie, I don't much care for your hostile attitude. Yes, you do a bang-up job, but I have never seen you smile once in the whole year you've been here. If this job is a chore or if you hate it, you might want to think about moving on. I don't like negative people. It tends to rub off on one. You need to pitch in. Office work does not take all day. Since you're on a salary, you *will* do as I say. There are four doors in this house, a front door, a back door, and the two side doors. What that means is, it's my way or the highway, ladies.

"Gertie, from now on I will be hanging out in the kitchen whether you like it or not. I like sitting at the table to eat and drink my coffee when I take a break. I do not, I repeat, I do not like to sit in the dining room. If I feel like making coffee or slopping up the sink as you put it, I will do it. I pay you an outrageous sum of money for the little you do. From now on, I'm taking a page out of my mother's book. I'll kick ass and take names later. As I said, there are four doors. What's it going to be?" Emmie sucked in her breath and waited for a response.

"Tell me what you want me to do," one of the young girls said. "I know how to plant flowers. I do it at home all the time for my mother. I can show Annie and Donna how to do it. I'm assuming you want us to start with the porch and work our way down to the gardens."

"Yes," Emmie said.

The office manager drew herself up to her full height. "Well, I never," she sputtered, at a loss for words.

"What's it gonna be, Aggie, the unemployment line or this nice cushy job here at Blue Diamond Farms? You might want to think about your nice 401(K) and that comfortable health insurance plan we have you on. It ceases the minute you walk out the door."

"I'll stay. Perhaps it would help both of us if you outlined what it is you expect of me, Miss Coleman. You never did say."

"That's true, I didn't say what you were to do. You said you were an office manager, and Smitty spent two weeks with you. You saw what she did and how she did it. You watched, but you didn't apply what she taught you. You will pitch in when needed and you will smile and you will treat me with the respect I deserve."

Aggie smiled. Emmie clapped her hands. "Good, now we're getting somewhere.

"Gertie?"

"I can't work in the kitchen with people watching me," the housekeeper said, wringing her hands in frustration.

Emmie pointed to the kitchen door.

"I can learn, Miss Emmie," she added hastily.

"Okay, that means we're all now on the same page. Let's get to it. I have a phone call to make and then you, Aggie, and I are going to lug all that junk by the back door out to the Dumpster. Feel free to start without me. I don't suppose any of you knows a good house painter, do you?"

"My dad's a house painter," Donna said. "He's always looking for extra work."

Emmie pointed to the phone. "Call him and tell him if he wants, he can start right now. I need all this done by the weekend."

"My brother helps out when Dad gets behind," Donna said as she dialed her home phone number.

Emmie waited, her face breaking into a smile when the young woman said, "My dad said he can come out at one-thirty and start scraping."

"That's great. Okay, disperse and make this place sparkle. Jenny, you're in charge of the planting. I don't want to see even one weed." She would have cheered if she'd been able to work up the energy.

"Yes, ma'am."

"If you ruin your clothes, I'll replace them," Emmie said generously. "From now on, just in case you're called on for something similar, keep some old clothes here." Her left hand massaged her aching right hand as she spoke. She almost swooned with the sudden relief she felt.

"Gertie, I'd like a tuna sandwich and some coffee in about thirty minutes. First I have a call to make, and I have to help Aggie. I'll be sitting right here at this table while you fix it, so get used to it."

"Yes, Miss Emmie."

"Gertie, skip the Miss and just call me Emmie."

Emmie flipped through the back of the phone book until she had the number she wanted. She punched in the numbers and waited. "This is Emmie Coleman at Blue Diamond Farms. I'd like to order a Serta Perfect Sleeper mattress. The orthopedic one. The firmer it is the better. I'd like delivery this afternoon if possible. Between four and five sounds great. Thank you."

Outside, she bent down to pick up a load of junk to drag to the Dumpster. When had she gotten so sloppy? When she first started to experience the joint pain, that's when. It was simpler just to toss something than to walk all the way to the Dumpster.

"I was never a sloppy person. I don't know why I kept tossing junk onto this pile. My mother is right, it looks like a bunch of hillbillies live here. Sometimes I get so caught up in what I'm doing, I forget the things I should be doing. If you see that happening, Aggie, bring me up short."

"I can do that, I guess," she said, jerking her head toward the kitchen. "Back there you were trying to tell us we weren't measuring up to Smitty. I'm sorry about that. I thought you wanted me to be professional. I didn't know you wanted us to . . ."

"Blend in with us, be a part of the family, is that what you mean? We're loose around here. There aren't that many rules. I'm not going to ride your asses. First of all, I shouldn't have to do that. If you see a problem, work on it. If I see a problem, I'll ask for your help. I can't be everywhere, and I can't do everything myself. I *need* you, Aggie, and I *need* the girls, and I *need* Gertie to make it all work."

"That's all you had to say, ma'am. None of us are mind readers. I thought we were doing what you wanted."

"Stop with the 'ma'am' stuff, Aggie. Call me Emmie. I want us to be friends. By the way, I think your blouse is ruined. I'll be happy to get you a new one. From now on, bring some old clothes and keep them handy."

"All right, Emmie. That's the last of it," Aggie said, throwing a trash bag into the Dumpster. "You might want to rake this ground a little and get all the little pieces of junk cleaned up. I think some bright pink petunias would look real nice here with a little border of sweet williams in white. What do you think?"

"What I think is you are one very smart lady." Emmie stretched out her hand. Aggie pumped it vigorously. The pain was excruciating. *Why didn't I do this months ago?* Emmie wondered.

Always honest with herself, she knew the answer. She'd spent all her spare time daydreaming about Mitch Cunningham. When she wasn't daydreaming, she had searched for ways to insinuate herself into his company, almost to the exclusion of all else. She'd screwed up big-time in her mother's eyes. And then there was the pain and the need to hide what she was feeling. Now she had to make it right. Realist that she was, she knew now that Mitch Cunningham viewed her as a friend and probably nothing more. And he was leaving in a few days for California. Long-distance romances never worked according to the slick magazine articles she read from time to time. *Tomorrow morning, no matter what, I'm going to go into town to the doctor. If I just show up and they see how miserable I am, maybe they'll see me on the spot and not make me wait for an appointment.*

Emmie walked around to the front of the house, where she picked up a trowel and a small rake along with a flat of petunias. An hour later she was sprinkling the freshly planted flowers and heaving a huge sigh of relief. Relief mostly because the pain in her knees didn't seem as bad.

Knowing her mother as she did, she knew when she returned to the farm on the weekend, she wouldn't say a word about the flowers, the fresh paint, or the removal of the junk pile. She probably wouldn't go upstairs either, just to make her point. "She thinks I'm lazy, that I don't care. She's thinking she made a mistake in turning the farm over to me," she muttered to herself as she made her way to the kitchen where, to Gertie's dismay, she washed her hands in the kitchen sink. The warm water rushing over her swollen hands felt wonderful. She held her hands under the water until Gertie looked at her pointedly. "I've washed my hands here in this sink all my life and I'm not going to stop now, so don't look at me like that, Gertie. Every damn time I do it, you give me the evil eye. I'm taking charge, and we're going to do things my way from now on so get used to it. Is my lunch ready?"

"I have it all ready. Would you like a slice of pie?"

"Maybe for dinner. I hope you made enough for everyone. I didn't know until recently that you haven't been making lunch for the girls in the office. They work here, so that means they get lunch, too. It's always been that way. So from now on, you will prepare lunch for anyone working here in the house, including me. You are not overworked, Gertie. You straighten up, dust, vacuum, cook, and that's it. I do mine and Gabby's laundry, and I take care of both our rooms. You're going to have to tape your soap operas and watch them at night when you go home.

"I'm not blaming anyone. I let this whole thing get out of hand. I probably would have done the same thing you and the office staff did if no one was watching me. I'm watching now. I want a day's work for a day's pay. That's the bottom line. Maybe I will have a slice of that pie."

As she chewed her way through the sandwich Gertie had fixed for her, Emmie's thoughts went to the phone call from Willow. Just the thought of what she might possibly want made her break out into a cold sweat.

The old Emmie would have called Nick, promise or no promise. But this new Emmie, who had failed so miserably in her mother's eyes, wasn't about to break a promise. Her mother had always been big on promises and handshakes. It shows a person's character, she'd said. And she was right.

It was time to go down to the barn and time to work at what she did best. She hoped and prayed the pain would allow her to do it.

"The pie was really good, Gertie. Next time, put more celery in the tuna. Make pot roast for dinner, please, and potato pancakes."

"I was going to make pork chops," Gertie said, her face turning red with the declaration.

"I really don't like pork chops, Gertie. Gabby has a hard time chewing them. Pot roast will be good. Mashed potatoes, wilted lettuce, and fresh string beans. Fruit cocktail for Gabby. From now on, I'll tell you in the morning what I want for dinner. That way I won't have to eat something I don't like so as not to hurt your feelings. Are we clear on this?"

"Yes, we're clear on it. You really got your panties in a wad today, didn't you? Is it always going to be like this when your mother comes to visit?" Gertie said boldly.

"God, I hope not. I think everyone gets the picture now. This is the way it's going to be from now on. I'd like some flowers here on the table and maybe some in the clay pots under the windowsill. You can water them when you do the ones on the front porch."

Emmie heard the housekeeper mumbling as she made her way out to the back porch. "Take this trash to the Dumpster, Gertie. Don't bag it and leave it on the porch anymore. Do it now before you forget!"

"I am my mother's daughter," Emmie said over and over as she made her way to the barn. "I don't know if it's something to be proud of or not."

Time will tell, she thought.

3

Emmie stared down at her sleeping daughter. How sweet and innocent she looked in sleep. She lowered herself gingerly to the bed. She really had to see a doctor about her back. Hot soaks in the tub and the deep penetrating ointments she rubbed on daily weren't helping at all. She'd swallowed bottles of aspirin, so many in fact, Gertie had asked her if she was hoarding them. Nothing seemed to be working. Her hand went out absentmindedly, to scratch Cookie behind his ears. The little fluff ball licked her hand before he settled himself more snugly in the crook of Gabby's knees.

Emmie continued to stare at her daughter, seeing a strong resemblance to Buddy, her ex-husband, in the sweep of her cheek and the extra-long curly lashes that fringed her bright blue eyes. Thank God she hadn't inherited his deafness.

Emmie had known Buddy from childhood; he was the son of a neighboring Thoroughbred horse breeder. When his parents were killed, Nealy took him into her home and cared for him. Buddy and Emmie had attended the same school for the hearing- and speech-impaired, where they learned to sign.

Buddy had been the perfect friend, and they had looked out for one another. It was inevitable that they would marry. At least her mother had said it was inevitable. Emmie could no longer remember what she had thought.

She leaned back against the footboard trying to ease the pain in her back as well as taking pressure off her knees. She looked at the tight stretch of the jeans over her knees and flinched. Because she didn't want to think about what she called "my condition," she switched her mental gears and thought about her ex-husband, Buddy.

They had been happy enough because of familiarity, but it

wasn't the happiness or love of romance novels. It was just a comfortable way of life. She supposed she'd been happy, but what did she really have to compare that happiness to? Nothing. Then, one day, fear had allowed her to cry out. Long months of speech therapy ensued, and eventually she was able to talk normally. Buddy had been furious. Not that he ever said so in words. She could see it on his face when she spoke with people, sometimes forgetting to sign in front of him and voicing her thoughts aloud. He'd drawn away from her, little by little, and she hadn't been able to recapture the old, easy familiarity. Maybe she hadn't tried hard enough. And sometimes she thought it was Buddy who hadn't tried hard enough.

Suspecting she might be pregnant, wary of telling Buddy, she'd planned a romantic cruise, hoping the time would be right to tell him then. It hadn't worked that way at all. Buddy had been surly and angry during the whole cruise, leaving her to fend for herself while he stayed in the stateroom and read stacks of books from the ship's library. Then, the day they disembarked, he'd left her standing on the gangplank, saying he was filing for a divorce.

Emmie squirmed on the bed, her body burning with shame at the scene on the gangplank. She'd clutched at him, begged him not to leave her. He'd shaken her off like she was a stray dog. Her hands went to her burning face. She'd screamed at him, promising she would stop talking if that was what he wanted.

"Too late," he'd signed back. "I don't love you anymore."

Then he walked away and didn't look back.

She'd gone back to the house they shared and licked her wounds, crying until there were no more tears. Her mother had been furious with her, and with Nick, too, because both of them were a week late returning to work at the farm. She'd been so angry she banished both of them for three long years.

Emmie blinked away the tears. She didn't want to think about those miserable years. She smiled at the sleeping child, patted Cookie, and left the room when she heard the phone ringing in her own bedroom. She hobbled down the hall and picked up the phone on the sixth ring.

"Mom!"

"Emmie, I'm sorry. I'm calling to apologize. I was out of line today. It won't happen again. I don't want any hard feelings coming between us. We've had enough of that these past few years. Is it too late to be calling? Are you getting Gabby ready for bed?"

"We were both wrong, Mom. We both overreacted. I know I did. It's all been taken care of. I wish you'd come back to the farm. I got a new mattress delivered today, so I'm back in my own room. Gabby's asleep. School really tires her out. I was sitting in her room thinking about Buddy. There are days when I think I should tell him about Gabby and days when I know keeping quiet is the best thing I can do. Sometimes he can be vindictive. In the past he was. I don't have a clue as to what he's like now. Maybe it's best to let sleeping dogs lie."

"I would never advise you on something like that, Emmie. You are the only one who can make that decision. One day, though, Gabby will want to know. It's hard to imagine what her reaction might be.

"Is it all right if Hatch and I come out to the farm tomorrow, Emmie? Will we be in the way?"

"Mom, you own this farm. You can come out here anytime you want. I'm sorry I let you down. I did, so you don't have to be nice about it. It's the house, not the barns and the horses, that kicks my butt. I don't know how you did it."

"We can talk about that tomorrow. I want to know the latest on the movie and how things went while I was away. You like Mitch, don't you?"

"What's not to like? He's handsome in a rugged kind of way. He's charming, and he's easy to work with. All his workers like him. That says a lot. He's got a sterling reputation. I've had to ask myself why no one snagged him. He told me he was married for ten minutes, and it didn't work. Maybe he's married to his work. Yes, I do like him, Mom. We had dinner not too long ago, and he asked me to dinner again tomorrow evening. I said yes. We're just friends. It's not going anywhere, Mom. He lives on one coast and I closer to the other. I gotta tell you, though, I was practically throwing myself at him the whole time he's been here, and he didn't give me a second thought. I think he feels safe where I'm concerned because he'll be leaving in a few days. No commitment, that kind of thing. Like I said, we're just friends."

"Men and women have overcome worse obstacles than distance, honey. Just look at Hatch and me. Think of it this way, it's his loss."

"I know, Mom. But Mitch and I aren't like you and Hatch. Mitch thinks of me only as a friend. I think he feels safe with me. Besides, he's going back to California in a few days, but he's leaving his crew here to film the Derby."

It sounded to Emmie like they were back on track. She imagined she heard forgiveness in her mother's voice. She laughed. "I'm glad you called, Mom. I would have gone looking for you tomorrow. Are you staying at the Inn? I love you, Mom."

"I know you do, and I feel the same way. Yes, we're staying at the Inn. We have a beautiful room with a sunken tub. I'll see you tomorrow, Emmie."

Emmie sat on the edge of the bed and pulled off her boots and socks. Her eyes widened as her feet swelled to twice their size in front of her eyes. She reached down to poke at her puffy ankles and noticed that her fingers were the size of little sausage links. It was almost impossible to pull her jeans down over her swollen knees. Her puffy fingers couldn't get a firm grip on the heavy denim. Tears streaming down her cheeks, she finally managed to push the jeans down to her ankles. It was another searing jolt to pull the pant legs past her swollen ankles and feet. A searing pain ripped up her back as she hobbled to the bathroom. Could stress make you swell up like this? A feeling of panic rushed through her. Maybe she needed to soak in a hot tub.

Emmie sat on the edge of the tub watching the water swirl and splash. She continued to stare at her feet and hands. For a month, she'd noticed that at the end of the day, her feet and hands ached and were a little puffy. She'd ignored it just the way she tried to ignore the pain in her back. Now, she could no longer ignore her condition. What would happen in the morning if the swelling didn't go down and she couldn't get her boots on? *Don't borrow trouble,* she cautioned herself.

She looked at the time before she removed her watch. She

had forty minutes before it was time for Willow to call. Maybe she should bring the portable phone into the bathroom so she could continue to soak while she talked to Nick's wife. All it took was three steps across the bathroom before she found herself on the floor, a look of shock and pain on her face. She crab-crawled into the bedroom and reached for the phone. It slipped out of her hands. She pushed it forward as she crawled back to the bathroom. She cried then as she pressed 0 for the operator. "Please, I can't dial the numbers. Will you ring the Inn and ask for Mrs. Littletree's room. This is Emmie Coleman. Yes, thank you."

Emmie almost fainted when she heard her mother's voice. "Mom, there's something wrong with me. You have to come out here now. Please, Mom. I'm in the bathroom, and I can't move. Hurry, Mom."

"We'll be right there, Emmie. Stay where you are. I'll call the doctor on the way."

The phone slipped away from Emmie. She cried harder when Cookie waddled over to her and flopped down next to her, waiting for Emmie to scratch his ears. "I can't, Cookie." Her tears soaked into the bathroom carpet just as the tub overflowed. It took every ounce of strength in her body to get to her knees and turn off the faucet, using her wrists. She was soaked to the skin when she fell back onto the mat that was by then dripping wet. *What is wrong with me? Hurry, Mom. Please hurry.*

Twenty minutes later, Nealy flew up the steps, calling her daughter's name as she went along, Hatch lumbering behind her. She ran straight to Emmie's bathroom and almost fainted at the sight of her daughter. Emmie's name ripped from her soul.

Hatch bent down to pick up his stepdaughter. He carried her to the bed and lowered her gently. "The doctor is on his way, Emmie."

Nealy sat down on the edge of the bed and stroked her daughter's head. "Emmie, oh, God, Emmie, how did this happen? I know this might be a stupid thing to say but did you eat something that might have caused a reaction like this? You were fine, earlier."

"No, Mom, I didn't eat anything different. I wasn't fine either. When I took off my boots, my feet started to swell. Sometimes they get puffy at the end of the day, my fingers, too, but never like this. The pain in my back has been getting worse. I've been hurting for a long time, but I didn't want you to know. You know your motto has always been work through the pain. I tried. I gobbled aspirin by the handful and took hot baths. Nothing seemed to work. Honest to God, Mom, I tried. I was going to go to the doctor tomorrow because it's been getting worse. What's wrong with me, Mom?"

"Emmie, I don't know. The doctor should be here any minute now. Hatch, go down and wait for him. Bring him right up."

"If I was a horse, what would this be, Mom?"

"Off the top of my head, I'd say arthritis. Emmie, I just don't know. Why did you wait so long, honey?"

"I guess I was stupid and thought it would eventually go away. Mom, I can't get sick. I have Gabby to take care of. I'm all she has. Oh, God, you don't think this is God's way of telling me I should have told Buddy about our daughter. Am I going to die, Mom?"

Nealy sucked in her breath and was saved from a reply when Hatch ushered in the doctor. She stared at him. "Where's Dr. Ward?"

"Dad's on a fishing trip, ma'am, and won't be back till the end of May. It's his first real vacation in fifteen years. I'm Luke. I'm an internist and practice in Lexington. It might be a good idea for you and your husband to wait outside while I examine my patient."

Nealy nodded.

"He's too *young,* Hatch. My God, he looks about Emmie's age. What's wrong with her, Hatch? You don't think it's serious, do you? She said she did what I told her to do, which was work through the pain. Never give in. I didn't mean for something like this. I meant for an ache or just plain old tiredness. I think she's saying this is my fault."

"That's not what she's saying. Young is good, Nealy. That means he's up on all the latest medical news. Sometimes the older doctors are so busy they tend to let things slide. I do think it's serious, and I think it's rheumatoid arthritis. A lot of the elders on the reservation have RA. She's not going to die if that's your next question. I'd say she's had this for a while and ignored it. That's just my opinion, Nealy."

"That means she'll be crippled. Like Maud. Like Sunny. Oh Hatch, she's too young for something like this." Nealy threw herself into her husband's arms and wept.

"Nealy, honey, children get rheumatoid arthritis. It doesn't just strike old people."

Nealy whirled around when the door opened. She wiped at her eyes, knowing her heavy makeup was going to get smeared—the makeup prescribed just for her, to cover the scars from all her facial operations because of the fire at Blue Diamond Farms. Her eyes were full of questions.

"I'm going to admit Emmie to the hospital. We need to run tests, do a lot of blood work, and try to reduce the inflammation. We'll be testing for rheumatoid arthritis."

"How could she get something so serious, just like that?" Nealy said.

"No, not just like that. She's had a lot of symptoms she tried treating with aspirin. Sometimes people think if they ignore something, it will go away. This is not going to go away. She doesn't want to go in an ambulance to spook the workers, she said. So, Mr. Littletree, if you can carry her down to the car, I'll take her in myself. She wants both of you to stay here with her daughter."

"She doesn't want us to go with her?" Nealy asked, dismay written all over her face.

"She wants you to stay with her daughter. She said there's nothing you can do for her at the hospital, and she's right. The little one might wake during the night. She'll want you even though she has a nanny in the next room. Stress is not good for someone with RA. Can I tell her you agree?"

"Yes, of course," Nealy said.

"Mr. Littletree, if you'll do the honors, we can be on our way."

"Mom, I don't want to go to the hospital. One day, that's it. Mom?"

"Emmie, you have to do what the doctor says. A day, two days, even three. We need to find out what it is so you can be treated properly. Don't worry about anything."

"Hifly?"

"I'll take good care of him, Emmie. Just do what the doctor wants. We'll see you tomorrow. It's going to be all right, Emmie."

Nealy was standing by the front door when the phone rang behind her. She walked over to the little alcove and picked up the phone. "Hello."

"Emmie?"

"No, this is Emmie's mother. I'm sorry, but Emmie is on her way to the hospital. Can I take a message?"

"The hospital?" the voice queried. Nealy frowned.

"Just for some testing. Can I ask who's calling? I'll be happy to give her a message in the morning."

"Just tell her Mary Ann called. I'm a friend of hers. I'll call again."

"All right, Mary Ann." Nealy replaced the phone, a frown building on her face. She looked at her husband. "I don't know anyone named Mary Ann, but her voice sounded familiar." She shrugged. "I guess she's a new friend. Or maybe she's with the film crew."

"Come on, honey, let's make some coffee and sit on the porch. Like it or not, Nealy, it looks like you're back in the saddle. We need to talk."

"Yes, I guess we do," Nealy said, reaching for the coffee canister.

Hatch watched his wife from a distance. He knew she was in her element but sad and unnerved at the same time. She was back—back where she felt she belonged. He'd taken her away after her recovery from the awful burns, and she'd gone with him willingly. Never by word or deed did she even allude to the possibility she might be sad or that she was homesick for Blue Diamond Farms. But he knew, because you always know when the one person you love more than anything in the world is hiding something from you. Even when it was as simple as an emotion or a smile.

Nealy looked up, shading her eyes with the palm of her hand. She motioned him to join her. He did.

"How's everything looking, Hatch?"

"Great. The porch is done, everything is scrubbed and sparkling. The flowers are blooming just the way they're supposed to. The gardens are really pretty. The girls did a good job. I think your family will enjoy sitting out on the porch. You might need a few more chairs, though. I checked the barbecue pit, and everything looks good to go. I told Aggie to come and fetch us if the doctor or hospital calls. How's it going down here?"

"I'm too old for this, Hatch. My stamina is gone. I'm good at supervising, but that's about it. Emmie has some good people here. They know what they're doing, and they're dependable. Everyone on the farm is rooting for this runt." She grinned as she pointed to Hifly. "They all know how much she loves him. He's starting to grow on me, too. We should have heard something by now, Hatch."

"Maybe later when we go into the hospital they'll tell us something. It's only been a few days. Sometimes they have to wait for the blood results. You know, it has to sit or mix or they have to put stuff in it. It all takes time. RA can go along nicely for periods of time and then flare up into full-blown episodes like what Emmie is going through now. There are medications, and I'm sure they're doing everything humanly possible for her. If they definitely diagnose her with RA, then we can, if you want, find a specialist, a top man in his field, to have a look at her. We'll get a handle on it, honey. Think about it, Nealy. After the fire when you were so horribly burned, you almost gave up until Cole Tanner told you about Dr. Vinh in Thailand. Look at you now. You're beautiful. We'll find someone to help Emmie. It might be rough going for a while, but I think your daughter is up to it. Look who her mother is."

Tears burned Nealy's eyes. "Maybe that won't be enough, Hatch. She feels about that horse the way I felt about Flyby," she said pointing to Hifly in the paddock. "I don't want that taken away from her. I won't let it happen," Nealy said fiercely.

"I guess that means we're staying on as we planned." Hatch grinned.

"Do you mind, Hatch?"

"Nealy, this is where you belong, and nothing will ever change that. If you need me to say we can stay forever, then I'm saying it. I just want to be where you are. I only want to help. Semiretirement leaves me a lot of free time."

Nealy threw her arms around her husband. "I was hoping you would say that. I think we can pull it all together until . . . until Emmie gets on her feet. If . . . if it proves to be . . . more serious than we thought, then we'll deal with that, too." She looked across the land dressed for summer. The rolling hills, the luscious bluegrass and the barns that housed her beloved horses. This was where she belonged.

"I finally figured out a word to describe Emmie's horse. He's *stubby*. Each time I look at him I either smile or laugh. Emmie was right, he's got heart. This is just a guess on my part but I think he's going to be easy to train. I've never seen a meaner horse than Gadfly. Emmie was right about that, too. Sometimes you get one like that. You hardly ever get one like Hifly. The bloodlines are too clean. I keep thinking about John Henry. Hifly could be his twin. What do you think, Hatch?"

"What I think is it's time for lunch, and then a trip to the hospital. Come along, Mrs. Littletree."

In the kitchen, while they waited for Gertie to set lunch on the table, Nealy called out to Aggie. "Were there any calls, Aggie?"

"One, ma'am. I gave her Emmie's number at the hospital. Said she was a friend of hers. The other calls were farm-related. There's a huge bouquet of flowers in the foyer for you to take to the hospital. The girls picked and arranged them. Tell her we all hope she gets well soon."

"I'll do that, Aggie. Was it Mary Ann who called?"

"Yes, ma'am."

"Has she ever called here before?"

"As a matter of fact, she called yesterday. Do you know her?"

"No, I don't think so. Her voice did sound familiar, though. I'll tell Emmie she called. I'm not sure her phone is connected yet. They want her to rest, and talking on the phone isn't considered rest according to the doctors. I think dinner around six-thirty will be good, Gertie."

"Yes, ma'am."

"I hate hospitals, Hatch. I swore I would never go into another hospital as long as I live. So, what am I doing? I'm trooping through a hospital is what I'm doing. I hate the smell, I hate the blue chairs in the waiting room. Most of all, I hate the tattered magazines and the smell from the coffee shop. All they sell in the way of food in hospital coffee shops is egg salad and tuna salad sandwiches. I didn't know that until someone told me. And licorice. They sell a lot of licorice in the gift store. I didn't know that either. Did you know that, Hatch?"

"I think I did. People do get better in hospitals, Nealy. Everyone doesn't die. That's what you're thinking, isn't it?"

"More or less. It's almost impossible not to think things like that when you come here," Nealy said, jabbing at the elevator button. "We should have brought something besides these flowers. Why didn't we, Hatch?"

"Because we brought everything yesterday. Candy for Emmie's sweet tooth, magazines, books, lotions, clean gowns. I don't think you missed anything."

"Do you think we should have called Mitch Cunningham? I had this feeling Emmie wouldn't want him to see her . . . not looking her best. I think she had a bit of a crush on Mr. Perfectly Wonderful."

"A person's first reaction to something is usually the right one. I say we keep quiet unless Emmie instructs us otherwise. Wait, we're going the wrong way. We should have gone right instead of left. We need to follow the red arrows. Be cheerful, Nealy."

Nealy took a deep breath before opening the door to her daughter's hospital room. Before she could say hello, Emmie spoke. "They don't know why I puffed up like this, Mom. Maybe a bad reaction to the meds they've been giving me. They're running more tests. I know I look like the Pillsbury Dough Boy. Some of the inflammation in my joints has gone down but not enough. I hurt, Mom, all over."

"It's always worse before it gets better, Emmie. Has Dr. Ward been in yet?"

"Around six this morning. He comes back either before or after office hours. How's Gabby? Does she miss me? How's Hifly? I know he misses me. You should give him something of mine to smell, Mom."

"I did, Emmie. He snorted and tossed his head a bit. Yes, he misses you. And Gabby misses you, too. She sang 'Hey Diddle Diddle the Cat and the Fiddle' for me last night. Of course she giggled all the way through it. The flowers are from the girls.

Oh, by the way, Aggie said your friend Mary Ann called twice. She gave her your number here in the room. Is the phone connected?"

"Yes, but no one has called."

"Is Mary Ann a new friend? Her voice sounded familiar the night she called. She called just as Hatch was carrying you to the car. I don't know if I told you that or not. Do you want me to call her for you? Do you want me to call Mitch Cunningham?"

"No, Mom, don't call him. Mary Ann will call back. It's not important. She's someone I bowl with. It's not like we're best friends or anything like that," Emmie lied. "I want to go home, Mom."

Nealy looked around the hospital room. No matter what the hospital volunteers did in the way of decorating, it was still a hospital room. The floors were still hospital floors that were mopped twice daily with disinfectant and the hospital bed was still a hospital bed even though it had a flowered blanket. The colorful drapes were on steel rods with no cornice board and no sheer curtains underneath. The brown-leather chair was ugly as were the sink and the steel-framed mirror over it. The flowers on the windowsill gave off a sickly, funeral-like odor. She breathed through her mouth.

"Emmie, it's not like you have some bug that is going to go away in a day or so. We have to find out what exactly is wrong with you. For now, and I'm sure it won't be too much longer, this is the best place for you. If it's any consolation to you, I felt the same way you're feeling when I was in here."

"Mom, what if I can't walk? What if I end up in a wheelchair? I'll be no good to you at the farm. I won't be able to pull my weight. That means you're either going to have to hire someone or do it all yourself. I know you can't do it anymore. All those operations took their toll on you."

"Let's not worry about that now. We're managing just fine. You hired good people, and they're loyal and dedicated. We can always call on Ruby and Metaxas if we get jammed up. Or I can call my brothers."

"Mom, your brothers are older than you are. I think you need to call Nick."

"No, Emmie. Calling Nick is not an option. I don't want you

worrying about this. We'll deal with everything as it comes up. Are you hungry, honey?"

"No. I'm on a restricted diet. No root vegetables, no this, no that. I eat a lot of Jell-O. They're experimenting on me. I know that's what they're doing. When I ask questions no one has the answers, and that doctor doesn't have any answers either. They can send someone to the moon, but they can't interpret my blood work. Explain that to me, Mom. I want to go home."

"It sounds to me like you're whining, Emmie," Dr. Ward said from the doorway. "We're treating her like royalty, and she still complains. I have good news, and I have bad news. The good news is you had a bad reaction to one of the meds we gave you yesterday. The swelling and puffiness will start to dissipate rather rapidly since we took you off it right away. You only had one dose. The bad news is your blood work came back. You do have rheumatoid arthritis. We talked about this yesterday and the day before. It's going to take some time for the inflammation to subside, and it won't go away entirely. I'm working up a course of treatment, and you will have to be monitored very carefully. You'll need blood and urine tests once a month. Sometimes more than once a month. I want to see you once a week until we get this under control. In time, Emmie, you'll be able to pick up your life, but that isn't going to be for a while. I will discharge you tomorrow, but only if you agree to a wheelchair for the time being. I want you to stay off your feet until the major part of the swelling and inflammation subsides. I'll send a physical therapist who will work with you daily out to the farm."

Emmie asked the question Nealy had been dreading. "I'm not going to get better, am I?"

"If you mean cured, the answer is no. As yet there is no cure for RA. If you mean, will you be able to do mild activity, the answer is yes. You'll experience bouts of this from time to time. Some will be mild, some will be hellacious like this time. That's why you have to be monitored carefully. In time you might be able to play a little tennis, go for long walks, swim. I'm sorry the news isn't better. New medications, new testing is ongoing. Is there anything any of you want to ask me?"

"What about diet and exercise?" Nealy asked.

"I'll be sending Emmie home with a diet. There are certain foods she'll have to stay away from, and yes, moderate exercise is necessary. Emmie will have to be the judge of what her body can tolerate. I'll let her know when the time is right for that to begin. I'll sign your discharge papers when I make my late-night rounds, and you can leave here around ten tomorrow morning. We'll want to draw blood before you leave. Everything will be waiting for you at the desk, your prescriptions, your appointment card, and the Do's and Don't chart.

"There is one other thing I'd like to discuss with all of you. I want you to listen to me very carefully, Emmie. I want to recommend a rehabilitation center for a while. I think they could get you up and moving faster than home care can. Six months. The only problem is, there are only two or three in the country I would recommend, and they have waiting lists miles long. I'd like to put your name on one of those lists for consideration. The best one is right outside Las Vegas, but your hopes are slim to none of *ever* getting in there. It's the best-run facility in the country. I'd like to put your name on that list."

"Is that the center Fanny Thornton started for her daughter?" Nealy asked, drawing a deep breath.

"Yes, it is. How is it you know about it?"

Nealy smiled. "The Thorntons are family. As a matter of fact, they're coming on Saturday for a family reunion."

The doctor threw his hands in the air. "There you see, it's a miracle! Think about it, Emmie. It would be just six months out of your life. A good chance to become as whole as your body will allow if they can accommodate you."

When the door closed behind Dr. Ward, Emmie said, "I'm going to end up like Sunny Thornton. I know it. We can have wheelchair races." Her voice choked up as tears rolled down her cheeks.

Nealy turned to Hatch, a desperate look on her face. Seeing no help there, she turned back to face her daughter. "I don't want to hear any more talk like that, young lady. He said to think about it. We will think about it. We can ask Fanny if there's room for you at the center providing you decide to take that route. You can talk to Sunny and her husband. It's a thought, Emmie. You don't have to do anything you don't want to do."

"What about Gabby? She needs me. I'm her mother. She won't understand me deserting her."

"The young are very resilient. She has school, she has her nanny, and Hatch and I will be at the farm. We can bring her to see you on weekends. Just think about it, Emmie."

"Okay, Mom, I'll think about it. Why don't you go home now? I'm very tired, and I'd like to take a nap."

"Fine. We'll go down to the coffee shop and come back in a little while," Nealy said.

"No, Mom, I don't want you to come back. Like you said, I need to think about all this. Pick me up in the morning."

"All right, Emmie, if that's what you want," Nealy said.

"It's what I want. Give Gabby and Hifly a hug for me."

"I will, but you can do it yourself tomorrow when you get home."

Nealy leaned over the bed to kiss her daughter's puffy cheek. She wanted to cry, just the way Emmie wanted to cry. She knew that the moment the door closed behind her, she would howl like a banshee. She knew because she'd lived it.

Neither Nealy nor Hatch spoke until they were in the car heading back to the farm.

"She's not going to get better, Hatch."

"Nealy, for God's sake, didn't you hear what the doctor said?"

"Of course I heard what he said. You weren't watching his eyes. I was. If nothing else, I'm an authority on doctors. All you have to do is look at their eyes. The eyes, in case you don't know it, are the mirror of one's soul. Dr. Lucas Ward is full of compassion. That's probably why he became a doctor. The eyes never lie. What they do first is throw you a crumb. Emmie's crumb is being allowed to go home in a wheelchair and a therapist coming by every day. Then, just when you start to believe that's the way it's going to be, they throw in the clinker. Emmie's clinker is the rehab center. Are you following me, Hatch?"

"Yeah. Yeah, I am."

"And guess what? We didn't even touch on the fear element. That's a whole other story."

"Are you for or against the rehab center?" Hatch asked, his eyes on the road in front of him.

"I don't know. I guess I want whatever is best for my daughter. I have to think long and hard about all of this. Emmie will be looking to me for guidance, and I want to be sure I give her the right advice."

Emmie leaned back into the pillows the nurse had made a production out of shaking and fluffing. The minute she was gone, she let the tears flow. How in the name of God had she gotten something so devastating? She'd seen that strange look in Dr. Ward's eyes. He was trying to hold out hope. Mind-set was all important. The right attitude with lots of good food and plenty of sunshine could work miracles. Bull*SHIT*. She'd heard it all before when her mother was in the hospital burned over a third of her body. They were just words. They said whatever they had to say to get the patient over the worst of it. Dangle the old carrot and then wham, jam home the fact that you're going to be crippled for life.

Gabby was going to grow up with a handicapped mother. *If* she was around to raise her. Otherwise, her grandmother would raise her. She thought about Sunny Coleman and how her brother had taken her son Jake to raise because Sunny couldn't take care of him or his sister. According to her mother, they were happy, well-adjusted kids, and Sunny was happy with the arrangement.

Emmie wiped her eyes on the sleeve of the hospital gown just as the phone rang. She knew who it was even before her swollen hand picked up the receiver. Her hello sounded cautious.

"Emmie?"

"This is Emmie, Willow. Why are you calling me? What's wrong?"

Willow ignored the question to ask one of her own. "Why are you in the hospital, Emmie?"

"The other night while I was waiting for you to call, I pulled off my boots and my feet started to swell. My hands, too. My back has been hurting me a lot lately, but I thought it was from lifting. I have rheumatoid arthritis. They've been doing tests on me since I got here, but I'm going to go home tomorrow and then I'll probably have to go to a rehab center for therapy. I think my case is what they call advanced and will require extensive therapy. Not that it's any of your business, Willow. Now, why are you calling me?"

"I need to talk to you, Emmie. Can I come by the hospital this evening?"

"Tell me why. Leaving Nick like that was a terrible thing. How could you do that to him? I don't want to get involved in your business, Willow. You need to make things right with Nick."

"I'm in a lot of trouble, Emmie. I need someone to talk to. You and I always got on well, and you were always nice to me. I just want to talk to you. Please say it's okay to visit with you."

"I don't know what I can do for you, but okay. Dinner is usually over by six-fifteen. Come then. Aren't you going to ask me about Nick?"

"I figured I didn't have the right to ask about anything where Nick is concerned. Yes, I would like to know how he is."

"He's a lawyer now. A very good one with a top-notch firm."

"That doesn't surprise me. It's what he always wanted. He opened up to me, Emmie, told me all his hopes and dreams and shared his secrets."

"And what did you share with Nick?" Emmie asked coldly.

"I'll see you after dinner, Emmie. Can I bring you anything?"

"No, thank you."

She was just as pretty as Emmie remembered. She also looked wary and frightened. She was dressed in a pale yellow linen dress with matching sandals and string bag. Her straw hat had a wide yellow ribbon around the brim. She took it off, fluffed up her auburn curls, and sat down.

"I'm sorry you're in here, Emmie. You look . . . awful. I don't mean you look awful awful. I mean you look sick. Is there anything I can do for you? I know what hospitals are like. The year . . . the year I left, Mom died. She got sick and she just didn't get better. I used to go to the hospital around noon and stay till after eight. All I could do was sit there and talk to her if she was awake. You're young, Emmie. They'll get a handle on it and treat you aggressively. They have nuclear drugs these days, wonder drugs, and all kinds of stuff. I'm certain they have something that will fix you up. I'm babbling, Emmie, and I'm

sorry. It's just that I never know quite what to say when someone is sick."

Emmie clenched her teeth. Mitch Cunningham would like
Willow. The very idea made her angry. "We've established that
I'm sick. What do you want, Willow? As you can see, I don't
think I can be of any help to you.

"By the way, Nick knows all about that guy you married in
Bermuda. He even saw your wedding album. I saw it, too. I
guess that means you divorced Nick, huh?"

"No, I didn't divorce Nick. There are only two things in this
world I'm good at. One is cooking, the other is marrying rich
men. I'm a bigamist. It's what I do for a living. I make money at
it. It is not an admirable profession. I take everything they
shower on me, then I go on to the next mark. There's no feeling
to it at all. I'm not making excuses for myself, I'm telling you
like it is."

"That's disgusting," Emmie said.

"Yes, I can see how you would think that. Your mother figured it out real quick. If you stop and think about it, I did Nick a
favor by leaving. Think about that, Emmie."

"You broke his heart, Willow. I can never forgive you for that.
Which brings me to my original question, what is it you want
from me? How many husbands do you have anyway?"

"They aren't legal husbands. Nick is my real husband."

"Nick filed for divorce on the grounds of desertion and
bigamy. Hatch and that guy you worked for in Bermuda testi-
fied in court. You're divorced, and it's legal."

"I thought Nick would wait for me forever," Willow said.

"Boy, you don't know Nick very well. Your charms wore off,
Willow."

Willow twirled the straw hat around and around with her
index finger. "I need a good criminal lawyer, Emmie."

"If you're thinking Nick's going to help you, think again. So,
don't even ask."

"I may be a lot of things, Emmie, but I'm no murderer."

"Murderer! Who did you murder?" Emmie squealed.

Willow sighed. "I didn't murder anyone. The authorities
think I did, but I didn't. I was cooking in a big casino in Las

Vegas. The one that's tied to your family. I was living with this high roller. His name was Junior Belez. He had a lot of money, and he was very generous. I was about ready to move on and probably would have in another month or so. He bored me. Anyway, I went home after work one night, and he was lying in the living room. Dead. I didn't touch a thing. I did check his pulse, and he was still warm. I gathered up my stuff and took off. I drove up to Reno and hung out there for a while. I bought all the papers, listened to all the newscasts, because Junior was news. For months there was nothing. Then I just happened to hear on the news that I was wanted for questioning. I took off and have been hiding out ever since.

"I've made a lot of discreet phone calls, and I know where Nick is. His firm has a great criminal department. I want you to call him for me and arrange a meeting. He'll do it for you, Emmie; but if I call him, he won't. Please, I need you to do this for me. I didn't kill Junior. I swear on your mother, Emmie. On my mother and all the saints in heaven. I didn't do it. My . . . ah . . . lifestyle isn't exactly going to endear me to the police. I don't want to go to jail. I like my life."

Emmie shook her head to clear it. She couldn't believe what she was hearing. "You must be out of your mind, Willow. I'm not calling Nick for you. You caused him enough heartache. Find yourself another lawyer. They're a dime a dozen, good ones and bad ones."

"He'll be here this weekend for your family reunion. Please, Emmie, arrange a meeting for me. That's why I came to Kentucky. I know all about the reunion because I heard the Thornton twins talking about it in the dining room one evening. I remembered the conversation because they were talking about going to the Kentucky Derby race the weekend after the family reunion. I swear to you, Emmie, I didn't kill Junior. He had some weird friends, but I always stayed away from them. I didn't want to get involved. All I wanted was his money and the presents he gave me. That's the truth.

"Think about this, Emmie. How would you like to be locked away in a jail cell for something you didn't do? I'm only thirty-two years old. My whole life is ahead of me. Will you help me?"

"No, Willow, I will not be a party to this. I am not going to mention this to anyone. Not to my mother and certainly not to Nick."

"Then you leave me with no other choice except to get in touch with your ex-husband. I'll tell him about Gabby. Oh, yes, I know all about her. All I had to do was go to the courthouse and look it up. Her last name is Coleman. That told me all I needed to know. You told me the day your mother booted you out that you were pregnant. Remember? When he sees the condition you're in, he'll snap up the kid in nothing flat. Your mother's money isn't going to work. The courts always favor the natural parents, and you never told him about Gabby, now did you? Of course you didn't. I can see it in your face. Now are you going to help me or not?"

"You are a living, breathing bitch, Willow, whatever your last name is."

"It's Clay. Mrs. Willow Bishop Clay. What's it going to be, Emmie?"

"I can turn you in to the police. I have a phone right here."

Willow settled the straw hat on her head and tweaked the ribbon that trailed down her back. "Yes, you could do that. I will still call Buddy. If you arrange a meeting for me with Nick, I promise I won't call him. Gabby will be safe."

"How do I know I can trust you?"

"You'll just have to take my word. If Nick doesn't agree to help me, then I'll call Buddy. Make sure you tell him that. Tell him to meet me at the Inn on Sunday morning at ten o'clock. Tell him to come alone. If you screw this up, Emmie, it's bye-bye Gabby."

"Get out of here. I said I would do it. I don't ever want to see you again. If you don't leave, I will call the police."

Emmie could hear Willow's laughter as she strolled down the hall to the elevator.

Emmie wanted to beat at her pillow, at her mattress, but her hands were too swollen and hurt too much.

4

Emmie watched the arrival of her family from her wheelchair on the front porch. Hatch had constructed a makeshift ramp for Sunny Thornton and her husband Harry, and she would be using it herself once she got the hang of maneuvering the cumbersome chair. Everyone was smiling. They seemed so happy to be reunited there in Kentucky. Somehow, her mother had cajoled her two uncles to leave SunStar, their farm in Virginia, to join the family reunion, and they would be arriving momentarily.

She watched as the family broke ranks to allow Sunny and Harry to turn their chairs around to head up the ramp.

"Hi, Emmie!" Sunny said cheerily. "I don't think you've met Harry. Emmie, this is Harry. Harry, this is Emmie Coleman. Should we line up or should we disperse?" Sunny giggled as she waved her arm about. "They're going to take the tour, so that leaves the three of us alone. Your mom thinks the chairs might spook the horses. Oh, you have a manual chair. No, no, no, you need one of these babies," she said, pointing to the motorized chair she was sitting in. "You can really zip around in these. So, what's your problem?"

"Rheumatoid arthritis. *Aggressive* rheumatoid arthritis. The doctors say I'm going to need rehab. At least six months, but for some reason I don't quite believe that."

"How long have you had your condition? Mom never said anything about it to me," Sunny queried. "Gee, this porch is pretty. I love all the flowers and the hanging ferns. Do you spend a lot of time out here? We have a little patio and it's chock full of flowers. We can't take care of them ourselves but that's okay. We get to sit out there and look at them. We have a lot of hummingbirds, too, that like to sip the nectar."

She was like a runaway train, Emmie thought. Suddenly she wanted to cry for Sunny and her husband and their disabilities. According to her mother, they were fighters and did everything they could to the limit their bodies would allow. They were both incredibly thin with stick-like legs and arms, their hands crooked and deformed. Sunny used a hook to move the lever on her chair while Harry still had some mobility in his right hand and could maneuver his chair with relative ease.

"The arthritis . . . I guess you could say it sort of crept up on me," Emmie said referring to Sunny's first question. "I suppose I was in denial, and I sure didn't do myself any good. What you're seeing is the result of that denial. They have me on a regimen of this and that but even I know I need rehab. I hate this chair. I'm used to going full tilt but I can't even stand up now. It just came on that quick. It grabbed me and wouldn't let go. As to the porch, I used to spend a lot of time out here when I was younger. It's Mom's favorite spot on the whole farm. All the flowers and the plants are new and so is the fresh paint. In honor of all of you. I let everything die so it all had to be replaced. Everything just got away from me. Do you understand what I'm saying? My God, how do you two do it?" The tears in her eyes did not go unnoticed by Sunny and Harry. She couldn't have stopped them even if she wanted to.

Sunny giggled, and Harry smiled. "Very carefully," Sunny said. "Like you, I was in denial. When I found out I had MS, I went berserk. I was always a tomboy. I could beat both my brothers at everything. Then it all stopped, and I was lucky I could hobble around. I made everyone's life pretty miserable for a long time. I was married at the time, and my husband couldn't handle it so he left me. He didn't want the kids either, so my brother took over and later adopted them when I moved into the center permanently. It was the best thing for everyone."

Emmie wiped at her tears with the sleeve of her shirt. "I think it would kill me if I had to leave my daughter with someone else to raise. That bothers me more than my actual condition. It bothers me that I might not be able to raise her myself. I'm not used to sitting around either. It's just all so new, and I have to adjust. I can't believe this is happening to me."

Sunny looked at her husband. "This is one of those rare times in life that you're going to have to think of yourself first. If there is even the slightest chance that rehab can make you reasonably whole, you have to go for it. Your child will survive. I didn't think my kids would, but they did, and so will your daughter. Your first step is believing that."

"I hate this chair!" Emmie blurted for the second time.

"I hate it more than you," Sunny said vehemently.

"I hate it worse than both of you," Harry said.

An easy familiarity developed for the threesome as the morning wore on. Sunny and Harry regaled Emmie with tales of their adventures in snowy Vermont and then with their participation in a survival course for handicapped people.

"Oh, look, here comes my son Jake. Before, Emmie, when we were talking about what was best for the kids, Jake was always okay with me in this chair. He would wipe my mouth if I was drooling, he'd clean up if I spilled something, and he would always wear a smile. Unfortunately for both him and me, we seem to have some bad genes. He has that disease where he didn't grow properly. He couldn't wait to get here. He's thinking he might want to become a jockey."

"Mom! You have to come down to the paddock to see the horses! They're awesome." Jake turned to Emmie, stretched out his hand, then noticed her swollen and puffy fingers. He dropped to his knees and placed his hands on top of hers. "I'm Jake Thornton. Sunny's my mom. Guess you know that. I'm so glad to meet you. Grandma Fanny talks about all of you a lot." He smiled.

Emmie looked into the boy's eyes and smiled back. He was the right height, the right weight, and his touch was as gentle as a feather. "Training to be a jockey is a lot of hard work. It's also dangerous and scary at times. Did you meet Hifly?" she asked wistfully.

"Yes, and he came right up to me. I think he liked me. I don't know anything about horses, but I sure would like to learn." He turned to look at his mother. She nodded. "I want to apply for the job. The training. Whatever you call it."

"Sit here," Emmie said, motioning to a small stool next to her wheelchair. "I wasn't kidding when I said the training is a lot of hard work. You have to love the animals first. Hifly is easy to love. The funny thing is, no one wanted him but me. I think he can be trained to race. Unfortunately, I'm not going to be able to do that training. I don't know if Mom has the stamina anymore. We have other trainers, but Mom is the best. With the right jockey and the right trainer, I think Hifly could make a run for the Derby. If you think you'd like to be part of that, then I'd say we have an even better chance of making it happen. The most important thing of all is the fear factor. If you even think you're going to be afraid, then it isn't the right profession for you. It's a lot to think about, Jake. You've never been on a horse, have you?" His negative shake of his head made Emmie smile. "We have a couple of horses that can carry you up and down the track so you can get the feel of being on a horse's back. You're pretty high off the ground, believe it or not. Once you feel comfortable, then it's on to bigger and better things. I'll talk to Mom later today to see what we can arrange."

Sunny's eyes filled with tears and thanks as she stared across the porch at Emmie.

"Mom, did you hear that? Harry, do you think I can do it?"

"Jake, you can do whatever you set your mind to doing. Emmie is right, it won't be easy, and you have to give a hundred percent. What did your aunt Nealy say?"

"Nothing. I didn't ask her, Harry. I wanted to run it by Mom before I said anything. You know I never make a decision on anything unless Mom approves. Grandma Fanny thinks it's a wonderful idea. I think she's going to talk to Aunt Nealy. Uncle Sage thinks I can do it, too. What about you, Emmie?"

He is a handsome youngster, Emmie thought as she reached for his hand. *He has unruly blond curls just like his mother and the same bright blue eyes. It's obvious he loves his mother, and her handicap doesn't bother him at all.* "I think your grandmother and Sage could be right. I think you would make a great jockey."

The boy let his breath out in a long explosive sigh. "I'm going back down to the barn. Mom, can I get you anything before I go?"

"No, honey, go ahead. Maybe later we'll take a spin down there to see what's going on."

Sunny waited until Jake was out of earshot. "See, Emmie, that's what I mean. I am his mother. He's never forgotten that even though Iris and Sage raised him. He's my son. I'm his mother. It will always be like that for us. Thanks for what you did just now. I'm sure your mother told you Jake's story, about how he wanted to be a navy pilot from the time he was five years old. It was the most crushing blow when he finally had to accept that it could never be. But," Sunny said philosophically, "when one door closes, another one opens."

Emmie stared off into the distance. Would she ever be able to accept a less than normal life the way Sunny appeared to accept it? She didn't know.

Nealy looked around at her entourage and smiled. "That's pretty much it as far as the barns and horses go. As you can see, everyone has his or her job, and I'm proud to say we have quite a few women working here. Emmie has developed a smooth-running operation. I'm going to have to hire a few more people because she isn't going to be able to . . . to . . . work for a while. I'll be moving back here shortly myself." She looked around at the interested faces of her family. "If any of you would like to go riding, I can have some riding horses saddled for you. If not, we can go up to the house and settle down on the front porch until the barbecue gets under way."

Maggie Coleman Tanaka spoke first. "Would you mind, Nealy, if Cole, Riley, and I just walk around? We won't touch anything and won't go near the horses. I'd like to walk barefoot through the bluegrass so I can tell Henry how it felt when I get back to Hawaii."

"By all means. Take as long as you like. Sawyer, what about you?"

"I think I'm going to take you up on your offer of the front porch. I want to talk to Emmie and Sunny. Harry, too."

"Nealy, if you don't mind, Rhy and myself are going to take Sage and Birch over to the stallion cemetery," Pyne said.

Nealy nodded as she linked her arm through Fanny's. "That leaves just the two of us. Let's sit down over there in the shade. You look tired, Fanny."

"That's because I am tired. Approaching seventy-five might just be a number, but try telling that to this old body. Oh, look, here comes Jake. I love that boy. If Ash were alive, he would be devastated at his grandson's condition." A look of sadness settled itself on Fanny's deeply wrinkled face.

"I want to apply for jockey training," Jake blurted.

Nealy looked him over from head to toe. She smiled. "You do, do you?"

"Yes, ma'am, I do. I've read everything I could get my hands on in regard to Thoroughbreds. I'm sure there is tons more to read, but hands-on should work just as well. I know how to work, Aunt Nealy. I'll do whatever you say. I'd like to be part of this business. I'd like to work with Emmie's horse."

"First, you have to get over your fear. I watched you when the horses came up to the fence. You backed away. If you're afraid, it will never work. We can work on the fear. Did you talk to your family about staying on here and training to be a jockey?"

"I did, and they all think I can do it. Mom thinks it's a great idea, and so does Harry. Emmie pretty much said the same thing you just did."

"I'll be working you like a mule. Can you handle that? We get up at four and are usually in bed by eight if we can keep our eyes open that long. Is your health going to present any problems along the way? I'm not real big on surprises."

"My health is good. I just didn't grow properly. I'm used to working hard on the mountain. I can do it, Aunt Nealy. If I don't cut it, you send me back home. I think that's fair."

"That's more than fair, Jake. You might as well get your feet wet right now. Walk along the fence line, whistle for the horses. They'll come right up to you." Nealy fished in her pocket for a handful of mints, her secret treasure for the horses. "Let them feel your touch. Talk to them. Don't get up close and personal with Gadfly, he's mean as hell. Monday morning we'll start to work with a vengeance."

Jake pocketed the mints. His hand shot out, and Nealy grasped it. She was surprised at his firm, hard handshake.

"You know the boy better than I do, Fanny. Can he do it? I'd hate to see him fail with everything that's running against him. It would be devastating to him. I can do just so much, and the rest is up to him. You need to know that going in, Fanny."

"I do know it, Nealy. Jake knows it, too. He gives a hundred percent to anything he does. Last year he made a birdhouse for me for my birthday. It was so perfect, so detailed and intricate, that it was worthy of a whole page in *Architectural Digest*. It was like a miniature hotel. The truth is, it was a birdhouse made to look like Babylon, one of our casinos. The day I hung it up on my fig tree I knew I was going to have to order birdseed by the ton. Jake's big on details. He's so good with his hands. Taking the boy on like this means the world to all of us, Nealy."

"If he can get past his fear, it just might work. No one can help him with that, Fanny. He's got to work through it, but I think he's already working on it. Now, how is Marcus?"

"Marcus is doing nicely. He was sorry he couldn't come. He said he will be ready to do some visiting by September, so if you invite us back, we'll be here. I'm really looking forward to seeing Ruby and Metaxas. They are two of the most wonderful people walking this earth. I'm glad they ended up here and love what they're doing. Oh, Nealy, you should see my mountain. It is the most beautiful spot on this whole earth, thanks to Metaxas. When it burned, I wanted to die. And just like that, when the conditions were right, and the ground cooled down, Metaxas replanted the entire mountain. When are you going to ask me, Nealy?"

Nealy looked bewildered. "Ask you what, Fanny?"

"If there's room at the center for Emmie?"

"No, Fanny, I'm not going to ask you. I won't say the thought didn't cross my mind. We'll manage. I think Emmie needs to be close to home. It's all so devastating. It doesn't look rosy. Everything happens in threes. First it was me, now Emmie. I wonder what will be next."

"You can't think like that, Nealy. I remember what we all went through with Sunny. I swear to you, I thought my heart broke in two. You never get used to it, but you learn to live with it. She was so young. Just like Emmie. There's room, Nealy. We can take her back with us. I'd like you to come along. We're family, and as such, we have to help one another. All I've done is think about Emmie since the moment you told me of her condition. Mind-set is all-important, Nealy. Iris, Sage's wife, suggested Gabby stay with them on the mountain so they can take her to see her mother on the weekends. Iris and Sage love children. The more the merrier. It worked so well with Jake. There's no reason it won't work with Gabby. You take care of my grandson, and my family will take care of your granddaughter. Will you at least think about it?"

Tears welled in Nealy's eyes. "Of course I'll think about it. In the end, it has to be Emmie's decision. I don't see her leaving here. She can be very stubborn. Then again, I could be wrong."

Fanny smiled. "Like the young people say today, I think it's in the bag. Sunny and Harry are revving her up as we speak. Sometimes, seeing the results of the center is worth more than a million words."

"Oh, Fanny, how did you handle it? I'm so torn up over this."

Fanny shrugged. "I had to take it one day at a time. I fell apart, too, but in the end, you have to be strong. Sunny's husband left her when he found out she had MS. Then he was going to sue her to get custody of the children. That's when I called in the big guns, and he went away peacefully. Jake hasn't seen or heard from him since he was four years old. He's married now, with children of his own. He's a doctor. You'd think he would have had a little more compassion where his wife was concerned. You learn to accept what you can't change. You have family now, Nealy. We're all here for you, Emmie, and Gabby."

Nealy knuckled her eyes. She squeezed Fanny's hand. "Yes, we're family. That pretty much says it all. I think it's time for us to meander up to the house. Before you know it, the barbecue will be ready. The band will be starting up, and the festivities will begin."

"I didn't know you were having a band, Nealy."

Nealy laughed. "They call themselves a band. It's a group of my employees. Ooops, Emmie's employees. They consist of three harmonica players, a drummer, and someone who whistles. Emmie said they're great!"

"Well, if you ever want a band, talk to Sunny. She's on a first-name basis with Dallas Lord and the Canyon River Band. According to her, they're right up there with someone named Matchbox and the Spiderlegs."

"God, I feel old," Nealy groaned. "I never heard of them. I'm a Sinatra and Elvis fan."

Fanny linked her arm with Nealy's. "I met both of them when they performed at Babylon. They were absolutely wonderful.

Frank was such a gentleman, and Elvis was so shy and polite. Magnificent performers. Sell-out crowds. Those were the days, but you know what, Nealy, I don't want them back. There was simply too much heartache back in those good old days. By the way, I love that husband of yours."

"Me, too." Nealy laughed. "He's the best thing that ever happened to me. Oh, look, there's Nick!"

"Ma!" He was running toward her, his arms outstretched. Nealy ran straight for him. Her feet left the ground as he swung her around and around until she was dizzy.

"Oh, Nick, it's so good to see you. Is everything okay? Are you setting the legal world on fire? How long can you stay? My goodness, where are my manners. Say hello to Fanny, Nick."

"Nice to see you, Aunt Fanny. You're looking prettier each time I see you."

"Now, this is a man with a keen eye," Fanny said, and laughed as the three of them walked up the path to the house.

Before they reached the back door, Nick looked down at his mother. "Ma, tell me what to expect when I see Emmie. I don't want to blow it here. Tell me the worst so I know what I'm dealing with."

Nealy told him and watched his face go ashen. "She's had it for a while, Mom. I remember once she couldn't hold the watering can when she was sprinkling her patch of grass. She never complained, though, and sluffed it off. She kept the aspirin bottle on the kitchen shelf, and I remember thinking she took a lot of them. God, how did this happen? What can I do?"

Nealy shook her head. "We'll talk later. Go on the porch and talk to her. I want to see about refreshments for our guests."

Fanny lowered herself to the top step on the back porch. She looked around. "It's so pretty, Nealy, with all the colorful flowers and hanging baskets. Most people don't do much with their back porches, but I like this. I think it's as nice as your front porch.

"There's something I don't understand. If Emmie had this condition, why didn't she do something about it earlier?"

"It's my fault, Fanny. From the time Nick and Emmie were old enough to understand, I drilled into their heads they had to work through the pain. I meant things like sore muscles, charley horses, and the like. Not *real* pain. This is all my fault. Emmie was doing what I taught her to do. How could I have been so damn stupid? How, Fanny?"

"You were doing what someone told you to do. I'm sure your . . . Josh Coleman told you to work through the pain. He didn't sound like a man who wanted to know anyone wasn't feeling well or was sore from working all day. Maud and Jess were old-timers and believed a shot of whiskey was the cure-all for everything. You can't blame yourself entirely, Nealy. Emmie is a grown woman, and as such she has to take responsibility for her own well-being. We're talking about denial here. I went through it, Sunny went through it, and so did the Texas branch of the family. I don't want you thinking you have a monopoly on stupidity here. Nor do I want to see you packing your bags for a guilt trip. I've been around the block more times than I care to remember, and I know what I'm talking about."

Both women watched as a hummingbird swooped down to suck at one of the luscious flowers. A pale yellow butterfly circled and swirled before it, too, settled on one of the colorful blooms. Off in the distance, one of the barn dogs let loose with a loud howl. The hummingbird and the butterfly took wing at the same moment. The barking continued, a sign that something was amiss in one of the barns. Nealy shrugged it off. It could be something as simple as a mouse scurrying down the breezeway, or it could be something as sinister as a horse in trouble. If it were the latter, one of the workers would have rung the bell.

"Is there really room at the center for Emmie, Fanny?"

"There's room. You won't like the rules at first, and neither will Emmie, but they work. Sunny is the living proof. She's getting worse. I would give my life for her if it would do any good. Through it all, she remains very brave. I think it's mostly for my benefit. I wish you could have known her when she was younger. She was like golden sunshine. There wasn't anything she couldn't do, and she was totally fearless. I have these horrible nightmares about her."

Fanny's voice turned fretful when she said, "I know I'm an old woman now, and Sunny is aging, too, so that may be part of it. Her prognosis is not good. I don't want to bury one of my children. I don't think I could handle that."

"Oh, Fanny, that isn't going to happen. Sunny is a fighter. You just have to look at her to know that. Every day modern medicine is making giant strides in cases like hers. You said it's all in the mind-set. You need to listen to your own words. And on that thought, I think we need to join the rest of the family. Oooh, look at that butterfly. I don't think I ever saw a pink-and-brown one before."

They watched as a steady stream of butterflies made an appearance in the little flower garden. White ones, yellow ones, blue ones tinged with black, and the beautiful pink one. Some were big and some were small and delicate.

"They're like our children, aren't they, Nealy? The big ones are robust and strong, and their wings are wide. The little ones look so fragile and delicate, like Sunny and Emmie. I suppose you can liken anything to anything. Does that make sense?"

"It does to me," Nealy said, standing up. She reached down for Fanny's hand. She, too, was thin and fragile, like her daughter. She shuddered under the warm sun as she wondered what the future held in store for her and her family.

"I think you're right, it's time to join the others. I think I hear your band warming up," Fanny said, a catch in her voice.

It was almost dusk when Nealy settled herself in one of the Adirondack chairs next to Maggie Tanaka. "That was a pretty decent softball game," she said. She patted her stomach. "I'm stuffed. I can't remember the last time I ate that much."

"I had doubles of everything. You throw a good barbecue, Nealy. Would you look at those guys?" Maggie laughed as she pointed to the ballplayers stretched out in the bluegrass. "I think the game kicked their butts. It's also probably the most exercise any of them has had in years. I am, of course, speaking of just our family. Your employees have it all together and won the day. Our guys were like slugs compared to the farm team. Twenty-seven to two is not a good score."

"They had fun. By tomorrow they'll put a spin on it that you won't recognize." Nealy grinned.

"It's so nice to have the whole family here. Next time we have to make sure all the grandkids, kids, and spouses can come. I never realized how busy kids' lives are. There's either some kind of lesson or some party they absolutely must attend. They have schedules. Do you believe that? I realize now I didn't give everyone enough notice. That's a failing of mine. I always say, next time I'll do better. I get so caught up in things and time gets away from me."

Maggie sipped from her glass of ginger ale. "We're all alike when it comes to things like that. I'm notorious for thinking I did or said something when all I did was think about it. It's called having senior moments. They usually hit you around the time you hit the big five-oh." She changed the subject abruptly. "Is there anything I or any members of the family can do for Emmie?"

"No, but thanks for asking. Fanny wants me to take her to that fabulous center they built in Las Vegas. It has to be Emmie's decision, not mine."

"It's really a state-of-the-art fantastic rehab center. It's been written up all over the world. If they can't help her, no one can. They have a top-notch dedicated staff. If Fanny can get you in, snap it up. I understand the waiting list is years into the future. It's just like everything else in life, Nealy. It's not what you know, it's who you know. RA is not something to ignore."

Nealy plucked at a blade of grass. "We used to whistle with these. I wish you could all stay a bit longer. A one-day visit hardly seems enough, and I'm glad you all agreed to come even if it was just for the day. I understand everyone has a busy life, but it would be nice to just lounge around and talk for days and days."

"Next year, let's do our family reunion in Hawaii. We have the room, and the Pacific Ocean is right below the house. You'll love it. The kids can run on the beach, and something is always going on for the young people. By the way, Nealy, I think it's wonderful what you're doing for Jake."

"I think he might have what it takes. Only time will tell. He seems like a fine young man."

"This family has certainly had its share of tragedies," Maggie said, her eyes on the ballplayers, who were moaning and groaning as they struggled to their feet. "It was a delightful day, Nealy, and for that, I'm grateful. It seems lately the only time the family gets together is when tragedy strikes or there's a funeral."

Nealy grimaced. "I think I have to find my husband so I can start playing hostess."

"Run along, dear, I'm going to join Fanny and Ruby and catch up on the latest gossip," Maggie said.

Nealy leaned over to kiss Maggie's cheek before she trotted off to find Hatch.

Nealy lay quietly, listening to her husband's even breathing. Hatch slept like a log, whereas of late she did little more than snooze her way through the night. Maybe it was the thin slice of moonlight on the bedcovers that was keeping her awake. Then again, maybe it was Emmie and her own feeling of guilt that wouldn't allow her to sleep.

She stretched out her legs and immediately regretted it. The cramp in the calf of her leg was so bad she bolted out of bed. She'd read somewhere that if you pressed your instep on top of the other foot, the cramp would go away. She did it and felt instant relief.

Maud's rocker beckoned. She hobbled over to it and sat down, her hands massaging the taut muscle. Wide-awake, she gazed around the room, her eyes coming to rest on her sleeping husband. He was so good, so kind, and she loved him with all her heart. And now she was going to throw him a curve by insisting they move back here to the farm. While her heart would always belong to Blue Diamond Farms, she had slowly weaned herself from it. Now, she was thrust smack-dab in the center of it again. Was she being selfish, thinking of herself instead of her daughter?

Nealy sighed as she reached for her robe hanging on the back of the rocker. She slipped into it and fumbled under the bed for her slippers. Tiptoeing out of the room, she closed the door gently and walked down the hall to the kitchen stairway. Maybe if she sat on the front porch with a cup of coffee, she could think better. Maybe it wasn't the front porch that she needed. Maybe she needed to go out to the stallion cemetery and sit.

While the coffee dripped, Nealy paced, up and down the

kitchen, then back and forth. In her entire life she'd never been so wired up. Things were out of control through no fault of her own.

Once life had been simple. She ate, she slept, and she trained and worked with the horses. That was before the fire that scarred her forever. Marriage had changed her, too. While she loved Hatch, there was something missing from her life, and that something was Blue Diamond Farms.

Nealy poured herself a mug of coffee and carried it outside. It was a beautiful evening with stars sprinkling the heavens. It was warm and balmy, not yet hot and sultry like it would be in a few weeks. A perfect May evening.

She walked across the driveway, stopping when she thought she heard voices. She tiptoed around to the side of the house. Emmie and Nick were on the porch talking. She smiled in the darkness. Nick, with his common sense, would make Emmie understand the seriousness of her condition. Maybe he could convince her to go to Fanny Thornton's center for treatment. She forced herself to walk away even though she wanted to join them.

In the cemetery, she sat down on the stone bench she'd sat on hundreds of times. From her pocket she withdrew a pack of cigarettes. She'd quit smoking so many times she'd lost count, but the turmoil she was going through called for a cigarette. She could quit again tomorrow. She fired up a cigarette and leaned back against the cold bench. In front of her, fireflies danced for her enjoyment. The air was sweet from the tea olive trees planted along the borders of the cemetery, Maud's favorite trees, which she'd gotten from South Carolina, guaranteed to die in Kentucky's climate. They hadn't died, though, because Maud had planted a buffer of hedges to shield them from the winter weather. And she'd always covered them in November. During a really cold spell she'd set out smudge pots, something Nealy herself had followed through with every year. She sniffed. Emmie always said the tea olives smelled like bubble gum. Nick said they smelled like cherry-grape candies.

"I don't know what to do, Maud," she whispered. "You always used to say, and Jess agreed with you, that when you don't know what to do, do nothing. How can I do nothing when Emmie's well-being is at stake? It has to be her decision in the end, but I should know the words to convince her to take this chance. I did it after the fire, but I'm not Emmie. I'm to blame for all this. Hatch and Fanny say I'm not, but I am. I swear, I wanted to lie down and die when Emmie said she was only doing what I told her to do all these years, which was to work through the pain. You did it, I did it, but I think both of us were wise enough to know the difference between an ache or a pain as opposed to what Emmie is going through. Then there's that part of me that can't understand my daughter's stupidity. She had to know she had a serious condition. Was she trying to be like me? I just don't understand."

"It's not your fault, Nealy. Stop being so hard on yourself. Emmie is a grown woman. You can't shoulder the blame for her condition."

"Hunt. Oh, Hunt, you haven't talked to me in a long time. I know, I know, this is just another dream. For some reason I always feel better when I dream about you. I'm so worried about Emmie."

"You have to cut her loose, Nealy. It's time for her to become her own person. I know how that sounds, like you're forsaking her, but you aren't. If she isn't tough enough to do it, you'll have to be strong and push her away. Do you want her to live on drugs for the rest of her life? Do you want to coddle her and watch her shrivel in front of your eyes? Fanny gave you the solution."

"Sometimes, Hunt, the solution is worse than the condition itself. I don't know if she can handle it."

"Her options ran out, Nealy. Right now she doesn't have any other choice. Convince her it's the way to go. Take her to Vegas."

"All right, Hunt. Aren't the fireflies beautiful?"

"Yes, they are. Let's talk about you, Nealy. Tell me what you want."

"Just to stay here where I belong. I'd like to train Hifly. You know what, Hunt, there's something about Gadfly that nags at me. That is one mean horse. I feel like I did something wrong. That's stupid but it's how I feel. Emmie said he's a horror and he is."

"That's because he's in pain. He has an ulcer. How come I have to tell you these things?"

"Because I'm stupid, that's why. I've only been back a little while. I kept looking at him and watching him. I think I might have figured it out, Hunt. Maybe not this quick but eventually."

"I know the way your brain is working, Nealy. You're already thinking about two horses in the Derby, aren't you? The kid on Hifly and you on Gadfly. You've made history already but two horses from the same sire running against each other in the Derby? Man, that would make the whole world sit up and take notice."

"For God's sake, Hunt, are you forgetting how old I am? Listen, I'm tired. I don't think I could do that again."

"Sure you could. You and the kid. That's smart, keeping it in the family. Come on, Nealy, you've been thinking about this. I know you have. Shoemaker did it, and a lot of others. They're men. For sure they'll put you on the cover of Modern Maturity *if you pull it off. You have two years to decide."*

Nealy stirred and opened her eyes. She must have dozed off. She looked down at the luminous hands on her watch: 3:33. The night was still warm, and the fireflies were still dancing in the velvety night. Overhead, the clouds dispersed to reveal a star-spangled sky. She sniffed the fragrant air and sighed. She was home.

Where she belonged.

"Thanks, Hunt," she whispered as she made her way back to the house.

Now she had a plan.

Nealy walked through the house and into the living room. The door was open enough so that she could hear Emmie and Nick talking softly. She turned to make her way up the stairs when she heard Nick's cry of anguish. She stopped and turned around. This time she listened to her children talking.

"What do you mean, Willow called you? We've been sitting out here for over two hours and you're just now telling me! That's unforgivable, Emmie! I can't believe you didn't call me when she visited you in the hospital. If the situation was reversed, the phone would have been in my hand the minute she walked through the door. You should have hung up on her, never given her the time of day. Damn."

"I'm sorry, Nick. I thought I could find out something that would help you, get some answers for you. I didn't know . . . how could I, what a mean person she is?"

"You read that report Hatch gave me. Are you blind, Emmie? Don't you think? Where in God's name is your head? This is your MO, Emmie. It's how you do everything. How many times did I tell you to go to the doctor? How many, Emmie? Six, seven, a dozen? You didn't listen. Now you have a serious medical condition, and you're being dumb-ass stubborn again. You need to grow up and take some responsibility here. So what if she goes to Buddy? So what? You should have told him about Gabby from the git-go. You didn't listen to me about that either. Or Hatch. He told you the same thing.

"You know what, Emmie, if Willow feels like putting the screws to me, she's going to tell Buddy anyway. You're in no condition to fight her or Buddy. This is the kind of thing that happens when you let things spin out of control. All right, I'll go to see her. Jesus, I just can't believe you let this happen."

Nealy had heard enough. She opened the screen door and advanced on her children. "I'm not going to apologize. I was on my way upstairs when I heard you two talking. It sounded like something was wrong. Can I do anything? Can any of us do anything, Nick?"

"Willow is my problem, Mom. I'll handle it. I'm going to go to bed now. I think the two of you have some talking to do. Good night."

"Good night, Nick," Nealy said.

Emmie whimpered into a tissue.

"I'm going to assume that Willow is the Mary Ann that called you. Emmie, why didn't you tell us? Did she say what she wanted? Surely she doesn't want Nick back, or does she?"

"Mom, I don't know what she really wants. She *said* she's wanted for questioning in a murder case. She said she didn't have anything to do with her husband's murder. She just goes around marrying men and leaving them. I think she wants Nick's firm to represent her. I don't really know. I'm just guessing. She threatened to tell Buddy about Gabby if I didn't arrange a meeting with Nick."

"That's blackmail. You could have called the police. Or me, Emmie."

"I could have done a lot of things, Mom. I didn't, okay? In your eyes I am never going to be able to do anything right. I've accepted that. I'll go with Aunt Fanny to Las Vegas, and Sage can keep Gabby for me. Now, if you don't mind, I'd like to be alone."

"Emmie, it doesn't have to be like this. All we want to do is help you."

"I don't need you, Mom. I don't want you coming to Vegas with me either. You stay here and run the farm the way you always did."

"Emmie . . ."

"Mom, go in the house and leave me alone before one of us says something we'll regret."

5

A light drizzle was falling as Nick Clay drove into the parking lot of the famous Kentucky Inn. He cut the engine and leaned back against the seat. An army of worms crawled around inside his stomach, and he was having difficulty breathing. Now, after all this time, he was going to come face-to-face with Willow, his ex-wife, the woman he'd given his young heart to. He closed his eyes, willing his mind to bring forth a picture of Willow behind his closed lids. He wished he was a little kid so he could cry. What was he going to feel when he finally saw her face-to-face? Would his feelings show? Would disgust wash through him? He wished he knew so he could prepare himself.

He looked out of the window and watched three plump bluebirds huddle under an oleander bush, raindrops spilling all about them. He wondered if the birds were related. What a crazy thought. Still, when had he ever seen three birds clustered together anywhere? Never, that's when. Was it an omen? He finally decided the birds were looking out for one another just the way he was going to have to look out for Emmie. *Son of a fucking bitch,* he seethed as he opened the door to climb out of the farm's pickup.

He was dressed casually in creased jeans, Nikes, and a Polo shirt. His hair was slicked back but still unruly. Emmie said he looked delicious, with his golden tan against the stark whiteness of his shirt.

In all the years he'd lived in Kentucky, he'd never been to the Inn. And it was *The* Inn. People from all over the world stayed at the Kentucky Inn when they came for Derby Week. He couldn't help but wonder how Willow had managed to snag a room since the Inn, according to the newspapers, was always booked a year in advance. It was obvious to him now that Willow got what Willow wanted when Willow wanted it. He made a mental promise to himself to come back another day and explore the famous inn.

His gaze swept the crowded lobby. He saw her one split second before she saw him. He had just that one second to realize she was just as pretty as he remembered. He made his way toward her, through the milling crowd of early *Derbyites.*

Willow motioned for him to sit down opposite her. A small table with a coffee service sat in the middle. "Black, one sugar, right?" Willow said.

Nick shook his head. "No thanks. Let's get to it, Willow. No games. What is it you want?" He was amazed at how cold and uncaring his voice sounded.

"I want you. We're still married, Nick." Her voice was still as soft as he remembered, almost a purr, mesmerizing. He fought the urge to clench his fists in preparation to slugging her in front of everyone.

"No, we're not married, Willow. I divorced you. I have the papers to prove it. Don't go down that road. Now, what is it you want?"

"A divorce is just a piece of paper just the way a marriage license is a piece of paper. We were married. We made love. We slept in each other's arms. You swore to love me forever. I want free legal counsel. I'm being set up for something I didn't do, and I want your firm to represent me. The man I was living with was murdered. They need someone to pin it on, and I'm their target. I didn't do it, but I can't prove it. I wasn't anywhere near the ranch when he was killed. I want you to head up the legal team, oversee everything. That's it, no more, no less, Nick. Consider it a favor for old times' sake."

"The firm doesn't do criminal law. I don't do criminal law. You need to get yourself a criminal lawyer for whatever it was you didn't do. Besides, we don't practice outside the state of New Mexico."

"Now, that's lie number two. Lie number one is, yes, you do handle criminal law. I checked it out. Your firm is the best of the best. Right now, I need the best and your firm is it. Hatch Littletree and Bode Jessup both defended people accused of murder, and they won their cases. Both are licensed to practice outside the state. Hatch can practice in any state of the union. Maybe you can't, but they sure can. I need an immediate answer, Nick."

"I'm speaking for myself, and the answer is no. Hatch is semiretired, and Bode is basically running the firm. We all have full caseloads. I'm also low man on the totem pole, and my opinion doesn't count for much, so I would suggest you go elsewhere."

Willow brought the delicate porcelain coffee cup to her lips. "This is your way of getting back at me, Nick. I suppose in the scheme of things, I can understand your attitude. I won't take no for an answer. Make it happen. If you don't, honey, I'm going to call Buddy Owens just the way I told Emmie I would."

"How can you be so spiteful, so cruel? Emmie never did a thing to you. She went out of her way to be nice to you. I never did anything to you either, and yet you walked out on me. Why did you do that? I want to hear you tell me why."

"Because your mother saw through my little charade. We both had a week of fun. You were so cute and such an apt learner once you got the hang of lovemaking. I still think of you fondly. If we had stayed together, you would have smothered me, Nick. I need my space. I like the challenge of . . . Look, it is what it is. Like I told Emmie, I may be a lot of things, but I'm no murderer. None of my . . . ah . . . husbands is going to make waves. Every single one of them has an ego that won't allow him to be made a fool of. I was very careful of my choices, so there's no problem there. You divorced me, so that's not a concern either. If there's no one to file charges on bigamy, I'm off the hook. Get me out of this and I'll disappear and you'll never hear from me again. I meant it when I said I would tell Buddy about Emmie's little girl. You help me, and I'll keep quiet."

Nick squirmed in his chair. "How do I know I can trust you? All you do is lie and manipulate." He couldn't believe he had said what he just said. Still, he had to consider Emmie and her wishes.

"That's a chance you have to take. What's it going to be?"

Nick looked around the plush lobby, at the chattering guests drinking mint juleps at noon on a Sunday morning. Doesn't anyone go to church anymore? Waiters in pristine white coats and immaculate gloves mingled among the guests with trays perched high over their shoulders. Piano music wafted his way, probably from the bar area. There was so much old money in the room, Nick thought he could smell it.

"I told you, Willow, it's not my decision to make. I have to talk to the partners." He leaned across the table and hissed between his teeth. "You say one word to Buddy Owens, and I'll hunt you down and kill you myself. Emmie has enough on her plate right now without worrying about you telling Buddy about Gabby."

Willow looked into his eyes and purred, "Ooohh, I love it when you get mad like this. You look so *manly*. I wouldn't object if you wanted to go upstairs and renew what we once had."

"I'd rather renew old feelings with a rattlesnake. I'll get back to you when I have something to report." He was on his feet a second later. He managed to thread his way through the gaggle of people clustered everywhere in the lobby. The minute he was outside, he took a deep breath of air. He felt drained and disoriented as he made his way across the parking lot to the pickup. Six cars were waiting for his parking space. He looked around, panic on his face, to see if the three birds were still huddled under the bush. They were, but farther back in the shrubbery. For some odd reason he felt relief at the sight.

"Shit!" he said as he backed out of his parking space and crawled through the parking lot and out to the highway. "Shit, shit, shit!"

Nealy clutched at Hatch's arm. "There's something about saying good-bye on a rainy day that doesn't sit right with me," she fretted. "I know I'm going to cry when Nick carries Emmie down to the car. How am I going to say good-bye to Gabby? The poor thing is so confused. Maybe it is the right thing but, then again, maybe it isn't. She's so little to be taken away and thrust among strangers, and they will be strangers to her even though they're family. I don't feel good about this, Hatch."

Hatch reached for his wife's hand. "You have to accept that this is what Emmie wants, honey." He squeezed her hand in a show of support.

"But Hatch, I'm her mother, I should be going with her. This feels so . . . so terminal. I think I'm scared. No, no, I *know* I'm scared. If I feel like this, imagine how Emmie must feel. Hang on to me, Hatch, or I'm going to run after her and drag her back."

"Easy, Nealy. Here comes Fanny. Smile, honey."

Fanny wrapped her arms around Nealy, and whispered, "I know just what you're feeling. We're going to take very good care of your daughter. Sage will pick you up at the airport first thing tomorrow. Emmie doesn't know you're coming, so let's keep it at that. We'll do . . . do what we discussed when you arrive. Jake will be ready with all his gear when you're ready to return. We're going to make it work, Nealy. I'll see you in the morning at Babylon."

Nealy wiped at the corner of her eye. "Okay, Fanny. Thank you."

Nick joined his mother and Hatch on the porch the moment the line of cars headed out to the main road. He looked at his watch. "Hatch, I need to talk to you. Mom, you need to hear this, too. Let's go inside. It's damp out here, and I can see you're shivering."

Nick looked first at his mother and then at Hatch. He reiterated his conversation with Willow and didn't spare himself when it came to recounting his emotions.

"That's blackmail," Nealy sputtered.

"Of course it's blackmail," Nick said tightly. "How else do you think she could convince me to help her? Emmie is . . . Emmie is wild about this. Now that she has this condition, and her activities are so limited, it is conceivable that Buddy could file for custody. A judge won't look kindly on Emmie for not telling him he has a daughter. He could get custody of Gabby if he knew. Am I right, Hatch?"

"He's on the money, Nealy."

"This is so like Emmie," Nick said. "She never thinks things through. I tried to get her to tell Buddy. The time to do it was when Gabby was born. Back then he just wanted to be rid of Emmie, so the chances of his wanting a child at that same time were nil. She didn't do it."

"Nick and I both tried to talk her into telling Buddy about Gabby," Hatch added. "I wanted to do it legally, with a letter and the courts, but Emmie was adamantly opposed."

Nealy twisted her hands in agitation as she looked from her husband to her son. "How do we know Willow won't tell Buddy even if you agree to help her? Say you do agree, and somehow it goes wrong with her even with your excellent representation. Just suppose she gets angry and tells him anyway just for spite. I knew that girl was trouble the minute I set eyes on her. I'm sorry, Nick. I wish things hadn't turned out this way."

Nick poured himself a cup of coffee. "Don't sweat it, Mom. There's more. When I got back from the Inn, I made some phone calls. Guess what I found out! Willow worked as a chef in Fanny Thornton's casino, Babylon. She just walked out one day. I guess that's her MO. She did the same thing in Bermuda. I asked Sage about it. I think I blew his mind when I told him I'd been married to his chef. Talk about someone's mouth going slack and agape."

Hatch stood with his back to the screen door. "Nick, what did he actually say?"

Nick cleared his throat. "He said to run as far and as fast as I could. He said I didn't want to be tarred with that brush. You know how it is in Vegas. Junior Belez is . . . was a high roller. There's a very large estate involved, but since Willow wasn't legally married, I don't know what the hell it means. All Willow said to me was that she's wanted for questioning. She said she was a lot of things but not a murderer. I don't think she's a murderer either. According to her, they're going to try to pin the murder on her. If she's arrested, they won't give her bail because she'll be considered a flight risk, which means she sits in jail. The thought doesn't pain me at all," Nick said coldly. "However, no one should spend time in jail unless they're guilty of something. She's staying at the Kentucky Inn, Hatch. I wish you would talk to her and see what you think."

Nealy continued to wring her hands. Finally, she stuffed them in the pockets of her slacks. "I can go to Ohio and talk to Buddy."

"No!" The single word exploded out of Nick's mouth like a gunshot. "That's the worst thing you can do right now. You didn't see old Buddy sending you any Christmas cards after he dumped Emmie, did you? You, Mom, are just as much a part of his problem as Emmie is. You never wake a sleeping tiger, just as you never ask a question unless you already know the answer."

"Nick's right, honey," Hatch said. "I'll call and arrange to meet with Willow. I'm not making any promises to either one of you. Let's understand that going in."

"Can you keep this quiet, Hatch? I don't want those film people finding out about this, or they'll want to include it in that damn movie. They're ready to go into the editing phase, but they can still shoot footage. Nick doesn't need that, and neither does this farm. And for sure Emmie doesn't need it."

"Nealy, you can't keep something like this under wraps. Sooner or later it's all going to get out. This family is newsworthy. In Vegas, the Thorntons are newsworthy just as the Colemans in Texas are newsworthy. The press loves stuff like this. I'll do my best to keep it quiet but don't count on any miracles."

"I'm going to pack my gear and head out to the airport," Nick said. "I have to be in court early in the morning. When you get to Vegas, give me a call so I'll know you arrived safely. Mom, promise you'll keep me up to speed where Emmie is concerned."

"All right, Nick. Are you okay with the Willow thing?"

"No, Mom, I'm not okay with it. I thought it was over and done with, and I was moving on. Now this comes up. Oh, another thing, Emmie didn't take her patch of grass with her. You might want to think about digging it up and taking it with you. I think she just forgot it."

"I'll do that, honey."

Nick nodded. He set his coffee cup in the sink, turned around, and clapped Hatch on the back. "I don't know if I should wish you good luck or not. Do you want me to fill Bode in on things when I get to the office?"

"Yeah. Tell him I'll call him after I talk to Willow. Have a good flight."

Nealy rinsed the coffeepot, not because she wanted to make more coffee but because it gave her something to do with her hands.

"It's just you and me now, Nealy. If I drink any more coffee, it'll be running in my veins. I know you want to go out there to dig up Emmie's patch of grass. While you're doing that, I'm going to call Willow. I guess we have no plans for Derby Day, right?"

Nealy shrugged as she set the empty coffeepot back on the counter. "I was only going to go because I thought the family was staying on to attend. Then Emmie's condition surfaced, her leaving for the rehab center, and this Willow thing . . . Derby Day is not on the top of my priority list. Next year."

"Hey, that's fine with me. We can watch it on television."

Nealy snuggled into the crook of her husband's arm. "Are you ever sorry you got involved with my family, Hatch? It seems there's one crisis after another."

"I'm loving every minute of it because I love you. It's all going to work out one way or another. It's called life, Nealy. Go on now, dig up that grass and pack it up. When we both wind up our tasks, I say we head into town for some Chinese."

Nealy smiled. "Now that sounds like a plan to me."

Nealy followed Fanny Thornton into the Harem Bar and sat down at a small table, her eyes wide in awe. "This is so exciting, Fanny. I've never seen anything like this in my life. It's so . . . *alive.* Don't people sleep when they come here? How is it this place can be open twenty-four hours a day all year round?"

"It just is. If you want it in one word, that word is money. Billions, not millions, of dollars go through this town yearly. There are no clocks either. I always found that amazing. So many things have happened here in Babylon. I met my husband Marcus right here in this very bar. I was sitting on this same chair at this same table. We're just babbling, Nealy. I'm . . . going to take you . . . somewhere in a little bit, but first I want to assure you that Emmie is in good hands. After we . . . after we do some, ah, business, I'll take you out to the center and give you the tour. You won't be able to see Emmie, but at least you'll know where she is and how things operate. Sage called earlier and said Gabby had a good night. Cookie is with her. They're all going fishing today. Jake is ready to leave with you. That young man is so excited. You've given him a new lease on life, and Sunny is delirious with joy that you're taking him on.

"Harry and Sunny will both be looking out for Emmie. She isn't going to be alone the way Sunny was. It's all doable, Nealy. Accept it, and things will move forward. Acceptance is the biggest hurdle."

Nealy leaned across the table. "Did you accept it, Fanny?"

"No, not at first. We had our rough patches just like you will."

"Is the casino in Atlantic City like this one?"

"Almost. If you mean just as lavish and decadent, yes. It's a tad smaller but we're the only ones who know that. Running a casino like this is a monster undertaking. The twins have it under control. I never did when I was running it. Things would just get away from me. I'm not comfortable here. I never was. I'll bet you don't know that handling money can make you sick. We have hydraulic lifts to move it from place to place. To me it's artificial and phony. Ash, my first husband, thrived in this atmosphere. See, I'm babbling again."

"Is something wrong, Fanny? You look so . . . jittery."

Fanny drew a deep breath. "That's because I *am* jittery. This place makes me crazy. All those bells and whistles, all those people milling about. It's time to leave, Nealy."

Nealy slid off the chair and picked up her purse. "Are we going to the center?"

"No. We're going . . . what we're going to do is . . . is, go to this dump and . . . wait. They have the best chicken soup and bread. They'll give you some to go."

"Can I ask why we're going there, Fanny? It's a little early for lunch, isn't it?"

"We're not going to eat. You'd think after all these years, I would be comfortable going there, but I'm not. I don't bother them, and *they* don't bother me. Or my kids. We work . . . in harmony now. They have their side of the street and we have ours. We . . . help one another . . . from time to time. One time I turned off the power and the water. The town turned black. From that day on, they knew I meant business. It's a mutual respect kind of thing for us. They helped Metaxas replant the mountain. Now when we get there, don't panic. They lock the door and pull the shade. Then they give you soup and bread. Somebody comes and . . . then things happen. You'd think in this high-tech age things would be different instead of ... of the way I do it. I know this doesn't make sense to you, but that's okay. Sometimes I think they just keep doing it this way to humor me."

"Can I ask how you arranged this ... whatever it is we're going to do?"

"I have this phone number. I just call it. Any time of the day or night. It's all because of Sallie, my mother-in-law. Don't ask me any more questions, Nealy. All right, here it is. I told you it was a dump," Fanny said nervously. "Don't say anything."

Fanny was right, it was a dump. The linoleum on the floor was cracked and peeling. The tables were lopsided with red-checkered oilcloth on top. The windows were fly-specked with greasy green shades. The chairs were battered and ragged-looking, but the aroma from the kitchen made it all worthwhile.

Nealy felt a presence, heard the snick of the lock going into place and the snap of the green window shade being pulled to the bottom of the door. She felt like she was taking part in a cloak-and-dagger movie. When she saw Fanny fold her hands in her lap, she did the same thing.

A fat little man in a snow-white apron set down a basket of warm, crusty bread. He returned a second later with two bowls of chicken soup. Fanny picked up her spoon. Nealy followed suit. "This is delicious," she beamed. "This bread tastes like the bread Maud's old housekeeper used to bake every Tuesday. The butter is fresh churned. Ohhh, this is just so good."

"When we leave, they'll give us some to take with us." Fanny fiddled with her spoon and finally placed it on the plate next to her soup bowl.

He was young, maybe Nick's age, and he was movie-star handsome. His suit was crafted by an excellent tailor and probably came from Savile Row. Nealy recognized the cut because that's where Hatch got his suits. Suits that cost a fortune. His shoes were just as expensive. The Rolex gleamed on his wrist.

"Mrs. Reed, it's nice to see you again. Are you enjoying the soup?"

"Very much," Fanny said breathlessly. "This is Nealy Clay Littletree."

Nealy didn't stop to think. Her hand shot forward. The young man grasped it.

"It's an honor and a privilege to meet you, ma'am. I watched you race. The oddsmakers on the street will love you forever."

Fanny had instructed her not to speak, so she nodded.

"Mr. Lucinelli asked me to tell you he's looking into the matter, Mrs. Reed. He also asked me to give you this," the young man said, withdrawing a white envelope from the breast pocket inside his well-cut jacket. He turned his attention to Nealy. "We hope your daughter has a speedy recovery. It was nice seeing you again, Mrs. Reed." He snapped his fingers. A moment later two paper sacks appeared on the table. And then he was gone.

"Our to-go order," Fanny said, getting up.

Outside in the warm summer air, Nealy said, "Fanny, what the hell was that all about? Was that man a gangster? What . . . how . . . I think we should talk, Fanny."

"Can't you walk any faster, Nealy?" Fanny fretted.

Ten minutes later, in the Harem Bar, Fanny signaled the waiter. "I'll have a double scotch on the rocks, and Nealy will have a double shot of Wild Turkey straight up."

Nealy did exactly what Fanny did. She gulped at the whiskey and downed it in two swallows. Both women wiped at their eyes with the bite of the whiskey.

Nealy eyed the two paper sacks on the table. "Are we supposed to eat this?"

"I always throw it away. I can never eat after I go there."

"Exactly why did we go there, Fanny? I don't understand any of this."

"I called . . . *the number*. I asked them if they would find out who killed Junior Belez. *They know everything*. Sometimes I think they know about things before they actually happen. He knew about your daughter. She just got here last night. They made millions off your races, Nealy. Not small millions. Big millions." Fanny signaled the waiter and held up her glass. "Their . . . their code says they have to return the favor."

"I didn't think you were the type to associate with gangsters, Fanny," Nealy said as she slugged at the bourbon in her glass.

"Shhhh. Don't ever use that word around here, Nealy. They're legitimate businessmen. They have their own codes. They . . . they . . . always took care of me. Ash was forever getting himself into one mess or another. They helped me bail him out. In turn I made them respectable. I go to their casinos, have dinner, play a little blackjack, and then I go home. I never . . . I never call that number unless . . . unless it's crucial. I thought . . . think the situation with Willow warranted a phone call. I don't want to see Nick get mired down in something he has no control over. They made money off you, Nealy. Like I said, their code says they have to return the 'favor' for want of a better word. Everyone in Vegas knows . . . knew Junior Belez. Tonight we have to go across the street to dinner. That makes it all official. It's an experience, Nealy. My goodness, our glasses are empty. Bring the bottles," she said to the waiter. Nealy blinked when the waiter set down a bottle of Chivas Regal and one of Wild Turkey.

Fanny slopped liquor into her glass. Nealy did the same. "This might be a triple," she said, eyeing the contents.

"Do you care? I don't care. Drink up. All we have to do is take the private elevator to the penthouse. It's not like we're going to be staggering around where people can see us. I hardly ever drink," Fanny said.

"Me, either," Nealy said, polishing off the amber liquid. She smacked her lips. "I did get drunk once, on my first date with Hatch."

Fanny laughed. "I did the same thing. Marcus showed up and cooked Thanksgiving dinner for my kids. I was . . . *polluted.*" She started to laugh. Nealy clapped her on the back as she poured from the bottle. "I think you just poured bourbon in my glass."

"Yep, I did. We'll switch up. This isn't working. I think it'll be easier if we drink from the bottle. I drink beer from a bottle all the time. Same difference," Nealy volunteered.

"I hardly ever drink. It's not ladylike. If you think we should drink out of the bottle, it's fine with me. I don't think it was full, do you, Nealy?"

"Noooo. The only person I ever knew who could drink a whole bottle of bourbon was Maud. I'm a tea toddler."

"Totaler. Me, too. I hardly ever drink. I said that before, didn't I?"

Alarmed at the way the ladies were slugging from their respective bottles of liquor, the waiter pressed a button under the bar. Within minutes Sage Thornton appeared in the doorway. He shook his head at the waiter to indicate he would handle things.

"Ladies, how are you?" Sage said, straddling a chair next to his mother.

"Sage! Look, Nealy, Sage is here. Honey, we brought you some lunch," Fanny said, pointing to the two paper bags on the table. "The best chicken soup in the state of Nevada. Take both bags. Nealy and I aren't hungry. We're just going to finish our drinks, then we're going to go out to the center. I want to show her around. Can you go with us? Wouldn't that be nice if Sage went with us, Nealy?"

"Yes sireee, that would be nice. We should go now, Fanny. I don't think we should drink any more until we get back. Isn't it getting late?"

Sage eyed the two bottles before he risked a glance at the bartender, who nodded. "Did you two ladies drink both these bottles?"

"Yes, we did," Fanny said smartly. "Neither one of us is a drinker. You know I hardly ever drink, honey. Sometimes, one needs to do things one doesn't normally do."

"You went to that dump, didn't you, Mom?"

"We went to an *establishment* down the road and brought back this lovely chicken soup for your lunch. I don't like it when you get cranky with me, Sage."

"I don't like it either," Nealy said. "You should never get cranky with your mother. You only have one mother. You always have to treat her with respect. I know that because I'm a mother. The dump was . . . it was *quaint*. Wasn't it, Fanny?"

"Yes, it was quaint. The bread was good, too. I love homemade bread. Maybe I don't like the bread as much as I like the smell of it baking. Do you like the smell, Nealy?"

"Love the smell, Fanny. Just love it. Aren't we going somewhere?"

"Yes, you are," Sage said, taking his mother's arm. He motioned for the bartender to help Nealy. "Let's take them up in the service elevator."

Fanny reared back in her seat. "I will not ride up in the service elevator."

"Ma, you and Aunt Nealy are drunk as two skunks. It won't look good if someone sees you looking like this."

"Oh. Do you mind riding up in the service elevator, Nealy? Do you care if anyone sees you like this?"

"I don't know if I should care or not. We didn't care when we went to that dump. This place is pretty fancy. Yes, I care."

Fanny sighed. "All right, we'll go up in the freight elevator. Ooops," she said as she fell against her son. "I'm going to take my shoes off, Nealy. You can take yours off, too. I have a story to tell you about shoes. Marcus sent me hundreds of pairs of shoes when he first met me. Will you remind me to tell you, Nealy?"

"Absolutely," Nealy muttered as she tottered after Fanny. "I probably won't remember till tomorrow, though."

"Okay."

Inside the elevator, Sage looked down at his mother. "Ma, what happened? It's only the middle of the morning, and you're skunked. What the hell happened?"

"Nothing happened. We brought some soup and some bread for your lunch. Why do you want to know?" She looked crafty.

"Because I need to know, that's why."

"We brought you soup and bread for lunch. If you don't want it, all you have to do is tell your mother you don't want it. She's your only mother, pay attention to her," Nealy said, waving her shoes around.

"I'm going to eat it. Ma, you're the only person in this whole damn town that ever gets chicken soup from that place. It's always closed for repairs. You decide to visit and all of a sudden there's soup and then things start happening."

Fanny rolled her eyes. "It's just your imagination, honey. Oh, look, we're here, Nealy. I lived here for a long time. I decorated it, didn't I, Sage?"

"Yeah, after you smashed it up."

"I might have *moved* things around a bit," Fanny conceded. "I have these two wonderful red chairs. We're going to curl up in them and talk, Nealy."

"After you drink a gallon of coffee," Sage said, heading for the kitchen. "You two stay put and don't move."

"She's the only mother you have. You need to talk gently to her," Nealy mumbled.

"I should fire him," Fanny said, flopping down on one of the red chairs. "Do ya ever notice, Nealy, how all of a sudden the kids are doing what you used to do for them. It's like overnight they become your parents. Is that a good thing? I hate it that I'm getting old, and they have to look out for me."

"Don't do it, Fanny. I did that once and regretted it." Nealy curled into a tight ball on the red chair opposite Fanny. They stared at one another as Sage clanked his way around the kitchen.

"We'll talk when he leaves," Fanny hissed.

"I heard that!" Sage bellowed.

"He heard," Fanny mumbled. "Shhh."

The minute the coffee machine made its last plopping sound, he grabbed two cups from the cabinet and poured the dark brew almost to the brims. He settled them on a colorful tray the way he'd seen his wife do and carried it into the giant living room with the wraparound windows that offered a magnificent view of the entire town. He felt like laughing aloud when he saw his mother and aunt sound asleep. He bee-lined for the kitchen.

Three minutes later he was talking to his twin in Atlantic City. "The two of them are shit-faced, Birch. Right now they're both passed out. Yeah, yeah. She brought back that damn chicken soup. She's the only one in this whole damn town that ever gets that chicken soup. She wouldn't tell me a thing. She only goes there when she's desperate, you know that. I have no clue what it means. My guess is she wants something, and they're the only ones who can give it to her. I heard her tell Aunt Nealy they'd talk after I left. Off the top of my head, I'd say it has something to do with our old chef Willow. Birch, I got this lump in my throat a little while ago when I looked at Mom. I felt the same thing at that last board meeting when I saw her. She's old, Birch. You need to come back here more often and spend time with Mom. I feel like bawling. You know what, I'm not sticking my nose in her business. If she wants to go to that dump and . . . do whatever it is she does there, then so be it. I'm even going to eat that damn soup. When the shit hits the fan, I'm going to look the other way. I don't even know why I'm getting so bent out of shape. Mom has been taking care of herself and us and this casino for as long as I can remember. I guess she knows what she's doing. And if she doesn't, then it will be up to us to pick up the pieces just the way she's picked up after us. Jeez, now I feel better. Nice talking to you, Birch."

Sage smacked his hands together in satisfaction. It always helped when he talked to his twin.

In the living room, he stared down at his mother and for a moment relived a few old memories. As far as he was concerned, she was the best mother in the world. He bent over to kiss her wrinkled cheek. "Be happy," he whispered before he left the room. The lump stayed in his throat until he made his way to the Harem Bar, where he picked up the two paper sacks and carried them to the kitchen. "Heat this up for me, will you? I'll sit over here in the corner and eat it."

It was seven o'clock when Fanny and Nealy sat down in the foyer of the rehab center.

"What do you think, Aunt Nealy?" Sunny asked.

"I think it's a beautiful place. It's very homey-looking. I like it that no one wears a uniform. I feel a lot better now that I've seen everything. I hope Emmie can adjust."

"It will take a while. There's a whole process you have to go through. It's like the stages of grieving. In the beginning, she'll fight it and do nothing to help herself. Then she'll give in and go with the flow. Then she'll get tired of feeling so bored and sick and decide to fight. At the fighting stage you literally fight and claw to get out of here. You do everything you're told plus more because you want to go home. Emmie isn't like me and Harry. This *is* our home. She'll want to get back to Gabby and back to her horses at the farm. She'll do it, too. You'll see."

Nealy leaned over to hug her niece. "Thanks for telling me all that. I'll come back next month to see her if she wants me to. I understand the rules are what makes this place work, so I'll obey them. I won't call or come until it's time to do so."

"Will you call me from time to time to let me know how Jake's doing?" Sunny asked.

"Of course I'll call you. He's going to do just fine. I don't want you to worry about him one little bit."

"He said he'll drive out here this evening to say good-bye." Tears filled Sunny's eyes. "I just want him to be happy."

Nealy nodded. "I'll send pictures. Will you . . ."

"I'll ride her tail every chance I get. I can be relentless. Harry can, too. I'll keep you posted. I gotta go, Mom. We have chapel at seven-thirty."

"It's very peaceful here, isn't it, Nealy? It costs an outrageous sum of money to operate this place. Just so you know, Nealy, the other side of the street helps. I couldn't have done this without their help. Every year they kick in millions so that people like Sunny and Harry can live here and not worry about cost. Half of all our revenues from both casinos goes to this facility and its sister center in Reno. The waiting list to get in here is mind-boggling. You might want to think about building a center like this in Kentucky. You have a ready-made setup already. You raise millions every year with your Derby Ball. Seven or eight acres of ground would do it. Metaxas would probably help you out. You could do it, Nealy."

Nealy rubbed at her temples. "I have the Queen Mother of all headaches. How about you? I could do that, couldn't I? I swear, I'm never, ever, going to drink like that ever again. I still can't believe I drank a whole bottle of bourbon."

"I guess we should start thinking about going back to the casino. I'm glad now I didn't give Sage an argument about the car service. I was seeing double there for a while. We still have to get changed and hit the other side of the street. That means we dude up in our finery and make nice. Oh dear, I forgot all about this," Fanny said, fishing the white envelope out of her pocket.

"What is it? A bill or a receipt for the soup?"

"None of the above." Fanny smiled. "It's *their* contribution for the second half of the year. They're always prompt. Sometimes they're actually early, like now. They don't have to do it at all, and that's what makes it so extra special." She waved the check in front of Nealy, who swooned at the amount. Fanny continued to smile as she tucked the check into her purse.

"We can go now. Are you glad you came, Nealy?"

"Very glad."

* * *

It was nine o'clock when word went out on the street that Fanny Thornton Reed and the most famous jockey in the world were going to visit the opposite side of the street. From windows high in the casinos, the owners watched the two women cross the street.

They were wined and dined like visiting royalty. They posed for pictures in each casino, pictures that would run in all the daily papers the next day. As they left each casino, they were handed small velvet sacks full of sterling silver dollars. "I have thousands of these," Fanny whispered. "I give them to the grandchildren at Christmastime. Save yours for Gabby." Fanny reached down to take off her shoes.

"I'm whipped," Nealy said, taking off her shoes, too. "This town is just now starting to jump and it's after midnight. Is it safe to be walking around a town like this at this time of night, Fanny?"

"Oh, yes. In case you haven't noticed, we have an escort, front and back. Sideways, too. I told you, they take care of me. Do you want to go somewhere and get an ice-cream cone?"

"I'd like that, Fanny. I really would. Do you lick yours from the bottom to the top or do you go top to bottom?" To Nealy it was the most serious question in the world.

"I bite off the top and then I lick from the top. How about you?"

"Isn't that amazing? I do the same thing. I like cherry vanilla. What's your favorite?"

"Chocolate. I always manage to drip."

"Me, too," Nealy said, going off into a peal of laughter. "I forgot to call Hatch."

"Oh, well," Fanny said. She slapped her thigh and burst into laughter.

Within minutes the word whipped down the street for the second time. Fanny Thornton Reed was back in town. So was the most famous jockey in the world, the owner of two prize Thoroughbreds and two-time Triple Crown winner—and she loved their town.

6

Cordell Lancer was as weathered as time itself. His skin was like old shoe leather, darkened by the sun and the elements, his legs so bowed a cow pony could have run between them. He watched now, his denim blue eyes speculative as Nealy listened to what he had to say. He hiked up one of his bowed legs over the board fencing so he could straddle it and stared off across the paddock. "I know I'm fairly new to Blue Diamond Farms, Nealy, but that don't change nothing when it comes to horses. Any horse man in this state will vouch for me, but then I think you already know that. It pains me to be telling you all these negative things about your daughter, but fact is fact. I told her I thought Gadfly had an ulcer, and she said no, he didn't. She told me to stay away from him because he was mean as cat shit. The *reason* that horse was mean as cat shit was because he was hurting. Once the vet came out and treated him, he started doing better, but that didn't change his attitude none toward Emmie. She must have done something to get his dander up because every time he saw her he pinned his ears back."

"Did you or anyone ever see her do anything to him?"

"Nope." He shook his head. "You know horses. Sometimes there's no figuring what they're afraid of. Some horses are afraid of everything from a rattling plastic bag to thunder. Others don't worry about anything. I'm thinking your Emmie was in a lot of pain herself and did something that Gadfly took personally."

"Let's you and me pay Gadfly a visit," Nealy said as she headed for the yearling barn. She rubbed at her throbbing temples. She'd had little, if any, sleep the night before, and the minute her feet hit the floor, a headache blossomed behind her eyes. She'd gulped aspirin to no avail. Emmie. Emmie. Emmie. All she could think about was her daughter.

"I think you might be right, Cordell. I'm having a hard time with all of it. Maybe all she did was raise her hand to him, and maybe she even hit him. When I got here, everything seemed, at least on the surface, to be right as rain. Then all this stuff rears up and slaps me in the face."

"Yes, ma'am, that's the way of it sometimes."

"Now that I think of it, every time I went near Gadfly, Emmie was with me. I guess he reacted. Did she mistreat him? What? I need to know."

Cordell pushed his hat farther back on his head. "If I knew the answer to that, I'd tell you. The best I can suggest is that you ask her. I never saw anything, and no one else saw anything. I would have heard something like that. A horse don't turn mean on his own. He's good with the grooms, with everyone but Emmie. You ain't gonna believe me until you see for yourself."

Nealy followed the farm manager to Gadfly's stall. She automatically reached into her pocket for a mint, holding it out, something she wouldn't have dared to do just days ago. Gadfly snorted as he pawed the ground. Nealy laughed out loud when the big horse tried to nuzzle her pocket for more mints. "Well, I'll be damned," she muttered.

"Told ya. Ain't nothin' wrong with this horse. When the vet gives the okay, you might want to train him right along with Hifly. The boy did well today, Nealy. His butt is hurting him some, so I sent him off with liniment and told him to take a good long soak. First days are always the worst. Tomorrow he'll probably be wishing he was dead when he has to work those sore muscles. Everything is in good shape. We can manage now that you're back in the saddle. It bothers me, to be telling a mama her offspring wasn't up to snuff. Didn't want to do it. Tried talking to Emmie a few times, and she told me to shut up or she'd give me my walking papers. I like it here, Nealy, and I'd like to stay as long as you'll have me. I'll try to live up to Dover Wilkie, but that's gonna be mighty hard. Good man, Dover."

"Yes, he is. I hope he's happy in his retirement. Do you think I should check on Jake?"

"No, ma'am, I don't think any such thing. Eighteen is just about a man around here. He needs to be taking care of himself. It was a good idea to put him up in the cottage so he fends for himself. Now if you want to be taking him a pie or something, I don't object to that. We'll see what he's made of tomorrow morning when he has to report to the barn at four A.M."

Nealy whirled around when she heard her name called. "Hatch! What's wrong?" she asked, running toward him.

It was then that she noticed her husband had shed his jeans and boots and now wore a business suit. "You look like you're going somewhere."

"Take a break, Nealy, and let's go up to the front porch. I asked Gertie to fix us some fresh coffee."

"Sitting on the front porch with my husband at this time of day is a real treat. Cordell said Jake did well, and he's soaking in a hot tub about now. Oh, Hatch, he told me so many disturbing things about Emmie. I wanted to cry. I still want to cry. He thinks she mistreated Gadfly, and the horse had an ulcer, something she refused to acknowledge. I'm having such a hard time with this. If we're going to blame all the neglect on her condition, and that seems to be what we're doing, how could she have been so stupid to ignore the kind of pain she was going through? I don't think I'm ever going to understand that."

"Who knows, honey? You can't change what's happened. All you can do is pick up the pieces and go forward. Placing blame does no good. Move forward. I'm sorry I took you away from here. I never should have done that. I know you said you were ready to leave and that you went with me willingly, but it was wrong. You belong here. This farm is you. Without you, it's nothing. We've seen the proof of that."

Nealy smiled at her husband. He always made her feel good. "I think you're giving me far too much credit. I'm only as good as the people who work for me. Now, tell me why you're all dressed up at five o'clock in the afternoon."

"I'm taking Willow back to Las Vegas. She's prepared to give a statement. At this point in time, I don't know what the police have in the way of information. There is every possibility they might arrest her. There's no way in hell she can get bail because she's a flight risk. Like she said, she's a lot of things, but she's no murderer. I'm taking the case because of Emmie and Nick, and that's the only reason.

"We have a seven o'clock flight. I'll call you later tonight.

Nealy, I don't know how long I'm going to have to stay in Vegas. Will you be okay here by yourself?"

"I'll be fine. Are you staying at Babylon?"

"Yes. Fanny insisted. She said I could use the penthouse as my base of operations. I'll call her this evening and tell her Jake had a good day."

"I'll miss you," Nealy whispered.

"Do you have any idea how much I love you, Nealy?" Hatch whispered in return.

Nealy giggled. "I know exactly how much because I love you the same amount. So there."

"Then, on that happy thought, I'm afraid I have to run. I really don't want to represent this young woman, Nealy. I don't like her or her lifestyle. She really thinks what she's done is okay. She says she didn't hurt anyone. It's the thrill of the chase and then the adrenaline rush when it's time to skip out. Nick is well rid of her, but try telling that to his heart. I suspect he still has feelings for her. He'll never admit it because it makes him feel the fool. I went into the law believing every single person has the right to their day in court and you are innocent until proven guilty. If they charge her with murder, it's going to be a different ball game."

Nealy shrugged. "Maybe she's missing something in her body chemistry the way I'm beginning to think Emmie is missing something in hers, too. I guess in time we'll know all the details. Travel safe, Hatch, and don't forget to call me when you land so I don't worry."

"Will do, lovely lady, will do. Nealy, I don't know how long I'm going to be gone. I need to hear you say it's okay. I feel like I'm deserting you."

Nealy stared down at the flower borders. She could feel her heart swell with love. "It's okay, Hatch. You aren't deserting me, so take as long as you need. I want you to represent Willow to the best of your ability because that's what you do. I don't ever want that to change. Now pucker up, Mister."

Hatch looked down at his watch and groaned. Nealy kissed him long and hard. "That's so you'll hurry back. Go on, honey, or you'll miss your flight. I'll be here waiting for you."

* * *

Jake crawled out of the bathtub. Every bone and muscle in his body protested as he dried off and wrapped himself in a robe. He eyed the bottle of liniment sitting on the vanity. He decided he wouldn't be a wimp or a *wuss* if he rubbed in the ointment. After all, Cordell had given it to him, so that had to mean others had experienced the same muscle pain after a hard day. He was exhausted when he finished rubbing the foul-smelling liniment on his legs, thighs, buttocks, and arms. He tottered over to the sofa and collapsed. How was it possible, he wondered, to be in so much pain, in every part of his body, all at the same time? He bolted upright, clenching his teeth. His mother was always in this kind of pain, and so was Emmie. What he was experiencing was *nothing* compared to what his mother and Emmie were enduring.

He clenched his teeth and forced himself to walk to the kitchen, where he fixed himself a pot of green tea. He drank two cups before he wolfed down the Kraft macaroni and cheese he'd prepared before his bath. He looked at the dishes piled in the sink. Tomorrow was another day. His mother's words rang in his ears. *Don't leave a mess behind you for someone else to clean up.* He sighed as he filled the sink with soapy water. *Damn, I forgot to hang up my towel in the bathroom.* His mother always said if you didn't hang up your towel, it would smell the next day. He retraced his steps to the bathroom to hang up the towel. He also dried off the vanity with tissues. Good. Maybe now he could sit down and think about his day. He groaned when he remembered the dishes.

Fifteen minutes later, his new abode tidy, he sat down in a recliner to relax. The moment he stretched out his aching legs, he remembered his promise to call his mother. He struggled out of the chair and dialed his mother's number from memory.

"Jake! Oh, sweetie, Harry and I have been sitting here willing the phone to ring. Are you okay? How did it go? Do you like it? Is everything okay?"

"Mom, today was the worst day of my life. All those bad days with the doctors and the hospitals can't hold a candle to what I went through. I'm okay, and I'm not complaining. I love it. I really do. Tomorrow I know I'm going to hate it because if I'm as sore as I am right now, tomorrow is going to be ten times worse.

Cordell gave me some liniment that smells like manure. I smell like manure, Mom."

"Oh, honey, the first few days are always the worst. Take it easy and work your way slowly into things. When you hang up you should go to sleep." Disappointment rang in Sunny's voice.

"Hey, Mom, it's okay. I expected it. Cordell said I did real good for the first day. He said I have a natural ability."

"Really?" Her voice rose an octave.

"Yeah, really. Big surprise, huh? If my body didn't hurt so much, I think I might have actually enjoyed myself.

"Mom, I'm afraid to go to sleep. What if I don't hear the alarm at four o'clock. No, three-thirty. I have to be in the barn at four. I sleep like Uncle Sage. Aunt Iris said we both sleep like we're dead. I'm going to have to get another alarm clock for backup."

"I'll call you, Jake. Put the phone by your bed, and I'll ring it till you answer." You know Harry and I don't sleep well, so it won't be a problem. But only until you get yourself a backup alarm clock. Is it a deal?"

"Oh, Mom, you're the greatest. You got yourself a deal."

"What did you do today? Tell us all about it. I have you on the speakerphone so Harry can hear at the same time."

"I did everything, Mom. You name it and I did it and if I didn't help, I watched. I started off riding this pony, a pony, Mom, and let me tell you I felt silly as hell, but I stayed on. Then I got on a bigger horse, a mare. She was real gentle but my rear end will never be the same. I helped groom the horses, I mucked stalls, picked their hooves, I swept the breezeway, fed the horses, helped the hotwalkers. I cooked two packages of macaroni and cheese and ate both of them. I also had two cups of green tea. I'm okay, Mom. I know I have to go to a store and buy vegetables and fruit and I will as soon as I settle in. Before you can ask, yes, I'm taking my medication. I'm going to watch some horse-racing videos, and if I don't fall asleep, I'm going to read up on some jockeys. Are you and Harry okay, Mom? Did you hear anything about Emmie?"

"Harry and I are fine, honey. Unfortunately, we know nothing about Emmie. You know how it works for the first month you're here. Sage called and said Gabby is having the time of her life on the mountain. My phone time is almost up, honey, the light is blinking. Take care of yourself. I love you."

"Mom?"

"What is it, Jake?"

"I can do this, can't I?"

"I don't know, Jake. I think you can, but that's the mother in me talking. I think you can do whatever you want within your own limitations. Don't give up, Jake. Even when you think you can't do it for another hour, another minute. Call on all your inner reserve and *do it*. That's what I had to do. It's what I still do every day of my life. Try and get some sleep, and Harry and I will call you at three-thirty. Turn the phone up as high as it will go and make sure you put it right by your head."

"Okay, Mom. Thanks. I love you. Tell Harry I love him, too."

"Good night, Jake," Sunny and Harry said in unison.

Jake hung up the phone, his eyes burning. Sometimes life just wasn't fair. He didn't care so much for himself, but he did care for his mother. No matter how bad things were, no matter what went wrong, her sunny disposition always came through. If he turned out to be half the person she was, he would definitely be ahead of the game.

He looked at the stack of videos and the pile of books and decided they would have to wait for another day. He was going to bed. He couldn't ever remember going to bed at eight o'clock at night. He also couldn't ever remember getting up at three-thirty in the morning. He had a whole new life now, governed by rules and regulations, just the way his mother lived. It wasn't a bad thing, all things considered. Not a bad thing at all.

It was like every other police station in the country, manned by overworked and underpaid police officers. The smell of disinfectant was strong, the coffee was black and bitter, the donuts stale. Empty sugar packets were scattered everywhere on the makeshift table along with the stirrers and Styrofoam cups. Hatch looked down at the mess and closed his eyes. This definitely was not the kitchen at Blue Diamond Farms, where everything gleamed and sparkled. He decided to pass on the coffee and walked over to the water cooler, where he filled a flimsy cup with water and gulped it down. He carried a cup back to his client, who shook her head when he offered it to her. He drank the water himself before he crushed the paper cup in his hand. He hit the wastebasket on his first try.

The detective was a tall man with a receding hairline and a face full of freckles. "Joe Sullivan," he said extending his hand. "Come with me, Mr. Littletree. You, too, Miss . . . Mrs. . . . What is your name these days?"

"The name I was born with is Willow Bishop," Willow said quietly.

A second detective joined them the moment they were seated at a scarred table that was totally bare. The room smelled of sweat, insect repellent, and Pine-Sol. Detective Sullivan introduced Noah Wately.

Hatch took the initiative, and said, "I want it on the record that my client has come here voluntarily today. Until a few days ago she didn't know she was wanted for questioning. She used those few days to seek out legal counsel. Are you filing charges against my client or is this a Q&A interview?"

"We just want to ask your client a few questions. For now. We'll see how it goes, Mr. Littletree."

If Willow was frightened, she didn't show it, Hatch thought. She appeared cool, almost nonchalant.

Detective Sullivan leaned his arms on the table. "Why don't you tell us your side of things, Miss Bishop. Were you married to Carlo Belez, also known as Junior Belez? Can you account for your whereabouts on the night of October fourteenth? And can anyone verify your whereabouts on the night in question?" His emotionless voice sounded like it had come out of a can.

Willow tilted her head so she could peep out from under the brim of her straw hat.

"I went through a wedding ceremony with Carlo Belez. We lived together at his ranch.

"The fourteenth of October was supposed to be my day off but I still had to make an appearance at the Emperor Room to make sure my sous chefs were doing what they were supposed to do. I left about nine-thirty that evening. I played the slots for about an hour, then I hit a few other casinos. I had a few drinks, listened to the music in one of the bars before I headed home. It was close to midnight. It was a clear night, a lot of stars in the sky. It was actually kind of cold. I remember because I had to turn on the car heater.

"I parked the car, entered the house through the kitchen, and poured myself a drink. I smoked a cigarette at the kitchen counter and nibbled on some cheese and crackers. I remember taking my shoes off. I was tired, but I did remember to fix the coffeepot for the morning. Junior's car was parked in the driveway. I assumed he was upstairs watching videos. When he didn't go into town, he watched videos all night long. He was a very boring man."

"Did anyone see you? Did you speak to anyone?"

"A lot of people saw me, and I spoke to a lot of people that evening. I didn't exchange names with anyone if that's what you mean. If I had known I was going to need an alibi, I would have done so. That's all I can tell you."

"Then what happened?"

"Then I turned out the lights and locked up. I walked upstairs in my bare feet and headed for the bathroom to take a shower. I heard the television. I called out to Junior to tell him I was home, but he didn't answer me. He doesn't like to talk if he's in the middle of a movie. It didn't bother me that he didn't answer. I took a shower, washed my hair, and put on a nightgown. I was just about to tell Junior I was going to sleep in the guest room if he was going to finish watching the movie when I saw all the blood on his white shirt. I think I froze in my tracks and just stared at him. I was standing in the doorway of the bathroom, but even from there I knew he was dead. When I got my wits together, I walked over to check for a pulse. His body was still warm if that's important for you to know."

Hatch watched a cockroach walk across the floor. He was about to get up to step on it when Joe Sullivan beat him to it. Two more appeared and were squashed. The detective made no move to pick them up. Instead he used the edge of his shoe to slide them back under the makeshift coffee table.

"Why didn't you call the police? What did you do next?"

Willow looked at Hatch. He nodded. "I did what anyone would do in a situation like that. I panicked. I thought I would be blamed, so I packed my things, cleaned out the safe, and left. I drove up to Reno and slept in my car the first night. I don't know why I went to Reno, I just did. It was that panic thing in me.

"I bought the papers, watched newscasts, but my name wasn't mentioned at all. They did give a lot of play to Junior's lifestyle, his gambling habits, and his friends. After a couple of weeks of living out of my car, I drove to New York. I got a job working in a small, out-of-the-way restaurant. I have a laptop, so I checked the Vegas papers daily. There was still no mention of me, so I relaxed a little and then a short while ago I saw, for the first time, that I was wanted for questioning. I drove from New York to Kentucky and hired Mr. Littletree. That's all I can tell you because there isn't anything else to tell."

Hatch doodled on the yellow pad in his lap and waited.

"Can anyone vouch for your presence in Reno?"

"I don't think so. I ate at fast-food places and paid cash. I pumped my own gas and paid with cash. I cleaned up at gas station bathrooms. I told you, I was panicky. I didn't know what to do."

"We'll need the name of the restaurant in New York and where you stayed. It would help if you could come up with the names of the gas stations you stopped at on the way to Reno."

"I didn't buy any on the way. I bought it after I got there. One place had a Taco Bell on one side and a Burger King on the other side. I remember because I ate at both places. The name of the restaurant in New York was La Grotto."

"Where are you staying here in Vegas, Miss Bishop?"

"Babylon."

"And you, Mr. Littletree, where are you staying?"

"Babylon. Is my client free to go?"

"For now. We need a signed statement before you leave. We also want a list of all the men you married along with names and addresses. Don't leave town, Miss Bishop." Detective Wately slid a yellow pad across the scarred table along with a pen.

Willow grimaced as she risked a glance at Hatch. He nodded. She started to write.

An hour later Willow and Hatch walked out into the warm, summer night.

"I think I'll walk back to the casino," Willow said.

Hatch stopped in midstride. "That isn't a good idea. Those two detectives in there are not stupid. They are going to have a tail on you. From here on in, don't even think about leaving. They're probably getting a warrant right now to seize your car back in Kentucky. You are a suspect, Willow. You admitted to finding the body, to touching it, to stealing Belez's belongings from the safe. And you didn't call the police. That's what's going to do you in."

"Are they going to arrest me?"

She's too damn calm, Hatch thought. A chill washed up his spine. "My guess would be yes. I just don't know when. You must realize, if you skip out, they'll find you. You need to cooperate."

"I appreciate your honesty, Hatch. I think I'd like to be alone for a little while. I'll walk back to the hotel and get a little dinner and head for bed. Do you want me to check in with you before I go nite-nite?"

And she's cocky, too, Hatch thought. "If you're serious about clearing your name, you'll do the right thing and not make waves. I'll check with you in the morning after I come back from police headquarters."

Willow nodded. "Good night, Hatch."

Hatch's eyes narrowed as Willow walked away. She blended in with the crowd of vacationers, and within minutes he lost sight of her. He realized how hungry he was a moment later. And he had to call Nealy. He was glad now that he'd called Sunny earlier. Nealy had warned him to call early so as not to upset Sunny and Harry's nightly routine.

Hatch hailed a cab and returned to Babylon. He headed for the Harem Bar, where he ordered dinner and a bottle of Foster's beer. He kept glancing at his watch while he waited for his dinner. Even if Willow was a slow walker, she'd make the casino in under an hour. If she didn't bolt and run. His gut told him that was exactly what she was going to do. He was on his third beer when his salmon primavera was set in front of him. He ate slowly, savoring each mouthful. The moment he finished, his cell phone was in his hand. He rang the hotel and gave Willow's room number. He listened to the phone ring. He broke the connection on the thirteenth ring.

Conceivably, Willow could have stopped to eat somewhere just as he did. She said she was going to get some dinner. She might have decided to do a little gambling on the way back. Or, she could have cut and run.

A moment later the palm of his hand slapped the tabletop. The beer bottle moved three inches with the force of the blow. Willow had traveled light—just her backpack and purse. She had both with her at the police station. There would be no need for her to go back to the hotel. She could have hitched a ride somewhere, picked up some high roller and coaxed him into taking her somewhere. Obviously she was very good at enticing men into her life. He rang her room again. There was still no answer.

Where would she go? He realized he didn't have a clue. The detectives had warned her not to leave town. He reminded himself that he was her lawyer, not her keeper.

A waiter appeared at his elbow with his dinner check. He scrawled his name and room number across the bottom and left the bar.

Life was going to get complicated. He could feel it in his bones.

Willow hailed a cab and asked to be taken downtown. She'd been there many times and knew the area well. She headed for the bar at Sassy Sally's and looked around. Her experienced eyes raked the long bar until she saw what she was looking for.

His name was Lute Granger, and he was a hair away from being cut off at the bar. He was a pretend Texan with pretend cowboy boots and a real Stetson. He lived off a trust fund, or so the scuttlebutt said. "Hey, Lute, how's it going?" Willow asked, sitting down on a stool next to him.

"Do I know you?"

"Not really. We played pool once down the street. I beat you. It's pretty smoky in here. Let's go for a walk. They're going to cut you off any minute anyway. I can get a bottle, and we can sit in the car. Unless you have other plans. You up for a little fun? The night's still young."

"Well, sure. What'd you say your name was?"

"I didn't say, but it's Bertha. Whoops, watch it, you almost fell there. Hold on to my arm, okay. Where's your car?"

"Why do you want to know?"

"So we can sit in the car and drink. They won't serve you any more liquor here. If you don't want to go with me, that's okay."

Willow linked her arm with Lute's to steady him. "You ever been to Mexico, Lute?"

"Nope. Why?"

"I was thinking it might be nice to drive to California and cross the border. You want to go for it?"

"Hell, why not. I don't have anything else to do. Okay, here's my car," he said, pointing to a classic Cadillac with a pair of Texas longhorns attached to the front grille. "I filled it up earlier this evening. You want to drive?"

This is too easy, Willow thought. *Either that or I'm even better than I thought.* "Sure. Why don't you curl up in the backseat and sleep off all that booze. I'll pick us up a bottle and wake you. You okay with that idea, Lute?"

"Sounds like a *suuuperbbb* idea," Lute said, crawling into the backseat.

Willow settled herself behind the wheel, adjusted the seat, and fixed the rearview mirror to her liking. She looked around to see if anyone was following her, then pulled into traffic slowly, her eyes going from the rearview mirror to the side mirror. She paid careful attention to the road, knowing how the Vegas cops operated. If there was one thing she didn't need, it was to be stopped by a cop. She felt her adrenaline kick in. She was on the run again. She started to laugh. It sure beat sitting in a dirty police cell.

Hatch was right about one thing, the police were going to arrest her in the next few days. At least now she knew what was going on. With no other suspect, she was going to be their prime target. It didn't matter that she'd told the truth. They would never give her bail, never in a million years, and there was no way she was sitting in jail for the rest of her life. She'd been on the run before, and this time was no different. She could get lost in Mexico and live well with her stash in the backpack. She could hide out there for years and years. For the rest of her life if she had to. She still had three identities she'd never used. Life was suddenly looking a lot less stressful.

Willow looked at her watch when she drove across the bridge to Tijuana the following day. Lute was still sleeping in the backseat, snoring loudly. He would probably be fresh as a daisy when he woke, and she'd be whipped. She also needed to ditch the pimpmobile she was driving. Lute would pitch a fit, but life was tough sometimes. There had to be chop shops all over the area. Maybe all she needed to do was park it and cross her fingers that someone would steal the flashy Caddy.

She stopped the car in front of a cantina whose windows were so fly-specked you couldn't see inside. The entire street smelled of grease and urine. She climbed out of the car, glad now that she'd stopped along a lonely stretch of road to change her clothes just before dawn. She now wore flowered slacks with a matching blouse. Her hair was piled high on her head under a curly red wig. She looked like all the other bargain-hunting tourists walking up and down the street.

Inside she bought a bottle of root beer and asked for directions to the nearest realtor.

Lute was still sleeping in the backseat when she slid back into the car. She was careful to follow the directions to a real-estate office that was just as dirty as the cantina. A weasel of a man with greasy hair and a pencil-thin mustache said he had just what she was looking for in the way of accommodations. For $250 she could get a four-bedroom house fully furnished and for another $50 a month his sister would keep house for her. "Cash," he said, rubbing his hands together.

Willow nodded. "No lease. I'll pay cash for one month. If I like it, I'll stay. Drive us to the house and show me what it looks like. We'll leave our car here."

Outside, she opened the back door and shook Lute's shoulder. "Wake up, honey. This nice man is going to show us a lovely house, but we're going to go in his car. Step lively."

In a daze the pretend cowboy climbed out of his car and into the Chevy Nova that groaned and sputtered all the way up a steep winding road.

Willow took one look at the long sprawling ranchlike house

and opened her purse. She would be safe there from the long arm of the law. At least for a while.

"I'll come by for the car later today. Is that all right?"

"That will be fine," the realtor said, pocketing the cash. "When I get back to town, I will tell Rosa she is to keep house for you. She will arrive in the morning to cook you breakfast. Will that be satisfactory?"

"Yes. Come on, honey, let's see our new home. We just got married," she whispered to the realtor.

"Ah, yes, honeymooners. Very good, *señora.*"

"So, Lute, what do you think?" Willow asked.

"Who are you?"

"Your brand-new wife. Don't you remember? We got married last night in Vegas and drove here." She lied with a straight face. "We're on our honeymoon."

Hatch crawled out of bed the minute he hung up the phone from his wake-up call. He immediately dialed Willow's room number, knowing there would be no answer. He swore under his breath.

He showered, shaved, and dressed and was on the fourteenth floor thirty minutes later. He looked up and down the hall to see if a maid was anywhere near. He turned when he heard the service elevator doors open. The floor maid worked her cart until she had it free of the doors, then looked up at him expectantly.

"Can you please check on the guest in Room 1409. I'm not sure if the guest checked out or not. I'll wait here," he said when the little woman looked at him suspiciously.

"There's no one in the room, sir. The bed hasn't been slept in, and the towels haven't been used."

Hatch thanked her and handed over a ten-dollar bill. Willow was gone, and he knew it.

He didn't bother with coffee. Instead he walked outside and grabbed the first cab he saw.

"I hope you're not in a hurry, Mister. Traffic's a bitch at this time of morning. I'll take all the back streets, but it's still going to be thirty-five minutes."

"It's okay. I'm not in a hurry." Hatch leaned back into the seat. His job there was over. There was nothing more he could do. He felt relieved. Now he could go back to Kentucky and Nealy.

The driver was as good as his word. Thirty-eight minutes later, Hatch paid him and got out of the cab. He felt a hand on his shoulder almost immediately. "Detective Sullivan. I was about to go inside to look for you. My client seems to have disappeared sometime during the night. If you didn't have a tail on her, she's gone. Don't look at me like that, Detective. I'm her lawyer, not her keeper. I warned her not to leave town. For whatever it's worth, I don't think she killed Junior Belez. She knows you're going to try to pin the murder on her. She is not a stupid woman."

Hatch watched as police officers of every size and description walked from the parking lot to the front steps of the station house. He looked down at his watch. Almost seven. Time for the good guys to start catching the bad guys.

"Son of a bitch!" the detective seethed. "I knew this was going to happen. My guys were about two minutes too slow last night. They picked you up the minute you got in your cab, but your client was already gone. They did some pretty fast scrambling, but they screwed it up. We'll put out an all-points bulletin on her. You staying or returning to, where was it, Kentucky?"

"No point in me hanging around here. If I hear from her, which I don't think I will, I'll call you."

The detective held out his hand, and Hatch shook it. It was so civilized he wanted to puke. He offered up an airy wave before signaling for a cab. While waiting for a cab to stop, he pulled a pair of sunglasses out of his breast pocket and made a production out of putting them on.

"Hey, hold on a minute." Four long-legged strides brought the detective next to Hatch. "We have the warrant to seize Miss Bishop's car," Sullivan said.

Hatch shrugged. "If you have no objection, I'd like to be there when the police check it out."

"I don't have a problem with it. Check with the locals when you get back. I've got your card. Let's agree to share information."

"Sure." Like he was really going to have information to share. Oh, yeah.

What mattered was calling Nick to fill him in on the latest developments.

The forty-minute ride to the airport allowed him the time he needed to call Nick, who listened until Hatch finished speaking. When there was no response on the other end of the line, he said, "Say something, kid."

"Do you think she did it, Hatch?"

"No, I don't. She ran because she knew they were going to arrest her. She couldn't face being locked up, so she took off. They're going to issue an all-points on her. I don't know how much good that will do. She seems to be an expert at going to ground and hiding out. There's nothing we can do, so I'm on my way to the airport to catch a flight home. Try and put it out of your mind. She has no hold on you, Nick, other than an emotional one. No one can help you with that but yourself. I'll call you when I get home and if anything comes up, I'll call you first."

Hatch's cell phone snapped shut. He leaned back in the seat and closed his eyes.

7

It didn't look like a doctor's office, but it was and she knew it. Even though Dr. Ian Hunter wore beige twill shorts and a white tee shirt, he was still a *shrink*. And he was waiting for her to bare her soul. This particular session had been scheduled for outdoors on one of the many flower-decked patios but at the last minute, Ian, as he liked to be called by the patients, said simply, "We're going to talk indoors today."

Emmie looked around Ian's lair as she thought of it. His diplomas and certificates lined one wall. The opposite wall held watercolors painted by his patients. Some were beautiful and some were downright ugly. She fixed her gaze on one that was full of vivid splashes of orange and yellow. She didn't know why she was drawn to it, she just was. From where she was sitting she couldn't make out the initials scrawled across the bottom.

She hated it there, resented being in his office, resented being told what to do and when to do it. What she really hated, though, were the words: *cooperate, join in, accept.* She wished she could cry, but all her tears had been shed when she first arrived. There were none left.

She waited for the session to begin.

"What is it about this room you don't like, Emmie? Be as specific as you can." Ian's pen was poised over a yellow tablet, ready to record her response.

"For one thing, I don't like those pictures on the wall. They're the result of an illness, a disease or . . . something. Don't ask me to make one. I don't like all the bookshelves, and I can't understand why you have to turn on the lamps when there's bright sunshine coming in the windows. Most of the patients here can't hold a book or a magazine, yet you have them all over the place.

I don't care why. You could at least look professional. Wearing docksiders, shorts, and tee shirt makes me think you're trying to con me into something. You're a doctor, so look and act like one. You asked me a question, and I'm answering it." Emmie spoke in a cool, detached voice, a voice that clearly said I don't give a damn about this office or about you either, Dr. Ian Hunter.

Ian Hunter had had his share of difficult patients before, but Emmie Coleman was front and center this past month. He'd been treating her for five weeks with absolutely no results. He had yet to see a spark of interest. He leaned back and took a deep breath. "Okay. That was a good, detailed response. Now it's question and answer time. Before we start with the questions, let me say, again, that I know your history, but it was given to me by your other doctors and by your mother. I would really like to get your response to what I already know, so today the questions will deal with those facts that I do have."

Emmie grimaced as she looked down at her hands. Most of the swelling in her hands and the rest of her body had gone down, but her joints were still inflamed and painful. She could actually walk a little now and even hold things in her hands, but it had taken her two long months to get to this point. No quick fix, the rheumatologist had said. She nodded, indicating that Ian should ask his first question.

"If you could be anywhere in the world right now, right this minute, where would you like to be?"

Emmie looked at her watch and didn't hesitate for a second. "Back home in the barn, getting ready to exercise Hifly. *If* I ever get back there, he's not even going to know me."

Ian sat up straighter in his chair. Was this the spark he'd been waiting for?

"I'm the first to admit I know nothing about horses but why is that?" he asked. "Don't horses know your scent? Surely, they'll recognize you when you return home."

Emmie fixed her gaze on the window to the right of Ian Hunter's head to stare at a vibrant blue hibiscus bush. She carefully shifted her weight and her lips narrowed into a thin straight line. "Don't you mean *if* I go home? They *might* recognize me, but it's too late now for me to train Hifly. My *mother* took over that job, and Jake is in training to be a jockey, thanks to my *mother* and her little swap deal. She agreed to take on Jake and train him so I could come here. No one wanted that horse but me. Now they're going to train him for the Derby. That was to be my decision. I was the one who was supposed to do it. Just in case you don't know who Jake is, he's Sunny Thornton's son. I keep forgetting what her married name is. Her mother built this center. She probably pays your salary, too." She wanted him to look impressed, but he didn't.

"Are you at odds with your mother over the horse, Emmie?"

"That's really a stupid question and I'm not going to answer it, *Doctor* Hunter. My mother has nothing to do with my condition other than the genes she passed on to me."

"I think your father might have passed on a few genes himself. You can't hold your mother totally responsible for the gene pool." Ian paused for a moment. "Tomorrow is Visitor's Day. Are you ready for company?"

"No, I'm not. I told them I didn't want any visitors. You people can't force me to have visitors."

"Don't you want to see your daughter?"

"No, I don't. She's happy up there on that super-duper mountain that my mother arranged. There's no need to have her see me here like this." His expression told her he wasn't quite convinced. "I'm not going to change my mind, so don't even try."

Ian made a steeple with his fingers before he propped up his feet on an open desk drawer. "Let me throw out a question, Emmie. If your mother, your daughter, and Hifly were in peril, and you could only help one of them, which one would you choose to help?"

Emmie switched her gaze to the orange-and-yellow painting on the wall before she sucked in her breath. "That's another stupid question. You people drummed into my head from the day I got here that we don't deal with what-ifs. It is or it isn't. Don't try to trick me. That is one ugly picture," she said, pointing to the orange-and-yellow painting.

"I'm not trying to trick you. Add that question to the list that you will have to answer before you leave here. By the way, Sunny is the one who made that particular orange-and-yellow drawing. Do you have any idea how hard it was for her to do it?

You saw her hands. It took her hours and hours to make those slashes of color. Painful hours. She didn't give up till she filled the paper. The colors represent the sunrise on the mountain where your daughter now resides, and where Sunny grew up."

"I'm sorry," Emmie said.

"No, you're not sorry, but you should be. Sorry is just a word some people use when they don't know what else to say. Furthermore, I wasn't trying to trick you. You're on the defensive, and that has to make me wonder why. Your mental health is as much in jeopardy as your physical health. Until you face your problems, you won't heal. You refused visitors at the beginning of the month and you're refusing them again. That will go on your overall evaluation. You cannot leave here, Emmie, until all the doctors on your case sign off on you. You're fighting me, and I want you to stop it."

"Yes, sir, Doctor, sir!" Emmie said smartly. "Actually, I'm getting to like this place. When you people aren't poking and prodding and drawing blood and making me pee in bottles, it isn't half-bad. The food is actually delicious, and the bed is comfortable. With my mother's connections and money, I can probably stay here for the rest of my life. Now, what other questions do you have for me? We still have twenty-five minutes to go."

Ian Hunter wanted to haul off and give his patient a good swat. Until he saw the tears in her eyes. He looked away, pretending not to see.

"Talk to me about the horses. You grew up with them, didn't you? Just ramble, say whatever comes into your mind. Think of it as educating this ignorant equestrian mind. I consider myself ahead of the game if I learn one new thing each day."

This is safe ground, Emmie thought. Horses were one thing she could talk about from morning to night. Until that moment she hadn't realized she was perched on the very end of the deep, comfortable chair. She squirmed backward and took a deep breath.

"I was pretty young, but the first horse I really remember was Stardancer. He was the one who threw Maud Diamond off his back and crippled her for life. My mother managed to train that horse, and she loved him dearly, probably more than she loved *anyone.* Then Flyby was born, and she raised and trained him from a colt. She trained him herself and ran him in the Kentucky Derby, the Preakness, and the Belmont. She won the Triple Crown. Flyby's colts sold for millions and millions of dollars. Then along came Shufly, Flyby's son. She gave him to Metaxas Parish as a gift. She trained and ran him in the Derby. She won, and Shufly has a Triple Crown, too. And she raced one of her brother's horses, too. My mother, she's one of a kind. To know her is to love her." Her voice was so snide, so bitter-sounding, that Ian stopped doodling on his pad to stare at her with wide eyes. She ignored him.

"There was a really bad fire at Blue Diamond Farms a while back. My mother was severely burned trying to save the horses. Flyby got her out of the barn, but she was disfigured. She spent a long time in a special hospital in Thailand and went through many, many operations. She saved the horses at a great cost to herself. We were all brought up and taught from an early age that the horses came first. She has to wear this thick, muddy makeup to cover all the scars. She said the horses don't care what she looks like.

"My brother Nick used to work with the horses, but they weren't his life like they were mine. He went off and became a lawyer. My mother said Nick had *the touch*. But you know what, he didn't *want* the touch. I, on the other hand, wanted it so bad I could taste it. My mother has it. Somehow or other, it skipped me. I know I could have trained Hifly for the Derby. I know it."

Dr. Hunter leaned across the desk. "Did you just want him to run in the Derby or was it that you wanted to train him to run in the Derby? Does it make a difference?" he asked, a blank look on his face.

Emmie snorted. "Of course it makes a difference. A horse is only as good as his trainer. I would have made a good one. Hifly is mine. I bought him when no one else wanted him. I bonded with him just the way my mother bonded with Flyby and Shufly. I had my jockey all picked out and was going to have him come to the farm and work with Hifly, so he would be comfortable with him on his back. I even gave some thought to riding him myself. I think I'm good enough. Now, *she's* training him and *Jake* will probably end up riding *my horse*. The horse no one wanted but me. My mother actually chastised me for buying Hifly. I wasn't trying to prove anything to anybody when I bought him. I saw him, liked him, and I felt something. At that time I didn't know if he was Derby material or not, and it wouldn't have mattered either way. I fell in love with the horse. That's the bottom line."

Ian digested the information, scribbled a few notes, and followed up with another question. "If the horse is yours, and you feel so strongly, why don't you tell your mother how you feel? Knowing the circumstances, don't you think she would defer to your wishes? If you don't care, that's something else entirely."

"You don't know my mother, Dr. Hunter. She made a deal with Fanny Thornton. Jake for this place. Now she has to prove Jake can do it, and the only horse she can do that with is Hifly. Gadfly is a lost cause. He's mean."

Ian scratched his head. Talk about a crash course in horse breeding. "What makes a horse mean? What's the difference between Gadfly and Hifly?"

"A world of difference. Different mares for one thing. Gadfly never liked me. Maybe I was too hard on him. He's huge. Huge and mean. It was hard to control him. I had . . . to . . ."

"What? What did you have to do to him?" Ian was sitting up straight and literally holding his breath.

"I hit him. I had to hit him. I didn't want to do it. I've never hit a horse in my life. That's the first thing my mother taught Nick and me. No matter what, you never strike a horse. I don't have my mother's sterling record. Hell, I can't even come close to it."

"Do you want to tell me why you did something so foreign to your nature?"

Emmie paused to marshal her thoughts. "Gadfly did intimidate me because of his size. I tried to overcome the feeling, but I was in pain the first time. I was going to give him an apple and when I stretched out my arm, I had this excruciating pain ricochet down my arm and into my hand and fingers. I dropped the apple. When I tried to bend down to pick it up, my right side seemed to lock up on me. Gadfly pitched a fit because he didn't get the apple. I thought he was going to kick down the door of the stall. No one was around to help me. The pain didn't go away. In fact it got more intense, so intense, I couldn't move.

Gadfly wanted the damn apple, and he wasn't about to give up on it, so I used my left hand and whipped it across his face. It was hard enough that he felt it. I think I stunned him, but he did quiet down. Right then, I started to hate that horse. Then I became afraid of him. I just kept whacking away at him. I couldn't seem to stop myself. Listen, I don't want to talk about this anymore," Emmie said, mopping the perspiration from her forehead.

Ian risked a glance at the clock on his desk. He could call it quits for the day or press on. The professional side of him said to stop the session and suggest a stroll around the grounds.

"Let's call it a day. If you like, I can push your chair over to the snack bar, where we can get one of those icy things that dribble down your chin. My treat. What do you say, Emmie?"

"No thanks, Dr. Hunter. I have a book I want to read. This next hour is free time for me. I can get back to my cottage on my own."

"Okay. I'm still going to get that *slurpy* thing. Maybe I'll get blueberry today," he said lightly. "I'll see you at ten sharp tomorrow morning. Remember, now, you have pending questions you have to answer. Not necessarily tomorrow, but soon."

Emmie spun her chair around and was out the door a second later. She didn't bother to respond. The moment she was inside her assigned cottage, she got out of the chair and walked around to exercise her legs. The chair was for outdoor travel and the rougher terrain of the grounds. Inside, she was to walk around as much as she could.

There was no book to read. Why had she lied to Dr. Hunter? The next day was Visitor's Day. That meant she had the whole day to herself since she wasn't accepting visitors. What would she do with herself? Sleep? Not likely. No visitors probably meant she would have all her scheduled therapies regardless. Somebody would be checking on her hourly. Maybe she could call someone. She had thirty minutes of accumulated telephone time she could use up. Nick? Her ex-husband? Her daughter?

Emmie sat down on the small love seat and propped her legs up on the ottoman. She realized she felt better than she had in months. Just last week Dr. Hunter had told her she was her own worst enemy. He'd gone on to say, *If the object of your being here is to get well so you can go home, why are you fighting all of us every step of the way? Is it for attention? Is it payback time to your family? Or is it that you hate who you are and what you've become?*

"All of the above," she whimpered.

Emmie closed her eyes and let her mind roam. Where was Nick, her half brother? *What's he doing right now, this minute?* Nick had always been kind to her, but she knew in her heart that he was her mother's favorite child. Her mother had been harder on Nick than she was on her, and yet Nick had survived, thumbed his nose at their mother's demands, and gone on to do what he wanted to do. She, on the other hand, didn't have the guts to do any of the things Nick did. She couldn't even stand up for herself. Maybe it was time to use those thirty minutes of telephone time to call her father. Her *real* father. Maybe that's what was missing in her life, a father. If she did call her father, and her mother found out, she'd probably disown her, and call her a traitor in the bargain. Did she dare risk it?

How many times in the past she'd fantasized about her father. She'd even dreamed about him. In her dreams he was always kind and loving. In those dreams, he'd bring her presents and put his arm around her shoulders and call her his little princess.

Sooner or later the shrink would get around to asking her about her childhood, her parents, and what it was like growing up. Maybe if she called her father, she could find the answers so they would be on the tip of her tongue, to be rattled off at the appropriate time. Or would she be calling her father only to piss off her mother? More than likely the latter.

"I hate this place. I hate it, hate it, hate it." Dr. Hunter's words echoed in her mind: *Then do something about it. Stop fighting everyone and give a hundred percent. It's all about mind-set, positive thinking, and looking forward to the future.*

"Okay!" The phone was in her lap a moment later. She dialed long-distance information, copied down the number, and placed a person-to-person call to Dillon Roland. No one was more surprised than Emmie when her father answered the phone.

Emmie jumped right into the conversation before she could change her mind. "I'm not sure what I should call you. This is

Emmie Coleman. You're my father. If this is a bad time, I can call you later."

"Emmie! I don't know if you'll believe this or not, but I've thought about you a lot over the years. It's nice finally to talk to you. Is something wrong?"

Emmie sighed. "I guess there's a lot that's wrong. Maybe I shouldn't have called you. I guess I wasn't thinking. You know what, let's just leave it at that and I'll hang up."

"No. Wait. Please don't hang up. You must have called me for a reason. Tell me what it is, but first tell me, does your mother know you're calling me?"

"No, my mother doesn't know I'm calling you. This is probably a mistake. I seem to be real good at making mistakes. I don't want to intrude on your life."

"The truth is, Emmie, I'm alone right now, and I could do with some intrusion. My wife passed away a while back and my children are scattered all over the country. Everything isn't all black or all white. I do have a side where you're concerned. Perhaps one day we can sit down and talk about it."

"How about tomorrow? It's Visitor's Day."

"Exactly what does Visitor's Day mean, Emmie? Where are you?"

She told him.

"I'm so very sorry. I watched my own father battle the same condition. I have a touch of it myself, but not like you've described. I'm also on medication. It's bearable. I'll tell you what. If I can get a flight out this evening, I'll be there first thing in the morning. I can find my way. You're sure now you want me to come there."

Oh, God, no, I'm not sure. "Absolutely," she said. *What's one more giant-size mistake on my record?*

"Then I'll do my best to be there. If for some reason I can't make it, I'll call you. I'm glad you called me, Emmie. I really am. You need to know this right up front. I would never have called you because of your mother. She's very powerful, and she makes herself understood quite clearly. Are you okay with that?"

"Yes, I'm okay with that."

When she hung up the phone, she was shaking so badly she

thought she was going to faint. She took huge, deep breaths, trying to calm herself. When the electronic buzzer went off by the front door to remind her of her whirlpool therapy, she almost jumped out of her skin.

All during her session with the swirling water, her mind raced. What would it be like to finally see her father? Would he put his arms around her? Would he talk nice and say how much he wished he could have been a part of her life? Most important of all, would she like him? Was it even remotely possible that they could become father and daughter at this stage in their lives? Did she even want that?

Later, after the session, the therapist handed his written report over to the doctor in charge of Emmie's care. The summary was simple: "Something came over Emmie while she was in the whirlpool. Some kind of transformation for lack of a better explanation. She stiffened and her eyes started to sparkle like she had a mission to fulfill. I feel this is a good thing. She was smiling and apologized for giving me such a hard time prior to today. I think she made the decision to stop battling us."

Emmie took extra pains with her makeup and even dabbed perfume behind her ears, delicious-smelling perfume given to her by Nick for her birthday. The dress she chose to wear was yellow linen with matching extrawide sandals with special grippers over the instep for extra support. Her hair curled naturally over her ears and forehead. She looked like her father. She knew that because she'd seen pictures of him at the Keeneland sales and at the Kentucky Derby.

Precisely at ten minutes till nine, she wheeled her chair toward Dr. Hunter's office, where she canceled her ten o'clock appointment.

"Emmie, you know the rules. If you aren't having visitors, your sessions go on as scheduled."

"I'm having a visitor. I have to go now or I'll be late. If you don't believe me, check for yourself."

"But you said you didn't want to see your mother."

"It's not my mother. It's not important for you to know who my visitor is, Dr. Hunter. I'm having a visitor, that's it. You all encourage this, and I'm complying. I'll see you for our session tomorrow."

She saw him first. He looked elegant, almost like a movie star, with his well-cut suit, deep tan, and white Stetson. Her father. She brought the wheelchair to a stop and stood up. "I'm Emmie," she said, holding out her hand. A hug was too much to expect. "Just don't squeeze my hand."

"Businesspeople shake hands. Father's hug their daughters," Dillon Roland said, wrapping his arms about his daughter. "Hmmm, you smell nice." Emmie swooned. She flushed and felt warm all over.

"Do we have a game plan?" he asked.

"I thought we'd go to my cottage. I have a nice patio outside, and we can sit there or stay indoors. First, though, you have to sign in. Please, use another name if you don't mind. I'll explain later."

"I understand. How does Dwight Holcum sound?"

"Like a phony name." Emmie giggled.

"Then, let's do it!" Dillon laughed.

They talked of everything and nothing. They laughed, they smiled, and touched hands from time to time. Emmie felt at peace for the first time in years. She knew if she closed her eyes, she would fall into a deep, dreamless sleep.

"Now that you know everything there is to know about me, how about telling me all about you. Start with when you first met my mother. Please don't leave anything out because you want to spare my feelings. I just need to know. My book of life has always had missing pages."

He sat back against the cushioned patio chair and gazed at the desert landscaping that surrounded the facility. "I used to sit across from your mother on the school bus. Not every day because I was involved pretty heavily in sports and everything was after school. Your mom had to get right home to do her chores. I never had chores or responsibilities other than to play sports and excel. I managed to get myself pretty banged up over the years and had knee-replacement surgery a few years ago. My father expected me to be the best of the best, and I did my damnedest to become what he wanted. It wasn't easy a lot of the time because there was another side to me, a noncompetitive side. I used to be a secret poet. In fact, I wrote a lot of poems for your mom."

Emmie's mouth fell open.

Dillon nodded. "Yeah, I know. It probably sounds pretty sappy to someone your age, but the truth is I fell pretty hard for your mom. She was shy and didn't mingle with the other kids. Most of the time she looked frightened and tired. She was prettier than a newborn filly. I wanted to get to know her, so I used to sneak over to the barn. I slipped her a note on the bus one day and the next day she slipped one back to me. We'd meet in the barn late in the evening. She'd sneak down to the barn, and I'd sneak out of the house and ride my bike to meet her. In the beginning we'd just talk and laugh and hold hands. I'd read her my poems, and she'd smile. I didn't have a mother and neither did she, so we had a lot in common. My father was every bit the tyrant her father was. Over a period of months, we became close so it was inevitable that we . . . we made love. It was wonderful. She was my first girlfriend and I was her first boyfriend. I think we were in love or as much in love as two youngsters can be. Then the roof fell in. Nealy told me she was pregnant. I just stood there looking at her when she told me. All I could think of was that my father was going to kill me. I didn't think about her at all. I didn't take the bus home after that. I didn't take it to school either. I lived in mortal fear that she would tell her father, and he would come gunning for me. I saw my whole life going down the drain. Again, I didn't think about Nealy at all or the baby she was carrying."

Me, Emmie thought. *She was carrying me, not "the baby."* It was only when she saw her father's anguished expression that she realized that she was being self-indulgent, thinking only of herself.

Dillon continued his story. "Then the day came when she wasn't on the bus. I knew because I used to lurk in the bushes to get a look at her. That very day, I skipped school and sneaked over to her house and cornered her in the barn. I told her . . . what I told her was I would blow her head off with my father's shotgun if she ever told anyone I was the father of her baby. She just stood there looking at me. She didn't say a word. Not one word. I went home and bawled my head off.

"I went off to college that year. When I went home for breaks or holidays I would hear the rumors. The story was some vagrant attacked her in the barn. The second year when I went home, I heard she had left with her baby. I was sick all over again. I occasionally thought about her over the next few years, and she more or less faded from my memory, but I could always resurrect her when I wanted to. I'd get out my book of poems and read them and remember how she looked or what she said when I read them to her.

"I eventually married Allison. We had three sons. They're pretty much worthless, thanks to their mother spoiling them. None of them has ever worked a day in his life thanks to trust funds. I never loved Allison, and I don't think she loved me. Our parents considered it a merger. She died from breast cancer. Everything I inherited from her I donated to breast cancer research. The boys howled and yowled, but I did it anyway. That's pretty much the story of your mother and me."

"She hates you," Emmie said.

"Yes, I know. She has every reason to hate me. I abandoned her, left her to fend for herself. I was mean, selfish, and hateful. But, I've changed. People can change, you know. I don't want you to hate me. Do you think we can work through all that? I have a lot of regrets, regrets I'm going to have to live with for the rest of my life. I'd like to try if you're willing. It will be nice finally to acknowledge you. Not having done so is my one true regret in my life."

Emmie swallowed. She had regrets, too. Regrets about Buddy, about her mother, about Gadfly, about life. She looked down at her puffy hands. "I don't know what to do."

"Well, I know what you have to do, young lady. You have to get better, and then I'd like it if you'd come to live with me in Virginia. We have a whole lifetime to catch up on. I'd like to get to know my granddaughter as well. I want us to start out right. I think you should tell your ex-husband about Gabby. If you want that horse you love so much, we'll get him back for you.

We can train him together if that's what you want. You are the only one who can make these decisions, and they don't have to be made right now. We have all the time in the world."

Emmie smiled. "Are you as hungry as I am?"

"I'm pretty hungry," Dillon said.

"They go all out in the dining room on Visitor's Day. The food is really good."

"In that case, allow me to escort you to the dining room. I'd like it if you called me Dad. I know you have to earn a title like that, but if you can say it and mean it, I'd sure like to respond."

"Okay, *Dad*, let's go to lunch."

Ian Hunter flipped the pages of the Visitor's Book until he came to the name Dwight Holcum. Next to the name was Emmie's signature. Who in the hell was Dwight Holcum? He looked familiar.

He carried his salad and iced tea from the buffet line and settled himself across the room. He deliberately chose a table that would allow him to observe his patient and her guest. He was finishing his tea when Emmie looked up and waved. They were both facing him. He was stunned at his conclusion.

Like father, like daughter.

PART II

8

The mansion had always reminded her of the white-pillared Tara in *Gone With the Wind*. Even the sweeping grounds and the ancient oaks dripping Spanish moss were reminiscent of the movie. Emmie Coleman, now Emmie Roland, was mistress of all she surveyed, thanks to her indulgent father.

She was back in the swing of things, working a few hours a day in the barns with her father's Thoroughbreds and acting as his hostess when he entertained. She was happier than she'd ever been before.

The year she'd spent in the Thornton rehab center had flown by, thanks to her father's monthly visits. He spurred her on to challenge her limits and took great pride in even her smallest accomplishments. These days she had no regrets.

At the end of her stay, with Dr. Hunter's help, she'd made important decisions that would affect the rest of her life. She was comfortable with her new life. If she missed her mother or Blue Diamond Farms it wasn't noticeable to anyone who knew her. She refused even to think about the ugly scene with her mother when she told her of her decision to live with her father.

Her health had improved greatly. Knowing someone cared about her enough to monitor her well-being constantly meant more to Emmie than all the riches in the world. And she owed it all to her newfound father, who was also a doting grandfather.

Emmie surveyed the lunch table, adjusted one of the fine linen napkins before she stood back to admire her handiwork. Lunch was always special for her father because he only had black coffee early in the morning and was starved by lunchtime. A pretty table was something he liked. She always made sure there were fresh flowers in the center of the table, and every single day, when lunch was finished, he plucked one of the flowers and handed it to her with a low, sweeping bow.

They were having potato-crusted salmon, a garden salad, and a fruit compote for dessert. For her brother Nick, who would be arriving shortly, there would be a large T-bone steak and a twice-baked potato.

Nick had invited himself to stop by on his way to visit their uncles, Rhy and Pyne. "It will just be for lunch. I'm anxious to see Gabby and to meet your father," he'd said on the telephone. She looked down at her watch at the same time she heard the doorbell. She didn't wait for Caruthers, her father's houseman, to open the door, she ran to it, thrust it open, and jumped into her brother's arms.

"Whoa, Nellie." Nick laughed. "If I had known I was going to get such a greeting, I'd have come sooner. You look good, Emmie. Real good. Are you happy? Don't answer that. I can see for myself that you're glowing and sparkling. I'm happy for you," he said, hugging her. "You feeling okay?"

"Yes, I'm feeling fine these days. I still have to take medication, but look, I can make a fist again, and my feet and most of my joints are back to normal. I go once a month to be checked from head to toe. Dad makes me go. In fact, he takes me and waits to get the reports. So far so good. What's new with you? Dad's running late today, so let's go into the sunroom and talk a bit. I want to hear everything. I know you didn't just come here to see me and our uncles. What's up? Is it Willow?"

Nick flopped down into a deep recliner. "Damn, you always did manage to home in on the crux of something when it involves me. Yeah, it's Willow, it's Mom, it's Hatch. Hell, it's everything. Willow was picked up in Chula Vista and arrested last week. She was hiding out in Tijuana. Mom's real pissy. Hatch is glowering about Willow and doesn't want to defend her. I'm in the middle of a kick-ass case I know I can't win, and how is your life going?"

"Wonderfully. Nick, I am so happy. Gabby is happy. Cookie is happy, and Dad is . . . wonderful. We get on so well. I call Mom once a week to say hello. She's civil, and the conversation is usually about Gabby and lasts no longer than five minutes. I do call, though. You know you were her favorite, don't you?"

"That was your imagination, Emmie," Nick hedged. "She treated us both the same."

"No, she didn't, but it's okay for you to think that. I learned a lot during the year I spent in Las Vegas. I've come to terms with everything. I had bags and bags of guilt I carried around. I tried so hard to be like Mom, I made myself sick. And in the end I managed to screw everything up. I learned something Mom has yet to learn. I love my daughter because she is my flesh and blood. I know that I'm capable of killing to protect her if that need ever arose. Mom . . . Mom used me as her penance for what she thought she did wrong. She took care of me, fed me, clothed me, but she didn't allow herself to love me the way I love Gabby. She smothered all her feelings and channeled them into working like a mule. That was her choice. The mind is an amazing thing. All my life she made me feel guilty. It was like I ruined her life in some way. The way she treated me, acted with me, is the way she treated your father, Hunt. If anyone needs a shrink, it's our mother. Going to the core of your being and pulling out all the *uglies* for someone else to see, in my case, Dr. Hunter, is what it's all about. You talk it through, work at it, then one day you wake up and go, yeah, that's what happened. Then you ask yourself how you can fix all those *uglies.* When your mind and body are healthy, you can deal with anything. It worked for me. I love Mom, but not the way a daughter should love a mother. It's a different feeling. I can recognize the differences in everything in my life these days."

Nick stared at his sister, a stunned look on his face. "Jesus, Emmie, you just put into words what I've been feeling guilty about for years. I bet if we were horses, she would love us to death. You're right about my dad, too. Sitting in his office, I think about him a lot on my downtime. I feel really close to him there. When I'm sitting in his chair, I remember little things he said, remember the way he looked at me or Mom like he couldn't believe what he was hearing or seeing. Guilt is a terrible thing. You're free now, aren't you?" His voice was so full of awe, Emmie smiled.

"Yes. Oh, God, yes, Nick."

Nick rubbed his chin, his eyes on his sister. "Think about this, Emmie. Your happiness now comes from your dad. My only happiness was with my dad. Even now, just sitting in the chair that was supposed to be his makes me happy. I know he's watching over me. I know it as sure as I'm sitting here. Why couldn't Mom give us that? Both of us busted our asses to be what she wanted. When we went back, it wasn't because of Mom. We went back because of the place. Because of Blue Diamond Farms. It was the only home either one of us ever knew. Our roots were there. You didn't take anything personal with you that concerned Mom when she booted us out. You took a patch of grass."

"I know all that, Nick." Emmie smiled. "Dr. Hunter helped me figure it all out. Do you know what else he told me? He told me it's okay if I don't love Mom. He said if I cared about her it was enough. No one on this earth can force you to love someone if the feeling isn't there. And, by the way, my patch of grass is still growing. I have twelve blocks, and it's thriving. There's a greenhouse here, so it's growing under perfect conditions. Boy, you should see my Gerber daisies!

"Now, what's wrong where Hatch is concerned? I wish you could stay longer. We didn't even talk about Mom's movie." Her voice was so wistful, Nick hugged her.

"I don't know what's wrong. He's pissed because I can't win this case I'm on even though the other partners agree with me. We never should have taken it on to begin with. He said his firm doesn't lose cases, and maybe he made a mistake hiring me. He said I must have screwed up along the way, but I didn't, Emmie. He's like a wet hen, and now this thing with Willow came up. I'm thinking, and I could be wrong, that things down on the farm aren't what he thought they were going to be, which brings it all back to Mom."

"Tell Hatch he doesn't have to take Willow's case if he doesn't want to. I don't care if she tells Buddy about Gabby. I'm prepared for it. I told you, I can deal with anything these days."

"I'm glad I came here. You saved me a lot of money in shrink bills. I'm so glad it's working out for you, Emmie. What are you going to do about Hifly?"

"Nothing. After the race, I'll take him back and put him out to stud. Who knows, I might get a real winner one of these days, one I can train myself. I realized I couldn't yank him away from

Jake. The boy needs to do what he's doing, and if I can help, so be it. It's more important to him than it is to me. I know I keep saying this, but I learned how to sift through stuff, to analyze and make the right decisions. You have to look at the whole of something, look at the pros and cons and decide what's best for everyone concerned and if you can live with it, you go for it. Jake is important. If it's meant to be, it will be. Hey, I hear Dad's car. Come on, I can't wait for you to meet him.

"Nick, I know you heard Mom's side. He had a side, too. He loved her back then, but he was a kid, just like Mom was a kid. Kids screw up and don't always make the right decisions. You have to look past all that to the person he is today. Can you do that?"

"You bet! And speaking of the movie, I really wanted to go to the private screening, but my time was just too tight. Did anyone in the family go?"

"I didn't. I had the time but . . . I didn't want to see Mitch Cunningham. Dad was willing to go, but since I didn't know if Mom was going or not, I thought it would be best if I stayed away. I found out later she didn't go. I didn't watch the video they sent me either. It didn't seem like the right time. Too much was going on. Besides, it's all about Mom. It was her story. Maybe I'll never look at it. It did get good reviews from all the women's organizations. It's going to get a nomination. The truth is, I don't care. How about you?"

"They sent me the video, too. Those movie people made a big deal about no one from the family showing up for the private screening. It was in all the papers. Medusa pointed it out to me. She stays on top of stuff like that. If the movie really does get a nomination, I guess we'll be invited to the Academy Awards. I'm afraid that's not my bag either. How about you?"

"Nah. I lived it, so did you. Why would I want to see all that stuff played out on the big screen?"

Emmie linked her arm with her brother's. "I hear the car. Let's go meet my dad."

Nealy perched on the paddock fence and watched Jake put Hifly through his paces. He had progressed rapidly, going beyond her expectations. She was almost giddy with the realization. The boy was so comfortable in his skin now. He might be considered a runt by the other workers, just the way they considered Hifly a runt, but he was all heart, just the way Hifly was. To say Jake had bonded with the runt horse was to put it mildly. Hifly wasn't quite as accommodating to her or any of the others as he was to Jake. And Jake loved it.

The fear had left him early on, and from that moment, he took off like a rocket. She hoped it was because of her encouragement and his mother's support. Like Hifly, Jake only wanted to please. He'd never complained. Not once. He sucked up the ribbing, sucked up the early morning hours and all the hard work that went with raising Thoroughbreds.

But more than anything, it was the look in Jake's eyes when he looked around at the lush bluegrass, the paddocks, and the horses. She'd never seen that look in Nick's or Emmie's eyes. Hunt, her first husband, had never had it, either. For sure Hatch didn't have it. Maud and Jess did, though. It was obvious to everyone that Jake loved Blue Diamond Farms with a passion.

She loved it when he came to her for advice, loved it when he asked her to watch a particular video of a jockey so he could learn from it and not make mistakes. And she loved it when he linked his arm with hers, and said, "Aunt Nealy, you're the greatest. If I turn out to be half as good as you, I'll really be flying."

In the night, in the darkness of their bedroom, Hatch said she was trying to clone Jake to be like her. She didn't think she was doing that, but if she was, it wasn't a bad thing in her opinion. Confidence, ability, and the love of the animal was something Jake had earned. She was free and yet stingy with her praise. They both knew his shortcomings and worked together to overcome them. She must be doing something right because Sunny and Fanny both said the boy had never been happier. His reports to the family were full of love and praise for her. Always in the wee hours of the morning, while Hatch was still sleeping, she would tell herself Hatch was jealous.

In the beginning, she'd had a hard time understanding how a grown man could be jealous of a boy who had the same intense passion, the same intense love for the horses that she had. Sometimes she felt almost drunk with the knowledge that finally, at last, there was someone she could truly communicate with, share the love of Blue Diamond Farms.

She knew in her heart that Maud and Jess were up there somewhere watching her progress with young Jake, just the way they'd watched and instructed her so many years ago.

She had become more and more aware of her age and her limitations. Her body protested every night when it was time to call it a day. She knew she was a disappointment to Hatch in the lovemaking department, and she worked hard to overcome what Hatch called her ambivalent attitude. She couldn't seem to help herself, and she did try, but it had been the same with Hunt. She loved Hatch, but she loved the farm and the horses more. And Hatch knew it just the way Hunt had known it. And, now, Jake knew it, too.

Jake came up behind her. "Is something wrong, Aunt Nealy? Are you missing Hatch?"

Nealy whirled around. "I guess I was woolgathering, as Maud used to say. She was such a wonderful woman, Jake. She took me in, nursed me back to health, gave me and Emmie a life here, and when she died she left all this to me and Emmie. Sometimes I feel guilty. I guess that's why I work so hard. I don't ever want her to think she made a mistake by doing all she did for me. She was the mother I never had. I suppose that sounds a little weird to you, but I believe she can see and hear everything that's going on down here. Either you believe or you don't."

Jake dropped to his haunches. He stared up at his aunt. "I don't think it's weird at all. In the past when I would get really discouraged, I always thought my grandfather Ash was around. Sometimes I thought I could smell his aftershave. I always felt better afterward." He reached into his pocket and pulled out a pair of gold aviator wings. "This is what kept me going. They go where I go. I put them under my pillow at night, and first thing in the morning they go in my pocket. He used to tell me such great stories. We'd sing, *Off we go, into the wild blue yonder,* till we were hoarse. Then we'd go fishing. If we caught a fish, we threw it back. I really loved him.

"I wanted to ask you a question, Aunt Nealy. Don't tell my mom I asked, okay?" Nealy nodded. "If you decide that I'm good enough to ride in the Derby, do you think it would be okay to tell my dad? He pretty much crossed me off his list, and he has a new family, so I don't know if it's the right thing to do or not. I think I need to prove to him that I am important, that I count for something. If it's going to hurt my mother, I won't do it, though."

For one second, Nealy saw red. Why did it always come down to this? First with Nick, then Emmie, and now young Jake. Fathers. She searched her mind for the right words. "I don't think anyone can give you advice on something so important. You have to search your heart and do what's right for you. I will say this, if you do ride in the Derby, the world will know. Your father will read about it or hear about it in some way. Your picture will be plastered all over the newspapers, the Internet, and television. Mainly because you'll be riding for Blue Diamond Farms. They'll hash and rehash my victories, they'll show the pictures of the president and me, and it will be a circus. Trust me when I tell you, he'll know, Jake. You won't have to tell him unless you want to."

The young man sighed. "You know he dumped my mother when she got sick. I can never forgive him for that, and yet I want him to know I count. He's a doctor, too. What kind of man is that?"

"I don't know the answer to that, Jake."

"Well, I know the answer," Jake said vehemently. "He's a jerk."

Nealy laughed. "The world is full of jerks, Jake. Just make sure you don't turn into one."

The boy laughed. "Fat chance."

"Here comes Gadfly. We really turned that horse around, didn't we?"

"Not we. You. I love racing against you. His time is as good as Hifly's. I've been wanting to talk to you about something, Aunt Nealy. Is there any rule in the Derby book that says you can't enter two horses in the Derby?"

"Nope. Why?"

"Why don't we run both of them?"

Nealy jerked to attention "Gadfly and Hifly? Are you serious?"

"Damn straight," Jake responded, using his mother's favorite expression. "I read about this young guy who is just a year and a half older than me. He's a good jockey, but everyone is afraid to take a chance on him. Maybe afraid isn't the right word. More like they don't want to hire him."

"Because . . ."

"Because he's foreign, Oriental, Asian, something like that. I watched hours and hours of training videos, and, Aunt Nealy, he's good. He used to live in Thailand. He trained in Japan. He's a United States citizen now, but he is the nephew of a famous surgeon, Sinjin Vinh, who lives in Thailand."

Nealy took exactly three seconds to digest Jake's statement. She spent another five seconds reliving her reconstructive surgery in Thailand after the fire. Dr. Sinjin Vinh. Her savior.

Payback time.

"Call him, Jake. Do you know how to get in touch with him?"

"Jeez, Aunt Nealy, no, I don't."

"It doesn't matter. I know how."

Jake's jaw dropped. "You do?"

"Yep. I'm going to do it right now. Come with me."

Twenty minutes later, after exchanging greetings, Nealy waved a slip of paper under Jake's nose. "I have here the telephone number and the address of what Dr. Vinh says is the second best jockey in the world. He thinks I'm the best."

"Lee Liu," Jake said looking at the slip of paper. "Are you going to call him, Aunt Nealy?"

"Right this minute. Miracle of miracles, he lives right here in this glorious state. I bet, if he's interested, he could be here by tomorrow morning. Maybe later tonight."

"Aunt Nealy, are you sure we can run two horses?"

"I'm absolutely sure. This is so exciting. Okay, okay, I'm dialing the number. Oh, damn, it's an answering machine."

Jake drew in his breath and held it while Nealy left a detailed message. When she hung up the phone, she slapped her hands together. "Two horses from Blue Diamond Farms running in the Derby. That means, if it happens, there will be a winner and a loser. If you ride and lose, can you handle it, Jake? Remember now, it's not a given that you'll be ready, but if you are, can you handle losing?"

"Well, sure, Aunt Nealy. I don't plan to lose if it happens. More to the point, can you handle one of your horses losing?"

Nealy felt a grin stretch from ear to ear. "I don't know. I've never had a loser before. You really think that pissass runt can run the Derby, eh? When they get a good look at him, they're going to laugh both of us right off the track."

"Before or after the race and on the way to the bank?"

Nealy collapsed laughing. "All of the above. He's got heart, I have to give him that. Plus, there's no denying that Hifly loves you, Jake. Right there, you won half the battle. Gadfly now, that's an entirely different story. That stomach ulcer he had is all healed now, and he's fine. He's not exactly warm and fuzzy, but he isn't mean. He tries to please, too. And, he loves running against Hifly. It would be so great if Hifly and Gadfly go to the Derby and pull adjoining gates. Can you just see them blasting out of the gates at the exact same moment?"

"I can, Aunt Nealy. I really can." Jake looked down at his boots. "When are you going to make your decision, Aunt Nealy?"

"In March. It's weighing on your mind, isn't it, Jake?"

"Yes. I know my weaknesses, and I know my strengths. I'm working on both."

"I know you are. I am so proud of you, Jake. You know, you remind me of myself when I first came to Blue Diamond Farms. I was about the same age as you when you first got here. It was all new to you, whereas I had grown up on a farm much like this one so I can respect the time and effort you've put into working for me. I was around horses all my life, so it came a little easier to me than it did to you. I learned the workings of this farm real quick. I had to. I didn't want Maud to toss me out on my ear, so I worked hard to prove myself. Sometimes I think I'm still trying to prove something. I guess what I'm trying to say to you is keep doing what you're doing because it's what I would have done in your place."

"Thanks, Aunt Nealy," Jake said, hugging her. "I'm going to run to the cottage and call my mom. She has afternoon telephone time this week. She worries about me, and that's not good for her. I won't be long."

"It's okay, Jake. Hatch is supposed to be calling me about

now. I'll let you know if Lee Liu calls. Take your time. You deserve a break."

Nealy poured herself a cup of coffee and carried it out to the front porch, her haven. She was almost to the door when she turned around and went back to the kitchen for the portable phone.

As she sipped her coffee, her gaze strayed to the phone, willing it to ring. She leaned back in the old wicker rocker and let her thoughts scurry in front of her. She hadn't really dealt with what she called Emmie's defection. Nor did she want to deal with it at the moment. Maybe she would never deal with it. Maybe she should be grateful that Emmie was finally happy. What did her own unhappiness matter? She'd dealt with Nick's defection and lived through it. There was no reason to believe she couldn't handle Emmie's new life. Maybe it was the shock of that last encounter. That horrible time in the sunroom at the rehab center when Emmie marched right up to her and said . . .

". . . I'm not going home with you, Mom."

"But, Emmie, the doctors said you're being released. I don't think it's such a good idea for you to go back to your own house. That is what you meant, isn't it?"

"No, Mom, that's not what I meant. I'm going to Virginia to live with my real father. Look, I know this is a shock to you but it's what I want. It's what Dad wants, too. Dr. Hunter has given his approval. He's talked extensively to Dad, and he thinks it will benefit me and him both. Since you were too busy to come to the sessions or even talk to Dr. Hunter on the phone, and I'm not blaming you, Mom, it showed me what I needed to know. Now, you can get angry, you can spit and snarl, or you can walk away and go back to the farm. It's your choice."

Bile rose in her throat. "What about Gabby?" was all she could manage to squeeze past her tight lips.

"He's looking forward to meeting her. Of course she's going with me. I can bring her to visit you whenever you like—holidays, summers, whatever."

"I think I'd like to know why, Emmie."

"He was the part that was always missing from my life book. There were too many missing pages in the book, Mom. I've had nothing to do but think this past year. I had to pull out, for inspection, every single dumb-ass thing I've done during my whole life. After I did that I had to write down those dumb-ass things and then I had to show those same dumb-ass things to Dr. Hunter so we could discuss them. You probably don't know too much about shrinks, Mom, but they do not tell you what to do or how to do it. I was the one who had to figure it all out and work from there. This, Mom, is not one of my dumb-ass decisions. This one is as right as it can be. I'm sorry if you have trouble accepting it."

"Why wouldn't I have trouble accepting it? That man, your father, threatened to blow off my head with a shotgun if I ever told anyone he was the father of my child. Yeah, I'm having some trouble with that. I carried you, I gave birth to you, I made sure you were taken care of. I did it all. Me. Not him. Now, you're telling me that wasn't good enough. Now, you're going with *him? That*, I will never understand."

"Yes, Mom, you did all those things. But you forgot something. You forgot to love me along the way. There's a big difference between taking care of someone and loving that person. You're the one who needs to talk to someone about her feelings. I'm okay with mine. I'm just sorry I screwed up your life."

"He doesn't love you, Emmie. He wants one of my horses, and he thinks if he cozies up to you, I'll sell him one. Don't you get it? Stop being such a fool."

Emmie took a step backward. "Mom, he didn't call me. I called him, and he came right away, the very next morning. He does love me. I feel it. It's what's been missing all my life. I feel it, Mom. Everything in your life and mine, up till now, has been about horses. He doesn't want one of your horses, so rest easy on that score. He doesn't want anything from you."

"Yes, he does. He wants you. You belong to me, Emmie, not him."

"Mom, I don't belong to you. I'm your daughter, just like Nick is your son. You don't own him either. He's his own person. I'm my own person. I spent half my life trying to be like you and the other half trying to please you. I wasn't able to do either, so I moved on. I will always care about you, Mom. I'll make sure Gabby visits so she can maintain a relationship with you."

"Don't bother, Emmie. You made your choice. And I've just made mine."

"Mom, wait! I want you to think about something. If things hadn't worked out the way they did, you wouldn't be who you are today. We probably wouldn't be standing here having this conversation. You'd probably still be back in Virginia with Rhy and Pyne. You would never have come to Kentucky, you would never have met Maud and Jess. You wouldn't own the biggest and best Thoroughbred racing stable in the state of Kentucky and you sure as hell wouldn't be a two-time Triple Crown winner. Nor would you have met and danced with the president of the United States. You wouldn't have Nick for a son either. And, by God, you wouldn't have had a movie made about your life that just might get nominated for an Academy Award. You think about all those things, Mom. Oh, yeah, you wouldn't be married to Hatch either."

"You're a fool, Emmie . . ."

. . . Nealy's eyes snapped open when the phone shrilled. She reached out for it with one hand while her free hand wiped at the hot tears scalding her eyes.

"Nealy?"

"Yes, Hatch, it's me. How are you? What's going on? I have so much to tell you, but you go first." She continued to knuckle her eyes.

Nealy watched as a small brown bird flew into one of the evergreens by the front steps. He seemed poised for flight on the tip of the branch. He was so tiny, so fragile-looking. How could such a tiny bird fly and soar? Once Emmie had been a tiny baby. She couldn't fly, though, and for a long time she couldn't talk either. When the bird took wing, Nealy concentrated on what Hatch was saying.

"Well, we had the court hearing, and Willow has been bound over for trial. Bail wasn't even an option. They had her shackled, which is never nice to see. She's not doing very well right now, but her options ran out when she skipped town. We'll get a court date, probably tomorrow or the next day, and then I have to prepare my defense. I don't know when I'll be home, Nealy."

"I'll be here whenever that is. Just be the best lawyer you can be, Hatch."

"You said you had a lot to tell me . . ."

"Jake thinks we should run both Gadfly and Hifly in the Derby. We think we've found a jockey to ride Gadfly. Actually, Jake found him, and you'll never guess who he is. He is the nephew of Dr. Vinh in Thailand. Well you know me, Hatch. I ran with the news. How perfect this is. The young man trained in Japan and is right here in Kentucky running minor races with minor horses. You know how Jake is glued to those training videos he watches all the time. He said Lee Liu is good. That's his name, Lee Liu. Isn't it wonderful, Hatch? Two horses in the Kentucky Derby from the same farm. Racing against each other. It doesn't get any better than that. I cannot tell you how excited I am. I think Jake is going to make it. I wish you were here today to see him ride Hifly. That boy looks like he was born to ride that horse. Hatch, you aren't saying anything."

"Nealy, does all of this mean our trip to Paris is off?"

Nealy blinked into the late-afternoon sunshine. The small brown bird was back, along with several companions. Her gaze went to the bird feeder hanging from a tree. It was full. Her attention returned to Hatch and what he was saying. "No, no, the trip is not off, just postponed. How could we go with Willow's trial coming up? The Derby is closer than you think. Before you know it, the time will be here, and you know what it's like. As soon as the racing season is over and as soon as you can wind down the trial, we'll go to Paris. I don't see any other way. Do you have some ideas you want to run by me?"

The birds were clustered around the feeder, eating the sunflower seeds ever so daintily. She wondered if birds flew in families. Did they go their separate ways once they left the nest? She should know that, but she didn't. She made a mental note to add more feeders to the trees and possibly some birdbaths.

"I'm sorry, Hatch, what did you say? I think the battery is getting weak on the phone."

"I said, no, I don't have any ideas. Have you spoken to Nick or Emmie?"

"Oops, there goes the battery, honey," Nealy lied. "I'll talk to you later after it charges."

Nealy clicked the OFF button. She looked around for the birds, but they were gone. She stared off into the distance, at the lush bluegrass, almost cobalt blue in the late-afternoon sunshine.

She walked back into the house to replace the phone, aware that she had just done something underhanded where her husband was concerned.

She sniffed the delicious aromas coming from the stove. "What's for dinner?" she asked Gertie.

"One of your favorites, Miss Nealy. Stuffed peppers, mashed potatoes, coleslaw, and string beans with bacon. For dessert, blackberry cobbler and yes, I made two, one for you to eat before you go to bed. I know your sweet tooth. I hope your dentist doesn't come after me with all the sweets you eat."

"Dr. Eugene Katz has a sweet tooth himself. Don't fret over it, Gertie. I won't eat any dessert tomorrow. Instead of walking back and forth to the barn, I'll run or jog. Did you make an extra one for Jake?"

"Yes, it's in the oven now."

"Okay, I'll see you at suppertime, Gertie. It will just be me."

It's not a bad thing being alone, Nealy thought as she made her way to the barn. *Not a bad thing at all.*

9

~~

Willow Bishop saw her opening and didn't think twice. She moved in a slow, straight line and followed the pest-control technician out the front door of the police station. Five minutes later she was nowhere to be seen on the streets of Las Vegas.

Dressed in sneakers, jeans, and white tee shirt, she blended in with the throngs of tourists. It took her an hour to maneuver the back streets and finally hitch a ride with an old gentleman with poor eyesight. She knew he had cataracts because the pupils of his eyes were pearly white. "I know I shouldn't be driving, and that's why I stick to the back streets. The police are always hauling me in, but I can drive these roads blindfolded. Lived here all my life. Lost my license a year back. Can't afford the operation," the old-timer said.

"If you take me to where I want to go, Mister, I'll give you the money for the operation. You have to promise not to tell anyone where you're taking me. I ran away from my husband. He beat me so bad I just got out of the hospital. I have to try and get my kids back before he does something to them. I really need your help. Will you promise not to tell?" Willow dabbed at her eyes.

"Well, sure, little lady, just as long as you don't tell anyone I'm driving."

"I'd appreciate it if you'd lend me that fishing cap you're wearing, sir. Just in case someone remembers seeing me riding along with you. I'll pay for the cap, too. The place I want to go to is about ten miles out past the Chicken Ranch. Do you know the way?"

"Should. Been a regular customer out there for a good many years. Got real lonely when my wife passed on. Nice bunch of gals. You got a name, gal?"

"Mazie. What's yours, old-timer?"

"Zack. Zack Leroy. Used to mine some. Did a bit of farming. Did a whole bunch of a lot of things. Don't do nothing much these days but watch game shows and think about the good old days. I was just funnin' with you about the operation. I have money to pay for it. I just don't want to go to the hospital because old people like me die when they go to a hospital. That's what happened to my wife. You need to be saving your money for your young'uns. I'm happy to take you to where you're going. Terrible thing when a man abuses his wife. Some men are just no-account. You gonna be all right, little lady?"

"I hope so. My biggest problem right now is getting some kind of vehicle. I just ran away and left everything behind. The place you're taking me to is my mother's house that has been closed up for a long time. I have some money hidden there, but it's doubtful Mom's car will still be there. If it is, it might not start up. You got any ideas, Zack?"

"Can help you with the gas. Always carry a spare five-gallon can in the back. Can't see good enough to work on the engine, though."

"I'll figure something out. You're sure now, you won't tell anyone you picked me up?"

"Swear I won't," the old man said solemnly. "Never go back on my word. Never!"

They rode in companionable silence until Willow waved her arm, and said, "Okay, slow down, we're coming up to the driveway now. It's about a half mile back in there. You can't see the house from the road. Oh, my goodness, everything is all grown over. It doesn't look like anyone has been here for a long time. I don't remember the ruts being this bad in the road. Are you sure you'll be able to find your way back?"

"Got some peripheral vision in my right eye. I'll make it back. You got a key to get in the house? I can stay long enough to make sure you're okay."

"I hid a key in the garage a long time ago. I'll be okay. Are you sure I can't pay you for bringing me out here?"

"Nope. Glad to do it. Nice to have someone to talk to once in a while."

Willow climbed out of the truck and started to walk away. On the fifth step, she turned around, walked back, and climbed back into the truck. "Listen, Zack, I lied to you a little while ago. I was desperate to get out here, and I didn't want the police to find me. I guess you could say I'm a fugitive. This house belongs to a man I lived with for a while. He was murdered out here, and the police think I did it. I swear to God, I didn't. I ran away because I thought they would try to blame me. They finally caught up with me. Twice. This is my last chance to get away. I can't be locked up for the rest of my life. They're looking for me now."

"I know all that. I always play the radio in the truck. I heard all about it on a breaking news bulletin and then you showed up ten minutes later. Your giveaway was asking for my hat. Now, Mazie, what can I do to help you?"

"My name's Willow Bishop."

"Know that, too. I kinda like Mazie. Used to know a girl up to the Chicken Ranch named Mazie. Made my blood sing, she did."

Willow laughed. The old-timer joined in.

"That was smart of you to come back here. They're never going to think you'd head back to the scene of the crime. But you best be doing whatever it was you came here to do and get out of here as fast as you can. Where you headed if you don't mind me asking?"

"Santa Fe. My ex-husband lives there."

"You said there was a car here."

"In the garage. There were three or four at one time. I don't know if the police took the keys or not. Look, the yellow tape is still across the doors, and it even goes around to the back. I'll get the key. I need some clothes and some of the stuff I left behind. Can you see well enough to check out the cars, Zack?"

"Keys would help, Mazie."

"Junior kept a spare set in the garage, taped to the back of motor-oil cans. I found them once when I was looking for something in the garage. Stand back, Zack, I have to break the glass to open the door. Let's just hope the police didn't figure out how to set the alarms when they closed it up. Junior had all kinds of systems in place. Okay, door's open. Good, the cars are still here."

"Mazie, what were you doing with a man like that?"

Willow turned around. "Having some fun and lining my pockets. In the beginning, I thought he was just a high roller. I didn't have any problem taking that kind of money. I didn't kill him. That's the truth, Zack. I was getting ready to split anyway. Another week, two at the most, and I would have been out of there."

"Nice vehicles," Zack said, tilting his head to the side to better observe them with his limited vision.

"Here are the keys. You do what you have to do while I check the house. I want to make sure none of the alarms are set."

It was eerie, Willow thought as she walked through the bare, stainless-steel kitchen. It looked just the way it had looked the last time she'd been there. Her wineglass was still sitting in the sink. The box of opened crackers was still on the counter. She picked up the phone and was surprised to hear the dial tone.

It was a one-of-a-kind house, a drug house built with drug money. It was decadent, lavish, and over the top with the custom furnishings, rich marble floors, and pricey Oriental rugs. She'd never paid much attention before simply because those things would do her no good when it was time to leave. Jewelry and hard cash were her forte.

She walked up the steps to the second floor, her gaze sweeping the intricate panel that housed the alarm system. Good, it was off. She made her way down a thickly carpeted hallway to the bedroom she'd shared with Junior Belez. She looked at the bed and then looked away. The bedding was still on the bed, the blood long dried and dark brown. She skirted the bed and walked into the bathroom. The first time she'd seen it, she'd been stunned. It had been crafted to look like a grotto with real stone. Moss grew out of the cracks and crawled toward the ceiling. The fixtures weren't gold-plated, they were solid gold. The thick Egyptian towels that Junior favored hung limply on the racks. His shaving gear was still on the triple vanity.

She dropped to her knees and opened the vanity doors. She pulled out toilet tissue, soap, stacks of toothpaste, toothbrushes and mouthwash. She yanked at the extra shaving cream, razors, and aftershave. The nine bottles of Grecian Formula that Junior used to darken his hair went on top of the vanity. She was going to need it later.

Willow sat back on her haunches, remembering the day she'd seen Junior pry up the floor of the vanity and either take something out or put something in. She'd been so scared, she'd turned and run down to the kitchen. As far as she knew, Junior had never known she'd seen him that day. The question now was, how to pry up the floor.

In the bedroom in the little Victorian secretary, there was a pearl-handled letter opener. She ran to get it and started to pry and gouge. It took her twenty minutes to lift out the entire floor in one long piece. She stared down at the contents, her jaw dropping. Half of the entire opening, six layers deep, were stacks and stacks of money held together with tight rubber bands. A single sheet of paper said, ALDON'S MONEY. Aldon was Junior's brother. She'd never seen so much money in her life. She inched along the floor until she was in front of another section of the flooring. Again, neat stacks of money were lined up, six deep. Everything was neatly compartmentalized. Notes on top of the stacks of money designated winnings from different casinos. She flopped down on her rump and hugged her knees. She turned when she heard Zack enter the room.

"I guess this is why he was killed. Whoever did it wanted *that*," she said, pointing to the neat stack of white-plastic bags. "I'm sure it's cocaine, but I'm not going to touch it. This is what we're going to do, Zack. See all this money, here on the left side? I'm pretty sure it's drug money. I'm going to give it all to you to play Santa Claus with. This money, from here to the white bags, is gambling money. That, I'm taking. Are you okay with this?"

"You mean you want me to give all that money away?" Zack asked in awe.

"Yes. The homeless, soup kitchens, orphanages, animal shelters. Wherever there is a need for money. Do it at night or figure out how to do it anonymously. Maybe you do need to think about getting your cataracts removed. It's a one, two, three kind of operation. You shouldn't be afraid. Think about how much fun you'll have giving all this away. And if you can see while you're doing it, think how much better it will be."

"I never seen so much money in my whole life. There must be millions of dollars there. How did the police miss that?"

"They didn't know about it. Guess they didn't bring any

drug-sniffing dogs in here. If they had, the dogs would have found it. I'll get some bags, so we can carry all this money out to the cars. By the way, how are the cars?"

"All the batteries are dead. I'll give you my truck, and I'll pick up a secondhand one. Engine is sound as a dollar. The body ain't much to look at, but it will get you to where you want to go. The registration and insurance card are in the glove compartment. Don't even ask me why I'm doing this, or why I'm believing you. Maybe because you came back and told me the truth. You don't look like no killer to me."

"I'm not. I appreciate you helping me, Zack. Listen, do you mind loading up the money while I hack off my hair and add some of this color juice to it?"

"You go to it, little lady. Just get me the bags."

"Be sure to keep it separate. I don't want anything to do with drug money. That's not what I'm about. I want you to give it all away. Every last cent. When I get to where I feel safe, I'll call the authorities and tell them about the cocaine. I don't want you to do it, Zack. You're too old to go to jail, and I'm too young."

As Willow sawed and hacked at her long, curly hair, she risked a glance at Zack, who appeared to be having the time of his life.

Sixty minutes later, Willow cleaned up the bathroom and flushed her shorn locks. She was dressed in a long navy blue linen dress with matching straw sandals. Her hair was still damp when she settled a denim hat with a huge yellow sunflower on it. "What do you think, Zack?"

The old man tilted his head to the side. "You look like you could be my granddaughter. I got the money all packed up. The blue suitcase goes with me. The green is yours. That's a lot of money to be toting around. Do you want me to keep some of it for you in case you head into a spot of trouble? Sort of like a safety blanket."

"That's a good idea. You're sure about the truck now?"

"Lord, yes. I've been hankering for a new one. Might get one of those Range Rovers I hear about all the time. They're a bit pricey to my way of thinking. Then again, I might get a used one. Depends on my mood."

"You know what I always say, Zack. Either go first-class or

don't go at all. Here," she said, tossing him a packet of money from her green case. "Be sure to keep it separate. I don't want to have nightmares about you spending drug money. This," she said, tossing more bundles of money into a plastic bag, "is my reserve in case I get short of cash. If you give me your phone number, I'll stay in touch. Just tell it to me and I'll remember. If I ever have to call you, I'll say I'm Mazie, okay? Remember, you promised to get that operation. Use the gambling money."

The old man laughed. "I always do what I say I'm going to do. I think we should lock up now and get out of here."

Willow looked around. Satisfied, she followed the old man out of the bathroom, across the huge bedroom, and out into the hall. In the kitchen, she let her gaze swivel around. She hadn't touched anything in the kitchen. "Okay, we're good to go. I'll drive. How far do you live from here, Zack?"

"Just a spit. Maybe a mile or so back the other way. I moved out here after Melba died. Didn't need a big old house anymore. Don't really know the neighbors. I got a dog and a cat to keep me company. I'm ready to go if you are."

"You could go to jail for helping me like this. You do know that, don't you?" Willow said, climbing into the truck.

"Yes, I guess I could. Haven't had this much excitement in over twenty years. Don't worry about me getting to town either. I can use Melba's old Chevy. I keep it gassed and running. Just drop me off at the house and get out on the highway."

They drove the short distance in silence. Willow thought it strange that she wasn't getting her adrenaline rush the way she normally did when she was on the run. She genuinely liked the old man and hoped he wouldn't get into trouble.

"Whoa, little lady, slow down. Make a right, and my house is down the road."

It was a neat little house with window boxes full of yellow Gerber daisies. She found herself smiling. Her mother had loved Gerber daisies. When she was little there was always a veg-etable garden as well as a flower garden. Until her father would get in a drunken rage and rip everything out, after which he would slap her mother around and beat her with his belt.

"What are you thinking about, Mazie?"

"My father. He was a drunk. He used to beat me and my

mother. I used to dream about him frying in hell. When he died, my mother and I had him cremated. It was the closest thing to hell we could think of. If I had a father, I'd want him to be like you."

The old man screwed up his face into a grimace. "I don't know as how I'd like to have a daughter doing the things you do. I like you, but I don't approve of all these shenanigans. You could end up in jail again. Murder is something to take seriously."

"I am taking it seriously, Zack. I'm not going to jail for something I didn't do. The best I could possibly hope for is some kind of plea bargain and some serious jail time. For something I didn't do. No thanks. I'll help you carry in the bag."

"I can do it. You go on now and get out of here."

"Thanks, Zack. I'll be in touch."

Willow shifted gears and peeled out of Zack's driveway. She waited for the usual adrenaline rush when she was on the run. When it still didn't come, she shivered in the intense heat of the Nevada desert. An omen?

Ninety minutes later she was cruising down a back alley, looking for a warehouse she'd visited once before. For the right amount of money, she could get a driver's license, a passport, a credit card, and a new Social Security card, that would pass muster anywhere in the world. As a bonus, for an extra incredible amount of money, she would walk away with an A-1 credit rating. It paid to explore the seamy side of any city you were going to live in for any length of time, which was exactly what she had done within a week of settling in Las Vegas. Two hours at the most and she could move about freely. All it took was a fistful of money, and she certainly had that.

She drove around the block twice before she parked Zack's battered maroon truck around the corner from the house she wanted to visit. Her watch told her it was 3:10 and she was bone tired. She set out on foot, the heavy bag dragging down her right shoulder.

It was probably a mistake to go there, but for some reason she couldn't help herself. She wanted to see Nick Clay one last time.

She'd made so many mistakes in her life that one more could hardly matter.

Willow took a moment to admire the house in the moonlight. It was an impressive structure, with white columns running across the front porch. Obviously, Nick Clay was doing very well for himself.

She walked around to the back of the house. It was easier to pick a lock on a kitchen or a garage door than to muddle around with dead bolts on front doors. Of course, if Nick had an alarm system, she was going to be SOL.

It was a quiet night, no dogs barking anywhere to announce her arrival, and for that she was thankful. She looked around to make sure there were no nocturnal neighbors sitting on their decks or patios. A moment later she almost jumped out of her skin when she felt something brush up against her leg. Sucking in her breath, she looked down to see an orange-and-yellow tabby cat. She purred loudly as her back arched. Willow scratched her behind the ears for a minute until she felt her breathing return to normal.

The tabby continued to purr as Willow fished inside her breast pocket for her new Visa card with the ten-thousand-dollar limit. She worked it quietly until she heard the snick of the lock. She smiled in triumph. People went all out with bolts, chain locks, and double locks on their front doors and forgot about the flimsy locks that were usually on kitchen doorways. She was glad she didn't have to crack a pane of glass, a dead sure giveaway on a quiet night.

Leading a life on the run had taught her a lot of things. She could break and enter using a credit card or a pick. She knew how to hot-wire a car in under three minutes, and she was so good at being a decoy in times of acute danger that she even amazed herself.

She bent down to put the credit card with her airline ticket inside the green bag. Her heart picked up an extra beat when she entered Nick's kitchen and locked the door behind her. The tabby had followed her inside and looked at her forlornly. She waited in the darkness to get her bearings from the slivers of moonlight creeping through the blinds over the kitchen window, then set the green bag down in a corner so it was out of the way.

Even in the semidarkness she could tell the house was just a place to sleep and perhaps eat on rare occasions. There were no plants, no knickknacks, no flowers, just dark, bulky shapes of furniture.

She headed for the stairs that led to the second floor. She walked softly, crossing her fingers that the stairs wouldn't creak and groan. At the top, she looked left and then right. All the bedroom doors were open. Nick must require a lot of room. Five bedrooms and, she had to assume, five adjoining baths, was a lot of room for a single guy. Maybe the house was a tax write-off. She took off her sandals and left them by the top of the stairs before she started down the hall.

She saw him in the second bedroom. Something tugged at her heart as she stared at the man she had married when he was still a boy. He looked vulnerable in sleep, his right arm thrown up above his head, the rest of his body sprawled across the king-size bed. His breathing was light and even, indicating a deep, peaceful sleep. She stared at him for a long time, her mind willing him to wake. He continued to sleep.

Willow turned to leave, wanting to stay, wanting to make love to the man who had once been her husband, but the commonsense part of her told her to leave quickly. She had enough emotional baggage to tote around.

Why didn't he sense her presence? The morning he walked into the Inn back in Kentucky, she knew he still loved her. A small part of him would always love her because she'd been his first love. The thought pleased her. If she'd ever loved anyone, it was Nick, but she knew she wasn't capable of loving any man the way a woman was supposed to love a man. Thanks to her drunken, brutal father. Maybe someday when she had time, she'd go into therapy and try to work it all out. Maybe.

Willow walked over to the bed and sat down on the floor, Indian fashion. She stared up at Nick. She was close enough to see the freckles on his naked shoulders. How lean and hard he looked. He wasn't that same awkward boy she'd taught the art of lovemaking. This was a man. A man she wanted. For now.

"What are you doing here, Willow?"

"How long have you been awake? What gave it away?" she whispered.

"I heard you come in the back door. Lately, I've become a very light sleeper." He rolled over and sat up. "Did you just happen to find yourself in the neighborhood?"

"No. I came here deliberately. I just wanted to talk to you one last time. I don't know why. It's not something I can explain. Maybe I came to say good-bye. Are you going to call the police?"

"Yes."

"Why? To get even with me? Because I was smart enough to elude the law, to walk out on the cops twice? They aren't very smart to have let me get away twice. I didn't kill Junior Belez, Nick. I have no intention of going to prison for the rest of my life for something I didn't do. Maybe someday they'll find the person who killed him. No one deserves to die like that."

"What do you want, Willow?"

"Five minutes ago I thought I wanted to make love to you. Now I just want to talk, to try and explain something to you. I don't want you to ruin your life thinking there was something wrong with you. It wasn't you. It's me. I really liked you, Nick. I liked the fact that you were rich even more. I grew up dirt poor. You know the old story, the other kids had everything and I had hand-me-downs. I didn't have any friends because I didn't want them to know where I lived and how I lived. My father was always drunk. He'd drink up his paycheck and come home and then beat me and my mother. Once he tried to molest me, but I got away from him. I had to run screaming out of the house half-naked. I don't think I ever got over that.

"We never had enough money because my father either drank it up or gambled it away. My mother was a wonderful cook. She taught me how to cook. She worked for rich people, cooking for their dinner parties. I'd go along with her to help clean up. Without her, we would have starved. I saw how other people lived and what money could buy. As soon as I was old enough, I split. I worked, got enough money together, and helped my mother get a start on her own life. We had a good thing going, cooking in famous restaurants, meeting wealthy people. Mom stayed straight, and I took off in another direction.

I didn't ever want to be poor again and I didn't want to be be-holden to some man. So, I beat them to the punch. I played the game, took their money, and moved on when I got bored.

"You were different from all the rest, Nick. You were fresh and young. You loved with your entire being. In a million years I could never be what you wanted or what you deserved. I knew that the day we returned to Blue Diamond Farms. I knew it even before your mother pounced on me. What I'm saying is, I would have left you in a few weeks. You were just too nice. Believe it or not, I didn't want to hurt you."

"Well, you did."

"I know, Nick. I'm sorry. I realize they're just words but I mean them. Well, I guess I better get going. Would you mind giving me a little bit of a head start before you call the cops? Six hours should do it."

"They'll find you, Willow. If you didn't do it, let Hatch clear your name. If you don't, you'll be running for the rest of your life."

Willow untangled her legs and leaned toward the bed. "No, this time they won't find me."

Nick looked into her eyes and believed her. "It's going to be light soon. You better get going." His voice was so husky sound-ing he couldn't believe it was his own. "I won't call the police."

"If you don't call them, that means you're aiding and abet-ting me. Can you live with that?"

"Yeah."

Willow smiled. "I wouldn't have called Buddy about your sister's baby."

"I know that, too," Nick said.

Willow leaned over and kissed him full on the mouth. "Forget about me and be happy, Nick. You're a wonderful human being and you deserve to be happy. Tell Emmie I said good-bye."

He didn't want to ask but he did. "Will I ever hear from you again?"

"No."

Nick wiped at his eyes when he heard the door close behind her. He held his breath, waiting to hear the kitchen door close. A minute later he saw a yellow tabby cat he'd seen in the neighborhood leap onto his bed, a piece of sticky paper stuck to her head. He pulled it off and read the scrawled note. "This little girl looks like she needs someone to love her. Her name is Mazie Breckenbridge."

Nick laughed until he cried.

It was midafternoon when Willow packed her bag for the last time. She'd spent the entire morning cutting out the middle of ten rare first-edition books and stuffing Junior Belez's money inside them. She'd picked up a gadget in a Super Kmart that allowed her to encase the valuable books in plastic. The rest of the money went into three money belts she fastened around her body. The long, flowing Indian-style dress gave no hint as to what was underneath. The backpack and straw purse she'd purchased in the same Super Kmart held the balance of the money securely placed in other books and magazines.

At 5:10 she walked through customs and boarded a British Airways flight to Switzerland.

The land of numbered bank accounts.

Willow Bishop didn't look back.

10

Even though he was Asian, his appearance was as American as apple pie, with his blue jeans, Timberline boots, and Red Sox baseball cap. He said his name was Lee Liu. He grasped Nealy's hand and gave her a bone-crushing handshake.

"Welcome to Blue Diamond Farms, Lee. I'm Nealy Littletree, and this is my nephew, Jake Coleman."

Everything about the slight young man was exuberant. "I never, ever, thought I would be standing on such hallowed ground, ma'am. It's an honor to be here, and I'd be more than honored to ride one of your fine horses. When I drove through those gates it was the most awesome feeling with those two bronze statues of Shufly and Flyby guarding the entrance. I feel like I'm making history, and all I'm doing is standing here. It's a real pleasure to finally meet you, ma'am. I've seen all your races. I bought tapes and studied them. If I had one wish, it would be to be half as good as you were."

Nealy was so flattered she preened. "I appreciate the compliment, thank you. It takes a lot of hard work and dedication. Just ask Jake here.

"I'm glad you don't have a problem with staying here and getting to know Gadfly. No one rides my horses until they're comfortable with them and a two-minute ride in the Derby isn't going to do it. I don't like riding for hire. It just doesn't work for me. Jake showed me a few of your tapes and you're good with the horses. I like that.

"Jake's going to get you settled in. You'll be bunking in with him while you're here. Come down to the barn when you're ready, and I'll show you around."

"This sure is a pretty place, ma'am. Do you ever wonder if

Paradise is like this? I guess that sounds kind of corny," the young man said.

"Not at all. I've always thought of it in those terms." Nealy shielded her eyes to look across the vast expanse of bluegrass and white board fencing, then looked squarely at Jake. "I made my decision last night. You're going to ride Hifly in the Derby under one condition. You work your tail off from now till Derby week. I mean it, Jake. I want you and that horse to be one when you blast out of that gate. Now is the time to tell me if you have second thoughts. I think you're good enough, but you're the only one who really knows if you can do it. You have to feel it, live it, eat and sleep it. I want your answer by tomorrow morning."

"I can give it to you right now, Aunt Nealy. Jeez, I can't wait to call Mom and Grandma Fanny."

Nealy smiled. Was she ever that young, that enthusiastic? "As for you, Lee, you have one week to prove yourself. I've seen what you can do on tape, but I want to see what you can do with one of *my* horses. If you're ready in my opinion, then we're running two horses in the Derby, both of them from the same sire."

Lee Liu's eyes danced in excitement. "Fair enough, ma'am."

"Call me Nealy. Before this is over you'll be calling me a lot of things, and none of them will be flattering, but that's okay."

In the barn, Cordell Lancer was hitching up his jeans over his bony hips, his eyes on Gadfly, who was trying to nose his pocket. "Do you see what this dang horse is doing, Nealy? You damn well went and spoiled him. All he wants is peppermints. Won't take an apple or a carrot anymore. No, sirree, this gentleman wants candy. Saw your new rider up there a bit ago. Whatcha think of him?"

Nealy slipped the big horse a mint. "He's got a lot of enthusiasm, that's for sure. You know I never make a rash decision. I have to think about it, stew about it, then fret on it. I think he's going to do just fine. This is all new to me, too, Cordell. Two horses in the Derby by the same sire is the stuff dreams are made of. The only downside is there will be one winner and one loser."

"Assuming one or the other wins," Cordell drawled. "They

could both lose. You aren't the rider this time around. How old are you this year?"

Nealy bristled. "What does age have to do with anything? Are you telling me I should be put out to pasture?"

Cordell burst out laughing. "I wish you could see the look on your face right this minute. I calculate you to be around fifty-seven, give or take a year or so. Now I'm not saying that's *real* old, I'm just saying you're on the shady side of fifty and the sunny side of sixty. In my opinion, that's too old to be running a race like the Derby or the Preakness and the Belmont as well. Leave that to the young ones. Women's bones are different than men's bones. You could have that condition women get when they get to be a certain . . ."

"Enough!" Nealy roared. She was about to stalk away when she changed her mind and turned to Cordell. "For your information, I do not have *that condition* all women of a certain age get. Chew on that, Cordell Lancer! Furthermore, I could ride that Derby with my eyes closed and probably win it. I don't want to hear another word about my age. Do you hear me, Cordell?"

"I hear ya, Nealy. Testy today, aren't we?" He grinned.

Nealy flipped him the bird and left the barn. She headed for the stallion cemetery, where she always went when she needed to calm down and think. *It's quiet and peaceful here,* she thought when she sat down on one of the small ornate benches.

Overhead the branches rustled and whispered in the late-afternoon breeze. Before long it would be dark, and the day would end. Ever since Emmie's discharge from the Thornton rehab center and her decision to move in with her father, Nealy had been out of sorts. She hated the darkness, hated being alone. Yet she had always reveled in her aloneness. Even with people around her, she was alone. She'd never understood how that could be. It just was.

She closed her eyes and thought about the last meeting she'd had with Emmie's shrink, Dr. Ian Hunter. He'd gotten right in her face and told her she was responsible for Emmie's mental state. She knew she'd said a lot of things in her own defense, but she couldn't remember even one of them. She did remember running from his office, tears streaming down her cheeks. From that moment on she had refused any and all contact with the pyschiatrist. What in the name of God had Emmie told the man? When she finally calmed down enough to ask Emmie, her daughter's response had been, "I just told him the truth."

The truth as Emmie saw it or the real truth? Were they mixed up in Emmie's mind or were they mixed up in her own mind as Dr. Hunter had implied?

Nealy started to shake. She dropped her head into her hands and bit down on her tongue so she wouldn't cry when her daughter's words thundered in her ears, *You forgot to love me along the way.* And then the crowning insult—*Nick feels the same way I do.*

It must be true since Nick's phone calls were almost nonexistent these days. She had thought it was because of Hatch and his tirade about a case he was working on. Now she knew better.

Alone. Always alone.

The shadows in the cemetery were deepening. How easy it was to lose all sense of time in this place. Here, unlike the world outside that quiet place, things were neither black nor white, they just were. Beyond the low wall, a sharp line defined her life, and it was black or white. There were no gray shadings, no maybes, no what-ifs. It was. She wondered if she tried to explain her thoughts to anyone if they would understand. Probably not.

Fifty-seven!

It was a number.

In the barn, Nealy's mood changed instantly as she walked with Lee Liu and Jake up and down the breezeway. "And this big guy is Gadfly. He's the horse you'll be riding in the Derby if things work out. Let him get your scent. Talk to him, stroke his head. When you're finished talking, slip him this mint. Always keep them in your shirt pocket, but be stingy with them. They're a sweet reward for a job well-done. He already knows this, so he'll be looking for them. Praise goes a long way with this horse. Later, Jake can fill you in on the story of Gadfly, who, by the way, is the biggest horse ever to come out of Blue Diamond Farms.

"This small baby is Hifly." She waited to see if Lee's reaction was the same as her own when she saw Hifly for the first time. It wasn't.

"He reminds me of John Henry," Lee said. "He's got a good configuration. The question is, can he run?"

"No!" Jake said. Then he grinned, and said, "He flies! And I'm his pilot." He fingered the gold wings in his pocket.

"Ah, I see. That has to mean he's very good."

"Yes, he's very good," Jake said.

"And Gadfly?"

"He's like greased lightning," Nealy said. "In my opinion, he's as good as his daddy, and that says it all. I'm going to leave you two now and go up to the house. Hatch is due home any minute. I'll see you both bright and early in the morning."

Nealy was sitting in the kitchen having her after-dinner coffee when Hatch walked through the kitchen door. She set her coffee cup down carefully and got up to greet him, not liking the grim set of his jaw or the cold look in his eyes. He barely grazed her cheek when he kissed her. He walked over to the coffeepot, poured a cup, then reached up into the cabinet for a bottle of bourbon. He poured generously into his cup. He drank it in two gulps, then fixed a second cup. He carried it to the table and sat down, his expression the same as it was when he walked through the door.

Nealy sat down opposite him. "Would you like some dinner, Hatch? You look awful. Tell me what's wrong."

"I'm not hungry. Your son is what's wrong, Nealy. Willow went to visit him in Santa Fe. He didn't have the good sense to call the police. They're probably hauling his ass into jail as we speak. I had this gut feeling she was going to head for Nick. The minute I found out she walked out of the jail, I knew. I can't believe it, but, by God, that's what she did. No one saw her, no one tried to stop her. She had a good fifteen-minute head start before they knew she was gone. Nealy, she just up and walked away. What the hell was Nick thinking of?"

Nealy was so agitated, she spilled her coffee all over the table. Some of it dribbled onto Hatch's lap. She tried to mop it up with paper napkins. "I don't know, Hatch. His heart, I guess. Are you sure he didn't call the police? How do you know all this?"

"I told you, I had a gut feeling. I called one of the guys in the investigative firm we use and told him to watch Nick's house. I didn't want the kid getting into trouble, Nealy. I thought he had more damn sense. The whole thing is a big mess. The bottom line is, she's gone, and Nick is on the hook, unless he came to his senses and made the call later on. You need to give him a call, Nealy. For all I know his ass could be in jail."

Nealy paced back and forth in the kitchen, wringing her hands. "This is terrible. I'm probably the last person he wants to talk to right now. I'll do it, I'll do it," she said, reading the angry expression on her husband's face.

"You're his mother for God's sake."

"Apparently, if you are to believe Emmie, I hold that title in name only. I'm calling him, Hatch. Just let me get my wits together."

Hatch got up from the table and snagged a piece of celery from the cutting board. He chomped on it as he poured coffee into his cup for the third time. He tilted the bourbon bottle and poured. Nealy watched him out of the corner of her eye.

"Nick, it's Mom. I need to talk to you. Hatch just came back from Las Vegas and told me that Willow is on the run again. An investigator the firm uses says she visited you and that you didn't notify the police. Is that true, Nick? If it is true, you could be in big trouble. Hatch is here now. Do you want to talk to him?"

"No, I don't want to talk to Hatch. Why is it so easy for you to believe I would do something like that, Mom? Yeah, and why is Hatch so quick to believe I would break the law and damage the firm's image? You're both pissing me off here. Yes, Willow was here. She broke into my house in the middle of the night. She stayed till it was almost light, then she left. She asked me if I would give her a head start before I called the police. I told her I wouldn't call the police, but I did call them. If you want to stretch that hour into getaway time, then go ahead. I got up, took a shower, shaved, got dressed, drove to the police station, and filed a report. I did what I was supposed to do, so get off my back. And you can tell your husband to get the hell off my back, too. If you two are having sticky problems, don't lay them on me. I didn't do anything wrong. I'm going to hang up now before one of us says something we'll regret. Good-bye, Mom."

Nealy turned to Hatch. "It appears you were a tad premature.

Nick did go to the police station, and he did file a report. He wouldn't lie about something like that. He also said we're both, as in you and I, pissing him off. You're angry, Hatch, I can see that, but why are you taking it out on Nick and me? Clients burn their lawyers all the time. It goes with the job, doesn't it? It can't always be a hundred percent in your favor. It's called human error, being human, whatever. I'm starting to think you might be sorry you got mixed up with my family. Nobody forced you to take on Willow's case. I was grateful that you did, but when she ran away the first time, you could have called it quits and filed something with the courts. You didn't have to go back the second time."

Hatch sat down and rubbed at his aching temples. "Nothing like this has ever happened to me before. I never had a client like Willow. She's a wild card. Some small part of me admires her guts. The girl is a survivor. By now she's probably halfway around the world. She had help along the way, that's for sure."

"Why don't we just lay it to rest? She's gone, and there's nothing you can do. Let's get back to our lives and move forward."

"By moving forward, do you mean the running of the farm and training the horses for the Derby?" Hatch asked carefully.

Nealy answered just as carefully. "I guess that's what I mean. Lee Liu arrived today. He's with Jake. I made the decision to let Jake ride in the Derby. I really think he's good enough. All his fear is gone."

"He's never run a race, not even a stakes race, Nealy. He's so damn young. Are you sure he's ready?"

"He's as ready as I was at that age. He's really come into himself these last six months. He's got perfect balance, and that's what I was looking for. Cordell says his stance is a mixture of dynamic imbalance and ballistic opportunity. Jake has that. He's also got that exquisite sense of pace over each furlong. To you that means an eighth of a mile. It's such a pleasure to work with him. I'm seeing myself all over again from way back when. This is not a decision I made lightly, Hatch. The boy is ready. Hifly is ready. It remains to be seen about Lee Liu. I'm hopeful though." Excitement ringing in her voice, she said, "In my wildest dreams

I never, ever, thought I would have two horses running in the Derby. I get giddy just thinking about it."

Hatch eyed his wife over the rim of his coffee cup. He remained silent, wondering how much time they would have together now that she had committed to the Derby. "I think I'll go back to Santa Fe tomorrow and check on things. I might have to mend a few fences where Nick is concerned. I want to talk to the investigator myself. I don't want anything coming back to bite me later on. Do you mind?"

"Nope. I'm going to have my hands full with Lee. Stay as long as you like."

"Now that's a romantic statement if I ever heard one," Hatch grumbled.

"Oh, honey, I didn't mean it that way. I meant take as long as you need to make sure you're okay with everything. I'd rather you stayed here, but we did make a deal. We each get to do what we want to do as long as it doesn't interfere with our marriage. As in you and me. Seeing as how you're going to be leaving tomorrow, what do you say to us storing up some memories to draw on while you're gone?" Nealy stood and linked her arm with her husband's.

"I'd say that's the best offer I've had all day," Hatch said, leading her to the stairs.

"Nice to see you again, Cal." Hatch's hand shot forward. The private investigator pumped vigorously before he handed over a manila folder.

"It's not extensive. I didn't go out to the desert, but I did get the license plate number of the truck Willow Bishop drove here. As I told you, she parked it around the corner and walked to Nick's house. I don't know if she heisted the truck or if the guy gave it to her. He's one of the old-timers around here who live out in the desert. I ran his plate, and his license is suspended. Not because of anything he did but because he's legally blind and is still driving. He tries to elude the cops by using back streets. I didn't go out to his house or make any inquiries. I waited to see what you wanted me to do."

"I'll take it from here, Cal. Send your bill to the firm. Thanks."

Thirty minutes later, Hatch rang Nick's doorbell. "I was in the neighborhood and thought I'd stop by. I owe you a couple of apologies and thought I'd deliver them in person. You got a beer? If you do, I'm in a drinking mood."

"Yeah, sure. Come on in."

Hatch looked around. "You need to pretty up this place a little. Green plants go a long way. Put some junk on the tables and some pictures on the wall. Ask Medusa to help you."

"It's on my list of things to do." Nick uncapped a bottle of Hatch's favorite beer and handed it to him. "I got apples and cheese. That's it in the way of food."

"I'm not hungry, kid." He slapped down the report on the kitchen table. "I can pretty much tell you what it says. Willow somehow managed to borrow, and I use the term loosely, a pickup belonging to some old guy who lives out in the desert. I'm thinking, and this is just my personal opinion, that she had a little help. Some old codger that doesn't give a hoot about anything might have seen fit to help a little lady in distress. Seems he's legally blind, and his license was suspended, but he still drives. She could have seen him and helped herself to the truck. I'm thinking about taking a drive out there. It's about a mile after the Chicken Ranch. You want to go along for the ride?"

"Not really, but if you want some company, I'll go. Look, it's just like I said. She broke into the house and came in through the kitchen. I woke up, and she was sitting there staring at me. We talked for a little bit. And, no, I did not go to bed with her. I wanted to. She was agreeable. However, it didn't happen. She said I would never hear from her again. She's gone, and I don't know where she went."

Hatch looked down at his feet, where a yellow tabby was purring loudly. "I didn't know you had a cat."

"Yeah. Her name is . . . Mazie. I did what I was supposed to do. I told the police she was here. That ends my involvement."

Hatch reached down and picked up the tabby who settled herself in the crook of his arm. She continued to purr loudly. "How do you feel about it, kid?"

"I just want it to be over and done with. Every time I think I've put it behind me, she rears up, and it starts all over again.

She's gone now, and she won't be back. I think I can guarantee it. Well, I'm ready if you are."

"Then let's hit the road. Cal gave me a map, so we won't have any trouble finding the place once we hit Vegas. The flight isn't that long. I'll have you back in time for your morning shower. I want to be sure in my own mind that she's gone. We all need closure where Willow is concerned. There is every chance the old guy knows nothing."

"Why don't we just call him, Hatch? Wouldn't it be a lot simpler to call and talk rather than make the trip?"

"We could do that, but, as you know, seeing someone face-to-face and talking with them gives you a whole other perspective. If he doesn't know Willow, we pack up and come home. I have this gut feeling she had help. The other thing is this, Nick, Junior Belez's house is just a few miles down the road past where the old man lives. That almost tells me more than I want to know."

Nick sighed. "Okay, let's go."

"Do you have to let the cat out or anything?"

"I don't think so. I just got her. She uses a litter box. She'll be okay till I get back."

"I would have taken you for a dog man myself. It surprises me that you'd get a cat."

"Yeah, it surprised me, too. She needed a home, and I needed a roommate. It works."

It was almost midnight when Hatch drove the rental car up the gravel drive to the little house where Zack Leroy lived. "He must still be up; there are lights on in the house."

Both men climbed out of the car at the same time a huge black Lab blasted through the front door. Hatch backed up a step and then another when the huge dog's lips peeled back to reveal a vicious set of canines. "Whoa, boy, down. Mr. Leroy!"

"Stay, Stella," a creaky voice said from the doorway. "Whatcha want out here at this time of night?"

"I just want to ask you a few questions. My name is Hatch Littletree, and this is Nick Clay. We're attorneys in Santa Fe. We just want to talk to you. I know it's late, so we'll make it short."

"Come on in. I'm sorry about the lighting. I have to keep it dim for a few days. I just had my cataracts operated on yesterday. Bright light bothers me. Now, what's so all-fired important that it can't wait till morning?"

"We want to talk to you about your truck. Do you know where it is?"

"Nope. Someone stole it right off the street. Well, it wasn't a street but an alley. I went to get a haircut the other day and someone stole it. Wasn't worth nothing. Didn't report it because I'm not supposed to be driving. My license was suspended. Did you find it?"

"As a matter of fact, no. We spotted it, then it disappeared. In Santa Fe."

The old man laughed. "You must be thinking about someone else's truck. My old bucket would never make Santa Fe. I just use it for local driving. I mostly drive my wife Melba's car because the truck isn't dependable. I think you fellas are joshing with me here. That old clunker couldn't have gone all the way to Santa Fe."

"It had your license plate, and it was registered to you, Mr. Leroy. I have no idea where it is now."

"Even if by some miracle it was my old bucket, what does that have to do with anything? I'd like to have it back for sentimental reasons but if that isn't possible, I can live with the loss now that I can see again. Are you fellas trying to tell me something and I'm missing it or what?"

"Do you know a young woman named Willow Bishop?" Nick asked.

"Can't say that I do. I think you better ask yourself what would I be doing with a young woman?"

"Helping her," Hatch said. "She's wanted for murder. I *was* her attorney. Nick here was married to her at one time. If you did help her, you could go to jail for a very long time. Prison is not a nice place for an elderly man like yourself."

"No, I guess it isn't. I'm sorry but I can't help you. I never met a woman named Willow Bishop. Can't say when I met a young woman last. If you find my truck, will you give me a call? I'd like to claim it. I can write down my phone number for you."

"That won't be necessary. We already have it. I guess you can't help us after all," Hatch said.

"No, I can't."

Nick moved closer to the old man and stood eyeball-to-eyeball with him. "So, if we keep on driving and go out to Junior Belez's house, the guy who was murdered, we won't find your fingerprints anywhere around there, right?"

"Nope. Know the case, though. Saw it on television every night for a long time. It's my bedtime now. Good luck with your case and remember, now, if you find my truck, let me know."

"Thanks for your time, Mr. Leroy."

Outside in the dark on the way to the car, Nick said, "We made the trip for nothing. He doesn't know Willow. At this stage I don't give a good rat's ass if she's ever found or not. I'm sick of the whole mess. We gotta get back, Hatch. I have to be in court early."

"He was lying. Cal said he lifted the hood of the truck and the engine was sound as a dollar. The old man took care of the truck, and it had fairly new tires according to his report. The truck could have made it to Santa Fe. Five bucks says we'll find it at the bus station, train station, or airport. I'll get Cal back on it."

"Are we going to Junior Belez's house?"

"I think Willow went out there looking for something. More than likely she hitchhiked and Mr. Leroy picked her up. She probably gave him some song and dance and he fell for it. My thought is she either bought his truck or he gave it to her. It's just a guess. She might have had money stashed there, or Junior might have had some stashed and she knew about it. Don't forget, she walked out of the police station with nothing but the clothes on her back. Somehow she got to Santa Fe, and where she is now is anyone's guess. Whatever was at the house is gone now, so let's head home, kid, and put this whole thing to sleep. If we ever want to find Mr. Leroy, we know where he lives."

Nick threw his hands in the air. "This whole thing was stupid. We wasted a whole night and for what? Yes, he knew her, no, he didn't know her, yes, he helped her, no, he didn't help her. We're right back where we started."

"No, Nick, we're not. Something happened between that old

man and Willow. Sooner or later, one or the other will get in touch. I'll have Cal get some of his operatives out here in Vegas to take it on. We'll monitor him, his comings and goings, his mail, his telephone. Sooner or later, we'll come up with something."

"No you won't," Nick said. "She's gone, and it's over."

11

Emmie scanned her portfolio statement before she slipped it back into the envelope, then opened her checkbook to view past entries in the robust account. She fingered the six dividend checks she had yet to deposit. Her mother was always prompt about sending the generous checks that she normally transferred to a trust for Gabby. She really should go to the bank, but these days anything having to do with her mother annoyed her. Ian Hunter's words blared in her ears: *Don't procrastinate. Meet it head-on, deal with it, and put it behind you.* And he was right. She rummaged for the deposit booklet and ripped out two copies. She endorsed the checks, and filled out the ticket before attaching a paper clip to the little stack of checks. There, she'd met it head-on, dealt with it, and could close the checkbook. Done.

Dillon Roland came up behind her chair and put his hands on her shoulders. "Do I dare ask what is causing that ferocious look on your face?"

Emmie waved the stack of checks in front of him. "These. As half owner of Blue Diamond Farms, I get dividend checks every month. I put them in a trust for Gabby."

"That's a good thing, Emmie. You should be happy that you're lining Gabby's nest."

"I am happy about it, Dad. It's just that sometimes I get mad that I own something and have no say in the way things are done. Half the farm is mine. Mom never asks for my input. I understand that I screwed things up, but I'm okay now. She never asked for my input before I got sick either.

"When Josh Coleman died years ago, he left SunStar to me, and Mom made me sign it over to my uncles Rhy and Pyne. I did it because she said it was the right thing to do. I don't know if it was or not. I always did what she said. Then there was that awful court thing that dragged on with the Colemans before things were finally settled. The way Mom wanted them settled. I guess in some ways I was a little upset with the way she used the farm's money to pay off the Coleman loans and give them back their homestead. She didn't consult with me even once. I like to think I would have agreed, but I don't know that for sure."

Dillon walked around the table and sat down. "Something else is bothering you, isn't it? We said we were going to talk about everything. Dr. Hunter said that was the key to your recovery. So, Emmie, talk."

Emmie bit down on her lower lip. "We already talked about it, Dad. It was what Mom said that day when I was leaving rehab. She said you were just being nice to me to get one of her horses. She said you didn't love me. As Dr. Hunter said, once words are spoken, you can't take them back. You can't undo a mistake either, but you can work to make things right."

"I'm sorry your mother doesn't understand that people can change. Look, if you want to go back to Kentucky and talk to her, let's do it. It will be nice for Gabby to see her grandmother again. And if you want some say in the training of Hifly, I'm all for it. He's your horse. Nothing is ever going to change that."

"I'm not as good as she is. I wanted to try, though. I had such a good rapport with Hifly. Then I got sick. She's worked with him all the time I was gone. I don't even know if he'll remember me. I wish you could have seen her face when she saw him for the first time. Then she turned to look at me and that said it all. I'm not mom bashing here, it's the way it was then. You know what, Dad, let's go to Kentucky. I want to see my horse. I dream about him all the time." Emmie smacked her hands together. "When can we go?"

"Whenever you want to go, honey. This afternoon, tomorrow, the next day. It's your call. Just be sure it's really what you want to do."

"Oh, I do. What about you, Dad? Are you up for a visit with Mom?"

"Let's just say I'll stand on your end of the property as long as you show me which end is yours. I have no desire to upset your mother. There's every possibility she'll be civil to me, but I don't think either one of us should count on it."

"Tomorrow. Let's go tomorrow. We can stay at the Inn or at my old house. If you do the airline tickets, I'll pack for all of us. Should we take Cookie? Of course we have to take Cookie. Hifly loved him. He was his barn buddy there for a while. I'm so glad you're okay about us going back home. Thanks, Dad."

"My pleasure, honey."

Dillon Roland sat at the table for a long time after Emmie left to go upstairs to pack. Was he making a blunder by going to Kentucky with his daughter? Well, he'd had his share of screw-ups along the way, so one more wouldn't matter. He knew he could handle whatever Nealy threw at him, but he wasn't sure about Emmie.

True, Emmie had come a long way both physically as well as mentally because he'd been able to keep her free of stress and trauma. According to Dr. Hunter, Emmie was her old self again, and while he didn't know exactly what *her old self* meant, he was happy with the prognosis and her progress to date. To him she appeared absolutely normal in every way. She was so improved that she could ride daily and work as many hours as she wanted in the barns.

He thought about all the years he'd spent in a loveless marriage just to please his father. In many ways he was just like Emmie, and perhaps that was what endeared him to her. He didn't love his sons the way he loved her, and the thought saddened him. First, they had been spoiled by their mother, and then by his own father, who doted on them as they grew into tall, handsome young men. Young men who had never worked a day in their lives. They lived off huge trust funds and traveled around the world playing and partying. He shook his head when he recalled how he'd tried to intervene only to be shot down by his father and his wife. Sad to say, he'd just given up.

He looked around the great room he was sitting in and smiled. Cookie was asleep in her little bed near the fireplace. Toys were scattered everywhere, a doll buggy, a small racing car, and a basket of blocks that Cookie had upended before she conked out to sleep. He wasn't sure if the toys were Gabby's or the dog's. Not that it mattered. He laughed aloud when he remembered how Gabby had dressed Cookie in one of her doll outfits and taken her for a ride in the buggy. He'd never been happier in his entire life—except when he was seeing Nealy Coleman, back when he was a kid. He'd been so in love with her then, and so happy he could have walked on air.

A lifetime ago.

There was still one area of his daughter's life he had to work on: Buddy Owens, Emmie's ex-husband and Gabby's father. Dr. Hunter had said Emmie would never be one hundred percent until she faced her daughter's father. "If you have to, fight it out in the courts, but do something. Don't live with something like that hanging over your head. Gabby won't thank you as she gets older and finds out her father is alive and well and was kept from her. Now, if the child's father isn't interested and doesn't want visitation, that's a different story."

Emmie lived in fear that Buddy would sweep Gabby away, that the child would be lost to her. No amount of talking, cajoling, or wheedling could change her mind, even when her doctor told her, time and again, if she did it right, nothing would happen. She was simply too frightened. If she lost Gabby, she lost everything. Her favorite expression, where Buddy Owens was concerned, was, *Why stir up a hornet's nest?*

Dillon sighed. Maybe after the trip to Kentucky, he'd try again to talk Emmie into calling her ex-husband. Sometimes a miracle did happen if you were open to all things. He crossed his fingers the way he had when he was a little boy and made a wish.

"Grandpa, Grandpa! I'm home. Where's Mommy?" Dillon was off his chair in a second, his arms spread wide. Gabby ran right into him. He scooped her up as well as the whirling dervish called Cookie and hugged them both.

He closed his eyes, inhaling the warm, sweet smell of his granddaughter. He couldn't ask for more.

Nealy tilted the brim of her Stetson to shield her eyes from the early-March sun. Off in the distance she could see an expanse of gray clouds. By noon it would be raining, but for now it was a beautiful spring day. She whirled around when she felt a gentle hand on her shoulder. "Hatch!"

"That's my name. How's it all going?" he asked, shielding his eyes, too, against the glare of the bright sun.

"Take a look," Nealy said, pride ringing in her voice. "If those two young men keep this up, by Derby Day they're going to be superstars. I say this with all modesty, but they're as good as I was on my best day.

"I've always said a Thoroughbred is one of God's best miracles. Do you realize they can run forty miles an hour? They live for that one word, *run*. Hifly is a constant surprise to me. Jake is doing so well with him. I know you know this, but I'm going to tell you again. When a jockey is running a horse, he doesn't actually sit in the saddle. Jake had some trouble with that in the beginning. You have to crouch over, placing all your weight on your toes. The metal base of the stirrup hangs about a foot from the horse's topline, and that's where your toes go. It's tricky till you master it. When the horse is running, the only parts of the jockey that actually touch the horse are his ankles and the insides of his feet. All the rest is balanced in midair. Jake got it down pat, and it only took two good spills."

"I still shiver when I think about you racing those races."

"Sometimes I shiver, too," Nealy smiled. "Those two," she said, pointing her index finger at Jake and Lee, "are fearless. Jake actually turned green the day I put him on a pony. Just look at him now. You know, Hatch, everything about a jockey comes down to seconds. Just mere seconds. Some of the greatest jockeys in the world are called freakish because they have to be able to gauge pace to within two- to three-fifths of a second of the actual time. It all comes down to a fast faction and a slow faction. Jake has that ability, and from what I've seen from Lee, he's got it, too. I've got two fine jockeys here, Mr. Littletree."

"Did you ever get around to making your donation to the Jockey's Guild, Nealy?"

"Absolutely. I'm taking it a step further this year. All the proceeds from my Derby Ball are going to go to the guild. They're currently supporting over fifty riders who were disabled on the job. I think that's a wonderful thing for them to do. I just wish more people would donate."

Hatch turned around to look back toward the house. "I think you have company, Nealy."

Her eyes on the paddock, Nealy said, "It's probably some re-
porter. They're getting rather bold this year. We need to put the
gate down. The rumors are starting to fly. I expected it since we
have just two months till the Derby. I think the word is out that
I'm running two horses."

"Wonder how that rumor got started," Hatch mused.

"Cordell started it." Nealy laughed. "When the time is right,
I'm going to have both boys give an interview to the papers. So,
who's here?" she asked turning around.

"Emmie! Gabby! Come here, you little rascal, and let me look
at you. My gosh, you've grown half an inch. Well, hello, Cookie!
It's nice to see you, Emmie," Nealy said, reaching for her daughter. Emmie took a step backward to avoid her mother's outstretched arms. Instead, she climbed over the board fencing and
ran across the paddock to where Hifly was standing next to
Jake. She stopped halfway to where the horse was standing and
whistled. Hifly turned, swung his head about, and raced to her
side.

"Hello would have been nice," Nealy mumbled. She dropped
to her knees to hug Gabby, tears filling her eyes. The little girl in
her arms, she turned to watch the byplay in the paddock between Emmie, Jake, and Hifly. Lee Liu watched from a distance,
a frown building between his brows.

"Hi, Jake, how's it going with my horse?" Emmie asked, nuz-
zling the horse's head. Hifly whinnied in pleasure. "I've missed
this guy." She whispered in the horse's ear, and, to her delight,
he nudged her gently until her back was against the board fencing.

"Why is he doing that?" Jake asked.

"He wants me to get on his back. He remembers me. I was so
afraid he would forget all about me. Walk away and call him. I
want to see if he'll listen to you." Jake retraced his steps and
called out. Hifly ignored him. He called again. This time Hifly's
tail swished angrily as he waited for Emmie to climb on his
back.

"Okay, baby, show me what you can do," Emmie said, leaning down to whisper in the horse's ear.

"Emmie, no!" Nealy shouted. Hatch placed a gentle hand on

her arm as Gabby wiggled to the ground. A second later, Cookie leaped through the board fencing and raced after the galloping horse.

Up on the gravel driveway, Dillon Roland wiped at a lone tear in the corner of his eye. In his life he'd never seen such bliss as he was seeing on his daughter's face.

Exactly two minutes later, Emmie rode up to the board fencing where her family was standing. Hifly was snorting and pawing the ground as Cookie danced in front of him, happy to be back where he'd had so many good runs with his favorite buddy. Emmie's laughter rang in the air when Hifly bent down to pick up the little dog and held him high enough so Emmie could reach him. He took off again, his mane flying, his tail a straight line behind him. Dillon Roland's closed fist shot in the air as Nealy stood with her mouth hanging open.

Over the sound of the horse's pounding hooves, they could all hear Cookie's joyous bark and Emmie's laughter.

Gabby clapped her hands and shouted, "Mommy! Mommy!"

Hifly trotted over to the family, proud as a peacock. Jake helped Emmie dismount, Cookie in her arms. "The dog had a better seat than I did," Emmie said breathlessly. "How'd I do?" she asked Jake.

"You beat my time by two seconds," Jake said, his voice full of awe.

"No kidding!" She looked up at the driveway, saw her father wave to her. She waved back. "That's my dad up there," she said proudly.

"I'd like to meet him. Why is he standing up there?"

"It's a long story, Jake. God, I love this horse."

"It's easy to see he loves you, too. He likes me, but he doesn't love me. I can tell the difference."

"My mother was like that with Flyby. That horse was almost human. So's this guy. I'm going to cool him down and do what has to be done. Want to come along, or do you have something to do? You can meet my dad."

Emmie motioned for her father to join her. "How'd I do, Mom?" she asked, acknowledging her mother for the first time.

"That was a stupid, foolish thing you did just now, Emmie.

You could have gotten yourself killed. Hifly isn't the same horse he was when you left here. You couldn't know what he would or wouldn't do."

"Ah, but that's where you're wrong, Mom. I do know. Just like you knew with Flyby, or did you forget? Sometimes I think you have a selective memory, but only when it comes to me. Eventually, I'll figure it all out."

Nealy jerked her head backward. "I don't want that man on my property. I mean it, Emmie. Get rid of him."

"Easy, Nealy," Hatch said softly.

"That man? Get rid of him? Your property? I don't think so, Mom. Show me where my half is. My half, Mom. Is it down the middle? Is it crosswise? What?"

"This is not funny, Emmie. I want him out of here, and off Blue Diamond land. Now!"

Hatch tugged at his wife's arm. Nealy shook it off.

"Then maybe you should call the police or the sheriff or someone. Half this farm is mine. Hifly is my horse. I have the bill of sale. I didn't give you permission to train him, nor did I give you permission to bring Jake or that other guy here. You're supposed to consult with me. Sending a check once a month won't hold up in court.

"Jake, take Hifly to the barn and cool him down. I'll be there in a few minutes. Dad, go with Jake while I talk to Mom."

"He put you up to this didn't he? Can't you see what he's doing? What's gotten into you? Why are you behaving like this?"

"Because it's time. In case you haven't noticed, I'm not the old Emmie you can lead around by the nose."

Hatch watched in horror as mother and daughter went eyeball-to-eyeball.

"I'm going to ride my horse in the Derby so if you made any promises to Jake or the other guy, this would be a good time to cancel them out," Emmie said. "He's my horse, and I'll ride him."

"You don't know the first thing about being a jockey. You'll get yourself killed just to prove me wrong. I'm not wrong. Your doctors won't allow it," Nealy said desperately.

"Mom, they okayed me months ago. Do you think I spend

my time knitting and watching soap operas? I've been riding and training. I taught myself. I might not be as good as you were in your prime but I can damn well hold my own. Now, which half of this damn farm is mine? Draw the line now because I'm here to stay until after the Derby. Who knows, I might be here till after the Preakness and the Belmont. There's nothing you can do about it either."

"We'll just see about that," Nealy said.

"Yeah, I guess we will. Come on, Gabby, let's go find Cookie and Grandpa."

"Don't say a word, Hatch. I'm going up to the house to call Clementine Fox."

"That's a mistake. You'll make things worse if you go legal. Please, listen to me. I'm a lawyer. I know what I'm talking about. If you go legal, Emmie will be forced to get an attorney, and who do you think she's going to hire? Nick, that's who. Is that what you want?"

Nealy stopped in her tracks. "Nick wouldn't . . . you're wrong . . . no, no, that won't happen."

"It will happen. Fix it, Nealy, now, before it's too late. I'm telling you, don't go down that road."

Nealy sat down on the back steps and hugged her knees. "How in the hell did this happen? It's that man. I know it as sure as I'm sitting here. He's filling her head with all kinds of nonsense. She's no more ready to ride in the Derby than you are, Hatch. He wants something. I just know it."

Hatch stared off into the distance, his mind whirling. "Nealy, you could be wrong about Dillon Roland. He looks like a decent man to me. Gabby adores him, and I've never seen Emmie happier. If she's as sound as she said she is, then we have him to thank for it. Don't let your hatred for him drive you away from your daughter. And your son, if you insist on going the legal route. I think you need to backpedal a little right now."

Nealy threw her hands in the air. "She wants her half of the farm. Half. I'm the one who busted my ass all these years and now, just when Dillon Roland comes into the picture, she wants her half. Before she was content to take her dividend checks and never give it a second thought. Don't you find it all a little strange?"

"No, Nealy, I don't. Remember what she's been through. She came to a crossroads in her life where she had to choose which road she wanted to travel. This is the right road for her, her choice. You can't fault her for that. She has to survive, too, Nealy. You can salvage this if you think things through and don't do anything in haste."

Nealy got up and stared at her husband before she stomped into the house. "Whose side are you on, Hatch?" Bitterness rang in her voice as she crossed the kitchen to the coffeepot.

Hatch sat down at the kitchen table and stared at his wife. "There is nothing more important in this life than family, Nealy. Lately, you've hit a couple of rough patches, but somehow you've managed to avert some serious tragedies. This one facing you now is going to turn out to be the Queen Mother of them all if you aren't careful."

Nealy gulped at the hot coffee. "What you're saying is, my whole life has been wrong. I didn't do anything right. Yet somehow I managed to raise two kids, put this farm on the map, win two Triple Crowns, and breed Thoroughbreds that people stand in line to buy. That doesn't count for anything."

Hatch shook his head. "You are without a doubt the most stubborn female I have ever met. It doesn't matter where you've been. What matters is where you're going and how you get there. You can't get there, wherever *there* is, and destroy your family in the process. Is it your pride? Your ego? You don't have to prove anything to anyone, Nealy. Just yourself. Maybe you should think about consulting a therapist and talk all this out."

"So now you think I'm nuts, too. Somehow or other, I've managed to get this far in my life without talking to a shrink. I'll just continue to muddle through for the rest of my life, thank you very much. I'm going upstairs to take a bath." Her voice softened when she said, "Thanks for your input, Hatch."

Hatch recognized Nealy's tone of voice. She was going to do whatever she thought was right and live with the consequences. His shoulders slumped. He couldn't even begin to imagine where it would all end up.

It was dusk when Emmie said good night to Hifly. She gave him a quick hug before she joined her father and Gabby in the breezeway. "I guess we're going to my house. Is that okay, Dad?"

"Whatever you want, honey. I think this little rascal is ready for bed. I can make up the beds while you give her a bath. We should probably stop for some take-out food and maybe pick up something for Gabby's breakfast. We can do the rest of the grocery shopping tomorrow."

"Emmie, wait!"

Emmie turned around to see Jake running from the end of the breezeway. "You aren't angry with me, are you?" he asked.

"No, not at all. Why do you ask?"

"You know, Hifly . . . me riding him in the Derby. I wanted to but I had to wait for Aunt Nealy's approval. I just wanted you to know, I'm okay with you riding him if you were serious. We get along good, but he loves you and that makes the difference. To tell you the truth, I'm not sure I'm ready. I think I am, but like Lee says, if you have even one iota of a doubt, then you aren't ready. Are you strong enough, Emmie? Or did you just say that to make your mom mad?"

"I'm strong enough, health-wise, Jake. I feel like I'm stealing your thunder so to speak."

"No, don't think about it like that. I can use all the time I can get. I'm thinking I can only get better if I persevere. If you decide for sure that's what you want to do, I can show you a few little tricks I learned with Hifly. That horse has a mind of his own, but you already know that. I'd like to help you in whatever way I can."

"My mother might have something to say about that, but I appreciate the offer. I have to get Gabby home and to bed. We can talk tomorrow. I'll be here bright and early."

"Okay, I'll see you then. Nice to meet you, Mr. Roland," Jake said, extending his hand before he trotted off to his quarters.

"What do you think, Dad? You know, about what happened here today."

"It's not important what I think. What do you think?"

"I think I did okay. Boy, do I feel good. I can't remember ever feeling this good. Hifly didn't forget me. I was so afraid he would, but he didn't. Tell me the truth, Dad, do you think I can do it? If you have reservations, I need to know. You haven't steered me wrong yet."

"Emmie, you can do whatever you think you can do. It's what you think and what you feel. Listen to your heart. No one else is walking in your shoes, no one else can feel your heart or see into your head. You know what they taught you at the rehab center, stretch to your limitations. I hope I'm walking on your half of this farm. I believe your mother is ready to shoot me."

"No, she won't shoot you, but she'll do something. Mom never . . . let's not talk about Mom."

"A word of caution, honey. You better have a good attorney standing by in the wings."

"I got the best in the world, Dad, my brother. Now, let's go home."

From her bedroom window Nealy watched her daughter leave. Even from the second floor she could hear her laughter and Gabby's childish babble as the little group made their way to the car. One small part of her wished she was going with them and another part of her knew she could never belong to the little group. She was the outsider. She asked herself again how it had come to this. Maybe Hatch was right. Maybe she did need to talk to a shrink.

She was so deep into her thoughts, the phone rang six times before she actually heard it. Maybe it was Emmie calling to apologize. Her hello was brisk and cool.

"Nealy, this is Josh Clymen at SunStar. I'm afraid I have some bad news. I hate telling you over the phone, but there doesn't seem to be any other way. Rhy and Pyne were killed a little while ago. The roof collapsed on the new barn from all the heavy rain. They were standing side by side when it happened. We also lost four of the horses. We did everything we could, Nealy. Nealy, are you there?"

"I'm here, Josh. I guess I'm in shock. I just spoke to both of them the other day. I don't know what to say."

"What do you want me to do, Nealy? I know what to do about the horses, but they're your brothers. You have to make the decisions where that's concerned."

"All right, Josh. I need to think and to talk to Hatch. I'll call the kids. Let me get back to you when I have my wits about me."

Nealy pinched herself. No, she wasn't dreaming. She was wide-awake. She watched the spot she'd just pinched turn black-and-blue. Bruises didn't turn black-and-blue till later. Maybe it was a trick of light.

"Hatch!" she screamed at the top of her lungs.

On Nealy's orders, the funeral was small and private, with only the immediate family and the farmworkers. Both brothers were laid to rest next to their mother in the SunStar cemetery. Thanks to Josh Clymen's foresight, by nightfall, blankets of bluebells would cover both graves.

Nealy stood dry-eyed next to her husband and wondered why she couldn't cry. Out of the corner of her eye, she could see Nick dab at the corners of his eyes with his knuckles while Emmie sniffled outright. She cringed when she heard her daughter blow her nose.

And then it was over. Those who had been ahead of her in life were all gone now. Logically speaking, she was next. The thought frightened her.

They were almost to the house when a shiny black car pulled to a stop in front of the house. A small dapper man with sweat beading on his brow got out of the car, mopping at his face with one hand, his other hand holding what looked like a very heavy briefcase. "Ma'am, I'm Connely Brian, your brothers' attorney. I know you live in Kentucky, so I thought I would come right out in case you were planning on leaving after the service. We can do the reading of the will now or sometime later on. It's simple, and will take no more than ten minutes."

Nealy nodded and walked into the house. She led the way to the dining room and sat down. "I'm surprised my brothers made a will. Look, I know it's coming to me, so skip that part and read the bequests."

The dapper attorney frowned as he dug into his thick brief-case. He continued to frown as he smoothed out the crackly papers. He cleared his throat before he took one last look at Nealy.

"Both wills read exactly the same, so it doesn't matter which brother died first. As I said, aside from the usual bequests of twenty-thousand dollars to their foreman, the manager, and a few lesser bequests to some of the older employees, that's pretty much it. The farm, all the horses, and everything owned by both brothers goes to Emmie Coleman and her daughter Gabby

Coleman. There's a note here written by both Rhy and Pyne that says the reason for this particular bequest is that they both wanted Emmie to return to the place where she was born. Your brothers gave me an envelope and instructed me to hand it to Emmie after the reading of the will." He handed it across the table. Emmie reached for it with shaking hands. Inside was a penny. She ran crying from the room, the envelope clutched to her breast.

"When did my brothers make this will, Mr. Brian?" Nealy asked in a cold, brittle voice.

"Almost two years ago. A few months before Emmie got sick, I believe. A little time passed before they came in to sign the wills. I recall they were talking about her and her illness. The date is on the will. Is there something wrong, ma'am?"

"My daughter doesn't want this place. She gave it back once, and she'll do it again. It should have come to me."

"Are you questioning my integrity, madam?" Brian bristled.

"No. I'm just saying the farm was to go to me. I'm saying I don't understand."

"Well, I can't help you there. As for Emmie not wanting the farm, that's for her to say and dispose of whichever way she sees fit. This will now go to probate. I'll be in touch soon. Good-bye. I'm sorry we had to meet under these circumstances."

Nealy sat in the dining room chair and stared at the table. Hatch nudged her elbow. She ignored him. She didn't raise her eyes until Emmie came back into the room. She looked from her mother to her brother.

Nealy finally broke the silence. "Is it your intention to take up residence here at SunStar, Emmie?"

"I don't know. I think it might be a good place to bring Hifly after the race. I like it here. I can see myself raising Thoroughbreds with Dad's help."

"So he does get one of my horses after all," Nealy snapped. "I told you, that's what this is all about. You're such a fool, Emmie. Will you please wake up before it's too late?"

Nick stood up, his face angry and contorted. "That was uncalled for, Mom. What is it with you? Your brothers just died, and you're fighting over their farm. It's obscene."

"Let's go, Nick," Emmie said, tugging at his arm.

And then it was just Nealy and Hatch.

"The farm should have come to me. My mother is buried here. How could they do that to me? My own brothers. Damn them. I fought tooth and nail to make sure they got to keep this place, and this is the thanks I get. Damn them." She banged on the table with both fists to make her point.

"There's nothing you can do about it, Nealy. A will is a will. Don't even think about contesting it. Everything here will run smoothly. Mr. Clymen said he would take care of things until he heard otherwise. It's time for us to go home."

"This was my home for a long time. As hard as I try not to think about this place, I still do. It's so strange. Okay, I'm ready to go back to . . . to . . . Blue Diamond Farms, Hatch."

PART III

12

Nealy moved cautiously in the bed so as not to wake Hatch. If she'd gotten five minutes of sleep, it was a lot. She was so wide-awake she felt like her eyeballs were standing at attention. She looked over at Hatch, who was sleeping peacefully. She used to sleep like that. After a hard day's work, a good dinner, and a warm bath, she'd always slept like a baby. She couldn't recall when she'd last slept well. Probably sometime before the fire that had destroyed all the barns and left her scarred for life.

Satisfied that Hatch wouldn't wake, she crept from the bed and slipped into her robe and slippers. She headed for the kitchen and the coffeepot. While the coffee dripped, she munched on a granola bar.

The clock on the Capriccio coffeemaker said it was 3:47, almost time for the farm to come to life. When it came right down to it, that's when she came to life, too. Not so of late. She couldn't help but wonder why her life was going through such drastic changes. Was it because she was getting older, and it was the natural course of events? Or, was it something else? If it was something else, how did one go about finding out what that something was?

Nealy poured coffee into her cup and carried it out to the front porch. She was glad she had put on her cozy, warm robe. At best, it was probably fifty degrees. She sat down on the old rocker and tucked her legs under her. Above, the stars twinkled in the dark sky. Soon, though, it would be dawn.

The headlights were bright, round yellow orbs. Emmie reporting for work? Something tugged at her heart. In the time it took for her heart to beat twice, she knew what she was feeling. Jealousy. Of her daughter. She shook her head to clear away the horrible thought, but it wouldn't go away. Jealousy.

Hatch had hinted at it but had never actually came out and said the ugly word.

You were so busy trying to prove you could take care of me you forgot to love me along the way. Nick feels the same way I do.

Impossible. She did love her children. She did.

Did you ever tell your children you loved them? a niggling voice inquired.

Of course. I'm sure I did. Maybe not in so many words, but they should have known I loved them. I do.

Did you ever say, I love you, Emmie, or I love you, Nick? the niggling voice persisted.

I can't pick a time or a place but I'm sure I did. Of course I did.

When? Under what circumstances? When they were babies and didn't know what you were saying? When they were little and brought home good papers from school? When they were teenagers? When Emmie got married? Give me a time, a date, a place when those words passed your lips.

Right now I can't think of a specific time. I know I did, though.

How do you know?

I know because when they would tell me they loved me, I would have said the same thing back to them. So there.

No. No. You always said, I know you do. You never said the words. Not to them. They never heard you tell them you loved them.

No, that's not true. I know I said the words. I just can't remember when I said them. I was a good mother. I love my children. Every mother loves her children.

That's a lie. The only person you actually love is yourself, Nealy Coleman Diamond Clay Littletree. After loving yourself, you love the horses. Then maybe your children and your husband after that. You aren't capable of showing love. You fake it real well, but it isn't real. I know you, Nealy. I'm your conscience, so I know what's real and what isn't. You're going to end up a bitter, lonely old woman. Hatch won't put up with this bullshit forever. He wants a family because he knows how to love and he knows what a family is all about.

Nealy leaned back in the chair and closed her eyes . . .

On her way through the kitchen to the back staircase that led to the second floor, Nealy stopped when she heard her name mentioned. Thinking either Maud or Jess had called her, she walked across the kitchen to the small hallway leading into the dining room. Maud and Jess never used the dining room. The rare exceptions were Thanksgiving and Christmas. From time to time, if Maud had what she called monster paperwork, she would spread all her papers out, spit on the end of her pencil, bend her head, and do her paperwork, something she absolutely detested. Jess hated it even more, so they both let it pile up till they couldn't see each other across the table, at which point they would then do what they had to do.

She was about to call out when she heard her name mentioned again. They were talking about her, they weren't calling her. She leaned against the wall in the skinny hallway and listened.

"I love that girl, Jess, I really do. Since Nealy came here with Emmie, everything has changed. I've never seen a girl work so hard in my life and she's a little slip of a thing. She puts some of the men to shame. She never complains. Never. I think she's gotten real fond of both of us, but you'd never know it by the way she acts. It's like she's afraid to show what she feels. I'm thinking wherever she came from, affection wasn't the order of the day."

"I think you're right, Maud. The little one is different. She loves to be hugged and smooched, and she gives it right back. She's starved for love. I hate saying that, but it's a pure fact. You know it, too, Maud."

"I do, Jess, and it worries me. That little girl has enough to bear without thinking her mama doesn't love her. I'm sure Nealy does love her, but for some reason she's afraid to show it. She's good to her, that's for sure. She makes sure she eats well, gives the child her bath, makes sure her clothes are clean and pressed. You know what, Jess, it has to be hard talking to a child with your fingers all the time. She's never short-tempered with her, just weary and tired."

"What's going to happen to that child when she grows to womanhood, Maud?" Jess asked. "The outside world isn't kind to people with disabilities. Do you think after we're gone, Nealy will want her here to keep her safe from that outside world, or will she send her to one of those special schools? One of those places where you live there on the premises and only come home for holidays and such."

"I think she'll keep Emmie here, Jess. I don't think she would send her away. Nealy feels safe here. If she feels safe, her daughter is safe, too. She never wants to go to town, to a movie or to the Chinese restaurant. If she wants something, she just marks it on the chalkboard and counts out her money to pay for it. I think we both understand that she ran away from a bad situation and is afraid she'll be found. She's happy here, Jess. We're happier than we've ever been ourselves since they got here."

"Then I say we add Emmie's name to the will. Half to Nealy and the other half to Emmie. That way we'll be sure the child is taken care of and kept safe. We'll add a clause to the will that says Emmie is to live here until she reaches her maturity."

"I'm glad you said that, Jess. That's the way we'll do it. No need to tell Nealy. She might fuss up a bit."

"You're sure then that she loves the little tyke?" Jess said.

"Damn it, Jess, no, I'm not sure. I'm hoping she does. Just because she doesn't go around saying, 'I love you, I love you,' doesn't mean she doesn't. Nealy isn't all that verbal about her feelings. Sometimes she can be downright cold. Then there's the guilt attached to the little one. I don't know if that will ever go away. Add on the fact that she can't talk. Double guilt.

"What we'll do from here on in, Jess, is this. We will shower that little girl with love and affection. We'll tell her a hundred times a day how much we love her because we do, and it will come easy to both of us. We'll make sure she's taken care of for the rest of her life. Nealy will be okay because she's tough and resilient. I feel better now, Jess. Isn't it time for some *tea?*"

Maud's version of tea was a triple shot of Wild Turkey bourbon with an ounce of Lipton tea.

Nealy scurried across the kitchen and fled up the carpeted stairway to the second floor, where she collapsed on a stuffed ottoman next to a little table in the hallway. Her breathing was hard and ragged. Her face felt so hot, she thought she was going to burst into flames any second.

They loved Emmie more than they loved her. They appreciated how hard she worked, but they worried about her loving Emmie. They were going to make sure that Emmie was always kept safe from the wicked outside world. They loved her more. Well, she was never going to think about *that* again. Never, ever . . .

. . . Nealy woke with a start. She knuckled her eyes. She must have cried in her sleep. She looked around, aware that it would be light soon. Another new day. Maud always said a new day was whatever you made of it. You could waste it, or you could use it. She always used her days to the fullest, most times to the exclusion of all else that was personal.

Now she had to think about *that*.

In the kitchen she refilled her coffee cup and poured a cup for Hatch that she carried upstairs. "Brought you some coffee, honey!"

"Great. What brings you up here? Whoa, you're still wearing your robe. Is today a holiday or something?"

"I couldn't sleep so I went downstairs, made some coffee and sat on the porch, where I fell asleep. I just woke up. You know what, no one is missing me. Everything seems to be working. Oops, I spoke too quick. The phone's ringing. I'll get it. I'd kiss you good morning, but I don't want to get shaving cream all over my face."

"Hello, this is Nealy."

"I'd like to speak to Hatch please. This is Cal."

"It's for you, Hatch. He said his name is Cal."

Hatch wiped his face, rinsed his razor, and reached for the phone all at the same time.

"What's up, Cal?"

"Mr. Zack Leroy applied for a passport yesterday and booked an overseas flight to Singapore. They're rushing his passport through. This is a man who has never been out of the state of Nevada, and, as near as I can figure, the farthest he's ever gone is Reno. He made arrangements to take his dog, too. Bought him a seat and everything. First-class. Said he was legally blind, had the papers to prove it, and said he needed the dog with him at all times. He conveniently forgot to mention his cataract operation. It's one way of avoiding the cargo hold for the dog and I, for one, would *never* ship my dog in cargo even on a short flight. I'm thinking Miz Willow Bishop got hold of him and arranged this trip. What do you want me to do, Hatch?"

"When does he leave?"

"Tomorrow at noon."

Hatch's brain raced. "This is what I want you to do. Call Spence Wakley. Tell him I want him on the same flight as Mr. Leroy. I can't go since he might recognize me. There's every chance he might remember seeing you around, too, since you've been shadowing him. Then book two tickets on the next flight for you and me. Tell Spence not to lose Leroy. Make arrangements for us to meet up when we get there. I'll fly to Vegas this afternoon, hook up with you this evening at some point. I'll alert the authorities and, who knows, maybe they'll deputize me."

"You know, Hatch, there's a rumor here in town that someone is passing out free money. All good, worthy causes. Bundles of money to churches, the homeless shelters, hospitals, all kinds of places. The animal shelter out in the desert said they got a couple of million dollars. I just thought I'd mention it. The *really* funny thing is, all those lucky recipients were visited by Zack Leroy. He went to the animal shelter and donated fifty dollars. He wrote out a check. He sure goes to church a lot. One church after the other. All the churches he visited got money for additions, new roofs, new furnaces, and money to help their poor parishioners. Those soup kitchens . . . they're serving steak and roast beef, turkey, shrimp, and lobster. Mr. Leroy donated ten-dollar checks to each one he visited. My mind is always working three steps ahead of everyone else. I'm not saying it means anything. Maybe yes, maybe no. It sure is strange, though. I'll call Spence and get right on those tickets. See you tonight. You're staying at Babylon, right?"

"Yeah. I'll meet you at some point in the Harem Bar."

Hatch turned to Nealy when he hung up the phone. "I'm going to Singapore. I think we have a real hot lead on Willow Bishop. You don't mind, do you, Nealy?"

"No. It's okay. Is this *ever* going to be over?"

"Your guess is as good as mine. All I know is my client skipped out on me not once but twice. That doesn't look good for any lawyer no matter how good he is. She's as wily as a fox. I feel sorry for that old guy if he aided and abetted her. Why do people always think they're above the law?"

"Isn't it human nature to think you're smarter than the other guy?" Nealy asked. "I hope you find her and bring her back so Nick can lay it all to rest. If she's out there, living the good life, she'll always be in his thoughts. It will never end for him. He needs closure. Either she did it or she didn't. A court will decide that."

"Spoken like a true mother." Hatch grinned.

His words so pleased Nealy she reached up and kissed him.

"Now, now, none of that. That leads to other things, and I have to head for the airport." Nealy wiggled her butt as she sashayed over to the shower. Hatch groaned.

Nealy argued with herself all the way into town. *Do I really want to do this? No. Should I do it? Yes. Why? Because it's time to deal with that. In fact, it's way past time to deal with that.*

She'd searched the Yellow Pages after Hatch left for the airport and called three different psychiatrists. She asked for an appointment and was told there had been a cancellation and she could be seen at 1:30, the first appointment of the afternoon. She'd agreed.

It was a medical building in the heart of town. It looked like any other building that housed insurance companies, stockbrokers, or travel agencies. Dr. Elizabeth Shay's office was on the fourth floor.

Nealy climbed out of the car and walked across the parking lot to the front entrance of the building. Inside, she walked to the elevator and stopped, turned around, and walked back to the front door, where she stopped again. She took a deep breath and retraced her steps to the elevator. She pressed the UP button and gulped air again just as the elevator door slid open. Her shaky index finger jabbed at the number 4.

It was a quiet floor. Since she was ten minutes early, she walked down the hall looking at the names on the different office suites. Dr. Leland McEvoy and underneath, Urologist. Farther down was Dr. Anthony Bella, an obstetrician. Across from Dr. Bella was Dr. Nolan Prentice who was an ENT and an audiologist. At the opposite end of the hallway there were only two suites, Dr. Elizabeth Shay and Dr. Monica Lupinsky who was a dermatologist.

A tiny bell, barely audible, could be heard when she opened

the door. The waiting room was small but cozy and warm. Current magazines lay on the table along with a bowl of colorful hard candies. A luscious orchid plant rested in one corner. The paintings were subdued watercolors. A meadow full of daisies, a beach scene with tranquil water lapping at the shoreline, and a third painting of an apple tree loaded with bright red apples. The apples looked so real she wanted to reach up and pick one. Instead she sat down and waited.

A young woman appeared quietly with a clipboard. "Fill out both forms, and I'll need your insurance card to photocopy." Nealy complied and waited.

Ten minutes later the door opened, and the woman said, "Dr. Shay will see you now, Mrs. Littletree."

She'd been hoping for an older woman, a more motherly looking person. This fashionable woman, who was half her age, surely wouldn't be able to help her. She looked so chic, just like her fast-track attorney, Clementine Fox, with her designer suits and pricey high-end shoes. "You're so young," she blurted. Elizabeth Shay smiled, and it was suddenly all right.

"I'm Liz and you're Nealy. Is that all right with you?" Nealy nodded. "Now tell me why you're here."

Nealy looked down at her hands. "Because . . . of jealousy, fear, a dream, my daughter, my husband, the horses, and, of course, guilt. So much guilt."

"Where would you like to start, Nealy?"

Nealy smiled. "I guess the beginning is as good a place as any. I hope you have a lot of time."

"I have all the time in the world, Nealy. You were born. Then what happened?"

When Nealy walked out of the psychiatrist's office fifty minutes later she didn't know if she felt better or worse. Her throat felt scratchy from talking so much, and her eyes itched. She wanted to cry, but she fought the hot, threatening tears that were forming in her eyes. This was not going to be easy, that much she now knew. Well, if Emmie could bare her soul to a shrink, how could she do less?

The late-afternoon sunshine cast a glare on the beige console of her car, causing it to reflect on the windshield. She continued to sit, staring out the window. Why wasn't she starting up the car? Why wasn't she heading back to Blue Diamond Farms? *Because I don't want to go there now. I don't know why I don't want to go there. I just don't.* What should she do? Where should she go? Should she just sit and think about the past fifty minutes? She could do that back at the farm on the front porch. Or upstairs in the room she shared with Hatch.

What was it Liz Shay had said? "Don't expect me to give you answers. You're going to have to work to find those answers, Nealy. I'll guide you, that's my job. Your job is to be truthful and honest and delve into the past that you buried so deep you're going to need several shovels to unearth it all. I'll be with you every step of the way, but you're the one who is going to do all the work. We're going to start this very afternoon. Can you commit to this?" Of course she had said yes.

But did she really want to do it? Or did she *need* to do it? Maybe what she really needed to do was to go shopping. Women always went shopping when things overwhelmed them. If they didn't shop, then they drank tea. Maybe she could buy something and stop for a cup of tea. It sounded like a half-baked plan, but it was the best she could come up with at the moment. She put the car in gear, looked to the right and the left before she pulled out onto the highway. She drove several blocks before she found a parking spot.

The clock on Guerrin's Pharmacy said it was 4:59. The stores would be closed in an hour. Shopping in a drugstore was just as good as shopping in a department store. You could buy suitcases, cameras, and toilet paper in a drugstore these days. Hatch needed shaving cream and deodorant. She could use a new hairbrush. Toothpaste was always a good thing to buy in a drugstore. Shampoo was something else she could stock up on.

She was pleased to see the long soda counter where hot dogs, sandwiches, and coffee were sold. A sign said they sold nine different kinds of ice cream. The big question was, did they sell tea? One-stop shopping. Tea with lemon or milk? It seemed at the moment like a horrific decision.

Forty-seven dollars later, Nealy carried her shopping bag to the counter and sat down. A perky youngster in a yellow tee shirt and cut-off shorts bounced up to the counter. "Can I help you, ma'am?"

Ma'am. People used to call Maud Diamond ma'am. Ma'am meant you were old.

"Yes. I'd like a cup of tea."

"Lemon or milk?"

Here it was, the big question she'd been dreading. She eyed the three sugar donuts under a glass dome. "Plain. Three sugars." Ah, the world was looking brighter.

She felt a presence and looked up. "Nealy. You're the last person I expected to see in here. I know you don't want me to sit down next to you, but I'm going to sit down anyway. We need to talk, and this is as good a place as any. I was on my way out to the farm to pick up Emmie when I saw you come in here. It's a good thing, because Gabby needs some more Mister Bubble."

Dillon Roland sat down next to her. He placed the package with the Mister Bubble on the counter in front of him.

Nealy swiveled on the stool to stare into the man's eyes. The man she hated with every fiber in her body. "You're the last person on this earth I want to sit next to, Dillon. You aren't spying on me, are you?"

"No, I'm not spying on you, and I know I'm the last person in the world you want to sit next to. I've wanted to talk to you for years, really talk to you. That time you came to my office you were loaded for bear. It wasn't the time then because I was still doing all the things my father demanded of me. Just hear me out, Nealy, and I'll never subject you to my presence again. Just hear me out. Ten minutes. Eight if I talk fast. Surely you can give me eight minutes of your valuable time."

Nealy eyed the huge clock over the back of the counter. She could see powdered sugar on the oak frame. *The girls must dust the donuts under the clock,* she thought. "Okay, Dillon, eight minutes." She pointed to the clock. Dillon nodded.

"Let's get right to it. I can never excuse what I did or said way back then. Look, I was just a young kid of seventeen just like you were. I had a father that was demanding just the way yours was. The truth is, I think he was worse. I loved you back then, Nealy. You were the sunshine in my life. Those poems I wrote to you were from my heart to your heart. Back then I didn't know what to do. Call me gutless, a coward, whatever you want. I won't deny it. I was all those things and maybe more. I didn't think about you, what it was like for you. My mind couldn't accept it. I just thought about myself and what my father would do." He paused and checked the clock. "I never once measured up in his eyes. God knows I tried and tried. Jesus, my life was hell, and so was yours. Don't you remember how we told each other all our secrets and how being together for those little bits of time made it all better? At least for a little while.

"Some small part of me, the decent part, wants to believe I would have done something for you at some point in time. I thought about you all the time, day and night, wondering how you were, what you were doing. That shotgun business, that was bravado. Hell, we didn't even own a shotgun. I know it was worse for you. Much worse. If there was a way to unring the bell, I would.

"I finished school and got married to someone my father approved of. She came from an incredibly wealthy family. My father adored money. Actually, the man worshiped it. It wasn't a happy marriage. I had many affairs over the years. So did my wife. After our sons were born, we lived separate lives. I know now that I was looking for you in every woman I met. No, no, don't say anything. My children are worthless human beings. It pains me to say this, but it's true. My wife spoiled them and so did my father. None of them has worked a day in his life, and I don't expect that will ever change. They never call, and I never see them. Their trust funds will outlive them.

"When Emmie called me that night it was like my whole world turned around. I love her, Nealy. You did a good job raising her. She and Gabby are the sunshine in my life these days. I don't ever want to lose that. They're the reason I want to get up in the morning. No, I don't want your horses. I don't want anything from you. I never wanted one of your horses for myself. I wanted one for my father. Back then, I was still seeking his approval. When I finally realized I would never get it, I quit trying. I did love you, Nealy, with all my heart. If I close my eyes, even now, after all these years, I can still remember how you smelled, how you laughed, how good you felt in my arms, how your eyes would shine when I read one of my poems to you. At night I would lie awake in bed and ache for you. Then I'd get up and write a poem for you. Look," he said, pulling a tattered notebook out of his inside breast pocket. "I kept this in my car for years and years and never took it out until Emmie came into my life. When I saw you come in here, I went back to the car to get it. The dates are on the poems. I'm giving this to you so you can understand me a little better. I waited a long time to say these things to you. My shoulders feel better already.

"People can and do change. I know I have. Have a nice evening, Nealy. I have to get back so Gabby can have her Mister Bubble bath. Thanks for letting me talk to you like this. I won't bother you again."

Nealy watched him walk away. She looked up at the clock, but she couldn't remember what time it had been when Dillon sat down. Her teacup was empty, her shopping bag on the stool next to her. She sighed, then reached for the notebook Dillon had left on the counter and stuffed it in her purse.

Her head high, her eyes burning, Nealy left the drugstore that smelled of licorice and talcum powder and walked to her car.

"Hi, Dad, I'm home! Gabby! Where are you guys?" Emmie called out.

"I'm getting Gabby ready for bed, Emmie," her father called down from the top of the steps. "I picked up dinner from Chow Li's. It's in the warming oven. Gabby ate a little while ago."

"Okay, I'll set the table and then I'll be right up." Emmie smiled as she went about setting the table for two. When she finished, she took the steps two at a time and swooped down on her daughter to roughhouse for a few minutes. "Love you, love you, love you," she said, burying her face in Gabby's neck. The little girl giggled. "Okay, two pages of *Puff the Magic Dragon,* and then it's time for sleep."

"Three pages, Mommy. Please read three pages."

"Okay, but only because I love you." She winked at her father, who knew full well the little girl would be sound asleep by the end of page one. Cookie was already asleep at the foot of the bed.

"Are you ready, Gabby?"

"Yes, yes, yes, I'm ready."

"Close your eyes and here we go. Page one of *Puff the Magic Dragon . . .*"

An hour later, Emmie pushed back her chair. "I have a nice ripe melon, Dad, would you like some?"

"Sounds good. I'll pour the coffee. By the way I met your mother in town today, at the drugstore. We talked for a little while. That's not quite true, I talked, but she did listen. I feel like a load of bricks has been taken off my shoulders. I could be wrong, but I think your mother might be feeling the same way."

Emmie sliced the melon and cut the rind off. She lined the crescent moon slices on a bed of lettuce before she carried it to the table. "Was she her naturally ornery self or was she civil to you?"

"No, she wasn't ornery. Distant maybe. Maybe she was in shock that I actually sat down next to her. She said she would listen for eight minutes. I talked real fast, then I left. I'm just sorry it took me so long to talk to her. I wish I could have done it years ago. Perhaps if I had, things would be different. The next move, if there is a next move, is up to your mother."

"Then don't hold your breath. She won't make a move. She trenches in and burrows. I'm glad you feel better, though. Thanks for picking up the Mister Bubble.

"How did your day go, honey?"

"Great. Just great. I was actually able to get close to Gadfly. He didn't do a thing. I almost ruined that magnificent animal. Lee is wonderful with him. Mom was right about him getting to know the horse. Those two horses are so evenly matched it's uncanny. Jake is such a help. One of these days he is going to be a really good jockey. I think, and this is just my opinion, he's still a little afraid. He does love Hifly, though."

"What about you, aren't you a little afraid?"

His voice sounds so anxious, Emmie thought. "No. Dad, I've been riding all my life. I used to race out of the gate with Mom. I know what it's like. I don't care if I come in last. From the day I bought Hifly, it was my intention to run him in the Derby if he was good enough. He's good enough. I might not be good enough, but he sure is. I'm in good shape, all the doctors say so.

My weight is perfect. I feel positive and confident. What was Mom doing in town? She never goes to town. She left the barn around noon and didn't come back."

"I don't know. She had a shopping bag, and she was dressed up. Maybe she had some business to take care of. Her Derby Ball is coming up next month. It was none of my business, and it isn't your business, either, young lady."

"At forty you're still calling me a young lady. I like it. It's your turn to do the dishes. You know, Dad, we should start thinking about getting a housekeeper."

"I'm looking into it, honey. They aren't that easy to come by. In the meantime, we can manage. Since it's my turn to clean up, what are you going to do? Don't tell me you're going to watch me."

"Nope, I'm not going to watch you. I'm going to e-mail Buddy and tell him about Gabby. I'm ready to do it now. It took me about sixty phone calls to locate Buddy, but I finally found someone who not only knew him but also knew his e-mail address. I have his address and phone number, too. Even though he can't hear, he has the latest in high-tech phone equipment. I just thought I would do the e-mail."

"I'm proud of you, Emmie. Whatever his response turns out to be, you will want to print it out and save it for Gabby. Buddy could well turn out to be a wonderful father. It's the right thing to do, honey."

"Then I'm going to do it. Make sure you turn the dishwasher on. You load it, put the soap in, and forget to turn it on."

"Nag, nag, nag." Dillon grinned. "Call me if you need me."

Emmie walked into the room that had once been a downstairs bedroom. Now it was her father's study although he had yet to unpack the many boxes he'd had shipped from his own house in Virginia. The computer, however, was hooked up and waiting to be turned on.

Emmie flicked the switch and waited for it to boot up. She clicked on AOL and waited a moment. When she heard the words, "You've got mail," she smiled the way she always did. Nick was the only one who ever e-mailed her. She'd check it later. Now, she had a letter to write. Her fingers flew over the keys.

Dear Buddy,

    This is Emmie. I'm back at Blue Diamond Farms. I have some-thing important to tell you. I thought about trying to locate you and visiting you in person, but I thought you might not like me showing up on your doorstep. I opted for the e-mail so you can read it and Instant Message me, or respond by e-mail or regular mail.
    We have a daughter. I call her Gabby and I gave her my last name. I didn't tell you about her because I thought you wouldn't be interested. My thinking was, if you didn't want me, surely you wouldn't want our daughter. Everyone in my life tried to talk me into telling you, but I adamantly refused.
    I don't want anything from you, Buddy. I just want you to know you have a daughter. Two years ago I was diagnosed with severe rheumatoid arthritis and had to go to a rehab center for treatment. Part of the treatment had to be psychiatric therapy. If I am to move forward in my life, I need to clear away all the cobwebs and all the dark secrets. Hence, this letter.
    Attached to this e-mail is a picture of Gabby. She's on her pony Tick-Tock holding her dog Cookie. I think she looks a little like you around the eyes.
    I hope you're well and happy, Buddy. I am. In fact, I'm going to be riding my horse in the Kentucky Derby this year.
    Please respond when you have the time.

All best wishes,
Emmie Coleman

Before she sent off the e-mail, Emmie saved it to a file folder. The moment she was sure it was safe in her personal file, she clicked the SEND button.

While she waited to see if there was a response, she checked Nick's e-mail that was full of silly jokes, the kind that made her laugh out loud.

Her father appeared in the doorway. "Did you send it off, honey?"

"Yes. I'm waiting to see if there's a response. He might not be on-line this evening. Buddy is real good about ignoring things he doesn't want to deal with. In that respect he's kind of like Mom. In my opinion," Emmie added hastily.

"Are you just going to sit here and wait?"

"No. I was just about to go on the porch and jump in the hot tub. If an e-mail comes through, call me. You can have your study back now. By the way, I printed out Nick's latest jokes. They're worth reading today. See ya."

Dillon read through the jokes and burst out laughing. He was still smiling when he pulled out his checkbook to pay some bills. He kept one eye on the computer screen. An hour later, he closed the checkbook and walked out to the kitchen. If Emmie wanted to turn off the computer, she was the one to do it. Hope would always spring eternal where his daughter and Buddy were concerned. There was no doubt in his mind that Emmie still had a soft spot in her heart for her former husband. Just the way he would always have a soft spot in his heart for her mother.

Always.

13

 ৵

Hatch looked around at the lush surroundings. Willow certainly knew how to go first-class. The villa was exquisite, with its own swimming pool and closed-in walls. Walls that would provide safety for the young woman bent on eluding the law. Behind those walls were Zack Leroy and his dog Stella. He looked now at his two companions, Cal and Spence. "Look, my ass is dragging, and I know yours is, too, Cal. So, Spence, you're on guard duty until we catch up with our jet lag by getting some sleep. We're two villas down from this one. Stay alert and call if anything out of the ordinary happens."

"Will do, Hatch," the investigator said, sitting down at a round table where a drink waited for him. "Pricey digs, counselor. People like me only get to dream about places like this," he said, waving his arm to indicate the lavish villa and exquisite landscaping. "Take all the time you need. I can occupy myself for hours." The latest *New York Times* best-seller rested on the table, along with a camera that had a zoom lens attached.

Hatch squinted behind his sunglasses. Spence was far enough away so as not to attract attention, yet close enough to see into the villa if he wanted to use the binoculars resting next to the camera. Willow and Zack were in good hands. He trudged off, Cal in his wake.

Six hours later, Hatch and Cal relieved Spence. "Anything happen?"

"Nope. They're both inside. Willow went for a swim a little while ago. Great body by the way. The old geezer sat under the umbrella with his dog. He's got some real bony knees and a bathing suit that will give you eyestrain. The dog took a dip in the pool. Lots of everyday conversation. They fed the dog and had a garden salad and some crackers for a late lunch. Oh, yeah, they also had iced tea. She read the newspaper to the old guy. He soaked it all up." He pointed to a gadget hanging around his neck. It looked like a small camera but was really a high-tech listening device. A set of earphones dangled from the pocket of his flowered shirt.

"They're dining in this evening. I think the old guy might be tired. They're having rack of lamb, mint jelly, those little red potatoes with some kind of herbs, salad, and a mango sherbet for dessert. The old guy wanted bread with lots of butter and wanted to know if there would be gravy to soak it in. Willow said yes. The dog is getting a steak. You might want to move a little closer now that it's dusk. Don't worry, they can't see you. I'll be back in the morning."

"I feel like a butter-and-egg man," Hatch said sitting down and lighting up a cigar. He sniffed the air. It was so fragrant he immediately thought about Nealy.

"When are you going to pick her up?" Cal asked. He hitched up his walking shorts before he sat down. "Good thing we pulled the night shift. I can't take the sun. I don't think there's such a thing as a moon burn, is there?"

"We pick her up as soon as the locals say it's okay. She's slick, so we have to make sure we cover all the bases. I hate involving the old man, but if he helped her out, he's in trouble."

"You could look the other way, Hatch. I'm sure as hell not going to say anything. You didn't even mention him to the cops, so they aren't on to him. I say let him alone if my vote counts. About that moon burn," Cal said, looking upward.

"No, you can't get a moon burn. We'll play it by ear. He reminds me of some of the elders back on the reservation. The law says . . ."

"Screw the law, Hatch. He's an old man. How many years can he have left? He's got his dog, and he's here in this lush paradise. The girl is probably like a daughter to him. So he helped her, so what? Old people like to help out. It makes them feel needed. If you turn him in, he gets separated from the dog, and he loves that dog. The dog loves him."

"All right, all right," Hatch said, mopping at his brow.

Before he attached the earphones, Cal asked, "Did you find out about the extradition?"

"Hell, no, I didn't. She isn't going to squawk to the law. What are they talking about?"

"Food. She's telling him some of the fancy dishes she's prepared at places where she worked. He's telling her how to make hush puppies that aren't like sinkers." He shrugged.

Hatch stretched out his long legs, the binoculars in his hands. He thought about Nealy and wondered what was going on back in Kentucky. Nick had a date with a new paralegal the firm had just hired. Her name was Annabel Lee, and she was a petite blonde with a mind like a steel trap. She had an infectious sense of humor and Medusa adored her. Within hours of hiring the young woman, Medusa had introduced her to Nick and arranged a date for the two of them. Medusa had said, "This one will give young Nick her heart. She will give him beautiful children and be at his side for all his life." Hatch believed her because she was never wrong. Still, the question remained, would Nick give Annabel Lee his heart or would there always be a part of him that would belong to Willow Bishop, his first love?

Hatch peered through the binoculars. How eerie to be watching someone when that someone didn't know they were being watched. Willow and Zack Leroy were sitting poolside, chatting about the time Zack's dog Stella broke her two front legs and how Zack carried her around until she healed. He continued to listen . . .

"I never had a dog. I always wanted one, though. I travel light, as you know. It wouldn't have been fair to the animal. As long as you let me love Stella, it will be all right. I think she likes me, Zack."

"She does like you, and she don't cotton to most strangers. But she sees I'm okay with you, so that means it's okay with her. When a dog don't like someone, that's when you have to pay attention. Dogs are keen judges of character. Mighty pretty place you set yourself up in, young lady. I've never been anywhere half this grand. We're halfway around the world. Is this where you're going to live for the rest of your life?"

"For now. I think I might like to live in Spain. Put some roots down there and hope for the best. You and Stella are welcome to stay with me forever or for as long as you like. Guess you didn't think I'd be getting in touch with you so quick, huh?"

"I was a tad surprised. How did the visit go with the young man you said you were going to visit?"

"It was okay. It didn't quite go the way I wanted it to. I didn't tell him half the things I wanted to tell him because . . . he hates me. I can't say that I blame him for feeling the way he does. I had some very strange feelings that night. For want of a better word, I'd say they were maternal. He seemed hard and brittle. He was never like that when we were together. He was always kind, considerate, and gentle. Kind of like a lovable puppy you want to take care of. You said he came to visit you with Hatch. What did you think of him, Zack?"

"Nice-looking young man. An angry young man. He has feelings locked in his heart for you. You shoulda cut him loose."

"I tried. Time will take care of everything just the way it will take care of everything back in Vegas."

"Maybe not. If the police don't have any other suspects, and it doesn't appear they do, they aren't going to be looking for anyone but you. I watch those crime shows all the time. Rather I should say, I listened to them when my cataracts were growing, and they always call in Interpol when a murder suspect goes on the run. In real life, I don't know how that works, do you?"

"No, I don't know. No one knows where I am. I managed to get here with a mediocre ID, but I'm going to have to get new identification that will *really* get me anywhere in the world. For the right price, I can get it. These people are masters at forgery."

"What's your plan, honey?" Zack asked. For the life of him he couldn't remember what her new name was, so it was safer to call her honey and let it go at that. "It's nice to be lazy and do nothing for a few days but after that, you got to do something. You can't afford to get careless."

"I know. I'm thinking and planning. Did you make up your mind to stay with me or is this just a visit?"

"I thought I'd stay on a while. My Social Security and pension go straight into the bank by electronic transfer, so other than that, there's no need to rush home. I can live anywhere as long as Stella is with me. I suppose we could do some traveling. I like taking pictures of things, now that I can see pretty good."

"Yes, we could do that. We could go around the world if you

want to. Actually, Zack, we could do whatever you want to do. It will be kind of like a dad and his daughter going on vacation. Just say the word when you're ready, and we can leave."

Hatch rolled his eyes as he looked up at the star-filled night. Willow going around the world was a scary thought. What was even scarier was the thought that the two of them could turn into another Bonnie and Clyde. He continued to listen.

"What I do best is cook. We could go to one of the bazaars tomorrow and pick up some pots. I miss cooking. Would you like to do that, Zack?"

"I'd like to taste your cooking, honey. My wife was a pretty good cook. She won a few blue ribbons in her time. She made the best blackberry cobbler in the state of Nevada. She's the one who taught me how to make *light* hush puppies. Stella here can eat a bushel of them."

"Then that's what we'll do tomorrow. We'll shop, market, and cook. This is turning out to be a very nice vacation. I know it's early, but you look whipped, Zack. If you want to turn in, it's okay. I'm just going to sit out here and think. A kiss on the cheek would be nice. You know, a dad kissing his daughter good night."

Hatch turned off the recording machine. His gut instinct told him Willow was secure for the evening. "Fetch us a beer, Cal. Better yet, get an ice bucket and load it up. I could do with some munchies, too." He repeated what he'd just heard to the investigator.

Cal lumbered to his feet. "Beer and munchies coming up. I wouldn't take my eyes off the chick, Hatch. Things just seem a little too ordinary for me."

"I was thinking the same thing," Hatch said, bringing the binoculars up to his eyes. Willow was still sitting in the same spot. Zack Leroy and his dog Stella were nowhere to be seen.

Hatch accepted the bottle of beer Cal handed him. He eyed the bowl of trail mix and grimaced. He'd been hoping for something a little more authentic and native to the country.

"It's good for you. Consider it roughage. My wife buys this stuff by the sack," Cal said, stuffing a handful into his mouth.

Hatch grimaced again. It was going to be a long night.

*   *   *

Emmie dusted her hands dramatically, her eyes sparkling. She wanted to jump up and down but felt silly doing so. "God, did you see how great he just did? Each day he gets better and better. I feel like I should do cartwheels. Mom looked stunned. Did she look stunned to you, Jake?" she asked. "Look, there she goes, and she's all dressed up. She's left the farm every day at this time all week. Did she say anything to you about where she's going? She doesn't talk to me much, but I know she talks to you and Lee."

Jake blinked at the onslaught of questions. "Hifly did really well today, but then so did Gadfly. They love racing against each other. Go ahead and do a cartwheel if it will make you feel better. Your mother didn't tell me where she was going. She talks to me, but it's always about the horses. Did I cover everything?" he asked anxiously.

Emmie nodded. "Okay, Jake, I'm outta here. I have to pick up Gabby at school. Cool Hifly down and be sure to give him his mint. I'll see you in the morning. If anything comes up you can't handle, call me. I want your promise. You call me, not Mom, if it has to do with Hifly. I want your word, Jake."

"It's not a problem, Emmie. You'll be the first person I call. Have a nice night."

Emmie waved. "You, too. Say good night to Lee for me. Tell him, for whatever it's worth, he's doing great."

She could hardly wait to get home to see if there was an e-mail from Buddy. She felt on top of the world when she blasted through her house an hour later. Gabby had detoured to the backyard where Dillon was getting the barbecue ready to grill chicken and steak for dinner.

Her heart pounded in her chest when she turned on the computer and waited, her foot tapping the floor impatiently. When she heard the familiar words "You've got mail," she grinned. Either Nick was sending her today's joke, or there was mail from her ex-husband. She clicked it on and waited. She knew instantly that BudO was Buddy. She sucked in her breath and held it until she read through the one short paragraph of e-mail.

Hello Emmie. I was surprised to hear from you after such a long time. I read your news with interest. I guess I understand where you're coming from. I wasn't exactly kind when we parted. It just seemed better for me at the time. I'm sorry I didn't consider you or your feelings. I sat up all night reading and rereading your e-mail. It is so hard to believe I'm a father. I won't interfere, so don't worry about that. I would like to see Gabby, though. Will it be all right if I come for the Derby race? I can stay at the Inn so I won't put you out. I don't want to cause chaos where none exists. I can't believe you are going to ride in the Kentucky Derby. Should I bet my poke on you? By the way, I saw the movie they made about your mother. It was closed-captioned for the hearing impaired. I didn't like it. I wasn't sure why I didn't like it at first, and then I realized it was the way they portrayed your mother. Even on the screen she came across as a control freak. I guess that was deliberate. I thought the actress who played your part did a good job. I'll wait to hear from you concerning my visit. I won't make any claims, nor will I try to snatch your daughter away. Notice I said, your daughter. A child belongs with its mother. Even I know that. If you need me to sign anything, I will gladly do so when I get there. Buddy.

Emmie blinked away her tears. She quickly saved the e-mail to her personal files before she printed it out. Then she ran to the backyard and waved the paper under her father's nose. "Quick, tell me what you think." She watched, her heart beating like a trip-hammer, as he scanned the printout of Buddy Owens's e-mail.

"Is it a positive or a negative, Dad?" Out of the corner of her eye Emmie could see Gabby playing with her dolls.

"I think it's more positive than negative, honey. He wants to see Gabby. That's good but in the same breath he's saying he isn't going to invade your world or try to take her away. I think, overall, this is very encouraging. He's willing to sign off on her, and that's what you wanted. It is what you wanted, isn't it, Emmie?"

"Yes. No. I don't know, Dad. I've had nightmares where he would *swoosh* in and scoop her up, take her away, and I'd never see her again. Then another part of me wants Gabby to know her father. On my terms, though. He lives in Ohio, so visitation would be hard if he wanted to go to court to battle it out. I don't think he does. Buddy was never comfortable in what he called my world. I just don't see him being comfortable around Gabby. Children are very demanding. And yet, he's willing to come here and see her. Do you think that's suspect? What if, when he sees her, he changes his mind?"

"That's something you'll have to deal with if and when it happens. You knew that was a possibility once you let him know he had a daughter. I think you can handle it, honey. So can Gabby. I'll be your buffer."

Emmie sat down on the bench by the picnic table. "It's going to rain. Maybe we should cook inside. He's not interested in me. I was sort of hoping he would say something like he missed me or . . . *something*. He could have remarried for all I know. I guess we just have to wait and see. Should I answer this, Dad?"

"I would. Wait till tomorrow or the next day, though, so you don't appear too eager."

"Okay. I'm going up to sit in the hot tub for thirty minutes. I might have overdone it a little today. Can you watch Gabby for me till I get through?"

"Of course. She's going to read to me while this grill heats up. Take your time, honey."

"Make sure you come in if it starts to rain. They predicted heavy spring showers for late today."

"Yes, Mother," Dillon drawled. "Run along and take a good long soak. Here, take your letter with you."

Emmie leaned back to allow the supercharged jets to beat at her tired, aching muscles. She'd held her ex-husband's letter carefully, so it wouldn't get wet. Within five minutes she had it memorized. Was it a good thing or a bad thing? Her heart said one thing, her mind said another. She closed her eyes and re-lived the horrible moment when she'd walked down the gang-plank beside her husband. They'd taken a cruise to try to get their marriage back on track. The moment they stepped onto the asphalt, Buddy turned to her and said, using sign language, that he was leaving her and would file for divorce. She'd cried and pleaded, hung on to him like a petulant child until he shook her off as if she were a mongrel dog. She'd screamed at him, begged him not to leave her. She'd made a fool of herself when she screamed, "I won't talk anymore. I'll promise to sign from now on. I swear I will, Buddy." Of course he couldn't hear her because his back was to her, but all the other disembarking passengers heard. She could still see the pity in their eyes. It had been the worst day of her life.

Even now, just thinking about that hateful day made her burn with shame. She had been such a fool. Hugging her pregnancy to herself, she had raced home and cried for days and days. She felt like crying now, just thinking about it.

Emmie shifted in the tub to allow the jets to pummel her aching lower back. She heard the rain then. She loved spring rainstorms. A fitting end to an almost perfect day. Another five minutes and she could get out and dressed.

Emmie pulled on her sweatpants as she stared out the porch windows. She burst out laughing as she watched her father roll up his pant legs, remove his shoes and socks. He scooped up Gabby and ran around the yard with her on his shoulders. The little girl squealed and shouted to be allowed to run in the rain with her grandfather. He obliged and took off her shoes and socks. Wherever there was a puddle, they stomped through it. Gabby's laughter wafted upward.

Not wanting to miss the fun, Emmie raced down the steps and outside. Arm in arm, they ran around the yard singing, "Rain, rain, don't go away. We want to play in the rain all day."

When the last raindrop fell, they ran through the garage to the kitchen, laughing like lunatics.

"I can't remember when I had so much fun," Dillon said as he brought out towels from the laundry room. Emmie toweled Gabby dry and sent her upstairs. "Put on your white sundress. The one with the yellow flowers on the skirt. Don't forget your sandals. I'll send Cookie up as soon as I dry him off." She watched as chubby legs bounced up the steps. Unwilling to be toweled off, Cookie escaped and bounded up the steps after Gabby.

"I don't think I ever ran around in the rain. It just wasn't something we did on the farm. I did like to sit on the porch and watch the storms, though. I still do. How about you, Dad?" Emmie asked as she towel-dried her hair.

"The only time I ever remember running around in the rain was one summer night a long, long time ago. Your mother and I were in the barn, one of those illicit meetings, and it started to rain. I looked at her and she looked at me and we ran outside. It was dark, so no one saw us. It was hard not to laugh because we were having so much fun. Your mother never had much fun. She had this funny little laugh. I shouldn't be talking about the old days with your mother. It's just this old man's memory. Go upstairs and put on some dry clothes, Emmie. I have some here in the laundry room for myself."

On her way up the kitchen staircase, Emmie smiled when she heard her father say, "Now, that was fun." She continued to smile while she changed her clothes. She was still smiling when she walked down the steps with Gabby and Cookie.

When had she ever been this happy?

Never, that's when.

She thought about her mother. Nealy didn't like driving in the rain. Her fear and dislike of rain stemmed from the night she was forced to leave her home in Virginia, years and years ago.

When the sun came out a few moments later, Emmie heaved a sigh of relief.

"What would you like to talk about today, Nealy?" Liz asked. "Tell me what bothers you the most."

"It all runs together. I guess what bothers me more than anything is the relationship I have with my children. I'm having a hard time talking about my feelings. Guilt is a terrible thing, but then so are jealousy and fear. How can a mother feel guilt, jealousy, and fear when it comes to her children?"

"Let's find out. Let's go back to the night you left your home in Virginia with Emmie in that old truck. Or, would you rather start with Emmie's father and how you felt about him?"

Nealy twisted the wedding ring on her finger. "I was very young and I knew so little about love and relationships. What I did know was when Dillon smiled at me, my whole body just melted. He was so kind and so gentle with me. I think he loved me. At least he said he did. At the time, I believed him because I needed to believe it. He wrote the most beautiful poetry. We would lie in the straw, and he'd read it to me. He'd hold my hand while he was reading to me. Sometimes he would lean over and kiss my cheek or my neck. I lived for those stolen hours late at night. It was all so wonderful until I realized I was pregnant. It took me days to get up the courage to tell him and when I did . . ."

Hatch looked down at his watch to calculate the time difference between Indonesia and Kentucky: eleven hours. It was eight o'clock in the morning here in Bali. Back home, Nealy would still be up. He missed her. It was that simple.

"Anything exciting happen?" Spence asked as he flopped down on the chair Hatch had just vacated. Hatch stared at the investigator, who looked fresh from the shower, a cup of coffee in his hand. He, too, was dressed in walking shorts, white tee shirt, and docksiders. He looked like all the other tourists visiting this colorful country.

"They're going shopping this morning to buy pots and pans. I'm assuming to the nearest bazaar. Then they're going to cook. Willow is a five-star chef. Being on the run the way she has been means she hasn't been cooking much. That's just a guess on my part. I'm going to shower, call my wife, and catch a few hours' sleep. You're the tail since she doesn't know you. Call my villa if anything happens. Anything at all that you think is out of the ordinary. I'm going to call the local authorities to see if I have the go-ahead to take her into custody as soon as I get back to the villa.

"No one is stirring inside or outside, so I guess they're both still sleeping. See you in a little while. She's slick, Spence, so keep your eyes peeled."

"Will do," the investigator said as he rustled the newspaper he'd picked up at the front desk. Hatch waved as he followed Cal down the path to the main lobby, where he also picked up a copy of the previous day's *New York Times*.

Forty minutes later, water dripping from his body, Hatch wrapped a towel around his middle and padded out onto his private walled patio. A silver service of coffee waited for him, along with a plate of sticky rice cakes that dripped honey. He poured with one hand while his other hand worked the phone to place a call to Nealy. He didn't realize how tense he was until he heard her voice. He relaxed immediately.

"Hi, honey, how's it going back home? God, I miss you. Tell me everything that's going on, and then tell me you miss me as much as I miss you." He listened, grinning as Nealy talked to him.

They talked for twenty minutes.

He hated to break the connection but it was imperative he get some much-needed sleep. The jet lag he'd experienced yesterday was still with him to some degree. "Love you," he said happily before he hung up the phone. He walked into the villa to replace the portable phone in the cradle. The sofa beckoned.

His last conscious thought before drifting into sleep on the colorful rattan sofa was that he hoped all would go well with Willow and he could be on a plane headed back home first thing in the morning.

Outside the orchid-lined path that led to Hatch's villa, Willow crouched low among the dense flowering shrubbery. She'd almost had a heart attack when she'd walked into the lobby to get the morning paper. She'd stepped back into a cluster of palms in heavy clay pots the moment she saw Hatch, just in time to avoid being seen. She waited, then followed him to the villa two doors down from her own. Her eyes narrowed to slits as she watched the big man stretch out on the sofa.

Hatch Littletree would not have come halfway around the world alone. That had to mean there were others watching her. They must have followed Zack. Her mind raced as she flew back to her villa, where Zack was pouring coffee into two cups. She put her finger to her lips to indicate silence as she quickly scribbled a note. They conversed for several minutes by writing notes back and forth.

The alarm she saw on Zack's face worried Willow. In the short time she'd known Zack, she'd come to love the old man, whom she thought of as her surrogate father. She wanted no harm to come to him. *I'm going to go with Plan B,* she scribbled. She continued to write. *We're going to take our coffee out to the patio and talk. Just follow my lead and go along with anything I say. You know where to meet up with me at some point. There's someone out there listening and watching. Don't say anything you will regret later. You and Stella are here on a vacation. That's the bottom line.*

Willow's voice was cheerful when she carried the coffee service out to the patio. "Isn't it a glorious day, Zack? The flowers smell heavenly. This is really Paradise as far as I'm concerned. I think we should stay here forever. I'm sorry you aren't feeling well this morning. I bet it was that rich dinner we had last evening. Well, you won't have to worry about that from now on. I'm going to be doing the cooking from here on in as soon as I get some pots and pans. I think I'll leave now before it gets too hot. I want you to sit here in the shade and read the paper. When I get back, you can tell me everything that's in it so I won't have to read it."

"I think you're right. I'm not used to eating lamb. I didn't even like it. Do you think you can make some noodle soup or something light today?"

"Of course. I'll get everything fresh and it will be the best soup you've ever eaten. Stella, watch your master till I get back. Whew, it's already hot. I guess I better wear my straw hat. What do you think, Zack?"

"I think you're right. I might even take a snooze here on the patio with Stella before it gets too hot."

"I won't be long, two hours at the most. If you want anything, just ask the maid to get it for you. I think she just got here. I'll tell her not to bother you. See you in a bit. Be a good girl, Stella," Willow said, bending down to pet the dog.

Inside the villa, Willow motioned for the maid to follow her to the bathroom where she whispered instructions and held out a fistful of money. The maid's head bobbed up and down as she stripped off her uniform to don Willow's flowered muu-muu and straw hat. Willow in turn put on the maid's uniform and tied a white scarf around her head, just the way the maid had worn hers.

In the little foyer off the bathroom, Willow said loudly, "Check on Mr. Leroy but don't disturb him. You can leave the coffee service. I'll be back shortly. Oh, I almost forgot, do you think you can fetch some extra towels? We used them all up this morning. It's so hot here, I like to shower a couple of times a day. We also need more pool towels."

"I'll get them as soon as I finish cleaning the bathroom, Miss," the maid responded.

Willow motioned for the maid to put on her sunglasses and leave.

She waited exactly twenty-five minutes before she left the villa. Her adrenaline pumping at an all-time high, Willow secured the backpack that contained all her worldly possessions underneath a heavy load of towels and walked away. She stopped once to check the milling crowds of tourists as well as her location. She took a full five minutes to mourn the loss of Zack and Stella before she bounced her way along the promenade and a waiting taxi. She slid onto the seat and said, "Take me to the airport, please." She boarded a flight within ten minutes. Her destination: Singapore.

The maid assigned to clean Willow's villa returned shortly before noon, her arms full of pots, pans, and fresh vegetables. She was wearing Willow's flowered dress, sunglasses, and straw hat. She exited the villa one more time to head for the laundry room shortly after the noon hour, where she donned a spare uniform she kept in her locker. The flowered dress, sunglasses, and straw hat were scrunched into her carry bag.

At four o'clock, when Hatch and Cal joined Spence, he could only shrug. "She did what she said she was going to do. She shopped and came back here. I was right behind her all the way. She didn't spot me, so stop worrying. I haven't heard a peep from either one of them since we got back. The old guy went into the house with the dog after the maid left. He hasn't come back out. Said he was going to take a snooze. It's all yours. This heat is a killer. I think I drank a couple of gallons of water today, and now I'm off for a swim."

Hatch looked down at his watch. It was 4:10. He looked at the investigator sitting next to him. "It doesn't feel right, Cal. Spence said no one is talking inside or outside. Doesn't that strike you as peculiar? Shouldn't we be picking up some kitchen noises or the dog's paws slapping on the tile floor?"

"Maybe the old guy is snoozing like he said. Maybe the chick is taking a nap, too. People do that over here. You know, sleep during the hottest part of the day. She'll probably start to cook soon and be banging pots and pans. When did the locals say we can pick her up?"

"First thing in the morning. No, no, something's wrong. What time did the maid leave?"

Cal looked down at the clipboard Spence had handed him before he left. "A little after noon. Why?"

"Bull*shit* she left at noon! C'mon, we're going over there *now*."

"Hatch, wait!"

"She's gone. I feel it in my gut. C'mon, I'll prove it to you."

For a big man, Hatch was light on his feet. He raced through the gardens and up the orchid-lined walkway to Willow's villa. He yanked on the bell that hung outside the door. Zack Leroy marched his way to the door, his dog at his side. He showed no surprise when he said, "Now, aren't you fellas a little far from home? Come in, come in, it's hot out there. Would you like a soft drink or some iced tea?"

"Where the hell is she, Zack? Come on, spit it out or you're looking at serious jail time here in a third-world country," Hatch snarled.

Zack drew himself up to his full height and stared at Hatch. At his feet Stella bared her teeth and growled. "If you mean where is Mazie, she went shopping. Said she'd be back in a couple of hours. I was just starting to worry about her. Oh well, she's a big girl, and I don't think she'll get lost. So, do you want that drink or not?"

"No, I don't want a drink. I want to know where Willow Bishop went and what time she left?"

"Don't know any Willow Bishop. I am just a guest here of Miss Mazie Breckenbridge. I'll be staying here till the end of March. That's all I got to say to you fellas."

Hatch ran his fingers through hair that was soaking wet with perspiration. "Son of a fucking bitch!" he seethed.

Stella clamped her teeth around Hatch's ankle and tugged, knocking him off-balance. He flopped down on a sofa that was identical to the one in his villa. He cursed long and loud, annoying Stella even more. She leaped onto the sofa and sat on the big man's chest, her lips pulled back to show a set of remarkably strong, white teeth.

"Call off this damn dog," Hatch snarled.

"Why should I? You invaded my temporary home. A man has the right to protect his castle. This is my castle for the time being. I'm an old man. For all I know you could be a couple of scam artists, following me around. You did follow me, all the way here from the United States. When I tell the po-lice that, who do you think they're going to believe, me or you?"

"They'll believe me, goddamm it. The police were going to arrest her in the morning, and I was taking her back to the States. Don't go getting cocky on me, old-timer. You're in this up to your neck, Mr. Leroy. Now, call off your dog."

"Don't know what you're talking about. I'd appreciate it if you'd go somewhere else and leave me alone. If you don't leave, I'll call the desk and ask them to call the po-lice. Stella, show the man you like him a lot." He cackled in glee when the big dog slobbered all over Hatch's face before she slid to the floor and waited expectantly for her next order.

"All right, we're going, but we'll be back."

"Won't do you no good. Good-bye."

Outside in the humid air, Cal said, "Tough old bird, isn't he? You aren't going to get one word out of him. I say we pack it in and head back home. It's too damn hot and humid for me in this country. I'll take desert heat anytime." He stopped along the path to pick a pink orchid. He handed it to Hatch, who automatically brought it to his nose. He was surprised to note that the flower didn't give off a scent.

"This is the third time she's gotten away from me. I'm starting to feel like a real loser here."

Cal clapped him on the back. "Don't take it so hard, Hatch. She does this for a living. You can't be expected to think and act like she does. Let's call it a day and head for home, but first we have to decide what we're going to do about Mr. Leroy."

Hatch threw his hands in the air. "We'll just keep quiet about him. He won't tell anyone anything. I saw that in his eyes. Let him live out his days free and clear. He's got his dog, and that's all he needs. Just let me call the authorities and my wife and we can head for the airport. She changed places with the maid. Damn, how did I let that get by me? Why didn't I think of that possibility?"

"Because you're a lawyer, and she's a broad on the run. Look at it this way, she'll be running for the rest of her life and looking over her shoulder at the same time. That's no way to live."

"Maybe you're right. She'll surface again at some point in time. Trust me on that," Hatch said.

"Who cares. Our job is done here. I just want to go home."

"Beautiful word, *home*," Hatch said.

Cal grinned. "None better."

14

Nealy watched the cascade of rain pouring from the roof. She was sitting, yoga fashion, on the front porch, Hatch on the chair next to her. It was late, hours past her usual bedtime. These days sleep was not something she craved or even wanted.

"A penny for your thoughts, honey," Hatch said, firing up a cigar. He blew an aromatic puff of smoke upward.

"I don't think they're worth even that much these days. I never liked rain. Did I ever tell you that?"

Hatch smiled in the darkness. "I suspected it. I'm not crazy about it myself. Too many accidents on the roadways. For some strange reason, people tend to speed up when it rains, and the roads are slick. I could never fathom that. Want to talk about it?"

"Yes and no. I think my brain is on overload. All I do is think and remember. Liz said I should write things down so we can discuss them. Sometimes I do, but for the most part, once I unlock a memory, I remember it. There's no time limit on this therapy. I do better when I know I have X amount of time to complete something. Liz just says it will be as long as it takes. I've been going to her every day, six days a week, for over a month. Right now I don't know where I am except maybe in a muddle. Liz sorts out each session and gives it a summary."

"It sounds to me like you're making progress. Rome wasn't built in a day. You repressed years of things you didn't want to deal with. Try to be patient."

"I do try. Maybe I'm trying too hard. I was hoping to have all this behind me before the Derby. It's less than a month away. Right now I feel like I'm two different people. One is the Nealy who lives and works here, and the other Nealy is someone I'm just meeting, and I don't like her. Yesterday I hated her. I thought I was perfect. I really did think that, Hatch. God, I wasn't even close to perfect. My insides just crumble when I talk to Liz. Sometimes I can't look at her when I'm talking. She said that's normal. I lucked out when I went to her. I don't know if I can handle the day we stack up all those summaries and I have to deal with them."

A thunderbolt boomed in the dark sky, followed by a streak of lightning that was so bright it lit up the night. Nealy shivered as she brought her coffee cup to her lips. She hated cold coffee but was too lazy to go indoors to get a fresh cup.

"You'll handle it, honey. I'm here if you need me."

"Have you heard anything about Willow? You haven't said a word about her since you got back."

"It doesn't pay to dwell on something you have no control over. I imagine one day she'll surface somewhere. In one way I feel sorry for her. I really did believe her when she said she didn't kill Junior Belez. She can't prove it, so she has no control. She doesn't want to go to prison for something she didn't do. She's a tough cookie. What you would call a street kid. She'll survive one way or another. I feel like I failed her. That's never happened to me before. I had her, Nealy. She was just feet away from me, and she got away. That doesn't say much for me. And you're right, I am taking it personally."

"You aren't law enforcement, Hatch, you're a lawyer. You couldn't be expected to act like a cop even though they deputized you before you went over there. I know how you feel though. Is Nick okay with all of it?"

Hatch watched the lightning dance across the sky. He puffed contentedly before he replied. "I'm sucking it all up the way a good lawyer should. Surprising enough, Nick was okay with it. I'm sure there's a small part of him that will never forget his first love, but he's happy now that he has someone else in his life. She's a sweetheart, Nealy. You're going to like her. She's crazy about Nick, and she's one hell of a paralegal. The firm is hoping she'll accept our offer to send her to law school. Then the two of them will have even more in common."

"Do you think Nick will bring her to the Derby?" Nealy asked.

"I think you can almost count on it. Why don't you tell me

what's really bothering you? Maybe between the two of us we can talk it to death."

Nealy leaned back against the porch pillar and hugged her knees to her chest. "When you go into therapy you always have to go back to what you perceive to be the beginning. For me, the beginning was Dillon Roland. I loved him, Hatch. At least as much as a girl can love a boy. Somehow or other I convinced myself he didn't love me, that he just used me and abused me and then let me hang out there to dry. I was wrong about that. He did love me. I blamed him for everything. That seems to be a trait with me, blaming other people for things I did wrong and still do wrong. Liz pointed that out to me, but by day three, I had figured it out myself.

"I spoke to Dillon about a month ago. He saw me going into Guerrin's Pharmacy and followed me. We talked for eight minutes. Eight whole minutes, Hatch. That's all the time I would give him. Just eight minutes for him to tell me about how he felt. He was the beginning and I only gave him eight lousy minutes. He did it, though. He handed me this little notebook with all the poems he wrote for me back then. I cried when I read them. He really did love me. I think he was more scared than I was. I spent so many years hating that man. And now he is the love of my daughter's life. She has what she always wanted, a father. I was so jealous of that, I wanted to kill him for robbing me of Emmie. He gave her what I never could. Love. That girl soaks it up like a sponge.

"I watch her out there every day, Hatch, and I'm jealous. I don't want to be, but I am. She's doing everything I did at her age, and she's doing it because she loves doing it. I did it out of guilt and out of fear. At the end of the day, she looks to Dillon for approval, not me. It's like a stick in the eye when she does that."

"Is she good enough to ride in the Derby, Nealy?"

Nealy smiled. "She's better than good. She bonded with that runt from day one. He is her horse, and together they are one. It was like that with me and Flyby. That horse can run, but then so can Gadfly. It's going to be a once-in-a-lifetime race. I'm rooting for her every step of the way."

"Maybe you should tell her that."

"The time isn't right. I don't want to do or say anything that will upset the current situation. She has Dillon, who will see her through it all."

"Maybe you need to talk to him, too."

"At some point," Nealy said.

The wind kicked up, and a spray of rain ripped across the front porch. Within seconds both Nealy and Hatch were soaked to the skin. "I think we just found a good reason to shed our clothes. What do you think, Hatch?"

"Here on the porch?" Hatch gasped.

"Do you have a better idea? There's a lot to be said for spontaneity." Nealy ripped at her shirt.

Hatch watched his wife. When she started to unhook her bra, he knew she meant business. "Hey, wait for me."

"I'm waiting," she singsonged as she stepped out of her jeans.

Down to his skivvies, Hatch shed them quicker than lightning. "I'm ready," he boomed.

Nealy kicked her panties across the porch. She doubled over laughing when they landed on top of a scarlet geranium. "You better hope that last sentence doesn't draw a crowd!"

"We could go in the house," he said, reaching for her.

"And spoil all this foreplay! No way."

Emmie looked over at Lee Liu and grinned. "Dead even, and it was a wet track! We both picked up a second," she said as she eyed the stopwatch Jake held up for her inspection. "This little boy just loves to run." She leaned over to whisper to Jake, "Did Mom see us?"

"Yeah. She clapped her hands and was smiling. She went up to the house. It's almost four o'clock. See, there she goes. Did you ever find out where she goes every day?"

"Nope. It's her business, not mine. If she wanted me to know, she'd tell me. We're getting along a lot better these past two weeks. She's even been civil to my father, which is a miracle in itself. Okay, I gotta go. You guys are in charge. Call me if you need me. I can be here in fifteen minutes. I don't know if this means anything to you, but I'm proud of you both. I know it would mean more if my mother said it, but she will when the time is right. She's always been stingy with her compliments, so when she does give one, you have to stop and go 'Whoa, did I hear that right?' I didn't get too many growing up, and I know how important it is to hear the words. Sometimes they can make all the difference in the world."

Jake nodded as he led Hifly back to the barn.

Emmie drove home slowly, repeating over and over, *Seventeen days till the Derby, seventeen days till the Derby, seventeen days till the Derby.* She was ready—so ready, she thought she was going to burst wide open with anticipation. And the anticipation had nothing to do with her ex-husband's promised visit on Derby Day. Absolutely nothing.

Just last night, while she and her father were watching television, he'd said, "Emmie, you don't need Buddy's approval. I think that's what you're looking for. Something to validate you, something to say, 'Hey, look what you gave up. I'm going to run the Kentucky Derby. I am worth something, and it's your loss that you didn't see it.' "

Was her father right? Probably. He was right about most things. She didn't love Buddy Owens. Way back when, her mother had told her she loved him. It was always easier to believe her mother than to disagree with her. Did she ever love Buddy? She'd certainly been fond of him because they'd grown up together, but it wasn't the bells-and-whistles kind of love she'd read about in magazines.

Dr. Hunter had said *Look it in the eye and deal with it.* Okay, yes, she wanted to rub Buddy Owens's nose in her accomplishments. No one liked to be rejected. No one. Even her own mother had rejected her to a degree. Well, she wasn't going to think about *that* and spoil what was left of the rest of the day.

There was something she needed to think about, though, and that was the farm her uncles Pyne and Rhy had left to her in their wills. She'd only been there once, but once was enough for her to know she never wanted to go back. SunStar was the root of all her mother's problems—hers, too, but she'd worked through her own problems. The logical thing to do was sell it, lock, stock, and barrel, and put the money into Gabby's trust fund. She'd mentioned it to her father and he'd agreed. The problem was, how was she going to tell her mother. Would her mother even care?

Damn. Where *did* she go every day at four o'clock?

The late-afternoon sunshine filtered through the venetian blinds and danced on the far wall above a tropical fish tank. The psychiatrist settled herself more comfortably and sipped her herbal tea. "We have thirty minutes left, Nealy. Is there anything special you'd like to bring up? Any cobwebs you need to clear away?"

Nealy eyed the fish swimming lazily around the tank, in and out of the evergreen decoration, through a mock tunnel and out the other side and then up to the top. "I think you need a bigger fish tank. It doesn't seem fair to keep them in such a small contained place. Don't they need more room? What kind of life is that?"

Liz eyed the fish tank. "You could be right. I'll look into it. How are things going with Emmie?"

Nealy beamed. "Very well. I never thought . . . never knew . . . she was as good as she is. I didn't know it rubbed off on her. She's got the whole thing down pat. I couldn't find one thing to criticize. Not that I would. No, that's not true, I would have, but I would have been more tactful than I used to be. I hate to say this, but I think she's better than I was."

"Why do you hate to say it?"

Startled, Nealy blinked. "I guess I didn't . . . don't want her to be as good. She didn't work half as hard as I had to. She sailed in and took over. She stared me down and said, 'I'm damn well going to do it.' I worked like a dog, all hours of the day and night. I was always exhausted, but I did it. I trained. She's just . . . doing it. Does that make sense to you?"

"The question is, Nealy, does it make sense to *you?*"

"No. I resent it. She just stepped into it, whereas I had to bust my ass to get where I am, and you're damn right, I resent it. Those horses are mine with the exception of Hifly, who is hers. Blue Diamond Farms is *mine*. I damn well earned it. My whole life is in that farm, and she's entitled to *half*. Half of everything I broke my back to build to what that farm is today. Half. On top of that, she inherits SunStar Farms. It's not fair."

"Why don't you sell your half to her? We already established that your attachment to Blue Diamond is mostly guilt and not love. You could sell out to her and move on."

"That'll be the day! Until just recently, she never showed any real interest in the farm or the horses. She was content to take her dividend checks and blow the rest off. While I worked like a dog to make sure she got those handsome dividend checks."

"Do you think your attitude might have something to do with all of that? Remember, she had and still has a medical condition that was building in her and will be with her for the rest of her life."

"So I wasn't a perfect mother. Who is these days? I made sure my children were well provided for. Maybe I didn't bake cookies, but I always made sure there were cookies to eat. Maybe I didn't take them to church, but I made sure they went to church on Sundays. Even though I didn't do their laundry, it got done, and they had clean clothes, and while someone else cooked the food, it was nourishing. I did make them take their vitamins."

"Did you ever kiss them good night? Did they ever kiss you good night?"

Nealy squirmed in her chair, her eyes on the fish tank. "I'm sure I did when they were little. Nick used to hug me. He was more attached to his father. Emmie always more or less stood on the sidelines. She was shy. Maud and Jess showered her with love and kisses. You can overdo a thing like that."

"Is that when things changed, when Maud and Jess started showering Emmie with love and simply thanking you for all your hard work? When you heard them say they were going to safeguard Emmie's life so that she wouldn't have to go out into the world with her disability?"

"Yes. That's what you want to hear, isn't it? Yes, that's when it all changed. They said I was tough, that I worked like a little man. They said I could take care of myself. Emmie couldn't take care of herself. She had to be provided for. I goddamn well earned that farm. Now, all these years later, I have to keep proving myself. I don't think so! I need a cigarette."

"You said you quit smoking."

"I did quit. I'm starting up again. Are you going to argue with me over that, too?"

"I'm not arguing. I just stated a fact, a fact that you mentioned to me. If you want to smoke, go ahead."

"I don't have any cigarettes."

"Then I guess you aren't going to smoke. Let's get back to Maud and Jess. It was your job to protect Emmie. That was your goal when you left SunStar in the middle of the night with a sick child on your hands. You got yourself pregnant and you had to pay the consequences. What you didn't know was the man you thought was your father threatened that little girl and almost strangled her to keep her quiet. She didn't speak for over thirty years because of that fear. You feel guilt because you didn't know about it. You thought there was something wrong with both of you because your father called Emmie a half-wit. The child's father threatened to blow off your head if you told anyone he was the father. How am I doing so far, Nealy?"

Nealy clenched her teeth, and nodded.

"You thought you failed your child. Your child. Not Dillon Roland's child. Your child. Then you found a haven at Blue Diamond Farms, and you failed again. We talked about this last week in bits and pieces. Now we're putting the flesh on the bones. You let other people take care of Emmie to wash away your guilt and you did that, how, Nealy?"

"By working nonstop from dark to dark."

"Then, after Maud and Jess died, what did you do? How did you replace them?"

Nealy licked at her lips. "With Buddy Owens. He and Emmie were like two peas in a pod. They were inseparable. Then they got married."

"Was it at your urging? Were they in love?"

"I assume they were. They certainly acted like they were in love. I arranged the wedding." Nealy was on her feet a second later, looking out at the busy street below. She could feel herself start to shake and didn't know why. She really needed a cigarette.

"So, once again, you transferred your daughter to someone else. That's what you did, Nealy, you transferred her to some other person. You just handed her over, and that was the end of Emmie. She was taken care of, again, but not by you."

"You make it sound so cold and calculating. It wasn't like that. I wanted her to be happy. I thought she was. No, I didn't ask, if that's your next question. She appeared to be happy. Buddy appeared to be happy. They had their life, and I had mine. I worked. They appeared to work. Neither one of them knew the meaning of *real, hard* work. They wanted to go on vacations, go shopping, eat out four nights a week, and they wanted to go to movies and concerts. Then they wanted to sleep in in the mornings and lollygag around till noon. The farm is operational at four in the morning. We don't shut down for the night till around eight o'clock. Yes, it's a long, hard day, but that's what it's all about."

"Where does that leave us now, Nealy?"

Nealy bit down on her tongue. Say what was in her mind or not say it. "With one spoiled, rotten daughter who doesn't know the meaning of sacrifice, hard work, or the value of money. Yes, she's good with this one horse, but she almost ruined another one. She's not dependable because she never had to be dependable. Someone always looked out for her, someone always made it easy for her. Don't you understand, she owns half the goddamn farm, and she didn't do one damn thing to earn it. My time is up, isn't it?"

"Yes, it is. I want to pose a question to you, Nealy. I want you to think about it this evening, and we'll talk about it tomorrow. This is the question: What is it you really want at this point in time? What is the one thing that will make you truly happy? You have to be honest to a fault. You can't dance around it. I will only accept gut-wrenching honesty from you, and I'll know if you aren't being honest. Is it a deal?"

Nealy thought about the question for a full three minutes before she responded. "Yes, it's a deal."

"Good, I'll see you tomorrow, same time. Have a nice night, Nealy."

"You, too."

Nealy sat in her car for a long time, thinking. She should go home to Hatch, but these sessions always unnerved her. She needed to be alone to think. Maybe thinking was her downfall. Maybe she needed to go with the flow, to not make waves, to simply exist. Then she might as well live in a fish tank, like the fish back in Liz Shay's office.

She turned the key in the ignition and drove out of the parking lot. She drove aimlessly until she realized where she was— Emmie's street.

Nealy stopped the car at the curb and stared at the house she'd picked out for Emmie and Buddy. She'd paid for it, too. Liz would say she'd done it to get rid of her daughter. Was that what she had done? Obviously.

She got out of the car and walked up to the front door. She was about to ring the bell when she heard peals of laughter wafting from the side of the house. They must all be outside. She walked around to the back to see Gabby running through the sprinkler with Cookie on her heels. Dillon had another hose in his hands and was spraying Emmie, who was spraying him with still another hose. They were laughing uproariously until they saw her standing at the edge of the walkway, then they stopped and stared at her. She'd never heard Emmie or Gabby laugh like that. She had, however, heard Dillon laugh the way he'd just been laughing. She wanted to cry.

"Mom!"

"Nealy!"

"Grandma!"

Cookie barked and circled her legs until she bent down to pick him up. He was soaking wet, but it didn't matter. He licked her cheek before he squirmed and wiggled to be put down.

"It's nice to see you, Nealy. Would you like to stay for dinner? It's just weenies and salad," Dillon said, a hopeful look on his face.

Like she was really going to eat at the same table with these three. "Yes, I would. I haven't had a hot dog in years. Can I have the works on mine and the bun toasted?"

"Of course. That's how we do them around here. We use paper plates, is that okay?"

"Sure, paper plates are fine. I meant to call you, Dillon. It's been rather hectic at the farm. I wanted to thank you for the . . . for the . . . notebook. Do you want it back?"

"Not unless you don't want it. Do you remember any of the poems?"

"Every single one except for the later ones. They're all beautiful. Thank you for giving it to me. I don't have any objections to you coming to the farm. I think Emmie wants you there, so feel free to come anytime you want."

"Thanks, I appreciate that. I'll be out tomorrow. Is there one side or the other that I should stand on?"

Nealy shook her head. "That was stupid of me. I suppose I meant it at the time, but I don't mean it now."

"Well, I'll go inside and get our dinner together. I guess you want to talk to Emmie. Come on, sport, let's get you dried off. You too, Cookie," Dillon said, slinging his granddaughter over his shoulder. The little girl giggled all the way into the house.

When the sliding glass door to the patio slid shut, Emmie asked, "Is something wrong, Mom?"

"I suppose there are a lot of things wrong. I see the questions in your eyes when I leave the barn in the afternoon. I'm assuming you're wondering where I go every day at four o'clock. To talk to a therapist. It isn't easy baring one's soul to a stranger."

Emmie blinked at this sudden shared confidence. "It's hard. I've been there. You know what they say, sound body, sound mind. You need both to function in this crazy world we live in."

"I came here to ask you if you would consider selling me SunStar Farms."

"You want that place, Mom?"

"I didn't think I would but, yes, I do want that place. I'll meet your price whatever it is."

"Mom, I'll give it to you. You don't have to buy it from me. I was just thinking about it today and I was going to put it up for sale. If you want it, it's yours."

"No, I don't want you to give it to me. I want to buy it. You were very kind when Josh Coleman died and left it to you. I appreciate you deeding it back to my brothers. It's so strange that twice it was left to you and you don't even want it."

"No, Mom, I don't want it. Make me an offer, and I'll accept it. Do you mind me asking what you're going to do with it? I thought you hated the place and all the bad memories attached to it."

"Things change. People change. Times change. The best answer I can give you right now is I don't want it to go out of the family. It's running fine as it is right now, and I don't have to make any quick decisions. I'll decide later on what I want to do with it. By the way, you did real well today, Emmie. I couldn't have done it better. I think you're going to shine in the Derby."

"Do you really think so, Mom?"

"I really think so. You might not have the touch, but you sure have the feel for it. Yes, I think you're going to do real well. I'm very proud of you."

"Here come the dogs! Emmie likes hers burned to a crisp. Gabby likes hers just barely warm, and Cookie likes them just right and cut into little pieces. I like mine scored and juicy but a little dark. What's your choice, Nealy?" Dillon asked.

"Very well done. Kind of crisp, you know, dark."

"In other words, burned to a crisp. I got it. Like mother like daughter."

Emmie smiled and linked her arm with her mother's. "Yeah, like mother like daughter."

Nealy felt a lump in her throat. *Yes, like mother like daughter.*

Nealy was stunned when she walked into Dr. Liz Shay's office the following day. Directly in her line of vision was the biggest fish tank she'd ever seen. There were two new fish swimming gracefully to and fro.

"I decided you were right yesterday. I did need a bigger tank, so I went right out and got one after my last patient yesterday. They brought it right over and set it up. I call the two new fish Frick and Frack. So far they're getting on well with Yin and Yang." Liz grinned. "How's it going, Nealy? Did you have a good night? Want some herbal tea or maybe some coffee?"

"I'll take the coffee if it isn't too much trouble." She sat down opposite the doctor and waited expectantly.

"You're my last appointment today, so we could have a glass of wine if you like. It's really raining out there, isn't it?"

"It's coming down in buckets. I hate driving in the rain. I'm careful, but I have this fear the other person isn't as careful as I am. I made it here, that's the important thing. No on the wine. Coffee is fine with me."

Liz pressed a button on the phone. "Kelly Ann, please bring Mrs. Littletree some coffee. She likes it black, and I'll have a cup of black currant tea with three sugars." Liz settled herself comfortably in her chair and looked at Nealy. "Let's get to it. Time is money as they say."

Nealy grimaced, her eyes on the fish tank. "You asked me if I had a good night. I did. When I left here I drove over to Emmie's house. I don't know why I went. I was just driving along and found myself there. I think Emmie and Dillon were surprised to see me. They welcomed me. I stayed to have a hot dog with them. Emmie was . . . Emmie. She's incredibly happy. So is her . . . her father. It was all so . . . so normal, so suburban. In some ways I felt like I was seeing a movie from an actor's point of view. I stayed about an hour and a half. I was only at Emmie's house once before. She never invited me when she lived there with Buddy. I always wondered why, but I never asked."

Liz Shay scribbled on her pad. "Didn't you tell me once that you picked out the house and bought it for Emmie? Did you consult her?"

"Yes, I did pick it out, and yes, I paid for it, and no, I didn't consult her. I guess that was the wrong thing to do, too. Maybe that's why she never invited me."

"Do *you* think it was the wrong thing to do?"

"At the time I didn't think so. Now, yes, it was wrong. It was wrong of me to . . . to arrange Emmie's wedding to Buddy. Arranging is one thing, mothers do that when their daughters get married. I . . . what I did . . . said was, it's time for you two to get married. And they did. They were joined at the hip. I thought it would be better if they married instead of just slept together. Emmie could have gotten pregnant, and I didn't want that unless she was married. My own guilt again. Buddy did just what Dillon did, he took off and left Emmie. I was right about him."

"But he didn't know Emmie was pregnant. Dillon knew. There's a difference."

Nealy felt flustered as she stared at the doctor. "Yes, that's true. But he would have bolted anyway, had he known."

"You couldn't possibly know that, Nealy."

"I do know it. I knew it just the way I knew Willow Bishop

was a conniving, manipulative young woman. Neither one of my children could see what was right in front of their eyes, but I saw it. If you had a daughter or son, and they were teetering on a high wire, wouldn't you try to save them from a fall?"

"That's apples and oranges, Nealy."

"All right. I screwed that up, too. Damn it, I was right, though."

Liz Shay stared across at her, pencil poised in midair.

"I should have kept quiet and minded my own business. I just said I screwed up."

"Can you make any of that right?"

Nealy's eyes popped wide. "No. I can't make Buddy come back to Emmie. I don't even know if she wants him. She thought she did at one point. It was my feeling that her pride was hurt when he rejected her."

"The way Dillon Roland rejected you. You felt validated when that happened, didn't you?"

Nealy's answer was a low, hushed whisper. "Yes."

"And Nick? He did what you did and paid the price just the way you paid the price for getting pregnant, right?"

Nealy offered up another low, hushed whisper. "Yes."

Liz Shay wrote on her legal pad, long sentences that irritated Nealy. She said so.

"Is it because when it's in black-and-white it makes everything more real?" Liz asked.

"I don't want to read it if that's what you mean. Admitting these things, saying them out loud, is about as real as it gets. Once you say words out loud you can't take them back. When you write something down and it isn't to your liking, you can erase the words."

"I see. That's an interesting way of looking at things. Now, tell me, did you think about what I asked you yesterday? Do you have an answer for me?"

"I'm going to smoke a cigarette."

"Go ahead, it's your lungs. Are you agitated?"

"Let me worry about my lungs, and hell, yes, I'm agitated. I'm starting to feel like some kind of monster. I bought these cigarettes on my way home from Emmie's last night. I didn't smoke them, though. This is the first one," she said, coughing. She kept on puffing.

"So, what's the answer?"

"It's not that easy. I thought about it a lot on my way to Emmie's house. I knew the answer when I was in the car, and I knew it when I walked around to the backyard. When I left my daughter's house, the answer wasn't the same."

"Well, then, let's hear it."

"You asked me what the one thing was that would make me truly happy. Truly is the word I had trouble with. My answer is shameful, and I can't believe I'm going to tell you what it is. I couldn't sleep all night just thinking about it. You said I had to be honest and you would know if I wasn't. Take out the word *truly* and I can respond."

"Forget I used the word *truly*. What's your answer?"

Nealy licked at her dry lips. She leaned over to crush out her cigarette. "This was my answer before I got to Emmie's house: *I want her to fail if she rides in the Derby.* I thought that would make me happy because it would prove . . . a lot of things. I know how that sounds. I hate myself for saying it. It was what I felt. If you want me to justify my response, then this is it. I had to train, bust my ass, go without sleep, and deprive myself of a lot of things. I paved the way. I had to put up with all the bad press and all the bullshit that went along with it. I earned what I got with my own blood, sweat, and tears. She prances in, says she's going to do it and that's the end of it. She's so good, it boggles my mind. She's just doing it. With none of the negatives. That girl has a will and a mind of her own. They were all wrong about her. She doesn't need to be kept safe, and she sure as hell doesn't need to be provided for. But it's still happening. They were all wrong about that, too."

"Well, that was certainly a mouthful. You said that was what you felt before you went to Emmie's. Did you have a change of heart later on?"

"Yes. I realized I was jealous of how easy it is for her. It was never easy for me. Maybe I made things hard because I didn't know any better, or I was trying to prove something. She doesn't give a good rat's ass if she wins the race or not. She just wants to run it. I was determined to win, and I did. It was like I had to keep proving myself over and over again. To whom, to what, I don't know. I'll probably keep on doing it till the day I die."

"What's part two?"

"It would make me very happy if my daughter turns out to be as good as I was. Not better, not worse, just as good as. If you don't like that answer, that's too damn bad. You asked for honesty, and I'm giving you honesty. By the way, I offered to buy SunStar from Emmie. She said she would *give* it to me. I don't want her to give it to me. I'll pay her a fair price. She can add it to Gabby's trust fund. She said she was thinking of selling the farm, so I made the offer. I think that's why I went there. No, that's not true. I *know* that's why I went there."

It was Liz Shay's turn to stare into the fish tank. There was nothing more relaxing or soothing than watching fish swim lazily about. She knew from past experience, if she stared too long at the graceful fish, she'd nod off. "And you want to buy SunStar . . . because . . ."

Nealy lit a second cigarette. "I suppose you're thinking I don't want Emmie to have it. I just think it should stay in the family. I can lease it out. It belonged to us, to my brothers and me. We earned that damn place."

"And twice that damn place was willed to Emmie and not you or your brothers. Emmie doesn't want it. Your brothers are gone, so that leaves just you. Are you sure the reason you want it is so Emmie can't get her hands on it? After all, even though she was little more than an infant, she, too, suffered trauma there. You weren't the only one, Nealy."

Nealy blew a perfect smoke ring and watched it circle the doctor's head. A wry smile tugged at the corners of her mouth. "It *does* bother me that SunStar was left to Emmie twice. I guess I wasn't good enough in Josh Coleman's eyes. Neither were my brothers. It was that hateful old man's way of paying for his sin against Emmie. At least I think that's why he left her the farm. I was shocked when my brothers' wills were read. I did so much for them. I made it all happen, and then they turned around and slapped me in the face by leaving it to Emmie. Where is the justice to all that? Just tell me that."

"I suppose they were trying to be fair. Emmie did sign it over to them. But she did it at your urging. You called the shots back then. You were a very powerful woman and still are. Sometimes I think you don't know just how powerful you really are. The flip side to all that is, your home is Blue Diamond Farms. You will never want for money. You're world-famous. My God, Nealy, you danced with the president of the United States at the Derby Ball. The president hugged you for the whole world to see. Now, that's fame. Your accomplishments are legion. You certainly don't need the farm or the revenue from it. The horses aren't half as good as yours. Why?"

"Because . . . because she already has half of Blue Diamond and didn't do a damn thing to earn it. On top of that she gets SunStar and didn't do a damn thing to earn that either. That makes her better than me and she isn't. She isn't. You want honesty, I'll give you fucking honesty. That's how I goddamn well feel, and sitting here talking to you isn't going to change one damn thing. My brothers, much as I loved them, were two tight-asses. If I hadn't stepped in, they would have lost the farm and ended up working for a weekly wage at some other farm. And what do they do to show their thanks? They kick me in the gut. My mother is buried on that farm. My brothers are buried there. It belongs to me and I want it. If I have to buy it from my daughter to get it, so be it." Nealy lit a third cigarette. "You still don't get it, do you? *She doesn't want it.* She didn't earn it. It means nothing to her. Think of it in terms of a very costly gift that will never be used. Just like Blue Diamond Farms. She just takes and takes and takes. She doesn't give back and when she tries, she screws up and says, 'Oh, well, I'll do better next time.' "

Liz Shay leaned back in her chair. "I didn't realize you hated your daughter so much."

"I don't hate my daughter. Where did you get an idea like that? I get annoyed with her. I admitted I was jealous of her. But I don't hate her. She's my flesh and blood for God's sake."

"Born out of guilt."

"Yes, born out of guilt!" Nealy shouted. "Don't you dare sit there and tell me I don't love my daughter. I took care of her. She was always sick. I sat up with her when I was dead on my feet. I didn't let that ugly old man put her in an orphanage. I did what I had to do. I took her and ran. I did the best I could. If that doesn't meet with your approval, tough luck, Doctor. I'm leaving now, and I won't be back. I'm sick of listening to you telling me what I should and should not feel. You aren't inside my head, and you sure as hell don't walk in my shoes. Until you can do that, don't you dare judge me. Don't you dare!"

Liz Shay bolted upright in her chair. "Nealy, I have never judged you. It's not my place to do that. All I can do is try to lead you in the right direction. It's up to you what you do or don't do. I would hate to see you walk out of here in anger. We're making real progress whether you want to believe it or not."

Nealy offered up a scathing look and left the room.

By the time she reached her car, her anger was spent. She turned around and walked back to the office. She poked her head in the door to the receptionist's office and said, "I'll be back tomorrow at four."

"Okay, Mrs. Littletree. See you tomorrow."

15

Hatch watched Nealy as she rode a horse named Ethereal to the starting gate. He was rambunctious, and she was having difficulty calming him down. He'd never seen anything but perfection when Nealy was handling a horse. Something was wrong. Was it the horse, or was it Nealy? He continued to watch as Lee Lui led Gadfly into the gate. A moment later, Emmie maneuvered a prancing Hifly into the third gate. She looked confident. Lee Liu looked nonchalant sitting atop Gadfly. Nealy looked . . . Nealy looked terrified. Or was it anger he was seeing on his wife's face? Maybe he was the one who was terrified. Maybe he wasn't seeing things correctly. He was about to climb down from the makeshift stand when he heard the gates clang shut.

His gaze swiveled to Cordell Lancer, who was acting as a clocker, his starting pistol aimed high in the air. When it went off, a lump the size of a golf ball settled in Hatch's throat. *Nealy is too old to be doing this.*

He turned when he felt Jake's presence. The boy looked upset. What the hell was going on here? The young man shrugged, as he, too, watched the horses race around the track. Gadfly took the early lead and moved like greased lightning, Hifly racing to keep up. In the time it took Hatch to suck in his breath, Nealy was alongside Gadfly and flying down the track; Emmie and Gadfly settled into her wake.

"They're holding back, Hatch. Why are they doing that?"

"Who? What are you talking about, son?"

"Emmie. She's holding back. So is Lee. Hifly can outrun both those horses. She's letting Aunt Nealy win. So is Lee." There was such disgust in Jake's voice that Hatch dropped the binoculars.

"Why would they do a thing like that? I was watching, and I didn't see that," Hatch grumbled.

Jake shrugged. "I can think of a couple of reasons. One, Emmie wanted to give her mother the pleasure of winning. She probably told Lee to do the same thing. I don't know that for sure, though. Winning is important to Aunt Nealy even if it's just a training race. Two, Hifly is having a bad day and she didn't want to tire him. Or . . .

"Or, what? Spit it out, Jake."

"Or, she doesn't want Aunt Nealy to see how good Hifly is. There's a lot of rivalry there, Hatch. I know you think I'm just a kid, but I'm here twenty-four/seven, and I see what's going on. Hifly could have taken that race by a good six furlongs if she'd let him. Gadfly is no slouch either. He can give Hifly a run for his money. Hifly is tuned to Emmie to such a degree it's mind-boggling. I don't think you should mention what I just said to Aunt Nealy."

Hatch nodded. "What about Lee Liu?"

Jake hung his head. "He threw it, too. Gadfly is neck and neck with Hifly. This is just my opinion, Hatch. Ethereal is a plug if you know what I mean."

Hatch used both his hands to shield his eyes from the sun as he stared down at the track, where Nealy was offering up a blistering commentary on the race. Even from where he was standing, he could hear the anger in her voice. So it wasn't terror after all. Anger was better than terror any day of the week. Especially where his wife was concerned.

"I will not tolerate this. Do you hear me? You held those horses back. I saw that little byplay between the two of you. Do you think I'm a fool? There's no way in the world I could have won. I wasn't racing to win. I was racing alongside both of you so the horses could get the feel of a strange horse. It's the run. Those animals were born and bred to run. You have to let them do what they do best, run to win. You didn't do either one of them any favors, and you sure didn't do any for yourselves either. I'm ashamed of you both. Do it again, Lee, and you're out of here. Emmie, if I ever see a shoddy performance like that again, you will rue the day. Now cool down those horses and get out of my sight because you just shamed me, and I'm having a hard time accepting it."

Hatch looked at Jake, who was grinning from ear to ear. "Aunt Nealy is back in the groove, Hatch. I was starting to worry about her. She hasn't been herself these last few weeks. Yesterday morning at six-thirty, she raced Gadfly with three other starters. She tied Flyby's time in the Derby. I was standing right next to the clocker and saw the time with my own eyes. That's how she knew, Hatch."

Hatch rubbed at his chin. "When they do these races, does Emmie always hold Hifly back? Look, kid, I know it makes you feel like a snitch, but I really need to know. If she is doing that, I want to know why."

Jake scuffed his boots in the dirt. Hatch looked down at the boy's feet. He already had a hole big enough to stick his foot in up to his ankle. He looked miserable.

"I don't know why she does it, but yes, that's what she's been doing for the past month. I'm thinking she doesn't want anyone to know how good Hifly is. Lee and I were talking about it. He thinks the same way I do. He's doing it by the book, Emmie isn't. That's the bottom line."

"And Nealy knows?"

"I think so. I talked to my mother about it, and she said it was a mother-daughter thing and to keep my nose out of it. My mom is real smart about stuff like that, so I always listen to her. I gotta get down to the barn."

Hatch waved him off and waited for his wife to join him. He stuck his foot in the hole Jake had left behind.

"Digging for gold, honey?" Nealy asked, straddling the fence.

"Kind of. What the hell was that all about, Nealy?"

Nealy shrugged. "My daughter is trying to be mysterious is what I think. I'm also thinking she wants to surprise everyone at the Derby. So far she has refused any and all requests from the newspapers for an interview. She took a page out of my book, so I can't fault her for that."

Cordell Lancer appeared out of nowhere. "Nealy, can I talk to you a minute?"

"Sure. What's up?"

"It's Lee. I know you think he held Gadfly back, but he didn't. The boy isn't feeling up to snuff. I was wondering if you'd mind if I took him to town to see Dr. Fritz. He don't look real good to me."

"Would you rather Hatch or I took him in?"

"No, I think he'd be more comfortable with me. I'm going to have to fight him to go at all. He just keeps saying he has a belly-ache and is blaming it on something Jake cooked up the other night for dinner. He's been peaked these past few days."

"Then hog-tie him and get him to the doctor. I don't want him pulling one of Emmie's stunts and have it turn serious later on. Nip it in the bud now. If he gives you any trouble, let me know.

"The race is only a week away. I'll work with Gadfly until Lee's feeling better."

"What will you do if it's something serious, Nealy?" Hatch asked, his face etched in concern.

"I'm going up to the house now to see if there are any jockeys available. I shouldn't have too much trouble. After I do that, I have to leave for town. Liz moved my appointment up today because she has a crisis patient scheduled for my usual time. Don't ask me how you schedule a crisis appointment. I'm like you, I thought you dealt with it right then and there. What are you going to do, honey?"

"I thought I would go down to the barn and talk to Emmie. You don't have a problem with that, do you?"

"Nope. See you at dinner."

Nealy could see the psychiatrist through the glass partition. She was so pretty in a wholesome way, with her short-cropped blond hair, her freckles and engaging smile. She was so insight-ful it was scary sometimes. It was also scary that she held peo-ple's minds in the palms of her hands. Did she ever make a mistake? Did she ever steer a patient in the wrong direction? Did she sleep at night or did she worry about her patients? As Nealy lowered her gaze to the tropical fish tank she remem-bered the day she'd stormed out of the office, only to return mo-ments later.

Hanging one's guts out to dry was not an easy thing to do.

She felt rather proud of herself these days. She'd flinched, she'd cried, and she'd bitten the bullet, but she hadn't faltered. She'd gone on to fight another day. She wondered what Liz would home in on today. As far as she could tell, they'd covered every single phase of her life. They'd discussed Maud, Jess, Emmie, and her brothers. Hunt, Nick, and Hatch had come into play along the way as a diversion, or so she suspected. It always came back to Emmie, though. Emmie, SunStar, and Blue Diamond Farms.

Nealy felt her shoulders slump at the thought of Emmie and the experience on the track earlier. She was going to have to talk about that with Liz.

Liz opened the door. Today she looked exceptionally pretty and professional in a pale pink suit with a frilly white blouse. Nealy felt dowdy in her ankle-length, loose-flowing dress.

"How's it going, Nealy? Coffee?"

"Sure. To answer your question, it's going, but barely." She quickly recounted the morning's events.

"Obviously the whole thing upset you. Why is that?"

"Upset is hardly the word. I was royally pissed. Now that I think about it, I'm not really sure why I was upset. I think my first thought was she let me win so I could stand back and say I'm the best no matter what kind of horse you have. Maybe at one time, I would have thought that. She did let me win, but I think it was because she doesn't want me to know how good Hifly is. She hasn't forgotten the mistake she made with Gadfly. The horse tolerates her now, but he doesn't really like her. It could be something as simple as the shampoo she uses that Gadfly doesn't like."

"What did you say to her, if anything?"

"I told her if she pulled a stunt like that again she'd rue the day. I was just saying words, but I was angry. At first I thought Lee held Gadfly back, too, but it turns out he wasn't feeling well. My manager took him to the doctor. Is this something I should apologize for? I can't seem to make the right kind of decisions anymore. I always feel like I'm under a microscope. It's like, do I keep quiet, do I say something, or what? What if I say the wrong thing? What if I say the right thing, and she takes it the wrong way? I'm damned if I do, and damned if I don't."

"Do you think you should apologize?"

"No, I don't think I should apologize. The rules are you race the horse as if it were the Derby. It's my rule, and Emmie knows the rule. She flaunts her disregard of the rules. She's forever breaking them."

"Is it because they're your rules, do you think?"

"I guess so. When you run a farm the size of Blue Diamond, and if you're going to run the Derby, there have to be rules in place. It was the first thing I learned from Maud and Jess. The rules were already in place. I simply kept up with them. Emmie thumbs her nose at rules. Is that why someone else has to take care of her, oversee her well-being?"

The hard edge in Nealy's voice did not go unnoticed.

"She's never been on her own," Nealy went on. "She probably couldn't survive. God knows what would happen to Gabby if she didn't have the nest egg set up for her. I was her protector in the beginning. Then it was Maud and Jess. Then she came back to me, and after me came Buddy. After Buddy it was Nick and Hatch. Then she got sick and the rehab staff took care of her. Before she left there, she had her father on the line as her backup, and once again, she lucked out."

"There are some people like that, Nealy. They have to have what you call a protector. They're afraid to be alone. Sometimes people like that can't function without someone overseeing their day-to-day life. I'm treating you, not Emmie. What is it that you want or expect from your daughter? Do you know? Do you want her out there busting her ass like you used to do? Do you want her to grovel to you in thanks for giving her a good life? Do you want her to be like you, or don't you? Which is it, Nealy? When did this turn into a competition?"

Nealy stormed to her feet. "You're the shrink, you figure it out. I'm just here to give voice to my feelings and actions. Right now you remind me of my first husband Hunt. He used to say I had a black heart. You ask me all this crap, and when I tell you, you do what you did a few weeks ago. You make me feel like a piece of scum. I don't like that. Who said it was a competition?"

The doctor looked straight up at her patient but was at a disadvantage because Nealy was standing, towering over her. "You didn't answer my question."

"You got me so riled up, I can't even remember what the question was."

"The question was, do you or don't you want your daughter to be like you?"

Nealy stared down at the doctor for so long Liz thought she was going to have to repeat the question.

"No. I don't want Emmie to be like me. She's weak, she's ineffectual, and you can't depend on her. She also whines. Sometimes I hate to admit she's my daughter because she's nothing like I am. She takes after her father."

"Is Nick like Emmie?"

"Of course not. Nick is tough. He has the courage of his convictions. I respect that. There's very little to respect with Emmie."

"Do you suppose she knows that?"

"I don't know," Nealy said, sitting down.

"In my opinion, it would be very hard to live up to the great Nealy Coleman, Diamond, Clay, Littletree. For heaven's sake, for starters you have four last names. It must be very hard to live with the knowledge that you don't measure up in your mother's eyes. A mother's approval is so important to a child and even a young adult. I have patients who are in their sixties, their parents in their late eighties who are still seeking parental approval. Some people just give up. Some keep striving. Some look for substitutes."

"So I failed my daughter."

"Is that what you think?"

"Yes, it's what I think. I failed her. I can't change or undo the past. I can't be or do something I don't feel. I'm not that way. I don't see myself changing either. I'm too old to go by a new set of rules. Emmie's happy now. She has someone to take care of her and love her. She has a daughter. Perhaps she'll be kinder to her daughter than I was to her. I think we have come full circle, don't you, Doctor?"

"Yes, Nealy, I think we have. I hope you'll check in with me from time to time. I'll always be here for you if you need me."

Nealy gathered up her purse. "That's nice to know. Are you going to the Derby?"

"I wouldn't miss it for the world. Who should I bet on?"

Nealy laughed, a strangely hollow sound. "Bet half on Hifly and half on Gadfly. Both riders are top-notch. Both horses are exceptional. They're up against some stiff competition, but I think our horses are the best. Look who their sire is. I guess I'll see you around sometime."

"Take care, Nealy." Liz held out her hand, and Nealy shook it. "You, too."

It didn't hit her till she was in the car. She was finished. Liz had discharged her. She was free. Almost two solid months of therapy, six days a week, and suddenly she was finished. Prior to the session that day there had been no indication her therapy was ending. She frowned. Had Liz given up on her? Was that why she was discharged? Or was it the statement she made about not changing? Did it even matter?

Nealy drove home with the windows down, the wind ruffling her hair. She turned the radio on to a Golden Oldies station and sang along with Frank Sinatra, who was warbling about doing it his way. Her fingers drummed on the steering wheel to the beat of the music.

It wasn't a long ride back to the farm, but she made it longer by driving forty-five miles an hour to the annoyance of other drivers behind her. When they blew their horns and passed her, she waved. She continued to sing along with Frank.

At the entrance to Blue Diamond Farms, Nealy brought her car to a stop to admire the bronze statues of Flyby and Shufly. She smiled, remembering how Hunt had given her the bronze of Flyby for her birthday and Nick had commissioned the one of Shufly before she ran him in the Derby. She was always in awe when she stopped to look at the sculptures.

Pictures of the two magnificent horses, father and son, had over the years graced the front covers of just about every Thoroughbred, equestrian, and Kentucky magazine printed. The memories of their races would go down in the annals of racing history. She felt her chest puff out with pride.

Whatever she was, whatever she'd accomplished in her reign at Blue Diamond Farms, was because of these two spectacular steeds.

Flyby was gone now, and Shufly belonged to Metaxas Parish.

All she had was Gadfly to remind her of her glory years. She wiped at her eyes with the sleeve of her shirt.

Trips down Memory Lane were for other people, not for her. What a lie that was. She stomped on the gas pedal, the BMW kicking up gravel and dust as she careened down the road.

An urgency she'd never experienced before overtook her. She bolted from the car and ran to the one place that had always calmed her—the stallion cemetery, a sanctuary that had soothed her so many times she'd lost count.

When she'd first arrived at Blue Diamond Farms, Maud had showed her the cemetery. She remembered how much in awe she'd been that day. Back then it hadn't been a pretty place. Now it was a long, narrow area with a circle in the middle with iron benches and colorful pots of bright flowers. The right side was the human cemetery, the left side, the Thoroughbred cemetery. Beautiful, pruned shrubbery grew between the graves, affording each site privacy. Each grave had a stone, lovingly carved by a stonemason. She walked the length of the cemetery, pausing at Dancer's grave. How she'd loved that horse. The same horse that had thrown Maud and crippled her for life. Without Dancer, she would never have been able to train his son Flyby.

Nealy dropped to her knees and dug a little hole in the grass at the base of the stone. She reached into her pocket and pulled out a handful of mints and dropped them into the hole. She carefully covered it back up, tears rolling down her cheeks. She did the same thing when she made her way to Flyby's grave, only this time hard sobs racked her body. She rocked back and forth on the grassy carpet, choking and sobbing as she let her misery overtake her.

She felt ancient when she finally got to her feet and made her way to one of the iron benches under the angel oak that she'd planted herself forty-one years earlier. Back then it had just been a stick of a tree with a few leaves. Now it was huge, at least fifty feet tall, with full, thick branches shading almost the entire cemetery. It always reminded her of a giant umbrella. She'd often sat on the bench under the tree in the rain and never felt a drop.

Nealy stared across at the three graves she'd visited so often—Maud, Jess, and her first husband Hunt. Once a month for as long as she could remember, she had flowers delivered for the cemetery, even in the winter. Daisies for Maud, Jess, and Hunt. A blanket of red roses for Dancer and Flyby.

Her bottom lip drew down in a bitter, hard line when she looked at Maud's grave. "I feel like you betrayed me, Maud. I feel like you used me. I gave you and this farm my heart and my soul because I was so grateful to you for taking me in and giving my daughter and me a home. I sacrificed my daughter and my life for you and this farm. I couldn't do it all. God knows I tried. I gave you my daughter, and I gave you two Triple Crowns. I think my debt is paid off now.

"This place was never really mine, and you know what, that's okay, too. I know that now. I think, and I'm not sure of this, but I think you wanted me to get to this point in time so that it could all go to Emmie, whom you loved with all your heart. I think you loved her as much as you loved this farm. I was just the means to get her ready to take it over. Right or wrong, Maud, that's how I see it. Things are still jumbled up in my mind, but I know I can sort it all out, and I will, sooner or later.

"I realize now I don't want this farm. There was a time when I thought I did. There was a time when I thought I wanted so many things. I should have left those things as just thoughts and never acted on them.

"I'm never coming back here, Maud, so I'll say good-bye now. Hey, Hunt, are you listening to all this?" Nealy leaned her head back and closed her eyes. . . .

"That was some speech you just offered up. What's got your panties in a wad this time?"

"Go away, Hunt. I'm not in the mood to talk to you today. I'm pissy enough without having to listen to one of your sermons. I'm saying good-bye to you, too. I'm never going to come back to this cemetery. You all betrayed me. I gave and gave and gave, and you all took and took and took. No more."

"No, no, no. It doesn't work like that. You did what you did because you wanted to do it. No one held your feet to the fire. You were hell-bent on proving you could do it all. You almost did, too. You were so busy trying to be perfect you forgot to have a life, and you forgot you had a family. You're human. Everyone makes mistakes, but if you learn

from those mistakes, you can go on with your life. I can see you're pretty damn miserable right now."

"Is this where you offer up sage advice? If so, I don't want to hear it. Go fluff up a cloud or something and leave me alone."

"Your brain is whirling and twirling. What are you going to do?"

"None of your business. I managed to get this far in my life, and I think I can get the rest of the way without your help."

"Get off it, Nealy. You see what you want to see. You also have selective hearing. All that crap you were handing out about Emmie and Nick is pure bullshit, and you know it. You had help along the way. Where would you be without Maud and Jess and all the people who run this farm? Where, Nealy? You could have ended up at some farm, cooking or mucking barn stalls and living in some scrubby trailer if Maud and Jess hadn't taken you in. Don't ever say you did it on your own. Maybe Emmie can do it, and maybe she can't. Nick did it. He's off on his own. You're real big on verbalizing how Emmie screwed up things but you're no shrinking violet to screwups yourself, now are you?"

"Leave me alone, Hunt. I'm too tired to talk to you. Why do you keep showing up when I'm feeling at my worst?"

"Because that's when you need me the most. How's it going with my buddy, Hatch?"

"That's none of your business either. Is Emmie going to win the Derby?"

"Like I know. Get real, Nealy. I think it's going to be one of those races that go down in history. There's a horse running that's every bit as good as Spectacular Bid. You must be feeling a little sad that you aren't racing. Did you hang up your silks?"

"Yes, I did. That was another life. I'm a senior citizen, and that means I'm old now in case you hadn't noticed."

"You're only as old as you feel, Nealy."

"What do you think about Gadfly?"

"Great horse. You did a good job training him. You gotta watch that rebellious streak in him. I wish Hifly had just a smidgen of that streak in him. Reminds me of a big pony, but he's all heart. I think he's better than John Henry on his best day."

"Aunt Nealy! Oh, there you are! I thought I'd find you here. I saw you drive in earlier and then you disappeared," Jake said, sitting down next to her.

"I guess I dozed off. Is anything wrong? How's Lee? What did the doctor say?"

"Are you okay, Aunt Nealy? You look like you've been crying. Is there anything I can do?"

Nealy patted the boy's knee. "No, nothing is wrong. I always cry when I come out here. You didn't answer me, how's Lee?"

"They wanted him to stay for some tests, but he refused. They gave him some antacids." He looked away when he said, "Cordell said he had a mess of trapped gas."

"Well, that's a relief. Are you sure he's okay?"

"He said he was. The whole family gets here tomorrow night. Somehow or other they all managed to get rooms at the Inn. I'm real anxious to see them all. I hope they aren't disappointed that I'm not riding."

"There will be other races, Jake. You've come a long way. I'm so proud of you I could just bust. I can't wait for your mom to see you riding out on Blue Diamond's track. That is going to be the highlight of her visit, not the Derby."

Jake reached for her hand and squeezed it. "If Emmie hadn't come back and taken over with Hifly, would you really have let me ride him in the Derby?"

"You bet I would have. You're good enough to ride Gadfly, too. What's your feeling on that?" Nealy asked curiously.

Jake laughed. "The same as yours. I didn't want to sound conceited." This time it was Nealy's turn to laugh.

"Spoken like a true jockey. Did Hatch say what he wanted?"

"No, he just wanted to know where you were because he saw your car and knew you were home. I said I would try to find you."

"I'm just going to sit here a minute longer. I'll be along in a few minutes."

"Okay, see you later, Aunt Nealy."

When Jake was out of sight, Nealy walked the length of the cemetery one last time. She offered up a snappy salute when she passed Dancer's and Flyby's graves. She knew she would never come there again. "So long, Hunt."

"See ya, Nealy."

Instead of going down to the main barn or up to the house, Nealy circled around the stallion barn and headed for the old structure that had been falling down when she first arrived there. The structure where Maud and Jess had hid the pickup truck she'd stolen from Josh Coleman. The old building had been renovated years ago but the truck, now over fifty years old, still sat in the building. She never knew why, but from time to time she would walk out, open the doors, and stare at the truck that had brought her to Blue Diamond Farms. It was a blue truck, and she thought the color appropriate. Once she had actually climbed into the driver's seat but had scrambled out a second later when harsh memories flooded back to overwhelm her.

It was an ugly, old Ford truck unlike the new Ford Rangers that were all over the farm. She turned on the light, walked over to the driver's side of the car, and opened it. She touched the leather, certain it would crumble and crack beneath her touch. She was surprised when the old leather rose up to meet her fingers. It felt supple and soft. The key was still in the ignition. She climbed in and grabbed hold of the wheel. Her hand went to the key, and automatically turned it. She was stunned to hear the engine turn over. It purred. Literally purred. She'd run out of gas when she arrived. Who put the gas in the tank? Who kept the engine primed? She whirled around to see Cordell Lancer standing in the driveway. She climbed out of the truck. Her eyes were full of questions.

"I can tell you what I know, Nealy. I don't know the why of any of it, though. It seems Mrs. Diamond left orders that this here truck was always to be maintained. Like forever and ever. The farm manager that worked here when she was alive was to see to it till he retired. He then passed the job on to Dover Wilkie, who passed it on to me when I signed on with Emmie at his retirement. Dover put a new engine in it the year he retired. It's always got a full tank of gas. We work on it from time to time, tune it up, and I take it for a spin every two weeks or so. Maintaining this fine old vehicle came with the job description. There was another part to that job description, Nealy. It said the cargo in the back was never to be disturbed and always kept covered. You could drive this car all the way to Alaska. Put new tires on it myself about eight months ago. Perfectly balanced."

"Why?" Nealy whispered.

"I don't know, Nealy. Dover just told me it was part of my job the way it was for him when he took over. The main order came down from Maud Diamond, and that's all I know. No, there's one other thing I do know, the cargo in the back . . . ain't never looked at it and don't know what it is. Not my business. Dover now, he said he didn't never look at it neither. Do ya want to take her out for a spin? I'm thinking this old truck has some kind of special meaning to you, Nealy. If you don't want to talk about it, I'll pretend I never seen you in here."

"Pretend, Cordell," Nealy said before her throat closed tight. She ran then, faster than she'd ever run in her life.

16

Nealy was waiting on the front porch, Hatch at her side, when the airport shuttle dropped off her family. She smiled from ear to ear as she watched Fanny walk toward her, her arms outstretched. The others followed behind, with Sunny and Harry bringing up the rear, Sage and Birch guiding their wheelchairs.

Her family was there. All of them this time, and this time they were all going to Churchill Downs to watch the Run for the Roses. Kentucky's most important event of the year. The Kentucky Derby was to Louisville what Mardi Gras was to New Orleans. A super mega event the whole world watched.

"Hurry, everyone, we have to get over to the track. Jake is going to explode wide open if he doesn't get to show off for you. He's been waiting for this moment all day long. He's saddled up and ready." Nealy stopped at Sunny's chair and bent low. "He wants to do this for you, Sunny, since he won't be riding in the Derby. This little Blue Diamond Farms race is strictly for you. I have to run ahead because I'm racing with him. Make sure you clap real loud and whistle between your teeth. And, Sunny, it doesn't matter if he wins or not. You okay with that?"

Sunny smiled. "I'm okay with it. He's happy, and that's all that matters."

"Okay, I'll see you over on the track." Nealy sprinted away like a young girl. Hatch watched her, love shining in his eyes.

It was Lee Liu atop Gadfly, Jake on a horse named Lucky Lew. She would be riding Ethereal. Cordell was the clocker.

Nealy rolled her shoulders, bent low, and totally relaxed. The moment Cordell fired upward and the gates clanged open, all three horses blasted from the gate.

Back in the makeshift stands, Sunny gasped, "Oh my God! Is

that my son out there on that *huge* horse? Mom, look at him go! Remember when he was afraid of the pony rides we used to try to get him to go on?"

Birch and Sage, Riley and Cole were like four young kids as they ran hooting and hollering down to the finish line to cheer Jake on. They clapped, whistled, and stomped their feet.

When he came in second, he stood up, his fists shooting in the air. "Yahoo!" he yelled.

"Good race, kiddo," Nealy said, reaching for his hand. "I kind of think that family of ours is pretty proud of you right now. Congratulations, Lee. You look like a winner to me."

"Thanks, Nealy. It's always a pleasure to race with you. This boy is getting antsy. I'm going to cool him down and turn in. Thanks for inviting me to dinner but my stomach is still on overdrive. I'll be ready to leave for Churchill Downs in the morning. You'll know me because I'll be the one with the bells on."

Nealy leaned down to speak to Fanny. "What did you think?"

"I think you did a magnificent job with my grandson. I'll be forever grateful. He's got the right stuff, doesn't he? My heart was in my mouth there for a few seconds. Don't let me forget to give you a letter that was delivered to me earlier this morning. It was addressed to you in care of me."

Nealy frowned, then shrugged. "Yes, he does have the right stuff, Fanny. For sure he'll ride the Derby next year. I think I can almost guarantee it. I just have to take this horse to the barn and wash up a bit, and then it's Blue Diamond Farms' version of a Derby dinner this evening, along with mint juleps and all the trimmings. I won't be long."

The dinner was delicious, the conversation even more delicious as Nealy laughed and joked with her family. Excitement was running high, and everyone was excited about a possible win in the Derby.

"Where's Emmie?" Sunny asked when dessert was being served.

"She said she would be late. Gabby had a play of some sort early this evening. She had to find a sitter among other things. I'm sure she'll be here soon."

"I'm stuffed," Sawyer said, loosening the belt on her slacks. "I liked that caviar. What kind was it?"

"It's a dark large-beaded roe taken from a type of sturgeon native to Kentucky rivers. It's best paired with oysters in a vodka vinaigrette like we did it tonight. Domestic of course. Did you like the toasted pecans dipped in concentrated bourbon and then rolled in crystalized sugar? They're one of my favorites. I can eat those things all day long. It's a good thing the Derby only comes around once a year," Nealy said, pointing to her hips.

Sawyer pointed to her belt. "I loved them, too. See, the dish is empty, but I think Cole and Riley ate more than I did."

"We categorically deny that," Riley and Cole said in unison.

"I particularly liked the fish spread," Birch said.

"You should. We only serve it during Derby Week. It's made from hickory-smoked Atlantic salmon and then we cure it in Old Rip Van Winkle bourbon and blend it with cream cheese. You can get drunk if you eat enough of it." Nealy laughed.

"Is *everything* made with bourbon?" Fanny asked.

"During Derby Week it is. Sometimes after Derby Week, too. Would anyone care for another mint julep?"

"We all would," Sawyer said, holding her glass aloft. "Bring it on!"

"Mint juleps are as symbolic of the Derby as the blanket of roses. Did you all bring your Derby clothes?" Nealy asked.

"We certainly did. I read up on everything I could find to make sure we don't shame you. We have some rather elegant attire, thanks to Ms. Billie Thornton and Billie Ltd. Our hats are one of a kind, straw of course, with bright spring flowers and ribbons. We even brought straw hats for the men and bow ties. What do you think of that?" Maggie asked.

"I think it's wonderful that you're all in the spirit of it. Hatch has promised to take pictures of all of us. I'll be changing in the barn and join you all in the box at the very last minute. Thanks for the hat, Maggie, it's gorgeous. I never wore a hat like that before. I'm going to feel like a real Southern belle. The Derby is the most exciting two and one-half minutes of racing you'll ever see. The Preakness and the Belmont are great, but the Derby is really special."

"What did you call this stew that I had three bowls of?" Fanny asked.

"Burgoo. It's the spices that make it. We have gallons of it in case you want to take some home. And our Kentucky hams are the best in the country. We have plenty of those, too, if you want to take some home or we can ship them to you in dry ice."

"Put me down for whatever you want to give away." Sawyer yawned. "It's not the company, it's the time and the mint juleps. If you all don't mind, I'm going to head back to the Inn."

"You aren't driving in that condition," Riley snorted.

"No sirree, you are not," Cole said.

"I'm driving them if you can lend us a vehicle," Maggie said.

The phone rang just as Nealy was about to respond. Hatch answered it. "It's Emmie."

"Emmie, what's wrong?" Nealy listened. "Oh, I hope she's feeling better. No, of course not. I'll explain. We'll see you in the morning then.

"Gabby was in this school play tonight. Emmie said she was so nervous she threw up. She doesn't want to leave her. You were asking about a vehicle. Of course. They're all lined up by the garage. Keys are in the ignition. We'll be leaving here around seven if that's all right with all of you."

An hour later, Nealy and Hatch found themselves saying good night to Fanny, who was the last to leave. "I wanted to wait till last to give you this, Nealy."

"Who is it from, Fanny?"

"*Them.*"

"You mean the *them* we got the chicken soup from?"

Fanny nodded. "Why don't you take it in the house to read. Sage is waiting for me. I'll see you in the morning. It was a lovely dinner, Nealy, and I enjoyed every mouth-watering bite. And thank you again for all you've done for Jake. I've never seen him so happy. Sunny just beamed all evening. Nothing can make a mother happier than seeing her children well and happy. Absolutely nothing."

Nealy frowned at Fanny's words as she hugged her good night, and then it was Hatch's turn. "We'll see you in the morning." Together they stood on the front porch until the headlights of Nealy's BMW were out of sight.

"What is it, Nealy?"

"I have no idea, Hatch. Let's go in the house to read it. Let's have a mint julep, there's plenty left in the pitcher, while we read it. It might be something we don't want to hear . . . see. You know what I mean."

"Nealy, who is the *them* Fanny was referring to?"

Nealy turned evasive. "You know, *them.*"

"No, Nealy, I don't know who *them* is. How about telling me."

"What they do is they make this . . . chicken soup in this . . . ramshackle diner. The bread is good, too, and then they give you some to . . . you know, go. Someone comes in, pulls down the blinds on the door, and . . . and they look . . . very, ah, collegiate. Very mannerly and respectful. They like Fanny."

"Are you talking about the . . ."

"Uh-huh. Fanny said we needed some help. She has this phone number on a little piece of paper in her change purse. She knows the number by heart, though. They know things *before* they happen. Isn't that uncanny? We dined out that night on their side of the street, and it was like we were royalty. It was unbelievable. Then we got an ice-cream cone and went back to Babylon. It was real late at night, but as Fanny pointed out, we had escorts, front, back, and sideways to make sure nothing happened along the way. It was about the Willow mess."

"I see."

"No, you don't see, Hatch. That side of the street gives Fanny money for the rehab. They want to do that. You know how everyone in Vegas looks up to Fanny. She's a legend. One time she turned all the lights and the water off in Vegas to show them they couldn't mess with her. She said she was never so scared in her life. After that, they became friends. They even helped replant her beloved mountain when it burned. The whole town shut down to help her."

"And they make chicken soup and really good bread to go."

"That's probably a sideline," Nealy said, fiddling with the envelope.

"All right. I don't think I want to talk about this anymore. Open the envelope and see what it says."

Nealy ripped at the envelope, unfolded a single sheet of paper, and read the one sentence typed in the middle of the page.

"Watch the eleven o'clock news."

Nealy looked at her watch. "It's 10:50." She walked over to the kitchen counter and turned on the small television set. They sipped at their mint juleps in silence, their eyes on the small screen while they suffered through ten minutes of Derby talk, the weather, and speculation on who was going to win the station's Derby pool when the announcer said, "We have breaking news this evening. The nationwide manhunt for Willow Bishop was called off earlier this evening in Las Vegas, Nevada, with the arrests of Raphael Santiago and his brother Jesus. Both men are being charged with the murder of high roller Junior Belez, and will be arraigned in the morning."

"Well, hot damn!" Hatch said, slapping his thigh. "Did you hear that, Nealy? She really was innocent. I have to call Nick and Zack Leroy. Have another drink, honey, while I make the calls. Shoot, I can't call Nick. He was taking a late-night flight. In fact he should be arriving at the airport any minute. That's okay, I can tell him in the morning. I do have to call Zack, though. If anyone can get word to Willow, he can. Don't look at me like that, Nealy. No one should have to run and look over their shoulder for the rest of their life for something they didn't do, no matter who they are."

Hatch lumbered upstairs to his briefcase for his Palm Pilot. He found the number he wanted, raced back downstairs, and placed the overseas call. Seven minutes later he was talking to Zack Leroy.

"Mr. Leroy, this is Hatch Littletree. I'm calling you with good news. The police in Vegas arrested and are charging two men with the murder of Junior Belez. If you know how to get in touch with Willow or Mazie or whatever you want to call her, tell her she's home free. Just call the NBC news station in Las Vegas, and they'll confirm it. This isn't a trick, Zack. Give Willow a message for me. Tell her I said to have a good life and to stop getting married. Take care of that dog of yours. Maybe I'll see you around some time, old-timer."

Hatch turned to look at his wife. "You did that. By going to that chicken soup place and meeting Fanny's . . . ah . . . friends, you were able to give Willow back her life. That's no small thing, honey. That's right up there as in a major happening. I'm wired now. You up for some intense lovemaking?" He leered at her.

"How intense is intense?"

"Like *really* intense." Hatch grinned as he gulped the last of his mint julep.

"I'm your girl then." Nealy drained the last of her drink, and set it down with a thump in the middle of the table.

Together they tottered up the back stairway. In their room, they both flopped down on the bed and were asleep within seconds.

Nealy hopped from the Ford Ranger, a smile on her face. Churchill Downs!

The land of hopes and dreams for every horse owner setting foot on its fabled turf. Herself included. She watched Jake as he twirled around and around, trying to take it all in at once.

"I can't believe I'm here! I'm really here! Someday, and I don't know when that day will be, but it's coming, and I'm going to fly out of that gate, and I'm going to fly across the finish line. Will you bet your poke on me, Aunt Nealy?"

Nealy hugged him. "You betcha. Come on now, we have to get these guys settled. Where did Lee go?"

"He's around here somewhere. He knows what to do. Look, there's Matrix, the favorite to win. He's stupendous. The one who's going to challenge us the most is Alpha Omega. He's got a great closing style. He can be running ninth and all of a sudden he's second and then he gives that last spurt and crosses the finish line with everyone watching with their mouths hanging open. I've watched all his races on video."

"Nealy, wait up," a voice called.

"Nice to see you again, Nealy. Sorry you aren't running this race today. I'm feeling kind of cheated. I got a great horse here," the jockey said, pointing to Alpha Omega.

"Ricky! It is nice to see you, too. I heard you were riding the odds-on favorite. I've been hearing good things about you. I want you to meet my nephew, Blue Diamond Farm's up-and-coming jockey. Ricky Vee, this is Jake Thornton. Jake, Ricky Vee."

"Wow! You're one of the best jockeys out there."

"Nah, this lady is the best jockey ever to come out of Kentucky. I'm just a poor second," Ricky joked as he pointed to Nealy. "See you around, Nealy."

"Yeah, see you around. Cup of courage to you, Ricky."

Nealy turned to Jake. "Not only is he a great jockey, he's a great human being. He has heart, and he loves the horses."

"You're feeling sad, aren't you?"

"A little. It's like everything in life, Jake, the time always comes when you have to let it all go. The trick is knowing when that time is. I could probably do it but . . ."

"But?"

"I'm too old now."

Jake guffawed. "Do you want me to tell you how old Willie and Eddie were?"

"No, we can skip that. Oh, oh, this isn't good."

"Oh, shit," Jake said, sprinting after Emmie, who was leading Hifly to his stall where a cluster of grooms and jockeys were heckling her about the horse's looks. Nealy was about to run to her daughter when she saw Ricky Vee swing around and jam his hand in the direction of the hecklers. His voice carried to Nealy. "Knock it off and grow up. And remember this, think back to John Henry. Now, get your asses out of here, all of you, or I'll kick them all the way to the clubhouse turn."

Properly chastised, the little group moved on. Even from this distance, Nealy could see her daughter's shoulders shaking. She watched as Jake draped a comforting arm around her.

Nealy looked around and smiled at all the activity. Horse vans, trainers, grooms, owners, blaring music, it was all music to her soul. She saw Lee Liu and sighed with relief. There were Cordell and all her people. She whirled around when she heard her family call her name.

"What do you think?" Nealy said, waving her arms about.

"Awesome," they responded as a group.

They would splinter off to tour the grounds, gaze upon the awesome track, and snap pictures of the twin spires, a must for any first-time visitor.

"Dinner is at seven; we do a tailgate picnic. Everything is throwaway. Afterward we sit around and tell tall horse tales. In between the tall tales, we either talk to the press or we go out of our way to avoid them. They're like a band of locusts, they're everywhere, and they don't give up. I'd appreciate it if none of you would talk to them. I'd like to be the one to introduce Jake to the media. Okay, go explore Churchill Downs, family." Nealy watched them straggle off before she walked back to the barn where Gadfly and Hifly were in stalls next to each other.

For three years, the two of them were barn buddies and while some said it didn't mean anything, others said it meant everything. The naysayers, though, had never run two barn buddies in the Derby. Two barn buddies by the same awesome sire.

Nealy let her gaze rake the barn area for a sign of her daughter. When she spotted her, she took off on the run. She was breathless when she finally caught up to her. "Emmie, what was that all about? Are you all right? You look upset."

"They were riding me about Hifly. I was about to tell them off when your . . . *friend* intervened."

"Then why are you so jittery? You need to calm down now. Hifly is going to pick up on your nervousness."

"Mom, I know that. I knew I was going to take some ribbing, I just didn't expect it the minute I got out of the truck. It threw me, okay? I'm not you, I react differently to things than you do. Everything is under control."

Nealy nodded. "Where's your father?"

"He's here somewhere. He spotted some people he wanted to shake hands with. He'll be back soon. Do you need anything else, Mom?"

"No, I guess not. We missed you at dinner last night. You're coming to the tailgate dinner, aren't you?"

"I'll do my best. I brought Gabby with me, so I have to see to her."

Nealy was dismissed, and she knew it. She turned to see Hatch loping toward her. She felt a sense of relief at the sight of him.

"Nealy," Hatch hissed in her ear. "Guess who I just saw. I know I'm not seeing things. I recognized a picture of him that Nick showed me a long time ago."

"Who, honey?"

"Buddy Owens. He's here. There!" Hatch said, pointing to a champagne-colored Lexus at the far end of the parking lot.

"Buddy Owens is here! Are you sure, Hatch?"

"I think I'm sure. If it isn't Buddy Owens, then Buddy Owens has a double. The car has an Ohio license plate. Doesn't Buddy live in Ohio?"

"Yes. Yes, he went back to Ohio. I can't believe he's here. I have to tell Emmie. Wait here, Hatch."

Nealy ran back to the barn. "Emmie, Buddy's here. Hatch saw him in the parking lot." At her daughter's vague, blank look, Nealy took a step backward. "You knew he was here, didn't you? That's why you're jittery. How did he find you?"

"I sent him a letter, Mom. He came to see Gabby and to see me run the Derby. He's going to sign off on Gabby. Give me sole custody. He's being decent about it. I can handle it."

"Emmie, are you sure? Are you really sure? What if he changes his mind or switches up after he sees Gabby?"

"Then I'll deal with it. My life these days is all about dealing with things and situations. If I flub something up, I'll get back up and try again. This has nothing to do with you, Mom. Well, maybe indirectly, but not now. I'd rather see him alone if you don't mind."

"Of course. I thought . . . I didn't know . . . all right, Emmie, I'm leaving. I hope it all works out the way you want it to." She walked toward Hatch feeling like she'd just been body slammed.

Emmie leaned against the stall and took great gulping breaths. She was ready for this, she really was. She wondered if her ex-husband was as nervous as she was. Probably not. Buddy was always laid-back and cool. Most times, too laid-back and too cool. Maybe it had something to do with the world of silence he lived in. How long before he made his way to the barn? Ten minutes? Fifteen?

And then he was there, less than three feet away from her. She longed for her father. Maybe she shouldn't have sent him away. She spoke then at the same time her fingers worked furiously. "Hi, how are you, Buddy?"

"Not bad all things considered. It wasn't a long drive. I can't believe you're going to ride in the Kentucky Derby."

"I'm a little surprised myself." *He looks almost the same* she thought. *Maybe his hair is thinning a little on top, and he's gained a few pounds around the middle.* She wondered how she looked to him.

"So where is this miracle horse you're riding?"

Emmie pointed to the stall where Hifly stood watching what was going on.

"You're joking, right?" Buddy shook with silent laughter.

"Would I be here if I were joking? Why are you always so negative, Buddy? You never, ever, saw the bright side of things. Even when we were kids you were like that. If you want to see Gabby, she's back at the motel with the sitter. I can leave here and drive you there if you like. Are you staying for the race?"

Buddy's fingers worked furiously, while a smirk settled on his face. "I wouldn't miss that race for anything. I can wait to see Gabby. How about later this evening at the hotel where we're staying. Say nine-thirty or so. Did you bring all the paperwork you want me to sign?"

Emmie jammed her hands in the pockets of her jeans. "I have all the papers in the truck. Tell me where you're staying, and I'll be there. Gabby will be sleeping by then, so I can't bring her with me. Your visit with her will have to wait till tomorrow."

She knew Buddy hated it when she spoke instead of signing. He didn't like reading lips because that meant the person speaking could actually talk and he couldn't.

"How is everything else?" Buddy signed.

Emmie deliberately turned away and spoke. "Great. I'm getting married to this really, handsome, rich guy who loves me and Gabby. Stick that in your ear, Buddy Owens, and I'm lying to you because you were stupid enough to make fun of my horse. So there, you big jerk."

Emmie felt his hand on her arm. He forced her to face him. She grimaced an apology, and said, "Damn, I keep forgetting you can't hear. I said everything is fine, I'm getting married to this really handsome, rich guy who just dotes on Gabby. I hope you're as happy as I am." She smiled brightly, hoping it would take away the lie she'd just told.

Buddy didn't bother to respond. Instead, he looked at Hifly again before he doubled over laughing. "Nine-thirty in the lobby of the Starlite Motel." He waved airily as he strode off.

Cordell Lancer had seen the little byplay, but he couldn't hear what Emmie had said. He ran to Emmie as fast as his crooked legs could carry him. "What's wrong, kid? Who was that guy, and what'd he say to you?"

Emmie slid to the ground and brought her knees up to her chest. "That guy was my ex-husband. He's deaf. He dumped me after I learned to talk. He's here to sign off on my daughter, giving me sole custody of her. On top of that, he made fun of my horse. He snickered when he said he couldn't believe I would be riding him in the race. He's a jerk, what can I say."

"Do you want me to go pop him in the nose for you?" Cordell grinned.

"He needs a good popping, but I don't want to do anything that might change his mind where Gabby is concerned."

Cordell shrugged. "Just wanted you to know I seen that moving picture guy up at the clubhouse. He recognized me. Asked if you and your ma were here. Told him yes, and that you were running the race tomorrow. You coulda knocked him over with your pinkie finger when I said that. Said he's coming down here to see you. He's doing a doc-u-mentry on the Derby."

"Oh, my God," Emmie said jumping to her feet. "How long ago was it that you saw him? I look awful."

Cordell reared back. "You're a horse person, you ain't supposed to look good. You're supposed to look good tomorrow. Ain't tomorrow yet. Want me to head him off till you pretty up some?"

"Yes. No. I don't know."

"Why don't I just head him off and tell him you're too busy and to come by tomorrow when you got yourself all fixed up?"

Emmie's head bobbed up and down. "Yeah, yeah, Cordell, that sounds good. Do that. Don't let him anywhere near this barn, and keep a sharp lookout that he doesn't sneak past you. I need to work up to seeing him. I had this . . . this crush on him when he was doing all that filming."

Cordell scratched his head. "Figured it was something like that. Don't go stewing and fretting, little lady. I'll take care of the moviemaker. You sure you don't want me popping that ex-husband of yours?"

"I'm sure. Thanks, Cordell."

* * *

"I'm glad you're with me, Dad. Our first meeting didn't go that well. Then again, maybe it's my imagination. He's still as cocky as ever. All I want is his name on these papers. What if he changes his mind?"

"Then we fall back and regroup," Dillon said.

"He's going to be watching the race, Dad. For some reason that unnerves me. It shouldn't, but it does."

"Honey, that man isn't worth your little finger. Any man that turns his back on his child isn't worth anything. I know all about that because I lived it. We're here, the Starlite Motel. The guy doesn't exactly go first-class now, does he?"

"No, he doesn't. He's secure though. His parents left him a small fortune, and he does work. He was always on the frugal side. Look, Dad, there's Mitch Cunningham. I told you about him. He's the one who made the family movie. Cordell said he was here to make a documentary of the Derby."

"Emmie! Imagine seeing you here!" Mitch picked her up and twirled her around. On the half-swing, she saw Buddy and a slim young woman staring at her. She forced a laugh she was far from feeling. She turned her back to her ex-husband when Mitch settled her on her feet.

"It's good to see you. It's what . . . well over a year, more like two. How are you?"

"Good. The big question is, how are you? I tried calling that place where you went when you got sick, but they would never put my calls through. I called your mother and she said they had rules, and she gave me a list of your telephone times but every time I thought about calling, it was the wrong time. I'm sorry, Emmie. You're looking real good. You must be feeling good if you're racing in the Derby tomorrow."

Emmie nodded. He'd tried to call her. She smiled. "Have you had dinner yet? Oh, Lord, where are my manners? Dad, this is Mitch Cunningham. Mitch, this is my dad, Dillon Roland."

"I was just going to hunt down someplace to eat. Will you join me?"

"We'd love to if you'll just give me a minute," she said, squeezing his hand for Buddy's benefit. "Just wait for us by the door."

"What do you think, Dad? Do you like him?"

Dillon smiled. "He seems nice. I assume he's the man you talked to me about when you were in rehab."

"He's the one. He tried to call. I wish I had known that back then. Oh, well, that was then, this is now. All I want to do now is get this over with."

Buddy stood up, a strange look on his face.

"Dad, this is Buddy Owens. Buddy, this is my father, Dillon Roland."

They shook hands briskly. Buddy motioned for his companion to get to her feet.

"This is Debra London, my fiancée." They all shook hands again. Buddy voiced a question with his fingers. "Who was that man?"

Emmie looked into Buddy's eyes. "The man I'm going to marry. I told you that down in the barn. Didn't you believe me? My father is going to give me away and Gabby is going to be our flower girl." She lied with a straight face. "Mitch made the movie, Buddy, the one you didn't like. All right, here are the papers. Just sign by the X."

Buddy sat down, a scowl on his face as he scanned the papers he was about to sign. He finally shrugged and scrawled his signature.

"Dad, you witnessed his signature, so you have to sign on the first line. Buddy, your fiancée can sign on the second line. Otherwise, we have to get a total stranger to be a witness and you'll have to sign all over again. She won't mind, will she?"

Debra London smiled and reached for the pen. She wrote her name neatly.

Emmie felt like dancing a jig. "It was nice to see you again, Buddy. I hope you have a wonderful life. I mean that sincerely. It was nice meeting you, Debra." She clutched at her father's hand and literally dragged him to the door, where Mitch Cunningham waited.

"My God, he signed the papers. He actually signed the papers," Emmie said when they were outside and walking across the parking lot. "I feel like ten years and a hundred pounds just came off me. He signed them, Dad. He really signed them."

Dillon nodded as he cupped her elbow in his hand. "He did. He can't take it back now. Gabby is all yours."

Emmie turned when she heard her name called. She strained to see in the darkness. She thought she recognized the voice. "Dr. Hunter! What in the world are you doing here?"

"I had to come after you gave me that crash course in Thoroughbred racing. I wanted to see my star patient do what I never thought she would ever be able to do. Mr. Roland, it's nice to see you again. Or should I call you Dwight Holcum?" He burst out laughing at the sound of the name.

Emmie grinned as she reached for the doctor's hand. "Dr. Hunter, this is Mitch Cunningham. Mitch, Dr. Hunter is the man who got me to this place in time."

More manly handshakes.

"We were on our way to a rib house, would you like to join us?"

"Sure. I checked in a while ago. I was just meandering around. God, it's good to see you both. Is everything okay, Emmie?"

"We'll tell you all about it over dinner."

17

Derby Day!

"It's going to be a beautiful day!" Hatch said, pointing to the sun creeping over the horizon. "The last time we were here it rained buckets. When you crossed that finish line, you and Shufly were covered in mud from head to toe. As I recall, you took three showers. That was a day I don't think I will ever forget."

Nealy sighed. It all seemed so long ago. She sipped at the coffee in the Styrofoam cup Hatch had brought her earlier. It was cold now, but she was used to swilling cold coffee. Sometimes she thought coffee and not blood ran in her veins.

Her eyes on the horizon and the new sun creeping higher and higher brought back so many memories. The first time she'd been there, Hunt had been at her side. He'd been such a rock that trip. He'd been with her the second time, too, but only in spirit. Today, she wasn't riding. Today she was alone. Even though her entire family was there, along with her husband, she felt terribly alone. Maybe it was because she wasn't racing. Maybe it was because she couldn't bring the past back into the present. Maybe she wasn't ready to let go of the past, but one couldn't live on memories. It was a new day, a new time. She had to let it go, she had no other choice.

"What do you think we'd have to do to get some *hot* coffee?"

"Not much. A kiss on the cheek will do it. They set up a stand over there," Hatch said, pointing to his left. "And it's free. It doesn't get any better than free."

"If you don't mind, honey, fetch some for everyone. I can't believe what a beautiful day it's going to be. Even the weatherman said it's going to be in the midseventies, and no humidity. Perfect, just perfect."

"Don't get in any trouble while I'm gone," Hatch called over his shoulder.

Nealy's gaze raked the milling people, some moving almost at the speed of light, others dawdling. She stopped in midstride when a strange, alien feeling overcame her. She shook her head and rolled her shoulders back and forth to ease any tenseness, but the feeling stayed with her. The feeling was similar to the time when a pack of youngsters tried to attack her and Flyby came to her rescue. A warning of some sort. What? Why? Finding no answers to her questions, she walked down the breezeway to Gadfly's stall.

Nealy reached out to stroke the horse's head. She talked softly as she handed him a mint. He tossed his head in approval. "This is your day. I hope you can run like your daddy. I don't know if you can beat that little pygmy next to you because he's real good. Real good, Gadfly. I almost wish I was riding you. I think you and I could eat up that track. You like Lee, and that's a good thing. Just do what he wants and head for that finish line." She handed over another mint and moved on to Hifly's stall. The little horse poked his head out of the stall and nuzzled her neck. Flyby used to do the same thing. Her eyes filled with tears. She brought his head down close to her own. "I know you can do it. I know as sure as I'm standing here that you can win this race. I'm not sure you can beat your buddy or vice versa, but I know you're going to give it your all just the way Gadfly is going to give his all. I'm keeping my fingers crossed, sweet boy."

"Are you telling *my* horse secrets, Mom?" Emmie said, coming up behind her.

Nealy turned around to stare at her daughter. "No. I was just wishing him luck." She frowned at the dark circles under her daughter's eyes. Her movements were less than fluid when she stretched out shaking hands to caress the horse's head. Even her speech sounded jerky to Nealy.

"Did you have a bad night, Emmie? For some reason our internal body machinery knows how important Derby Day is and it goes on the fritz. It happens to all of us. Go off by yourself to some quiet place and try to relax even if it's just for ten minutes or so. The pressure will start to build soon, so you need to be grounded."

"I know all that, Mom. You don't need to pep talk me. I'll be fine."

"You don't look fine, Emmie," Nealy said bluntly. "Your voice is jerky-sounding, and your hands are shaking. Hifly is already picking up on it. That alone is enough to throw him off his stride. If you don't believe me, watch how he acts."

"You don't know everything, Mom. Why do you always try to beat me down? I'm okay."

"The way you were okay before you got sick? Emmie, you ignore what is right in front of your face. If you want to be a martyr, be my guest, but think about this horse. He deserves your best. I'm not seeing your best right now. It's dangerous on the track. If you aren't one hundred percent, you could get killed or even kill someone else. You need to listen to me, Emmie."

"I'm sick and tired of listening to you, Mom. Go pep talk Lee, who I've yet to see by the way, and you sure as hell don't seem too concerned about him. I know what I have to do, and I'll do it. A lot of people have faith in me, Mom. Dr. Hunter came to see me race. Buddy is here, and so is Mitch Cunningham, not to mention Dad."

Nealy gritted her teeth. "Is that what this is all about? Performing for other people so they can see how wonderful you are? I can't believe I'm hearing right. Furthermore, Emmie, Lee is a professional. He's raced before. You haven't. He was here a minute ago because I saw him. I'm talking to you as a professional, not your mother. Emmie, you need to look deep inside yourself. Ask yourself if you're riding this race for the right or wrong reasons. That's the mother in me asking that question. If you're doing it for the wrong reasons, then you don't belong here."

"And you do!" Emmie said, stalking off.

Nealy kicked a stall door in frustration.

"Ooohhh, I felt that," Dillon Roland said, coming up behind her. "I'm looking for Emmie."

"She went that way," Nealy said, pointing down the breezeway. "Dillon, I'm worried about her. Her hands are shaking, and she has dark circles under her eyes. She can get killed out there. If you can, calm her down, okay?"

Dillon rubbed at his temples. "She's stubborn, Nealy. I'm sure it's just the jitters. She's ready for this, but of course I'll talk to her. And, you don't have to tell me how dangerous it is out there. Are you okay, Nealy?"

"No, Dillon, I'm not okay. I'm worried about Emmie. I think she has it in her head that she has to show off for certain people who came here today just to see her ride. If that is her attitude, it's all wrong. Look, I tried, now it's your turn. She sees me as a jealous mother who doesn't want her to succeed. I don't want her getting killed out there. Sometimes, like just now, she's *spacey*. When she's out there on that track, there are no buffers, no one to help her the way we've all helped her. It's just her and Hifly. If she's off her stride, if she isn't one with him, it's all over."

"You make it sound ominous, Nealy."

"That's because it *is* ominous, Dillon. I know what I'm talking about. Will you please do what you can?"

Seventy-five minutes before post time, Hatch arrived with a black, shiny garment bag—his wife's Derby attire. He found her pacing the breezeway, her eyes on an ambulance at the entrance to Churchill Downs. It was always in readiness. The moment she saw her husband approaching, she ran to him.

"What's wrong?"

"I'll tell you what's wrong. I have two horses here scheduled to run in the Kentucky Derby and I have no jockeys. No jockeys, Hatch." The wail of the siren went unnoticed as her eyes raked the barn for a sign of Lee and Emmie.

"Calm down, honey, they're probably getting dressed. You used to wait till the last minute to put on your silks. Where's Jake?"

"Maybe with his mother. I haven't seen him either."

"They're right over there, and there's Jake. Uh-oh, something's wrong."

Jake skidded to a stop in front of Nealy. He struggled to get the words out of his mouth. For the first time, Nealy saw the silks he was holding in his hands. Her eyes widened in alarm.

Jake's arm shot out, pointing to the ambulance leaving the grounds. "It's Lee. He doubled over. The EMS guys said they think his appendix ruptured."

"Oh, my God! Hatch, we have to scratch Gadfly."

"No! No, don't do that, Aunt Nealy. I'll ride him."

"Jake, no. He's way too much horse for you at this point in your career. We have to scratch him."

"Please, Aunt Nealy, I can do it. I'm not scared. I've ridden him before. He knows me. Not as well as Lee, but he does know me. I can do it. Please. I don't know if I can win, but I'd like to try."

"Your mother . . ."

"She's right over there, Aunt Nealy. Talk to her."

"Mom?"

Nealy whirled around to see Emmie and her father standing behind her. "What is it, Emmie? I kind of have my hands full right now. What?" she said, her eyes going from her daughter to her father.

"I can't do it," Emmie said, bursting into tears.

"What?" Nealy all but screamed.

Emmie held out her shaking hands. "I thought . . . I can't . . . Dad . . ."

"She can't do it, Nealy."

"Damn it, Emmie, you waited till one hour till post time to tell me. See, this is what I mean about you and how irresponsible you are. We talked after dawn. It's now almost post time. You said you could do it. You swore you could do it. You told me to mind my own damn business when I questioned you. What is it with you, Emmie?"

Emmie drew herself up tall. "I don't want all of them to see me fail. I'd rather not ride than go through that."

Nealy threw her hands high in the air. Sixty minutes. She had sixty minutes to make decisions. She ran over to Sunny and dropped to her knees. "Listen to me, Sunny, Emmie isn't going to race. Lee Liu has been taken to the hospital. They think his appendix ruptured. I can scratch both horses or I can let Jake ride Hifly. Tell me what to do, Sunny. I need to hear you tell me it's okay."

Sunny strained to see her son over the heads of the people milling about her. She smiled when he waved at her. She looked Nealy directly in the eyes. "Is he good enough to ride, to come out *whole?* I'm not talking about winning."

Nealy reached for Sunny's hands. "He's way better than good, Sunny. He's damn near perfect."

"Then tell him I said to go for it."

Nealy smiled. "I'll tell him."

Nealy sprinted back to the barn. "Get ready, Jake. You're riding Hifly. There's no time for modesty here, strip down," she said, as she grabbed the silks from Dillon Roland's hands. "We only have fifty minutes. What did you do with Lee's silks?" she asked, peeling off her blouse.

"Nealy, what the hell are you doing?" Hatch thundered.

"What's it look like I'm doing? I'm changing my clothes. Everybody, turn around, I'm bashful."

"Mom . . ."

"Be quiet, Emmie. I don't want to hear another word out of your mouth. Know this, young woman, it's going to be a cold day in hell before I ever believe anything you tell me again."

"Mom . . ."

Nealy turned around, one leg in and one out of her jeans. "Yes, Nick?"

He blinked. "I guess this isn't a good time to introduce Annabel Lee. Kick some ass, Mom. We'll meet you in the winner's circle."

Nealy paused to stare at her son for a few precious seconds. "I'll meet you later, but that's the guy who will be in the winner's circle," she said, pointing to Jake.

"Hatch, quick, go make the changes. Cordell, get your butt over here!" Nealy shouted. She could hear Emmie sobbing in the background. She turned to look at her daughter just in time to see Dillon Roland take a step away from her. Later, she would think about what that meant, if anything.

She was finally dressed. She looked over at Jake, who gave her a thumbs-up. All she could do was nod. *I'm not doing this. This is somebody else in my body. Some stupid person who keeps forgetting how old she is.* Her adrenaline kicked in when she heard her name over the loudspeaker and the roar from the crowd. It kicked in a second time when the announcer called Jake's name. An ear-piercing whistle sounded over the roar from the crowd when the announcer shouted that both horses were from Blue Diamond Farms and sired by Triple Crown winner Shufly.

"That was me!" Sunny shouted. "I can still do that!" Nealy threw back her head and laughed. *Age is a number. You can overcome anything and everything if you try hard enough. Just look at Sunny! She pep talked herself.*

"Hurry, everyone. Get to the box. They're going to call for Riders Up, and I want you to see Jake ride out into the sunshine."

"Nealy."

Nealy leaned down. "Just wish me luck, Hatch. You can still make a bet." She jerked her head sideways. "Bet it all on the kid, okay?"

"You got it. How about two bucks on you. You okay, honey?"

"I'm okay, Hatch. If you get a minute, call the hospital and see how Lee is. What *is* he doing?" she said, pointing to Jake.

"This is just a guess on my part, but I think he's pinning those gold wings he carries with him all the time on Hifly's tail."

The call came for Riders Up.

"You okay, Jake?"

"I'm okay."

"Then let's do it!"

When she rode out into the sunshine, Nealy looked up at the crowd, who roared and chanted her name over and over. She smiled from ear to ear. She suddenly felt like she'd come home again after a long absence. Almost sixty years old, almost, and she was riding in the Kentucky Derby. It was the stuff dreams were made of.

She half turned to see Jake ride into the sunshine. The crowd went silent for five full seconds as they tried to absorb what they were seeing. A pity that they couldn't see that Hifly's heart was as big as he was. Then they stood and roared their approval. Maybe they did see it after all.

Her mind raced as she listened to the playing of "My Old Kentucky Home." When the last note sounded, she drew a deep breath and blessed herself.

"Room for one more, Nealy?"

"Hunt? God, yes. Hop on. You sure you're up for this?"

"Yep. The kid's looking good."

"He could use a friendly spirit to spur him on."

"He's got one, Nealy. His grandfather is his wingman."

"You mean he's riding on Flyby's tail?"

"In the Navy they call it his six, but yep, that's where he is."

"That makes me feel a lot better. Does Jake know he's there?"

"I don't think so. It doesn't matter, Nealy, he'll keep him safe. Trust me on that."

"I do, Hunt. I do."

"Nealy, good luck," Ricky Vee shouted from her right. "Feels like old-home week."

"Yeah, it does. Same to you, Ricky."

The gates clanged open.

"And they're off in the Kentucky Derby!" the announcer blared.

"Alpha Omega comes out in stride from the outside and on the inside it's Gadfly and not two strides behind is Hifly ridden by first-time jockey Jake Thornton. Matrix is there and not far behind is Furlong Freddie and here comes Small Change on the far outside. Dark Star for the first time moves up and it is Gadfly who leads the way as Alpha Omega drops one length behind but Hifly moves up and is right there with Gadfly. Furlong Freddie is along the outside and is running in third place. Alpha Omega is there right behind but in fourth position now. Small Change is fifth. It's Furlong Freddie on the outside heading for the clubhouse turn and racing into position. Sundown has moved up and is racing between horses now while Gumbo is closing in on Small Change and five lengths behind. Up front it is Gadfly and Hifly five lengths in the lead while Down and Dirty is ninth and on the outside, Kid Flash is tenth and Lord Dallas is lumbering behind in position twelve. Then it's a break to Wild Boy and Dark Star followed by Mandola on the inside and here comes Temptation also on the inside and then a break of six to the running long shots, but they are twenty lengths from the lead.

"This opening half mile, ladies and gentlemen, is the fastest in Derby history," the announcer screamed. "We're at forty-four and four-fifths seconds. Gadfly's pace is blistering down the backstretch, but Hifly's pace is scorching with four and one-half furlongs remaining. Gadfly is leading by two lengths over Hifly, but what's this!" the announcer shouted to be heard over the roar of the crowd. "Look at that horse! He's got wings on his feet and what's that shining off his tail! I don't know, but he's up a length and now he's running neck and neck with his barn buddy Gadfly, who is burning up that track. I can see the smoke from here.

"Alpha Omega is now third and on the inside, but Matrix is in striking position as Hifly continues to fly down this red-hot track and is now neck and neck with Gadfly. Furlong Freddie is five lengths behind, and he's smoking, but he can't make up the time. Alpha Omega is starting to advance and Matrix is right there with him at the field's far turn. Thundering along on the outside is Furlong Freddie, who's now in striking position. They're all surging now, belching fire and moving at the speed of light as they reach the top of the stretch. Gadfly takes the lead but look out, there goes Hifly to match it, and on the outside is Alpha Omega at the top of the stretch.

"Those horses are flying, not running, and it's Gadfly and Hifly and Alpha Omega in second or is it third. It's Gadfly and Hifly and they're running neck and neck in a dead-even heat. Listen to that crowd!" he shouted.

"It's Gadfly and Hifly and Alpha Omega with four furlongs to go. It's a dead heat at three, at two and there they go, straight across the finish line in a dead heat with Alpha Omega coming in third. It looks to me like a double win in the Kentucky Derby! What we call a photo finish." The crowd roared and chanted, drowning out the announcer's words.

"Photo finish! Photo finish!" they chanted.

Down on the track, Jake looked over at Nealy. "Who won?"

Nealy gasped for breath. "I think you did! Looked like it to me."

"It wasn't me, that's for sure." Ricky Vee laughed. "Great race, Nealy. I should have known I couldn't win against you. Good race, kid. See you around."

"I think I'm gonna be sick!" Jake said.

"No, you are not going to be sick. Not in front of the whole world. Just sit there and wait for the judge's call. Your mom must be so proud! Give her a high sign, Jake."

Jake turned in his seat, waved both his arms, and whistled between his teeth, two sharp, shrill sounds that ripped through the air. "Mom used to whistle like that for me when it was time to come in for supper." He cocked his head and listened when two more sharp, shrill whistles blasted through the air. "Good, she heard me. What's taking so long?"

"They're going to announce it now, Jake. Remember, be gracious and humble."

"Ladies and gentlemen, can I have your attention please. We have here today, for the first time in Kentucky Derby history, a tie. It was a photo finish all the way, stride for stride, nose to nose. The winners of the Kentucky Derby are Gadfly and Hifly. Once again Cornelia Diamond Clay Littletree takes home not one but two wins to Blue Diamond Farms. You have just witnessed history being made, ladies and gentlemen," the announcer roared, his voice hoarse.

Stunned, Nealy could only stare at Jake as half the blanket of roses was placed over Gadfly's back, the other half on Hifly's.

"If you faint now, Jake, I'll fire you," Nealy hissed.

Jake sat up straighter. "We won! We both won! We did it, Aunt Nealy! We did it! I felt like I was flying. I felt like my grandfather was in front of me the whole way."

"Wrong, Jake. He was on your six all the way."

"Yeah, yeah, I think he was. I felt like he was there. That's where I pinned his wings."

And then it was over, the speeches, the comments, the handshaking, and the purse, double this race. She'd made history.

She smiled when she saw her family descend on her and Jake. In her life she'd never seen such happiness. She stared into the gaggle of people, looking for her daughter, who was nowhere to be seen.

"I aged ten years watching that race," Hatch said. "That kid is good. He was right there with you on that little runt. Man, can that horse run. Emmie was right, he's all heart."

"Have you seen her, Hatch?"

"No. She didn't come to the box. I haven't seen Dillon either. I'm sure she's here somewhere. Nealy, could she have run the race Jake did?"

"No, Hatch. I hate to say that, but no. She's good, don't get me wrong. In fact, she's real good. She was fearless and determined in the beginning. Jake was fearful and unsure. Isn't it strange how things turned around? I'm just glad I was able to help him find his way."

"What about Emmie?"

"I don't know, Hatch. I just don't know. All I want to do is get these guys settled so we can head back home. I'm going to ask Ricky Vee if he'll ride Gadfly in the Preakness and the Belmont if he gets that far. Jake's okay if Emmie agrees to let him run. I'm thinking that she's thinking a win would be secondhand. This is just a guess on my part, but I don't think she'll run Hifly again. It's a shame, too. He's a great horse. I didn't think so in the beginning until I saw what he could do. When I'm wrong, I admit it. Boy am I hungry."

"We're all going out to dinner so we can hash, rehash, and talk this race to death."

"Oh, good. That means I get to wear all those fancy duds Maggie brought for me. I'll see you in a bit, Hatch. I have things to do right now."

In the barn, Nealy held up her hand, palm out. Jake smacked it. "You are the man, Jake! Enjoy every single minute of it. You deserve it!"

Jake held his grandfather's wings in his hand. A lone tear gathered in the corner of his eye. "I hope you were proud of me, Grandpa," he whispered.

"How touching," Emmie snapped. "If you don't mind, I'd like my horse back."

Jake nodded. He walked away, knowing Emmie's eyes were boring into his back. He stopped a moment when he heard his aunt's voice. "Grow up and get over it, Emmie. Who are you going to blame for this? Life goes on.

"Hey, Jake, wait up!" she called to her nephew.

The sun was just creeping over the horizon on a hot, sultry day in late June when Nealy walked out onto the front porch, coffee cup in hand, the way she'd done thousands of times before. Today was different. Today was her last day at Blue Diamond Farms. Sitting near the top step were four suitcases. A slim envelope lay on top of the bags.

She waited until the eighteen-wheeler carrying the remains

of StarDancer, Flyby, and her first husband Hunt passed out of her sight. She smiled. "I'm taking you guys home with me."

She finished the coffee and walked back into the house. "I'm ready, Hatch."

"Me, too. Let's get this show on the road then."

"I have to go down to the barn to see Emmie before we leave. You can come if you like."

"No, I think I'll wait here."

Nealy walked slowly, her gaze taking in everything. She didn't feel sad at all, only a sense of relief.

In the barn she called out to her daughter.

"I'm over here, Mom. What is it? I'm kind of busy right now."

"I know that. This will just take a moment. I have something to give you. It's the deed to my half of Blue Diamond Farms. It's all yours now. I was never meant to have this place. Maud and Jess wanted me to build it up so you would have a safe haven. I did that. They wanted you to have it. I hope you have a wonderful life here. Give Gabby my love."

"Where . . . where are you going?"

"Back to the beginning. I'm going back the same way I came here, with that old blue truck and my bucket of dirt in the back. I'm going back where I belong." She stepped forward to hug her daughter, but Emmie stepped back. Nealy's arms dropped to her side. She would not cry. She absolutely would not cry. She turned to walk away. She was halfway down the breezeway when Jake called out to her.

"Hey, Aunt Nealy, you got room for one more?" He stood in the sunlight, his bags at his feet.

"Absolutely." Nealy smiled.

"Is there room for me, too?" Lee Liu asked.

"There will always be room for you, Lee."

"Do ya suppose there's room for this cranky, old curmudgeon?" Cordell Lancer bellowed as he trotted up the breezeway.

"For sure there's room for you, Cordell."

Nealy felt like the Pied Piper as she led the way out into the early-morning sunshine, where her husband waited for her. The old blue truck was parked behind Hatch's Range Rover. She itched to sit in it and then drive it. All the way back to Virginia.

Hatch led the way as far as the gate. He stopped, and Nealy

stopped behind him to watch the driver of the eighteen-wheeler dismantle the two bronze statues standing guard over Blue Diamond Farms. They belonged with her because she loved them.

The minute the eighteen-wheeler pulled onto the highway, Nealy scooted back to the blue truck. She turned on the ignition and followed Hatch.

She didn't look back.

Sitting next to her, Jake started to sing, *"Off we go into the wild blue yonder . . ."*

"Riding high into the sky . . ." Nealy sang along with him.

Epilogue

Blue Diamond Farms
Five Years Later

Emmie Coleman sat on the steps of the front porch and looked out across what had once been the beautiful, luscious landscape of Blue Diamond Farms.

Five years of neglect had reduced it to nothing more than a bunch of empty barns, scorched grass, and a house badly in need of repair.

All the horses were gone, sold off to the highest bidder. Only Hifly and a barn buddy named Omar remained. No dogs or cats roamed the breezeway the way they had when she was growing up there.

It was a sad testimony to her reign as sole owner of the famous Blue Diamond Farms.

She wondered where her father was these days. He called from time to time, but he was another sad testimony to family life. He had simply expected too much from her, and when she didn't do what was expected, he'd chastise her until ugly words passed between them. Like her mother, he'd finally given up on her. He didn't understand, or maybe he refused to understand, that she wasn't perfect like her famous mother. Even her daughter Gabby refused to understand the way things were. In a weak moment she'd allowed her to visit her father after she'd started to ask questions, something she never thought would happen. After her first visit to Ohio, she wanted to spend every holiday and all her summer vacations with him, or her grandfather, but mostly with her father. Just as recently as last month, she'd said she hated coming home to such a dreary place and would rather live with her father and Debra, whom she adored, along with her two little stepbrothers. It had been simpler to let her go than to cry and plead to have her stay.

Even Nick was a scarce visitor these days—or was it years? He said the farm depressed him and chided her for the way she'd run it into the ground in such a short time. He was busy with his new wife and twin daughters. The last time she'd seen him was two years ago. He did call every few months, but rarely said anything of interest to her.

Her mother called regularly, at least twice a week. They discussed the weather, Gabby's grades in school, or her visits to her father's house, always mundane things. Nealy constantly invited her to SunStar Farms, but she always had an excuse as to why she couldn't go. She never invited her mother back to Blue Diamond Farms.

None of them understood.

She wondered what would happen if she sat there on the steps and never, ever, got up again.

When she saw the cloud of dust on the long driveway, she brought her hands to her eyes to shield them from the bright sun. A visitor. She didn't have visitors these days. She hadn't had a visitor in over a year.

It was a battered pickup full of dust and mud, but she could see it was maroon in color. The truck was probably half as old as the man driving it. Emmie stood up the moment the truck clunked to a stop to watch a man as weathered as his truck get out, shake down his denim jeans, adjust his hat, and walk forward.

"Afternoon, ma'am. I was wondering if you might have some work for me. My name is Denver Caldwell. This is Blue Diamond Farms, isn't it?"

"Yes. What's left of it. What did you have in mind?"

"Well from the looks of things, maybe sprucing it up a bit. I'm real handy with a hammer. I know how to paint without making a mess. I'm good with horses, too. I'll work for my keep and a decent wage. If I might be so bold, ma'am, you look pretty as a picture standing there like that. This porch could use some flowers and maybe some of those hanging baskets. Real nice and shady in the summertime. It looks like just the place to drink a cold, frosty glass of lemonade. I just betcha in six months, I could have this place looking real nice."

"Could you now? Would you like to stay for supper, Denver? I'm not much of a cook, but I get by. We could talk about it over supper."

"I'd like that, ma'am. I think I should freshen up a bit. You got running water down at the barns, don't you? Been driving the better part of three days. I can't be coming to supper looking like this. You didn't tell me your name."

"Emmie. Emmie Coleman. Yes, there's water down at the barn. There's warm water if you want to shower. Just go into the little cottage across from the third barn. The door's open."

"Thank you, ma'am. What time is supper? I don't want to be late."

"An hour from now. Is that satisfactory?"

"Yes, ma'am, it is."

Emmie walked over to the screen door. She frowned when she noticed the screen was half off the door. Then she smiled. This was what had happened to Maud Diamond. Jess had ridden in and taken over just when Blue Diamond was about to fall around Maud's ears and she was about to lose everything. Jess had pulled it all together for Maud. A fairy tale.

She smiled all the way to the kitchen.

Maybe Denver Caldwell would be her Jess Wooley.

Maybe Denver Caldwell would take care of her the way Jess had taken care of Maud Diamond.

Maybe.

Fern Michaels likes to hear from her readers. You can e-mail her at *fernmic@aol.com*